The City Knows
by Jason Schneider

a novel

MONTAG

A Montag Press Book
www.montagpress.com
Montag Press
777 Morton Street, Unit B
San Francisco CA 94129 USA

Montag Press, the burning book with the hatchet cover, the skewed word mark and the portrayal of the long-suffering fireman mascot are trademarks of Montag Press. Printed & Digitally Originated in the United States of America
10 9 8 7 6 5 4 3 2 1

for Paul

Blurbs

"This thorny, elaborate novel takes shape like the offspring of Thomas Pynchon and Mike Wallace. Settling between a 60 Minutes episode, and the Lennon-spectacle-wearing, Pynchonian antics of people trying to make history before it happens, Schneider's novel packs a heartfelt punch."

Walker Zupp,
author of Morocconomics

"Jason Schneider has created complicated, compelling and utterly heartbreaking young mid-western characters drawn from their unhappy lives in small town USA to the glitter of 1970's Los Angeles--where they're little more than fresh meat for a city swarming with music industry con artists, Hollywood hustlers, drug dealers and charismatic radicals."

Rodney DeCroo,
author of Night Moves:
The Street Photography of Rodney DeCroo

Garnered from decades writing about and participating in the culture of musicians and their craft, Schneider's succinct style doesn't encumber readers with lengthy prose, rather he captures unique insights into the creative and social lives based in some of music's most legendary environments. A highly recommended romp into the underbelly of music and its compelling characters.

Phil Saunders,
Author of No Flash Please:
(Underground Music in Toronto 1987-92)

Acknowledgements

Thank you to Charlie Franco, Lindsay Krumbein, Mike Sauve, and everyone who inspired the characters in this story.

Chapter 1

West Hollywood / May 1972

Alex Felske swiped the cap off his Zippo and lit a Camel. Will had told him to be at the Troubadour's back door at 9:30, and a busboy would let him in. Sustained knocking with the meaty part of his fist produced a dull throb that ran up his shoulder, rather than the desired response from inside. More waiting, as usual, Alex mused. The bouncers stationed at the front door had put him on the shit list after last time, when he ducked out on a forty-five dollar tab. His excuse? You drink that much tequila, you tend to forget things. Pinching his cigarette between his thumb and index finger, Alex mentally scrolled through Will's instructions: "Once through the kitchen, you'll see the stairs leading to the stage. There'll be a dark spot in the corner where no one will notice you. After my set I'll take you to the dressing room and introduce you to James Taylor." All Alex knew about Taylor was his rep around town as a bleached out junkie, making him another potential client.

Alex stuck an index finger into a breast pocket of his jean jacket and felt the plastic bag nestled in the bottom. Too easy, he thought, leaning against the rough brick, closing his eyes and inhaling.

He heard the scuffle of cowboy boots a few seconds before they rounded the corner. One guy put Alex in a full nelson and the other cocked a fist, as if waiting for Alex to indicate where he wanted to absorb the blow. It landed on his chin and blurred his vision, with a second shot to the body prompting the man restraining him to release the hold. Alex collapsed on the concrete and lay balled in a fetal position for several seconds as the two goons proceeded to kick him in the stomach until he stopped moving.

"This deal ain't going down," one of them said through clenched teeth.

The other chimed in, "If we see you on set again, trying to sell your shit to Mr. Taylor or anyone else, you're not getting away."

Alex wound tight with his eyes welded shut as the clamor of boot heels faded down the alley, subsumed by the traffic noise on Santa Monica Boulevard.

He lay still until his ears tuned into the music coming from the other side of the door. Will was starting his performance, one he'd convinced Alex would be the most important he'd played to date. All Alex could do in that moment was let out an oxygen-deprived laugh, knowing he was missing it. Refocusing, he flexed each major muscle before dragging himself to the Troubadour's back wall and heaving his body into a sitting position. With some effort, he fished a Camel out of the soft pack that remained intact in the pocket of the blood-dappled western shirt he'd bought at J.C. Penney. But there was a bigger surprise as he searched his jeans for his lighter; the goons hadn't taken his money. Allowing himself a moment to savor this lucky break, Alex took a deep drag and strained to hear the sounds from inside.

He came to the realization that he must have passed out when the back door burst open and a busboy dragged two overstuffed garbage bags to the dumpster at the far side of the alley. He didn't notice Alex until completing his task.

"Jesus, man! You alright?"

Alex, the half-smoked cigarette still affixed to his lips, smiled and nodded. His appearance must have been more damaged than he imagined. Alex motioned to the kid to keep his distance, and summoned the strength to unstick the Camel from his mouth.

"Go back to work," Alex said with a smile he hoped would keep the busboy from telling his co-workers what he'd seen. "I'll be fine. Just wanted to listen to the music." The door slammed shut, and Alex tried to lose himself in what he could hear of Will on stage. "Ohio Valley..." he whispered, a warm glow spreading through his aching gut. As the muffled music was replaced by muffled applause, Alex tossed the Camel and started inching his back up the wall. His head felt as though it was swelling to the point of bursting out of his ears, but the wave passed and he stood without fear of collapsing. He couldn't take the risk of going inside in such a pathetic state.

Expelling a deep breath, Alex stepped toward the boulevard, pondering how many other ways he would have to pay for his plan going wrong.

Sweat started to drip into Will Mosley's eyes. He hated that. It was bad enough that the stage lights prevented him from seeing anything past the first row of tables, but his eyes shut tight as drops trickled down his face, and onto his denim shirt and his faithful Martin. His granddaddy had bestowed the guitar on him when he saw that the end was near. It was the only thing Will brought with him, along with a duffle bag of clothes, when he and Alex drove to L.A. two years before. After all that time, Will's goal of breaking into the music business, or at least a small part of it, was coming true. He was on stage at the Troubadour, the same stage he'd read about in *Rolling Stone* during hazy afternoons in Ashtabula's only record store, sneaking joints out back as Jimmy the owner played the latest releases. Will called in every favor he could to get that night's slot opening for Taylor, and the pressure left him feeling this was an all-or-nothing gambit, rather than another step up the L.A. musical pecking order. So far, the crowd was polite and allowed him to do his job. One more song, then he could relax.

"Thanks for listening, and I hope I'll see you again soon. This is gonna be my last number tonight. It's a song about the place I come from, and I'd like to dedicate it to the friend who drove out here with me. It's called 'The Ohio Valley.'"

A smattering of applause forced a smile across Will's face. A few whoops helped him believe that Alex was out there, and as the song took him over—the song that maintained his confidence that this crazy plan he and Alex had dreamt up would pay off—Will felt at home. The applause roared the second he strummed the last chord, fading by the time he opened the dressing room door. A small group, including Taylor, huddled around a tub of Coronas in melting ice, and they all offered praise as Will joined the circle. He took a drag off a joint, grabbed a Corona, and observed Taylor as he responded to the flurry of questions lobbed by people Will didn't recognize. Will thought about moving closer to eavesdrop, but remained where he stood, fascinated by how Taylor retained his poise.

As people started drifting out, Will accepted that his night was over. He placed the Martin in its case and put on his jean jacket, trying to catch Taylor's eye as a gesture of unspoken brotherhood. Taylor did glance at him, mid-sentence, and although he displayed no hint of acknowledgement, it was enough for Will to conjure his own interpretation. More appreciative nods and shoulder taps were offered as he headed to the bar, heightening his anticipation of seeing Alex. There was no sign of him, and before Will could start searching the room, he felt two gentle hands on his forearm. They belonged to a cute blonde, the kind he had encountered many times since he'd been in California, but the young woman's assertiveness set him on edge.

"You sounded great," she blurted out, then took a long gulp from a bottle of Pabst Blue Ribbon. Her blue eyes were inviting, but Will couldn't get past her obvious little sister qualities.

"Thanks. Yeah, I had fun tonight." He avoided eye contact, hoping to spot Alex or, perhaps, a record company executive. Neither appeared. Will brought his bottle of Corona to his lips and surrendered. "What's your name?"

"Cyndi."

"You hang out here much?"

"Yeah, I just started coming here. The music is fantastic. Did you see Jackson Browne a couple of weeks ago?"

"Uh, no."

"He's so dreamy! I can't wait for the Stones to come this summer though. You dig the Stones?"

"Um, yeah sure." Will tried to keep up as Cyndi droned on about her favorite groups. He knew that Taylor would soon be on stage.

"Do you have a record out?"

"Um, no, not yet. Hoping to soon though."

"What's it going to be called? I know most guys use their own name as the title of their first album, but I think that's so boring. What was that last song you did?"

"'The Ohio Valley.'"

"Well, that's not a very good title for an album. You should try to think of something original."

"Yeah, that's a good idea. Hey, it's great to meet you, but I should go talk to a friend of mine over there. I'll see you around, alright?" Will didn't wait for Cyndi to say goodbye as he made a beeline for Angela Carney, sitting in a corner by herself, two double rye and Cokes on the table in front of her.

"I got these for you," she said. "I wasn't sure if you'd notice me here. That was a great set."

"Thanks, and thanks for the drinks. Where's Alex?"

"I don't know. I haven't seen him all night."

"You mean he didn't make it in?"

"I don't know."

Will's brow furrowed, but he raised one of the glasses, taking a large sip, and chasing it with the last swallow of his Corona. Angela began paying attention to how much he was drinking. "How do you feel it went tonight?"

Will downed the rest of the rye before answering. "I'm sure everyone's already forgotten I was even here."

"What do you mean? Didn't you hear how much they dug it? Did you get to meet James Taylor?"

"Yeah, he's a good guy. Nothing feels right though."

"Like what?"

"I don't know. Alex should be here."

Will observed Angela craning her neck in a vain attempt to spot Alex, before raising the second rye to his lips. There was no reason for him to believe that Alex had even made it inside.

Angela returned to the tequila sunrise she'd been nursing for the past half-hour. "I liked that last song," she offered. "What's it called again?"

"'The Ohio Valley.' Where my family's from."

"Oh yeah, I remember. Cleveland, right?"

"Ashtabula. That's where Alex and I lived. It's actually on Lake Erie. But most of my relatives are farmers."

"I love towns with names like that. It probably feels more like America there than it does out here."

Will was caught off-guard by the remark, and pondered a response. "You mean, like, the people are friendlier?"

"No, I just always picture people there doing normal stuff. Meaningful stuff."

"You don't like it here?"

"No, I love it. I thought you might be homesick, that's all. The song makes it sound like you are."

"Well, it's not all it's cracked up to be back there. I guess I'm starting to forget the bad things. That's all that the song's about. Maybe it's too sentimental."

"No, it's great. It says a lot about who you are, and that's what's most important, right?"

"I guess so."

Will found himself losing interest in the conversation, and took another look around the room for Alex. He was growing accustomed to his friend breaking his word, but at that moment Will felt isolated, in spite of Angela being there. With an inaudible sigh, he turned back to her, and tried to focus on her tiny, fragile face behind a mop of natural gold curls. She had worried for Will from the day they had met, and he realized he was taking it for granted. He didn't know what to do about it.

"It's okay," she said. "You had a great night. Something's going to come of this."

Will looked down at the table, smiling, before flagging down the waitress and ordering another double rye. He'd taken his first sip when the room erupted in applause as James Taylor walked on stage.

Alex stood bloodied and doubled over at the front door of Carlos Montez's apartment on Hacienda, a stupid grin unable to mask his pain.

"Well, can I come in?" Alex spat out between gasps, as if he'd just completed a marathon.

Carlos turned and said, "Shut the door behind you."

Alex gathered his strength and followed into the main room, depositing himself on the stained couch underneath posters for two of the b-movies Carlos had appeared in—*Drag Strip Debutante* and *Revenge of The Mole People*. He sat across from Alex in an unwelcoming wooden chair. "What the fuck happened?"

"I got rolled behind the Troubadour." Alex tried to enjoy the comfort the sofa offered, but Carlos kept up the questioning.

"How many?"

"A couple Sunset cowboys. Didn't matter, I couldn't get away. I was going in the back and Will had it planned for me to meet James Taylor."

Carlos pressed on. "How much did those guys take?"

"That's the weird thing, they didn't want money. I've got today's take from the grass for the crew guys. Probably need it for the hospital bill now. Feels like a couple of ribs are broken, or bruised at least. All they said was to stay away from Taylor. They must have had their eyes on me when I was on set."

Alex handed over the cash and Carlos methodically counted each bill. "Fucking Monte," he said. "I should have talked to him first. What have I told you about making deals on your own? You didn't get to see this Taylor fellow in the bar either?"

The question raised Alex's hackles. "No man, didn't you hear me? I couldn't get inside!" Carlos finished his count in silence, separating four fifties that he stuck in Alex's shirt pocket. "You can crash here tonight if you need to."

"Thanks," Alex responded. "Can you fix me too? I'm in some pain here."

Carlos scowled. Alex eventually got the message and fished out the package of golden-brown powder he was supposed to sell to Taylor, tossing it on the table within Carlos's reach. Expressionless, Carlos got up and retrieved a leather pouch that was wedged into the top shelf of the bookcase. With automatic precision, he prepared the hit as Alex removed his ruined new shirt and tied off with his belt. He strained to steady his arm and make the blue bulging vein obvious to Carlos. Their eyes locked in brief hesitation—Carlos with the needle cocked and ready, and Alex with his teeth penetrating the tough leather, pleading to be delivered. Alex closed his eyes and anticipated the rush. When it came, it was like a bullet to his forehead. His body went limp and he collapsed on the sofa in an awkward position with the needle in his arm. Carlos gently removed it and replaced his gear on the shelf, then laid Alex out straight and placed a pillow under his head before turning out the lights.

It was the swimming dream that Alex had almost every time he did smack, like a cartoon he remembered seeing as a kid, Porky Pig getting lured to the bottom of a lake while he was fishing, and the fish in their little fish city getting their revenge on him. Except this time, it was like something he'd read about mermaids luring sailors to their underwater doom. Alex moved within the warm, milky water, strange sounds resonating in his brain. Breathing wasn't a concern. Ingesting the liquid made him stronger. He felt pure bliss until he brought his head to the surface and saw the tide taking him to a fragrant pool at the base of a canyon. Alex lingered there, but could not resist the compulsion to follow the water. Diving into darkness, he swam until he reached a cavernous tunnel lined with shiny walls. He leaned against the crystalline surface, every nerve in his body singing. The sounds dissipated as a dim light danced above his head, casting shadows around him. The tunnel was breathing, and each convulsion drew him further in until the distant echo of deep moans rose into a crescendo of horror, too much for his ears to bear. He was no longer in control of his movements as the light faded and the shadows grew deeper until Alex was fully consumed by darkness. His screams were drowned out as he surrendered to the abyss.

Will was unable to relax during Taylor's set. All he could think of was his own failure, as one song after another sent giddy murmurings throughout the crowd. The booze was starting to take effect, but didn't calm Will's nerves. Angela stole anxious glances at him. Will downed two more doubles by the time Taylor finished his encore and the crowd started thinning out. As the lights in the Troubadour came up, Will remained as stoic as he had been for the previous hour. Angela placed her hand on the arm that kept him propped up on the table. Will turned toward her, eyes glazed.

"Are you ready to go?" she asked.

As he was about to answer, the young blonde, Cyndi, led a group toward their table. "See, I told you he's still here," she exclaimed, pointing a pink fingernail at a slight young man wearing outdated hippie gear.

"Hey, you were great tonight," he told Will without hesitation. "I'm Lucas. I caught your last few tunes, but Cyndi kept going on about how much she dug you. I just started doing promo work for Elektra. You signed up with anyone?"

The kid was talking fast, trying hard to impress. Will had met enough of these young hustlers to know where the conversation was going.

"No, I'm not with anyone," Will answered. "Just doing what I can."

"Where do you normally play?"

"Oh, the Ash Grove, the Palomino. On my corner."

Will hoped his aloofness would deter Lucas, but the kid was persistent. "How'd you get this gig?"

Will sighed before answering. "I've been playing the open stage night ever since I moved out here. Doug seemed to like my stuff, so he put me on the bill tonight."

"You got plans to make a record?"

"I did, but I'm not really thinking about it anymore. I don't like my songs. Gotta write some new ones."

"Well, let me tell you, that one you closed with was killer. Better than anything Taylor did."

It was hard for Will to tell if Lucas was sincere, but for the first time in hours, his self-loathing subsided and he could feel himself warming up to the kid. Lucas took his cue, producing a card out of his fringed leather shoulder bag, and placing it on the table in front of Will. "Seriously, if you think I can be of any help, gimme a call."

Will examined the card, which bore the same logo he recognized from the first Doors album he'd bought back home. Placing it in his shirt pocket, he looked up to give Lucas a smile of thanks, but Cyndi and her friends had him surrounded. After a few seconds, she poked her head out of the circle to ask, "Hey, you guys got a cigarette?" When Will didn't respond, Angela went into her purse and pulled out her pack of Virginia Slims. Cyndi lodged one between her lips and leaned toward Lucas for a light.

Exhaling a deep drag, Cyndi deposited herself next to Will and Angela. "Thanks for the smoke. Isn't this place cool? All these great musicians. Man, it's been so great to meet you."

Will shifted in his chair and cast a deliberate glance at Angela as if to answer her original question about leaving.

"Yeah, it is cool," Will said, turning back to Cyndi.

"You guys going to party somewhere else now? We're thinking of going over to the Whisky. I really feel like dancing."

"That would be a good thing for you to do," Will responded in a sharp tone.

Cyndi didn't catch the drift. She was engrossed in her own revelry, launching into a detailed monologue on things she enjoyed about L.A. and how great Taylor had sounded. Each word ground into Will's skull like a dentist's drill.

Cyndi paused to extinguish her cigarette before asking, "Is she your girl?"

Angela snapped to attention, casting her eyes on Will after grasping that Cyndi had been ignoring her until that moment. Will's face hardened. "I think you'd better get the fuck out of here," he said, trying to suppress his growing rage.

Cyndi stared in half-disbelief, her lips on the verge of a sheepish grin. Will continued to stare her down, anticipating any response as a further opportunity to unleash another stream of bile. Cyndi was afraid to move, and sensing this, Will got up and stumbled toward the door without looking at Angela, dodging the loitering stragglers. She chased after him, and caught him as he was pushing open the front door. "Wait," she said. "You need your guitar!" She gripped his denim-covered arm, and Will turned toward her with his head lowered.

Without lifting his eyes, he asked, "Can you go backstage and get it?"

"Okay. Please wait here." He nodded, and Angela let go. She took a few steps backwards before turning and finding her way to the stage. The moment she was out of sight, Will cracked open the door and walked into the West Hollywood night.

The pavement turned to dust before Will's eyes. The suffocating darkness gave way to the omnipresent sunlight of the desert, and wind kicked up into his face. The path he was on was lined with Joshua Trees. Lazy coyotes observed his presence and did not approach. As his step lightened and pace slowed, he heard the voice.

Why did you storm out like that? That girl was just being friendly. She really liked what you were doing.

Will raised his head and his mind's eye took in the endless vista.

You blew it tonight, you know that right? Just keep walking away, that's always the easiest thing to do. Turn your back on everyone trying to help. That's why you came out here in the first place, isn't it? Don't give me that shit about how your hometown had nothing to offer. You couldn't accept that people there actually respected you, even loved you. But that's not what you want. What is it again? You want to be rich and famous? No, that's not it. You want freedom to create your art? Well, that's pretty noble, but that's not it either. Well, if you don't know, then I suppose no one else can expect to know. That's the deal, right?

The sky turned dark and long shadows fell across the path that gradually returned to concrete. Will was besieged on all sides by grotesque figures, recoiling as each one passed. His soul felt on display. Their murmurings grew louder, and the growing cacophony made his clothes seem more ragged and his gait more erratic. Will turned a corner and was paralyzed by the sight of his street in stark contrast to the bright vision he had beheld only minutes before. As he approached the apartment on Doheny that he and Alex shared, each step required intense concentration. His footfalls echoed up the staircase and down the dim hallway. Will's anxiety began to subside as he fumbled with the apartment key, his thoughts turning to what he'd say if Alex was inside waiting for him. The key clicked, the door squeaked. The apartment was unlit and empty. Will exhaled, locked the door behind him, and went to the bathroom where the porcelain amplified a scream that shocked him from his stupor.

Angela stood in front of Will's door on the verge of tears, not because her tiny arms had carried his guitar all the way to the dilapidated walk-up, but because of what she knew she would find when her spare key opened the door. Will lay naked in the bathtub, the tap running, and the water edging close to spilling over the side. His head was the only part of his body not submerged, and the strain in his face suggested a silent struggle over whether to keep it that way. Angela reached to turn off the tap. The water was freezing. As silence settled over the room, Will lay motionless in the cold, his face knotted in terror and sadness. Will opened his eyes, and upon seeing her, let out a piercing wail. Angela pulled his head into her chest, while reaching down with her other hand to pull the plug.

Will started shivering as the receding water exposed his skin. Angela threw a towel around his shoulders while raising him to a sitting position. He stopped crying as she resumed cradling him, now with both arms.

"You should go to bed," she whispered.

"Don't leave," he begged.

"I won't."

Alex woke with a start in the early Sunday morning half-light, his bones singing with every shallow gasp of air. The first thing he noticed was a skin mag lying on the coffee table near his head. He fixated on its distressed pages, thinking of Jessy and summoning a hard-on despite the pain he was in. He didn't dare touch himself in the middle of Carlos's living room, instead deciding to see her as soon as possible.

Sleep had restored some of Alex's strength, and he knew he would need it if he was going to see Jessy. The proof would be if he could get up and grab Carlos's gear from the bookshelf, and officially get his day started. Wrapping an arm around his midsection, Alex raised himself upright. After a deep breath, he got to his feet and forced his legs to move. Within an agonizing minute he was removing the leather pouch from the bookcase with both hands. Accomplishing this made returning to the sofa a lot easier. He surveyed the contents for a moment—several needles, clean and dirty, a well-used spoon, and three separate baggies, one being the shit Carlos had given him hours earlier. Alex picked it up by the twist-tie and pondered whether he needed the fix at all. He determined it would be best if he left as soon as possible, but as he put on his boots, he heard Carlos stirring in his bedroom.

The sounds forced Alex to zip the pouch, but he hadn't been able to replace it on the shelf by the time Carlos sauntered into the room wearing a bathrobe that barely spanned his paunch. "Did I say you could help yourself?"

Alex offered a guilty grin, adding, "Hey, I was thinking about it but figured it would be rude. No harm done man."

Carlos's eyes stayed trained on Alex as he picked up the gear. Turning his back and moving to the bookshelf, he asked, "How do you feel?"

"I'm okay. Still need something to get me going today."

"I'll take care of that. I need you to do a little work for me though." Alex winced, but waited for Carlos to elaborate. "You want coffee?" Without waiting for an answer, Carlos headed to the kitchen, returning in a few minutes with two steaming mugs of instant. He sat in the shitty chair across from Alex as he had the night before and watched him suppress a grimace as the hot liquid scalded the roof of his mouth. Carlos appeared to take brief pleasure in this as he proceeded to share his thoughts. "I've been trying to decipher this Monte situation. You obviously talked to the wrong people on set. Any ideas?" Alex responded with an innocent shrug. "Okay, let's start at the beginning. Who let you onto the set?"

"Gene, the assistant cameraman. Just like before. He made the buy for him and the crew guys."

"The money you gave me last night was from them?"

"Yeah," Alex said. "It was for the grass. Will tipped me off about Taylor and I set up the buy at the Troubadour, just as I explained to you. Someone must have seen me go into his trailer and ratted me out." Carlos paused, providing Alex with an opportunity to state his case. "Look man, I like our arrangement, believe me. I appreciate the help, but I've been doing the legwork for a while and I need to start getting some of those real jobs you promised."

Carlos appeared hurt by the accusation. "I told you I'd get your foot in the door, and I have. A lot of people have come to like you, although it seems that Monte doesn't, and that's a problem."

Alex rolled his eyes in frustration, sensing that Carlos missed the point. "Then it's my problem, and I'll have to figure out how to solve it. I don't want to work for you forever."

Carlos sat back, his skimpy robe shifting to reveal tight briefs rimmed with thick, dark hair. Alex looked away. "I'll tell you what," Carlos said. "Go to Rancho Deluxe today, and ask for Ronnie. He's a cameraman I worked with on *Motorcycle Invaders*. Just mention my name, and say you're looking for any part. He might be able to help you out."

Alex smiled.

"After that, you need to make a few drops," Carlos added as raised himself to gather the day's packages in the kitchen.

"Hey, while you're up, I think I'd be better off with some speed. Oh, and a clean shirt too."

Carlos cast his eyes down on Alex. "Sure man. Just don't forget me when you're famous."

"Can I take the Honda?"

Carlos gestured toward the keys hanging by the door, returning a minute later with a large bag of marijuana and a bottle of pink pills, two of which he dropped in Alex's palm.

"I'm starting to think you might be more trouble than you're worth."

Will didn't dare move after Angela rolled against him. The back of her tiny body nestled against his side, her heat filling the emptiness that existed a few hours before. After several blissful minutes, her soft breathing told him she was asleep. He remained motionless, except for his swollen penis. No, don't do it, his mind screamed, this is a perfect moment, enjoy it for what it is. If she wants it, she'll make a move. Time ticked by in excruciating increments, and she remained still, her breathing shifting to involuntary gasps. He was mesmerized, but with each passing second his hard-on receded.

He inched away from her until he could swing his legs off the bed and reach for some clothes. He tried to recall the moments before they succumbed to exhaustion. There had been more talk about Will's perceived failure. It was all in his head, she kept assuring him. Yes, it was, but he didn't know how to explain the full truth. He hadn't had the strength to unburden himself. Her presence was enough to keep him grounded, he realized.

Will rose and turned, catching Angela's smiling face poking out from under the sheet. He couldn't help smiling back at her, but moved to the window that flooded the room with sunlight.

"Sleep well?" Angela asked.

Her voice unlocked some of the lingering guilt over his behavior, and he started pacing. "Yeah. I feel good. Let me, uh, see what I've got for breakfast."

"Don't worry, I'll take care of it." Angela peeled back the sheet and Will couldn't resist catching a glimpse of the warm body that had been his for the taking. She put on the faded jeans and the tight t-shirt she had arrived in, before wrapping her arms around Will's waist. He remained immobile and Angela withdrew, tentatively stepping into the bathroom.

Will listened to the taps run, as the fog of the past twenty-four hours descended over him again. Angela returned to discover Will still hadn't moved.

"So, um, let's do that breakfast thing," she stammered. "Why don't we go down to the corner? It's on me."

Her offer elicited a smile before Will refocused his attention on the window. "Thanks, but I think I'm gonna try to do some work."

Angela took it like a slap. "Oh, okay. Well, call me if you need anything."

"I will."

Angela retrieved her purse and Will still couldn't move until the final echo of her heels faded down the stairs.

Jessy Robinson had to pull Alex aside when she saw him come through the bar's front door.

"What the fuck happened to you?"

"Aren't you happy to see me?"

"Yeah, but Jesus Christ, you look like you woke up in a ditch."

"So what if I did? I'm not any worse than anyone else in here. You going on soon?"

"Not for a bit. The after-church crowd isn't here yet."

"Good. I needed to see you."

"Well, here I am. You look like you need a beer too."

"I don't normally indulge this early—"

"Bullshit, your eyes are bouncing around like a pinball machine. What you been up to?"

"I got some good news, baby. I just got a legitimate shot at a speaking part."

"Really? Looking like that? Who'd you blow?"

"Very funny. Carlos hooked me up with this cameraman he knows, Ronnie. His next gig is this flick about a bunch of revolutionaries who hijack a B-29 and threaten to nuke Fort Knox!"

"Fuck, that sounds stupid."

"Whatever, the story's not important. All you need to know is that it's exactly the thing I need right now."

"But you haven't got the part yet. What the fuck is a cameraman gonna do?"

"It doesn't matter. Once he introduces me to the director, they're gonna love me."

"Oh, you think so? I think you need to get a grip. Drink that beer."

"Come on baby, this is gonna be my big break. Aren't you happy?"

"Why, what's in it for me?"

The speed still had a hold on Alex's nervous system, forcing him to repeat desperately, "Why can't you be happy for me?"

"I am, I am. Settle down. I'll be happier when you tell me it's a sure thing."

"Oh, it's a sure thing, believe me ... it's a sure thing."

"So is that all you came to tell me?"

"No baby, I wanted to see you even before this happened. I, uh, had kind of a rough night last night."

"Well that's obvious."

"If you've got a few minutes, why don't we go somewhere?"

"Shit, I only woke up an hour ago."

"C'mon, I've got Carlos's wheels. I'll pull into the alley. I need you right now, babe."

Jessy kept trying to talk him down. "Why don't you just hang around and I'll give you a good show."

"It ain't the same. When are you finished?"

"Eight."

"Okay, I'll be back then," he said.

"Bring me a treat, and we can do whatever you want."

"I should have thought of that this morning."

Chapter 2

Ashtabula / April 1970

Alex stared into the shifting darkness outside the kitchen window of his parents' house, the telephone receiver silent as he waited for Will to resume their conversation. There was a crackle in the line when his friend came back on.

"I can't go. My old man needs me to help him fix the fuckin' Oldsmobile."

"Why? You don't know anything about that shit."

"He said I needed to learn. It's gonna be mine soon, remember?"

"I can't believe you're gonna drive that tank."

"Well, what do you want me to do, tell the old man I don't want a car?"

"So you're really not coming?"

"What can I do? Have a good time."

Alex hung up the phone and pictured Will standing in his driveway, holding a lamp under the hood as his father examined the plugs and points he should have replaced the previous year. He'd witnessed this scene before, Will's father dragging out the process by explaining why each part did what it does. With a shake of his head, Alex bounded up the stairs to his room to make final preparations, now that he was going alone.

He pulled out the bottle of Jack Daniel's from his bottom desk drawer—a lift from his father's liquor cabinet during the last Christmas rush, when the clients rewarded his dad's good service with so much booze, even he couldn't drink it all. Alex took it straight out of the bottle, enough to at least give him a buzz until he got to the auditorium. Grabbing his jean jacket from the top of his dresser—ticket in the pocket as it should be—he took the stairs two at a time in hopes of escaping out the front door before his mother could block his way. She called out from the TV room as Alex's hand gripped the doorknob.

"Alex! What's the big hurry?"

"That concert's tonight down at the Aud. I told you about it. I gotta go."

"Get in here!"

Alex's face tightened in anticipation of the scene he knew was to unfold. His steps were quiet and deliberate, through the kitchen and into the room where he had played as a child, but now avoided like poison. Things looked as they did every night: his dad flat on the couch, beer within reach on the cheap TV tray, Kronkite on the tube. Alex's mother sat in her reclining chair, content in her idleness after completing her daily tasks. All of them, that is, except for poking her nose into her son's business. Alex halted at the dividing line between the linoleum and the plush carpet, avoiding eye contact.

"I don't recall hearing about this concert," his mother chirped in her usual patronizing tone.

"Jesus, Mom, I told you two weeks ago when you loaned me the money to get the ticket."

"Don't talk to your mother like that!" Alex's father didn't raise his head, but still managed a long swig from his Miller High Life. His mother didn't react, as if the comment was the least she expected in defense of her honor, as well as the honor of their Lord and Savior.

"You're going by yourself?"

"Well, yeah. But I'll be meeting people there. Will's supposed to go."

"You and your damn rock concerts. It's just an excuse to smoke dope!" Alex's dad spoke without averting his gaze from the television screen.

"Well Harold, I did say he could buy a ticket. It shouldn't go to waste."

"Fine. But this is the last time! At least until I start seeing some better grades out of you. You're making me a laughing stock with how you're acting lately. So get it all out of your system tonight, because believe me mister, this will be the last chance you get! You hear me?"

"Yes, sir."

Alex felt compelled to go to his room for one last shot of Jack Daniel's, but took the opportunity to vanish. His father's words stung until he got to the sidewalk and could light a cigarette. Alone in the night, his father's demands seemed trivial compared to the promise of what lay ahead.

A jarring clang echoed around the garage as Will's father dumped the bucket of engine parts on the oil-stained concrete. Will stared at them, and though resigned to the task before him, he refused to start until ordered.

"Well, there they are. Tell me what they're called and what they do."

Will took a deep breath and grabbed the most obvious part. "Carburetor. Controls the gas and air mixture to the engine."

"Good."

"Alternator. Keeps the battery charged."

"Close enough."

"Gasket. Seals the heads."

"Good."

"Oil filter ... fan belt ... timing chain ... Dad, do I have to do this every time you work on the car?"

"I told you, once this thing's yours, it's your responsibility. I'm not gonna help you with it."

Once Will completed the ritual, his father refilled the bucket and placed it under the workbench where it would remain until the next test. Will knew better than to leave, and instead, lost himself in the early spring breeze flowing through the open garage door. When the moment passed, he asked, "Can I go now?"

Will's father took his time answering, occupied with washing his hands at the filthy tap in the corner. "You know, I get the feeling you're not taking this seriously."

"Well, I did take auto shop last year."

"Oh, so that makes you an expert?"

"No, I just don't get why you keep making me do this."

"Believe me, when you're broken down by the side of the highway, you'll thank me."

"Maybe I don't want this piece of shit! Maybe I want a car of my own. You ever think of that?"

Hearing his own words, Will knew he'd just set a dangerous precedent with his father. They stared at each other for a moment, absorbing what had occurred, before Will bolted out of the garage.

Funny you should come here. But I guess it is the last place people would expect. Remember when you were talked into joining the football team? Just because you were six feet tall. What a crock! All that wasted time after school—breaking your neck in practice and getting sick walking home in the rain. And for what? Every time you'd go in the game you were useless. All those opportunities to show them what you're made of. Now here you sit, alone. Yeah, you're making some good decisions buddy. Why aren't you at that concert with Alex? Better to appease the old man? Look what that got you.

SHUT UP

He probably won't let you back in the house tonight.

I SAID SHUT UP

Okay, okay. You're right. Enjoy the surroundings. That's why you came. Not because you're a coward.

JUST LET ME BE FOR A WHILE

I've always tried to help you, and you never take my advice. Now's one of those times when you need me. Look what happens when you ignore me—your father hates you!

NO HE DOESN'T

You've disappointed him. So you've gotta get outta here as soon as possible.

Will heard voices approaching from the far end of the field. He debated what to do, but one in the group spotted him before he could act.

"Hey, that's a dude in the stands!" Will straightened his posture, knowing he had to face them. As they passed under the lights behind the school, he was relieved to recognize Keith, Matty and Wayne.

"It's fuckin' Will Mosley up there," Keith said. He pulled a can of Budweiser from the 12-pack under his arm and cracked it open.

Will replied, "Hey boys, what's happening?" He was uncomfortably aware there was no logical reason for him to be alone in the bleachers.

Wayne yelled, "Whatsa matter, get kicked out of the house?"

Will flinched when Keith and Matty started laughing. "Well, I guess I kinda did," he answered.

"Thought you'd be at the show," Matty slurred.

"Nah. Had other shit to do tonight."

"Well, in that case, have a beer." Keith tossed Will a can, before the trio stumbled up the bleachers and sat a row beneath Will. "Who's playing?" Keith asked.

"Grand Funk, I think," Wayne answered as he hurled his empty into the field, then helped himself to another. "See that? I coulda been the fuckin' QB."

"There's always next year," Matty remarked, to the further amusement of everyone, including Will. The beer was warm and scratched Will's throat on the way down.

"You guys not going either?"

"Why?" asked Wayne. "We've got our own rock and roll show here!"

Matty jumped in. "Grand Funk's alright, but I'm not paying five bucks to see them. I could pay that much to see a ton of better bands in Cleveland. How's the beer?"

Keith checked what was left of the 12-pack. "One left for each of us. We'll have to get some more." He handed out the last of the cans, then tossed the cardboard to the grass below. Will did the same with his empty before pulling the tab on the next.

They spent the next several minutes drinking in silence, and their lack of interest in Will's situation comforted him. Wayne was the first to finish his final beer, chucking the can the opposite direction this time, toward the parking lot. He got up and walked the beam of the bleacher as if he were balancing on a line of railroad track, yelling, "Grand Fuck! Who gives a shit?" Will snickered under his breath, but Keith and Matty didn't pay attention, until Wayne keeled over and fell two rows to the grass, and they all howled uncontrollably.

The drum solo went on and on with no sign of abating. Periodic cheers erupted around Alex until there was a rumbling crescendo. Most of the audience was sitting on the auditorium floor, affected by the smoke that hung in the air like a bad omen—a mix of the fog machines, weed, and cigarettes. Alex felt oppressed by the stifling smog, despite having accepted several tokes from people next to him. It was not the type of buzz he was used to, and it didn't help that Will wasn't there to guide him through it.

The biggest disappointment turned out to be how every attractive girl seemed to be with either a Jesus freak or some burned out biker in a leather vest. When a wineskin passed near him, Alex made a bold move to grab it. Thankfully, the intended recipient allowed Alex to take a healthy swig. The drums kept rolling, and Alex's anticipation rose in unison with the crowd, but as he gazed around the auditorium, there weren't many others who appeared to share his growing need to release the tension. The feeling festered the more he observed the many couples groping each other, and denim-clad fakes pretending this was some kind of bacchanal. Mark Farner kept screaming, "We love you people" from the stage, but Alex just wanted the drum solo to end.

The final roll built, and the crowd was lifted again, anticipating the return of the guitar and bass. It was not soon enough for Alex. Everyone in his immediate vicinity was on their feet, leaving Alex feeling trapped amid the crush of bodies. A surge from behind buckled his knees. He responded by pushing back, only to have the last dregs of a beer can poured over his head. Alex lashed out, his fists connecting with whatever was within range. The next second, angry hands reached for him from every direction, and hostile voices merged into an indecipherable roar. Alex tried to break free from the amassing mob, but he was boxed in until a cop yanked him toward an exit. A cheer rose up, echoing in his head as the cop dragged him into the sterile brightness of the lobby. Seeing a row of fire exits, Alex thought of attempting another break, until he felt the cold steel of the handcuffs.

"You were throwing roundhouses like Joe Frazier. That's assault, son."

Alex's mind was a cloud of confusion. "No, I didn't, it wasn't me."

"Everyone was pointing to you. There's at least twenty witnesses. You're stoned, too."

"No, I'm not. It wasn't me."

"Come on, you're under arrest. I've got to book you."

As the cop led him out of the auditorium to his cruiser, Alex heard another roar drift through the building when Mark Farner yelled, "We love you Ashtabula! Goodnight!"

The four of them stood in the 7-11 parking lot. "It's your turn to buy some skin mags," Matty told Wayne. "You know the rules, we take turns. Keith got 'em last month."

Wayne paused, as if hoping to detect any sign of Matty cutting him a break. When none was forthcoming, he strode through the glass doors without further objection. Matty gave Keith and Will a sly grin then motioned them to follow Wayne. Each headed in a separate direction, Keith to the cooler to grab another 12-pack, and Matty to the counter to buy cigarettes. Will lingered by the door. He didn't need anything, but he knew that whatever would transpire was better than being at home getting chewed out by his father. There would be plenty of time for that. He watched as Wayne deliberated in front of the magazine rack. He'd reach for a *Playboy*, *Penthouse* or *Cavalier*, then look over his shoulder. He knew Matty was keeping an eye on him. Wayne took a handful of the magazines to the counter and casually laid them down. At such a late hour, there was no fear of the sale being questioned.

Feeling a shared sense of accomplishment in the parking lot, Keith asked the pressing question. "Where do you wanna go?"

Matty turned to Wayne. "Are your parents home?"

"Nah, they went to Buffalo for the weekend to see my uncle in the hospital."

"You mean, you got the house to yourself? Why the fuck didn't you say something?"

"I dunno."

"We're out here all fucking night? What were you thinking?"

"I dunno, man. We always go out on Friday nights."

"Jesus!"

The walk to Wayne's commenced in silence. The streets of the affluent neighborhood were devoid of cars. Will had known Wayne and the other guys for a long time, but his real friendship was with Alex. Will had never been inside Wayne's house, and he was hit by a strange sensation of discovery as he passed through the side door. A sign posted in the front door reserved entry for only the mailman and milkman. Will followed the others to the basement. The walls, lined with Wayne's father's beer bottle collection, made Will wary of his movements, for fear of disturbing the magnificent array. Will couldn't focus on the swirling mass of color; images of moose, Vikings and tall ships converging as his eyes scanned the crammed shelves.

"Did your dad really drink all these beers?" he asked Wayne.

"Yeah man, I guess."

"How long did it take him?"

"I dunno. He's had most of these since I was a kid."

"Jesus Christ, these are just the singles. He drank at least six of each, eh?"

"Maybe."

Wayne, drunk and uninterested in Will's questions, collapsed on the couch and dove into the skin mags, while Will continued to take stock of the room, from a handful of magnificent bowling trophies to an array of exotic ashtrays.

"Hey Matty, gimme a smoke."

Matty choked on his beer. "Since when do you smoke?"

It was true that Will believed it was a filthy habit. He'd seen it turn his granddaddy into a wheezing paperweight who still managed to suck down a pack a day. Still, he couldn't resist the small act of rebellion. "Just gimme one, alright? Maybe this is all a dream."

Matty smiled as he reached for his pack of Marlboros on the coffee table, and threw one over, along with his lighter. Will held the cigarette for a second, hoping he wouldn't choke on the first drag. He exhaled most of the smoke immediately.

None of the others appeared to notice, and Keith tossed Alex a can out of the new 12-pack. "Kind of funny we're drinking Bud with all these fancy beers around. Hey Wayne, you ever tried any of these?"

"No, I'm not allowed to touch them," he replied, his attention fixed on a centerfold.

Matty was near the stereo, flipping through the records in search of anything that might be worth hearing amongst the Mitch Miller and Burl Ives. He settled on Elvis's *King Creole*. Keith instantly objected. "I can't listen to that shit. He hasn't made a good record since 'Jailhouse Rock.'"

"This one's pretty good," Matty retorted.

Will had heard a lot of Elvis's music, but had never thought to judge it until that moment.

Keith continued to argue with Matty. "Nah. Have you seen him lately? It's total Vegas, what he's doing now. He does songs that other old bastards want to hear so they can feel like they can still score."

"Look who's talking, you old bastard. When's the last time you got laid?"

The comment hit home and Keith clammed up. The side played on and Wayne, in order to break the tension more than anything, asked no one in particular, "Are chicks still into Elvis as much as they used to be? I mean, he's married now, so—"

Keith looked over to Wayne, replying in a drowsy drawl, "Of course they're still into him. What chick wouldn't want to fuck Elvis?"

"But he's old. For chicks our age, it'd be like fucking their father."

"So what? He's got it all. That's what chicks care about."

Matty chimed in, "Once you start playing rock and roll, you stop the aging process."

"Shut up."

"No really. Think about it. Elvis looks totally different now, but you liked 'Blue Suede Shoes' the first time you heard it, right? Some kid in ten years is going to like it the first time he hears it too. It'll always be cool, so we'll always be cool for liking it."

"What the fuck are you talking about?"

"Well, to say you like Elvis now isn't cool, right? But who's the best musician? Jimi Hendrix, right? He digs Elvis. I read it in an interview. When Elvis is gone, 'Blue Suede Shoes' will still be a cool song. You can't kill something like that. My uncle saw Elvis before he went in the army, and that's pretty fucking cool as far as I'm concerned. Kids might be saying the same thing about us someday because we saw Jimi in Cleveland."

Will allowed Matty's late-night logic to sink in. He'd lately been putting a lot of thought into his own potential to be a musician ever since his granddad gave him his guitar, and it was starting to influence every decision he made. Matty's argument was bringing some unexpected clarity to Will's personal struggle.

Keith still wasn't convinced. "So, you're saying that the music itself is all that matters?"

"Well, look at it this way," Matty continued. "What were guys like us doing twenty or thirty years ago? Most of 'em had families so they'd all get together on the weekends and play poker. Or they'd sit around and shoot the shit about baseball. Or they'd go hunting or fishing or other stupid shit our dads do. Being into rock and roll is the same thing for us. It's a part of being alive. Sure, everything gets boring, but this is who we are."

Wayne was passed out on the couch and Keith appeared ready to join him. Will asked Matty for another cigarette, but after one drag, he set it in an ashtray, where it burned down to the filter.

He noticed Matty nodding off during a break between songs. "Hey man, wake up."

"Huh?"

"Can I ask you something?"

"What?"

"Do you really feel cool?"

"You mean right now? Not especially."

"No. I mean all that shit you were saying, do you really believe it?"

"Well yeah. What else have we got?"

"Yeah."

Will reached for the extinguished cigarette before watching Matty sink into sleep. When the record crashed to a halt, the only sound was the needle skipping against the label. Will sat hypnotized by the ceaseless thump. Throughout his life, he had been careful to do the right things, know the right people, listen to the right music, and that none of it mattered, despite Matty's argument. It didn't matter that Will had camped out all night for Stones tickets to be first in line. It didn't matter that he stole a bottle of Wild Turkey from his dad, and he and Alex got drunk for the first time. It didn't matter that he'd been with Janet for two years when he found out she'd cheated on him.

"Matty, wake up. I'm calling Janet tomorrow."

"Yeah, sure man."

Will grabbed a Bud, pulling the tab as he walked up the stairs and headed home, not worried anymore about what his dad might have in store.

Alex and Will met at Sharky's, their usual Saturday afternoon routine. They got their regular table and began knocking the balls around with familiar precision. But from the moment he saw Alex stumble in without his usual swagger, Will sensed something amiss. The tension built when Alex didn't offer any comments about the concert.

"How was it?" Will forced his inquiry, expecting a disastrous answer.

Alex, poised to take a shot, stood erect and shook the unkempt head of dirty blonde hair his parents had allowed him to grow out the previous summer. He smiled and mumbled, "You sure missed a good one, man."

Will ran his hands through his own collar-length straight brown hair as he awaited details, but Alex returned to lining up his cue and dropped the seven-ball into a corner pocket. Alex admired his shot before saying, "I spent the night in the slammer. Can you believe it?"

"You what?" Will remained calm, as if saying anything would somehow implicate him.

"Ah, it was nothing. Some people around me wanted to mix it up."

"You got in a fight?"

"Nah, just defending my territory. I was kinda fucked up too."

"So you got arrested?"

"Well, yeah. They were gonna charge me with first degree assault, but the cop turned out to be alright. No one was hurt, so he figured I could plead guilty to public intoxication. I gotta see the judge on Monday. First offence. Lawyer I talked to this morning said I should just have to pay a fine."

Will couldn't determine what was more shocking, his friend's actions, or his sudden expert use of legal jargon. "Jesus, your folks must want to kill you."

"Yeah, but who gives a fuck? When they showed up to bail me out, I was expecting that too. But they both just looked kinda, I don't know, sad. I mean really, really sad. The kind of sadness I've never seen before. They listened to everything the cop told them about what happened and what I had to do, and just nodded. All the way home, I had my guard up, but neither of them said anything. I think my mom was crying in the car, but I couldn't really tell. When we got home, they left me standing in the kitchen. It was the same thing this morning. Neither of them said anything to me. I made my own breakfast and came here. Pretty strange, huh?"

Before he could answer, Alex changed the subject. "What did you end up doing?"

The question diverted Will's train of thought. "Oh, not much. Got into a big fucking blow-up with my old man and I took off. Ran into Wayne, Keith and Matty and had a few beers. It's funny, my dad had kind of the same reaction this morning. He wasn't pissed off, he just ignored me, like he couldn't be bothered to be angry."

They returned to the game. Will worked up the nerve to ask more questions after a few silent minutes. "So what was jail like?"

"It's the shits, man. It was me and a few bums, basically, but I couldn't take it. I had to keep telling myself to stay calm."

"Seriously?"

"Oh yeah. I never want to be locked up again. Betcha a Coke you'll miss."

Will was down to the eight ball and had a difficult cut in order to put it in the side pocket. They didn't often play for money, or anything aside from personal pride, so Alex's offer was worth taking a second to contemplate. "Since when do you wanna gamble?"

"It's not gambling. It's just a fucking Coke. You gonna take the shot or what?"

Will smiled as he leaned over the table, the smooth wood sliding between his fingers, and coming close to brushing his chin. Without taking his eye off the cue ball, he answered, "Yeah, you're gonna be buying." With that, he stroked the cue with just enough force to angle the eight ball toward the pocket. The aim was true, although the ball lingered on the lip long enough to taunt Alex, before surrendering to gravity.

"I guess that's the kind of luck I've been having," Alex said, setting his cue on the green felt and reaching into his jeans to count his change.

They sat in the lounge with their Cokes, face to face over a grimy Formica table. A few other kids with nothing to do on a Saturday afternoon sat at other tables, eating fries and watching the Indians play the Red Sox on the big television anchored to a corner of the ceiling. Alex kept turning away to check the score, a sign to Will that something was burning within his friend's thoughts.

It finally emerged when Alex looked Will in the eyes and said, "You know, man, I think I gotta split."

"Why, what's going on? Someone having a party tonight?"

"No, no. I mean I gotta get away from my parents. I gotta get outta town."

Will glared at Alex with a furrowed brow. "Where do you wanna go?"

"I don't know. Anywhere's better than here. Don't tell me you haven't thought about it too."

"Sure, but what can we do? Work in a fucking steel mill? An auto plant?"

"Come on, you know what it's gotta be. You've got songs, man, you're a musician. You've got to go to L.A."

Will shrugged aside Alex's blatant attempt at flattery. He didn't feel close to being ready to perform in public. At the same time, he couldn't help being captivated by Alex's idea.

"Fine, I can go to L.A., but what'll you do?"

"Doesn't matter, man, I can do anything. It's the land of opportunity."

"Why don't you just go by yourself?"

"Come on, you wouldn't want that to happen? Besides, strength in numbers."

Will smiled to himself, allowing Alex's unexpected proposition to fire his imagination. It sounded like something Janet would say. Why couldn't she have asked him to leave everything behind and go with her to San Francisco like everyone else did the previous summer? No, she had to fuck around on him, and now she was back at her parents' house stuck with a baby.

"Hey man, do you think I made a mistake breaking up with Janet?"

Alex looked deflated to hear Will bring up her name again. "Janet? What are you still hung up on her for? She screwed you over."

"Yeah, but she's paid for it. I know she's not doing so well right now. I've been thinking about calling her."

"Fine, but don't let it change your mind. We gotta do this. I know you want it as much as I do."

They tipped their bottles back as a cheer rose up from the television. Carl Yasztremski had put one over the Green Monster.

"Fucking Tribe," Alex said. "They're brutal."

Will wondered if the lights in the coffee shop were getting brighter. The staff must have been trying to get them to leave. He hadn't taken Janet here when they were together, so the possibility of an embarrassing scene weighed upon him. But he couldn't leave until he got the answer he needed.

"Do you want another?" he asked.

"Sure, I'm feeling a little sleepy."

He looked for a waitress but the only other person in the place was behind the counter. He got up and paid for two coffees. Janet was staring out the window when he returned, and faced Will when he sat down.

"Thanks. I guess I owe you a few the next time," she said.

"When will that be?" he asked, trying not to sound too anxious.

She didn't answer, just gazed into her coffee as she brought it to her lips. Words failed him, and he was grateful when she spoke up. "What are you going to do this summer?"

"I don't know. I'm not taking any classes this year, even though they say I have to."

"I'll probably go out west again," she said. "The commune folk have been writing, asking me to come back."

"What about the baby?"

"I can bring her. There's a lot of kids there. Everyone pitches in to raise them."

"That's cool. You know, I've always wanted to go to San Francisco. I'm probably the only person who hasn't been."

"It's beautiful. I'd like to move permanently," she said.

"What would you do? A waitress is a waitress no matter where you are." He heard how petty he sounded as the words passed his lips.

"Well, there are lots of other things I can do."

"I know, I didn't mean it that way."

"How did you mean it?"

"I think a lot of travelling is overrated. I mean, people believe they're going on these big spiritual journeys and after they go halfway around the world, all they discover is how much they miss home."

"What's wrong with that?"

"Nothing. I just think some people do it with unrealistic expectations."

"Well, I know I don't like living here."

"I'm not saying you shouldn't go, I'm just sick of all my friends leaving me, I guess." Will took a long sip, hoping these words would elicit a little sympathy.

"You should think about going then," Janet said.

"Maybe I will."

There was a lull as they both listened to the rain. "Do you miss the people out there?" he asked.

"A little. I just feel better when I'm there. I didn't have a boyfriend in the city if that's what you're getting at."

"What about the guy who knocked you up?"

"That was a mistake. It was a crazy night. I never saw him again. You dated anyone recently?"

"Not really. They've all gone away too. One married the first guy she met after me, and one was only here temporarily."

"Why didn't you go with her?"

"I don't know. I was too wrapped up in my own shit, I guess."

"Do you miss her?"

"No, it would have been too hard to manage."

"I don't mean it like that. I mean, forget about all the practical things, was she the one?"

He hadn't thought Janet cared that much about him to ask such a question, and his mind drifted to the handful of days he'd spent with Tara in the aftermath of Janet's departure. Tara was on vacation from Ireland, visiting a mutual friend, when Will met her at an Independence Day beer bash. He was smitten with her accent and asked her endless questions about Belfast. They talked for hours. He didn't need much encouragement after she revealed that her father had played with Van Morrison in the early '60s. Van had been to her house. Van had played her guitar. Van the Man. The creator of *Astral Weeks*, the album that Jimmy at Replay Records had turned him on to as soon as it had come out, and that had become the gateway to his own newfound creativity. Tara came with him to the beach at Lake Erie. They drank and laughed and her delicate Irish skin got sunburned. He wanted to fall in love with her, but knew she was as good as gone.

"No, she wasn't the one."

He wanted to ask Janet if she'd met the one, but was terrified of hearing her say yes. Instead, he asked when she was leaving.

"I write my last exam tomorrow, and I leave Thursday. I'll be back in September though."

"Yeah? You already know that?"

"Well, maybe I won't. It's just different with the baby. My parents don't think I can take good care of her. I don't want her raised in the same shit I had to go through. The thought of her being with them makes me sick."

He nodded, continuing to bring his mug to his mouth despite the coffee being cold.

"You should come out," she continued. "I can't promise you can stay with me, but you'll have a good time."

The girl behind the counter came over, as if sensing their conversation reaching its conclusion. "Sorry folks," she said. "Closing up."

Will glanced at Janet. "I guess I'd better take you home." He tried to enjoy the remaining moments as they put on their coats and walked into the rain. Nothing she could say would change how he felt. If he were younger, he would have spilled his guts as they walked home. Instead, both of them stayed silent.

When they arrived at her parents' house, Janet turned to him. "Write me and let me know if you're coming."

Will offered an awkward goodbye before stepping off the porch and racing into the downpour.

Once home and dry, he laid on his bed in the dark and listened to *Astral Weeks* through his headphones, like he'd done more times than he'd care to remember.

"How's the Olds?"

"It's fine. My dad took it out this morning, then gave me the keys."

"You didn't tell him we're leaving, did you?"

"Well, I had to say something. I couldn't just split the first day I had the car."

"What did you say?"

"We're taking Janet and the baby to the commune."

"You *said* that? We're not actually doing it, right?"

"We're taking Janet and the baby to the commune."

"Holy fuck! Good thinking."

"Well, what else could I do? Thanks for the wheels, see you in a few years! Believe me, this works best for everybody."

"Alright, I'll be ready at ten! Don't honk the horn, I'll hear you."

"Last Letter to Janet"

The night before we left, I painted graffiti on a box car
Each wave of my hand dug into the metal; my work stood jagged
like a deep scar
I stared and felt how skinny I was getting inside my clothes

Then I went to the playground with the broken slide
And thought of how, if I could replay all the games, I would choose neither side
Then I sat down on the riverbank and wondered where all that dirty water flows

We're going to California where the wild heather grows

As the miles wore on I thought if there's a way you can show me
Despite the towering walls of silence, if you can admit that you know me
Then I won't deny my name when I have to take the blows

And as we passed over the mountains to rest in the shade of tall pines
There was a moment when I knew we had crossed the fault line
Where we will be with the others falling off the edge when the whole thing finally goes

We're going to California where the wild heather grows

Now that we're here, all I remember are the stops for gas and food
And sometimes I pretend it would be nice to see you if you'd be in the mood
But then I get distracted by all the static on my radio

Still, I'm comforted knowing that we've left our cold room and iron bed
But once in a while I still wonder if you give in and bow your head
And think of how beautiful the world can be when it snows

We're going to California where the wild heather grows

Chapter 3

Las Vegas / May 1972

"**H**ey, have you ever had a dream where you feel totally in love, even though you don't recognize the person you're with at all?"

"I can't recall," Jessy said.

"Well, it sure is something."

"You're saying I wasn't in the dream with you?"

"Hell no!"

To prove he was joking, Alex pulled Jessy close and kissed one of her earlobes. He couldn't resist adding a lick, prompting her to roll over and entwine her tongue with his. In the full light of day, and with only traces of a lingering hangover, the moment took on greater urgency. Positioning himself above her, Alex was in full command of his senses, consumed by a surge of raw power. Each stroke fell into perfect rhythm with Jessy's intensified breathing. It took all his strength to hold back, but as he sensed Jessy reaching a crescendo, they were frozen in time, a Rodin sculpture made flesh.

Alex collapsed on his half of the bed, training his gaze on the ceiling fan. Jessy reached over to her nightstand and lit a cigarette, inhaling a sizable portion with the first drag.

"Was that better than your dream?" she asked.

"Almost," he said with a laugh.

Jessy finished her cigarette without another word, her coffee-and-cream skin beaded with sweat. The weekend getaway in Vegas was going well so far, despite the stares directed toward them. It was the first time they'd appeared in public outside L.A. and the reaction struck Alex in a different way, leaving him wondering how protective he should be. But, knowing Jessy could take care of herself, he grasped that the predominant question in peoples' minds when they saw them was, why was this statuesque Black woman with him?

"Will and Angela should be up by now," Alex said. "What time is it anyway," he added, unwilling to lift his head to look.

"1:30," Jessy said, setting another cigarette in the ashtray.

"Jesus." Alex raised himself again, rubbing his face and hair in mock disbelief. He drank in Jessy's magnificence one last time before inserting his legs into a pair of cut-off jeans. She was in no hurry to join him, and pulled the sheet up to her neck.

"Don't you wanna hit the Strip again, baby?" he asked.

"Not yet, honey."

"Well I'm starving. Let's get some eggs or something."

Jessy cringed and turned her face into the pillow, muffling her words. "You go and play for awhile honey. That's what you wanted to do. Come back and get me tonight. I'll be okay."

All Alex could see of his lover was a tussled nest of black hair. Her mind appeared made up, and of what little Alex knew about women, the only certainty was that he couldn't make her do anything she didn't want to. "All right. I'm gonna have a little kick start, and then I'm gonna go. Too bad for you."

Jessy turned to face him. "Hey, while you're getting some for yourself—"

Will sat on the edge of the bed counting the cash that was left in his jeans. It was less than he'd remembered when they'd returned from the Flamingo. He couldn't recall what had drained his gambling budget, but looking at Angela, still asleep, he saw the cheap necklace by the phone. Buying it for her seemed like a good idea at the time. They had both been caught up in the excitement when she'd come out a little bit ahead at the roulette table. It was her first time playing, and she started out laying bets on red or black. After twenty minutes, she began picking numbers, sevens and threes, moving on to birthdays. She'd lose a few in a row, but as she'd decide to take one last spin, the ball landed where it was supposed to, eliciting cheers from those gathered around the table. Angela was the star of the night, at least to anyone who made a profit by following her lead. Will had sensed they hated to see her walk away, but she was ready to move on to the next distraction. It had gone so well that Will felt she needed to be rewarded at the end of the night. As they passed the gift shop on the way to the motel, he gravitated to a fake gold necklace with a heart-shaped ruby. She accepted with grace, and as they embraced she leaned in for a kiss, but he pulled away, brushing the blonde curls from her eyes and admiring the gift resting above the low-cut neckline of her t-shirt.

Looking at it next to the bed, Will wanted to be rid of what now seemed like an empty gesture. He picked up the necklace without waking Angela, the thin metal sliding between his fingers like honey. He grasped the ruby heart, examined its details and wondered if this was all that Angela meant to him. If he'd put some thought into it, he would have bought her a real gift.

Angela stirred, and Will replaced the necklace on the nightstand. The early afternoon sun illuminated her smile as she saw Will sitting at her feet. She propped herself up against the headboard, and Will couldn't help being amused by her clumsy movements.

"How long have you been up?" she asked.

"A while. You were sleeping like a log, I couldn't disturb you."

"Have you been out?"

"Not really. You feel like going for a walk? Alex is probably back at the tables already."

Angela yawned and shook her blonde tresses.

Will stood up. "Alright, you relax. I'll see if Alex is around." He didn't wait for an answer before opening the door, allowing some of the punishing heat to enter the room. He shut it behind him, and stood for a moment on the asphalt, trying to see beyond the motel parking lot to the desert off in the distance.

In that instant, whatever was out there was far more intriguing to him than spending another day wandering Fremont Street. He'd heard stories of the desert from other musicians he knew, stories of tribal peyote and LSD ceremonies, which were accompanied by UFO sightings. These weren't treated officially as a rite of passage, but to Will it was another thing that excluded him from the company he wanted to keep. When Alex suggested the four of them go to Vegas for a weekend getaway, Will thought they would spend some time in the desert. So far, Alex had only wanted to gamble. Will could ill-afford to lose any money, but he had a hard time saying no, considering how little time they spent together anymore. Having the girls there put him at ease, but as Will continued to gaze down the highway that brought them here, he felt as empty as the expanse it cut through.

Will walked the short distance to Alex and Jessy's room. As he was about to knock, he heard a splash that drew his attention to the pool. Alex's head emerged from the water and he paddled to the shallow end.

"Hey," Will yelled.

"What's happening?" Alex yelled back. "You just get up?"

"Yeah. Didn't think it was so late."

"I know. What happened to you guys?"

"Angela got on a bit of a roll playing roulette."

"She come out ahead?"

"A little. Enough to walk away happy."

"That's more than I can say. I think I lost a hundred bucks in ten minutes."

"What happened? You looked like you were doing alright last time I saw you."

"I guess that's how it goes here, man. The dealer had it in for me. I stood on seventeen at least three times and lost every one. Fuckin' bullshit."

Alex raised himself up in the shallow end, the saturated cut-off denim hanging low on his emaciated hips. "Nothing to worry about, though. Me and Jess had a good time."

"Where is she?"

"Still sleeping."

"Yeah, Angela is too."

"What do you wanna do? I'm ready to take another shot."

"Yeah, I think I am too."

"Good. I'll get dressed."

They walked the short distance to the Flamingo with the afternoon sun raising mirages across their path. Traffic streamed by in a constant flow—Caddies, LTDs, Lincolns—cars that made Will's Delta 88 seem small, or more accurately, mid-western. With their long hair, t-shirts, and aviator sunglasses, the pair wasn't the anomaly they would have been on Fremont Street ten years earlier. A few other L.A. hustlers stood out, and displayed an innate ability to spot kindred souls from a far distance. To Will's surprise, Alex maintained a cool disposition whenever they were approached by one of these dime-baggers who expected sympathy. Will could imagine that Alex was feeling beyond that, since he'd finally been handed an acting gig. At least they had something in common again; they were both getting paid for what they'd come out to L.A. do. Will was proud of his friend, despite Alex indulging in every detail of his good fortune on the drive to Vegas—from how the casting director ignored Alex's fake SAG card, to how he said he liked Alex's look, even after he botched the lines during his first read-through. Alex had all of them laughing when he recalled, "The guy goes, 'Don't worry, the character would probably say it like that too!'"

Alex had then been granted a brief meeting with the director, Bill Naud. Will had heard Alex tell plenty of stories about meeting actors but as he described how Naud gave his approval, Will knew this was something that had the potential of changing the course of Alex's life, and even his teeth appeared to give off a glow that suited an actor. "I could definitely feel that we were coming from the same place," Alex beamed. "We smoked a joint together afterward. Did I mention that?"

They strode up to the front door of the casino, through the mob of middle-aged tourists debating where to get the best two-dollar porterhouse steak. The sliding doors parted, and the concierge tipped his hat. A rush of the air conditioning welcomed them inside. They stood for a minute, surveying the room, each forced to adjust to the artificial light and sound.

"Remember which dealer you had last night?" Will asked, removing his shades.

Alex removed his as well, positioning them on top of his shaggy head. "How could I forget that chiseler," he replied under his breath. They drifted toward the blackjack tables, scoping out one that wasn't too crowded.

"You see her?"

"Nah, must be her day off."

They chose a five-dollar table manned by an old dealer with the hard looks of a refugee. His nametag read Paulo, and he traded the pair's cash for chips with an air of impassivity. The first hand was over before either had managed to settle into their seats. Will gave Alex a bewildered look, as he placed his next bet. He drew a king and a queen, and won. Alex busted, drawing a jack on his thirteen. The other person at the table when they'd arrived had left after laying out all his chips on a losing hand, an act that appeared motivated more by boredom than anything else. That feeling began to take over Will's thoughts after an hour without any progress, as their dealer unceasingly reached for cards and chips without any cracks showing in his tanned facade.

Alex seemed compelled to talk as bets hit the table like clockwork. "This must be a lot better than where you came from, huh?"

"Yes, sir."

"Where are you from?"

"Brazil, originally," Paulo droned as if he had replayed the same conversation a hundred times.

Alex feigned a look of fascination. "I thought things were pretty good down there," he offered.

"No, not good. Maybe good now, but not when I was there."

Will sensed that Alex was digging into things he shouldn't, and marveled at how Paulo kept his composure.

"What was it? A woman? Somebody after you?" Alex glanced over at Will with a conspiratorial smile. Will remained quiet out of respect for the dealer.

Paulo kept up his work, replying, "Yes sir, a woman," as if to shut Alex up.

A waitress arrived with a round of complimentary bourbon and sodas, and Alex tipped her with a five-dollar chip. "Yeah, who the fuck needs 'em, huh Paulo? Like last night, I'm sitting at that table right over there, and one of your female compadres cleans me out in a few minutes with a fucking smile on her face the whole time."

"I'm sorry to hear that, sir."

"At least you do your job with a little dignity. So, what'd this bitch do to you? Fuck some gringo behind your back?"

"Something like that, sir."

"Well, I hope you did the right thing and killed that bastardo." Alex laughed and looked in Will's direction for support. Will kept his eyes on Paulo, knowing Alex had crossed the line.

"Yes I did, sir." Alex cut his laughter. Paulo stood motionless in mid-deal, aiming his opaque blue eyes at Alex until the younger man raised his arms in mock surrender.

Paulo resumed dealing, and Alex stood on fourteen, passing his open hand over the cards. Paulo busted, and a new dealer arrived to take over, a small, middle-aged woman with a beehive hairdo who took up her duties in silence. "I can see why you don't wanna talk," Alex said to her after several hands. "Bet you've got more horror stories than old Paulo." He laughed to himself, before downing the rest of his bourbon.

Sitting in the Flamingo's dining room, Will and Alex ate two-dollar prime rib from the buffet. Will was up twenty bucks and Alex was down forty. The losses didn't affect him; he was still thinking about Paulo. "I can't believe he killed a guy. You think he killed a guy?"

"Looked like a killer to me," Will replied, his mouth stuffed with potato and carrots. "Lots of people around here look like killers."

"Come on. What do you think is his real story? He's probably a mob plant. Everyone around here is. Maybe he's skimming off the top and sending it back to fucking Brazil, or wherever, to feed his kids. He seemed way too high-strung to be dealing an honest game. Doncha think? You saw how much I was losing after we started talking."

"I don't know. I ever tell you how my great-granddaddy killed a man once? It was over a woman, too. Granddaddy told me about it when he was dying. It was down in Kentucky just after the Civil War. It goes that my great-granddaddy's sister got pregnant by a man who'd raped her. They were gonna arrest him, but my great-granddaddy got to him first. Everyone knew he'd killed the man, but they never found a body. It all ended up getting swept under the rug, but granddaddy said great-granddaddy couldn't forget about it. You couldn't talk about killing around him, not even pigs or chickens."

Alex pushed the food around his plate, before dropping his fork, lighting a cigarette, and leaning back in his chair. "I thought all your family were farmers."

"Well, yeah. But people lived by different laws back then, I guess. Another story my granddaddy told me was about his uncle in Tennessee during the Civil War. He'd gotten up one morning to work in the fields and he could hear some kind of battle going on a few miles away. He didn't pay it much mind until he came back to the house for lunch and this Yankee soldier was laying on his doorstep all tore to pieces. He was by himself; must have wandered off looking for help and got disoriented. Granddaddy's uncle takes him into the house and tries to comfort him however he can. He tries to get the soldier to tell him his name, and where he's from, and what happened at the battle, but all the Yankee says is how he sees the gates of heaven and the angels coming to take him. He didn't last too long after that, and granddaddy's uncle kept that soldier's gun belt and his Colt .45. I think my family were southern sympathizers, but granddaddy's uncle was broken up enough about that Yankee that he took the body back to where that battle happened, and tried to see if anyone knew him and could give him a proper burial."

Will bit into another healthy portion of prime rib. Alex cocked his head and blew smoke straight up in the air. "That's quite a family history. What's happened lately?"

Will looked up from his food and smiled. "Well, we haven't made our fortune here yet."

"You ready for another go-round?"

"Actually, no. I should go back and see Angela. She should be up and ready by now."

"Up and ready for what?"

"I got tickets for Elvis at the Hilton."

"Elvis? Jesus, you might as well see Wayne Newton."

"What do you mean? One of the reasons I said I'd come was to see Elvis, and that's what I'm gonna do."

"I thought you were kidding."

Will went back to cleaning his plate, and Alex finished his cigarette. "Wow, I'm suddenly learning so many new things about you," he said in between drags. "Confederate relatives and Elvis? You're a bona fide, shit-kicking hillbilly, ain't ya?"

Will stopped eating. He pushed his chair away from the table. "I'll see you later," he said, before walking out of the dining lounge. Alex watched him slip into the crowd, feeling more alone than embarrassed. He lit another cigarette and imagined the scene at the Hilton; screaming housewives throwing themselves at the buffoon in the jumpsuit, a man who could barely remember the words to the songs that the rest of the world had long forgotten. No, he could find something better to do with Jessy and her sweet brown thighs. "Give my regards to the Pelvis, and try not to faint," he said to himself.

Elvis paused before signaling the band to start the next song. Will saw something was missing and Elvis needed a second to find it. His sweat-streaked, dyed black hair framed his classic Roman features like strokes of paint from a thick horsehair brush. His gaudy jumpsuit initially shocked Will's eyes, but it helped Elvis move with the elegance of a second skin. The audience had been in his palm from the moment they took their seats, and when the house lights dimmed, the bottled-up anticipation exploded, leaving Will hanging in mid-air, detached from Angela.

Song followed song, inducing wild swings of emotion, from unhinged hysteria, to collective laughter at the jokes— "Man, I'm tame compared to what they do now. I didn't do anything but jiggle." It turned an unreal place, a thousand miles from where everyone in the room came from, into something they all had a stake in.

Then Elvis paused again. He drank from a plastic cup and an attendant brought a dry towel for his face. It seemed to Will that in Elvis's younger days, he was much more vain about his hair, that perfectly sculptured pompadour. Now he allowed it to hang limp after a slight touch from the terrycloth, its symbolic qualities long since passed into other myths about his non-conformist attitude, along with the pink and black wardrobe he had once cherished.

When the bandleader nodded to begin a pastoral introduction, felt the show was building to its climax after close to an hour. The musicians moved quietly yet consistently, like a train pulling out of the depot in the small country town where Elvis had been born. Will was fixated as Elvis stood in place, allowing the music to swell up within him, to a degree that the introduction carried on for an extra measure. He turned to the band and smiled that beatific smile that made everyone in the room feel like children again. The band dug even deeper into the song, awaiting Elvis's entrance, at which point they could all settle in for the ride. Elvis turned to the audience with eyes closed. Once he got the first line out, Will knew the rest would tumble from his lips with the urgency of someone wanting the entire world to know their life story.

Will knew the song well. He had learned it after hearing someone else's version on the radio. The song wasn't simple; the fingerpicked guitar figure at first seemed too delicate, and the words were tricky to deliver. Depending on one's perspective, it could be a love song, albeit a love for something more meaningful than a woman. Will had felt that kind of love a few times in his life, a love of simply being alive. Hearing Elvis sing the song at that moment was one of those times. Will pictured himself and Elvis on the same journey, both sent out into the world with the simple goal of reclaiming the only thing that held any meaning for them. It could be anywhere— the wheat fields, the coalmines, the train yards, even there on stage in Vegas, the end of the road for those whose idea of success was based on outdated notions.

Will anticipated the last verse coming, and knew that unlike the rest of the program, this song would not conclude with a bombastic flourish, but fade into the distance without resolution. Elvis let the final words trickle off his tongue like raindrops off a tin roof in a summer storm. All that was left was for the band to take the journey a little further down the road. The outro was extended to give Elvis time to compose himself, and the applause sounded respectful, almost sedated.

Elvis drank again from a plastic cup and toweled off his face, but this time didn't smile at the band. He sent a stern, resigned look toward the drummer. "Well it's a-one for the money..."

The house lights rose after an announcer stated that Elvis had left the building. There was some of the old adoration evident in the women who congregated at the front of the stage, but the rest of the audience seemed happy to file out. Will was drained. He sat staring at the thick, regal curtain concealing the stage.

Angela looked at him with trepidation. "Ready to go?"

He took a deep breath. "Yeah, let's split."

Will remained deep in contemplation as they mingled with the crowd filtering up the aisles to the exits.

"You know," Angela said, "when you told me you wanted to see Elvis, I wasn't sure we could be friends anymore."

"You mean you didn't have a good time?"

"Oh yeah, I had a great time. It was just something I wasn't expecting."

He resisted the urge to act snobbish. He was beginning to recognize he did that a lot when they argued about music. But he kept his passion in check, knowing the communion he'd experienced would be tarnished by a frivolous debate over aesthetics. They reached the Strip without any further word on the subject.

"What do you feel like doing," she asked, as a cool evening breeze caressed their faces. "Get some drinks and play roulette again?"

Will looked down at her and smiled. Her free-spirited gait made her blonde curls bounce in an innocent fashion. "I actually feel like playing some blackjack. I was doing pretty good today with Alex."

"Alright, let's go." She had no qualms about hooking her arm around his, and he allowed her to do it, although it forced him to alter his sluggish walking speed in order to keep up with her purposeful stride.

They were at the Flamingo within minutes, scoping out the tables. Will found one with a non-threatening male dealer, and two middle-aged men seated at opposing ends; one was small, clean-cut and nervous, with horn-rimmed glasses and bad posture. The other was an overweight cowboy, complete with hat and bolo tie, a cheap cigar providing the strongest evidence as to why there were several empty seats on either side of him. Will chose sets in between the men, sensing both ogling Angela, and wasn't surprised when she edged closer to him, her hands searching for contact. She whispered to Will, "You go ahead and play. I'm just happy to watch."

Will glanced at her with a raised eyebrow, and traded the dealer forty dollars for chips. His luck from the afternoon held out, and his stack modestly increased. He played every hand by the book, weighing the odds based on the dealer's hand. In little time he had doubled his original stake. The warm glow of this small victory was accentuated by having Angela to witness it. More players came to the table, while others stood and watched. Will paid little attention to the gawkers; if you were able to focus, he told himself, at least it gave you a shot at walking out with your head up. Angela nuzzling his shoulder provided a steadying influence.

Will was dealt two aces. He split them, as Alex had told him to do. Then a third ace fell. Another bet was placed, and more curious onlookers seemed to appear out of nowhere. The fourth ace landed in front of him. Angela wrapped her arm around his waist as gasps of amazement rose in unison around the table. Will placed another bet. Half of his stake was in play, arranged in a symmetrical line of cards and chips. Even the dealer hesitated, seemingly unwilling to disrupt the miracle that had manifested itself on his table. Suppressing his humanity, the dealer reached for the deck. Will drew an eight for his first ace, a nine for the second, a seven and another eight. The crowd exhaled a sigh of relief in unison.

The dealer drew a ten and a jack. The amassed crowd then groaned as one, and several men gave Will consoling slaps on the back. He continued to stare at the cards until the dealer swept them away, as if the moment had never occurred. Angela squeezed Will's waist tighter in an attempt to get any sense as to how he was taking the loss. After a few moments he looked toward her, saying in a measured tone, "You can let go of me now."

She retracted, her eyes locked onto his as Will placed a large bet, drew a fifteen, and busted a few seconds later. He was down to ten dollars.

"Maybe we should go," Angela whispered in his ear. The dealer didn't wait for Will to post his ante. The hand was dealt without him.

"Yeah, you're right," he said under his breath. "Gambling is about the dumbest thing anyone can do." Will stood up from the table, both of his hands trembling. Angela clenched his wrist and guided him on an agonizing walk toward the exit.

"If I get the crook-eye from one more of these redneck motherfuckers, I swear I'm gonna unload on them."

Alex had never seen Jessy on the verge of losing control. "Take it easy sugar," he said, trying to calm her. "Remember, we ain't in L.A. They're all just jealous, baby." She was decked out in her finest Hollywood Boulevard cock-tease gear, consisting of stacked heels, fish nets, and red leather mini-skirt, and a matching push-up bra to top it all off. The shoes lifted her a couple of inches above Alex, giving the added impression that he was skulking beside her as they cruised Fremont. He kept thinking of how to distract her from the condescending looks. "How do you think we'd do if we lived here?"

"I dunno," she responded coldly. "You'd probably do alright. I'd have to get a lot better at blackjack. Why? You got something cookin' in that little head of yours?"

"No. I'm just starting to like it here. Something about how fake everything is."

They kept walking, Alex keeping tabs on men observing them as they passed. She let him run his mouth about Vegas fantasies before abruptly cutting him off. "Let me tell ya baby, you can never get away from the ugly shit in this country, not even here. It all catches up to you eventually."

They were heading to the Stardust, a change of pace from what they both agreed was a stale atmosphere at the Flamingo. For the occasion, he had on his only semi-formal item, a checked blazer from one of his first jobs as an extra. Alex didn't have pants or shoes to go with it, but felt like hot shit just the same, since the jacket reminded him of selling six ounces of weed to the movie's leading man, James Coburn, at the end of the day's shoot. Alex was aware that he didn't live up to the sartorial standard Jessy set. Their walk turned out to be further than he was expecting, and the cocaine Alex had snorted with Jessy was wearing off by the time the Stardust's blinding logo came into full view. The remaining gram in his inside pocket felt heavy. "Hey baby, let's do a line before we go in."

"Where we gonna go sugar? Why don't we just get there and use their bathroom?"

"Nah, they got cameras in there." Alex's head darted around desperately. Spotting a McDonald's across the street, he yanked Jessy's arm, dragging her through six lanes of traffic.

"Jesus! What the fuck's wrong with you?"

"Sorry baby, I saw an opening."

"Well, you ain't gonna see another opening tonight if you do something like that again." She composed herself before facing the harsh fluorescent light of the restaurant.

Everyone inside took a good look at them. Alex was too absorbed by his mission to care. "Get a coffee or something, I'll be back in a minute," he said, releasing her hand, and dodging the line-up at the counter that blocked the path to the men's room.

Alex barricaded himself in a stall and scooped out a bump with a plastic coffee spoon. Coke was the right drug for Vegas, he thought as he brought the tiny utensil to his nostril. Its power to heighten the senses while simultaneously deadening the nerves was in tune with this hyper-reality. The junk was best left back in L.A., Alex reasoned, and rewarded himself with another bump.

He returned to find Jessy talking to two white men in bad western suits, one sporting a Fu Manchu moustache, the other bearing a startlingly pock-marked complexion. She showed no signs of distress. The two men both flashed their teeth when Alex stood beside her. "Well, whaddya know? She really is with somebody," Crater Face said.

"And look at him," added the other. "Bet he don't know what to do with her."

Alex's temper rose. He reached for Jessy's arm. "I think I'm ready to go, baby."

"Wait, wait," Fu Manchu said. "Didn't mean to get you riled, son. Just saw your lovely lady here by herself, and thought she'd like some company. So, how much is her company worth? We'd like to get her when you're done."

Alex froze, his rage barely concealed. He released his grip on Jessy as his other hand grasped Fu Manchu's throat. The man's friend jumped to his aid, and in a quiet but forceful tone, said, "Look punk, she's your girl, we get it. Our apologies. You got a lotta fuckin' balls being with her, but let me tell you, you make another move on us, and they won't find you until next spring." At this, Crater Face opened his coat wide enough to flash his .38. "If you go now, we'll forget about it."

Fear mingled with anger. Alex remained motionless. Throughout the ordeal, Jessy kept cool, and now coaxed him out of the restaurant. "It's okay baby," she cooed once they had returned to the relative anonymity of the Strip, "You're a star now."

Alex's teeth were grinding, but he managed to laugh at what she said. "Yeah, you're right baby. Fuck 'em."

"The Dying Soldier"

One day I was working as the sun was still rising
When a soldier came stumbling through the evergreen trees
His side had clearly felt the sting of a rifle
And by the time I'd run over, he'd fallen to his knees

I raised him by the sleeves of his bloody blue jacket
And carried him to the cabin where he lay on the bed
When I asked him his name and how he came to join the battle
He drew a long breath and this is what he said,

"There were voices in the air singing glory hallelujah,
There were six white horses coming up the road,
I'm ready to take my place at the side of His throne,
There'll be peace in the valley when I get called home."

He asked for some water and drank it down slowly
I pulled off his boots and the gunbelt on his hips
Just then his body shuddered and his eyes stared wide open
And with his last breath these words passed his lips,

"There were voices in the air singing glory hallelujah,
There were six white horses coming up the road,
I'm ready to take my place at the side of His throne,
There'll be peace in the valley when I get called home."

I laid him in my wagon and I rode into town
The battle was all but over by the dimming of the day
Soldiers lined the road, all wounded and shaking
No one claimed to know him, but they all seemed to say,

"There were voices in the air singing glory hallelujah,
There were six white horses coming up the road,
I'm ready to take my place at the side of His throne,
There'll be peace in the valley when I get called home."

Chapter 4

Joshua Tree / May 1972

The only object in the sky was a bird, dipping and weaving as it rode the strong current blowing in from the south. It seemed to take forever to disappear on its lonely flight, becoming nothing more than an immobile dot, a speck of dust on the vast blue horizon. It is a perfect day for flying apart from the wind, Will thought as he stood against a barrier overlooking a long and deep ravine. He could detect no other sentient creature for untold miles in every direction. But in spite of the vast expanse surrounding him, he felt crushed by an irrational sense of responsibility.

Boy, someone sure is full of himself.

So what? Can't I be allowed a little freedom?

How much more freedom do you want? You've been doing whatever you've wanted to do for the past two years and look what it's got you. I guess this is the natural conclusion though, to finally be where no one can reach you. What if something happens right now? Like, if you fall into this ravine, or one of these mangy coyotes takes a bite out of you? No one knows you're here.

Who cares? If no one sees me again, that's how legends are born, right?

To become a legend, you have to do something worth remembering. People drop out, but have you heard of them? No! They end up becoming dirt farmers like that idiot ex-girlfriend of yours. Jesus, her friends make the Manson Family look like geniuses. Is that why you're in this godforsaken place? Because those losers you admire hang out here too?

That's not fair. Look at the Joshua Trees—have you ever seen anything like that before? And those coyotes; I could walk up and pet them.

Why don't you write a song about it?

I will, if you shut the fuck up and let me get to work.

Angela came to Alex and Jessy's door late that morning, upset that Will wasn't there when she woke up. He's a big boy, Alex told her, trying to bar her from seeing too much of what he and Jessy had been up to. But in that moment Alex could see how small and fragile Angela was, and understood how deeply she cared for Will. At the same time, Alex sensed how Jessy's presence made Angela nervous, and she eventually left without making a scene. Angela's anxiety lingered in his mind as he got into the shower. He had to admit that he hadn't been a good friend to Will lately, but if Angela was acting like his nursemaid, it was no wonder he'd taken off without telling her. There was something about Angela that made Will want her in his life, but Alex couldn't see what that was. Jessy could give Angela lessons on how to be a real woman.

Alex heard Jessy brewing coffee as he dried himself off, shaved and put on clean clothes. She placed his mug on the nightstand then sat cross-legged in a robe on the bed.

"What do you want to do about Angela?" Jessy asked.

"She'll be fine. I'm sure Will just needed some time to himself. How about you? You gonna get dressed?"

"No, still too early. You go back and see if you can win enough for us to have a good time tonight."

Alex smiled and blew Jessy a kiss as he shut the door and walked through the parking lot toward Fremont Street. He knew he had nothing to worry about with her by his side. Whatever was happening between Will and Angela wasn't his problem. He had a career to think about—first, getting an agent once they got back to L.A., then getting himself ready for auditions.

His mood turned sour back at a blackjack table, where the dealer pummeled him with fours, fives and sixes. "No luck today sir?" A floorman was talking to somebody behind him, but the question pierced Alex like a knife between his shoulder blades. He glanced over at a row of white-haired zombies playing the slots, envious of their ability to block out the rest of the world.

I just gotta write something, anything. Out here in the middle of this beautiful place, and I miss the beach. This is the spot everyone said. Cap Rock. Like something that could be on Mars. Maybe I don't even need to smoke this Mexican shit. Yeah, right. What else is there to do out here? Jesus, why do I put so much pressure on myself? It's not like anyone's given me fifty grand to make a record. I could go back to playing the Corral or the Broken Spoke and make enough to pay the rent on our dump for the next few months no matter what Alex ends up getting out of this acting gig. But what's it all going to amount to? I've been writing songs for so long, I can't tell what's good or bad anymore. I start out with three chords and it ends up like something Dylan said back in '63. Is my life that uninspiring that I can't make one lousy album out of it?

Smoke that joint, it'll be okay.

Why do you care all of a sudden?

Well, since you made it all the way here to try to get something done, at the very least I shouldn't allow you to waste a whole day.

Wow, that's a first.

Well, if you'd listen to me more often, you wouldn't be feeling this sorry for yourself all the time. Your songs have touched people. You're just too self-absorbed to realize. Think of that drive through the desert through those little towns, like the one at the base of that mesa where the little kids were getting on the school bus. Can you imagine growing up in a place like that? Or those soldiers you passed outside of Barstow? Two months from now they're gonna be knee deep in a rice paddy. But here you are, where you always wanted to be, right? Well, how does it feel? I bet it's really inspiring staring out at miles and miles of nothing, while the rest of the world is getting on with things you can't even comprehend because you're waiting for some kind of sign to give you the all-clear to be an artist. Like you forgot all the shit you left behind that brought you to this place to look for your all-powerful answer.

"How much did you lose today?" Jessy asked.

"What makes you think I lost?" Alex responded with a sheepish grin.

"Come on honey, I've seen you at the tables. You don't know when to quit. When you start to slide, you think you can pull yourself out of it, and it just don't work that way baby."

"Well, I guess I don't have to tell you what happened then."

Jessy jumped up from the bed in nothing but a bra and panties. She threw her arms around Alex's neck and kissed him as a gesture of reconciliation. "I'm sorry honey, tell me what happened."

"I'm down another forty." They both laughed, then kissed some more. Jessy fell onto her back, still holding Alex tightly. She locked her bare legs around his waist and tried to drag his jeans down. Alex unhooked his belt and completed the task himself, eliciting a contented moan from his lover.

"You really shouldn't leave a girl by herself all day. It can lead to nasty thoughts." Her hand found his cock. She was not in the mood for foreplay. Grasping it, she removed her own underwear in one motion with her other hand and guided him inside her. He was caught off-guard, but kept up with her thrusts until losing himself in the savage rhythm. By then he knew it was going to end too quickly, but she kept encouraging him.

After, they shared a cigarette, and then a healthy bump of cocaine. "Let's take a swim, baby," Jessy said. "It should have cooled down enough out there by now."

A tiny lone figure was sitting at the side of the pool wrapped in a towel. At first glance through his coke buzz, Alex perceived it as someone's abandoned child but then recognized Angela. "Hey gal, how's the water?"

Angela looked up at Alex and Jessy through drowsy eyes, and managed a weak shrug before returning to sulking. Jessy dangled her calves in the deep end and lit a cigarette. Alex drained a can of Miller High Life, then bounced off the diving board, the splash shattering the oppressive silence. The sun was going down behind the mesas outside the city limits, casting severe shadows across the sheltered motel court.

After a few more dives, Alex called out to Angela. "Heard from Will?" he said in mid-backstroke. He peered at her face, consumed by near-complete darkness.

"No," Angela replied from inside the shroud of her towel.

"Well, he oughta turn up soon. Maybe he's on a roll somewhere."

"No. He wouldn't spend a whole day gambling."

Alex looked at Jessy, bemused. She made no attempt to get involved, but he couldn't let the matter drop. "Look, what are you worried about? Why aren't you out having some fun yourself?"

"I'm worried about him, okay? He shouldn't be by himself."

Alex laughed in Jessy's direction again, "What makes you think he's by himself?"

Angela sat up at this, throwing the towel off her head. "Hey, you're supposed to be his best friend, but you don't have a fucking clue what's going with him, do you?" All of her rage was uncorked by Alex's remark. "Where have you been? I'd really like to know. You and your film career. Let me clue you in—you're a fucking extra!"

At this, Jessy pulled herself out of the water and appeared ready to pounce. "Look, bitch, you'd better watch your mouth before I come over there."

"This has got nothing to do with you. Your boyfriend has been a real prick, and it's about time someone told him."

"Hey," said Alex, "I don't know what makes you an expert on Will, but we've been friends since we were kids. I think I know him better than some clingy little groupie."

"Well, you obviously don't. He's got problems, problems your pea-brain can't begin to comprehend."

Alex resisted the urge to lash out over Angela's provocation, letting his fuse burn while staring at the tiny figure glaring down at him from the deck. He imagined the back of his hand connecting with her upturned nose. Jessy wouldn't care. But what would Will say? Alex swallowed his anger and submerged, hoping Angela would be gone when he came up for air. He swam to the deep end and touched bottom before heading in the direction of Jessy's legs swinging beneath the water. Grasping a thigh, he closed his eyes and felt the pressure build within his chest. At last, he needed to breathe, and as he broke the surface, the desire to put Angela in her place had dissipated. He looped his hands around Jessy's waist, feeling her sculpted curves. She stroked his heavy, saturated hair. "Come on baby," Jessy cooed. "We're obviously not wanted here."

Alex pulled himself out of the pool and followed Jessy back to their room. He took one last look at Angela sitting in the same position as when they'd arrived, her head again wrapped in the towel.

Will didn't notice the vanishing daylight until Cap Rock glowed bright orange, giving it an unworldly appearance. Minutes later, shadows from the Joshua Trees crept close to his boots as he sat in the dirt with his back against the rock, scribbling final thoughts in his notebook. When he finished, he reached into his shirt pocket and removed the half-smoked joint that had helped get him through the afternoon. He took slow, deep drags, holding the smoke in until he could picture it filling his lungs to capacity, before exhaling a satisfying cloud through his nostrils and then his mouth. Down to the roach, he made a silent commitment to remain motionless until the sun was cut in half by the horizon. His focus held steady on the endless vista, as the minutes extended in equal measure to the smoke's migration to his brain. If he had had a sleeping bag, he could have slept at that moment, although he dreaded the thought of waking up in darkness.

Instead, Will recalled the late summer sunsets on his granddad's farm, when he was allowed to ride in the wagon behind the combine and help stack the neat, square hay bales. By sundown, his arms would ache to the point of keeping him up all night listening to the immense country stillness. His granddad sympathized, and would try to ease the strain by passing him a small glass of beer at dinner, careful to keep it out of sight of the parents.

A few years later, when Will believed he had better things to do than spend an entire day with his family, he would still walk with the old man around the fences that had set the only boundaries his cows would know. It took a long time, enough for the old man to be hunched over and breathing heavily when the house would come into view. He wouldn't pause or ask for assistance from his grandson, and with the sun only a trace on the horizon, the old man celebrated their return by pouring each of them a shot of Johnnie Walker Red.

After a few more of those visits, the old man could no longer walk. He was in his bed, his body paying the price for early years spent on the sea, then harder years on land, scrounging a living—and a purpose—out of the unforgiving fields that had been passed down to him. Inevitably, Will's grandmother and other sundry relatives would urge him to go upstairs to see the old man. He wanted to, but at the same time he could not bear to witness his final stages, an end that Will had yet to accept could ever happen to anyone, much less someone this close to him.

But he convinced himself to mount the steps, each creak in the wood signaling his imminent arrival. When he opened the bedroom door, the old man was awake and grinning, his appearance unchanged since the time before— clean-shaven, hair neatly parted, and teeth handy in a glass on his nightstand. On the opposite nightstand were dirty drinking glasses surrounding a bottle of Johnnie Walker. Whatever state he was in, the old man was eager to engage the conversation.

After a few visits, Will's misgivings vanished. Grandfather and grandson would start out talking about the expected things: the weather, school, family matters. Sometimes, the old man would ask about that girl Will was seeing. After that, and perhaps a shot or two of whiskey, the old man would find a way to offer a story. Whether it was meant to inspire Will or to grease the wheels of his own memory was never apparent. Will came to believe he was doing an honorable duty by listening to the old man talk, since, as he often reminded Will, as long as he was talking, he knew he was still alive.

The routine altered one day when the old man revealed that he owned a guitar, and had, before his marriage, been known to associate with a group of traveling musicians. They came from a mining town in West Virginia. He met one of them, the fiddler, when they were both in the navy. They'd kept in touch, and when a guitarist was needed for a new string band, the old man saw no better option to stave off the inevitable call to take up the family business. He took every penny he had, and bought a Martin D-20, the guitar he spoke of like a lost lover. When Will asked what had happened with the band, his grandfather offered a wistful reply.

"I couldn't play as good as those guys," he said.

"What happened to the guitar?" asked Will.

"It's in the closet, where your granny couldn't touch it. Go fetch it."

With some hesitation, Will approached the old man's closet. Its dim interior revealed a row of shirts and pants that would never be worn again. When Will pushed those items aside, he saw the outline of a hide-bound case leaning in the corner. Its smell of neglect was overpowering before Will put his hands on it, and as he lay the case on the bed, the old man's toothless grin sealed the newfound bond between them. Will's grandfather sat up, seeming determined to open the case himself and caress the guitar's polished veneer. Will observed every detail of the magnificent instrument, from the mysterious insignia of Nazareth, Pennsylvania visible through the sound hole, to the auburn finish, a color he had never seen before. The strings were rusty and hanging limp, emitting a barely musical sound under the old man's trembling hand. But after that single motion, he passed the guitar to Will. "It's yours now. Do more with it than I could."

Will held the Martin without touching the strings, feeling its weight, and the weight of the old man's words. He kept his eyes on his grandfather, observing him in the particulate light of the room where he was bound to spend his few remaining days. He sat, naked to the waist, with a smile that told Will that they were now equals. This was his inheritance, a freedom within him, beyond the constraints of his family, not the land that would be nothing but a burden. He saw in the old man's smile that, despite the mistakes he'd made during his life, he had given his progeny the most worthy gift he could offer. Will could feel that the instrument would become his most important possession. The old man continued to smile, resisting the pain as he propped himself up with one hand and struggled with the other to tussle the young man's hair. Then with a deep exhalation, he reclined and said in a hoarse cackle, "Pour us a shot." They didn't stop talking until the sun went down and Will's grandmother called him for supper.

It took longer for Will to drive out of Joshua Tree National Monument than he had remembered going in. The road wound out in the darkness, forcing him to grip the Oldsmobile's wheel with both hands as the smoke in his brain blurred the edge of his vision. On the highway, the lights of the town shone dimly until he was on the main drag. Will was nearly through when he recalled the café he'd passed that morning. He turned the car around and crept along until the homemade wooden sandwich board, the one he'd remembered from hours earlier, re-appeared on the gravel shoulder. The young hippie girl behind the counter startled slightly when he set off the chimes attached to the door. He tried not to appear threatening entering the empty restaurant, taking a seat at a table against a wall adorned with hand crafted faux Native

American regalia. Will caught the waitress's smile as she set aside some paperwork.

"Welcome," she said, and handed him a laminated menu that listed a number of simple vegetarian dishes. "Take your time, but could I bring you something to drink? Green tea, maybe?"

She wasn't that far removed from girls Will knew in L.A., with her long, ironed hair, and patchwork wardrobe, but her bold choice to run a business in the middle of nowhere captivated him. "Yeah, that would be great. A glass of water too."

"I'll be right back." She exited to the kitchen, giving Will a moment to close his eyes and recall that he was still a few hours away from Vegas, and that his friends were surely worried about him. Those thoughts were erased when the girl returned with a small steaming pot and a glass of water.

"I'll get you a cup for the tea."

"Bring one for yourself," Will replied. "It doesn't seem to be that busy. Why don't you sit down?"

The girl blushed, but took the chair opposite Will as if she did the same with every customer. He asked her name as she poured the tea. "Dawn. Dawn Redwood."

He was taken aback. "That's beautiful. But that's not your real name, is it?"

She put down her cup, feigning embarrassment. "Well, Dawn is. But my boyfriend started calling me Redwood when we first came out here and were staying up north. We had a cabin, and our first night we saw the sunrise over the trees. It was so amazing. He told me to change my name right then.

I guess I always give my full name when people ask, just to remind myself of what it was like there."

"Why aren't you there anymore?"

"My boyfriend's an Air Force mechanic and he got stationed down here last year. I opened up this place for something to do, since he's working all the time."

"Has he seen any action?"

"Not really. He's supposed to get on a carrier next month when he goes on rotation. Those pilots will do a lot of air strikes on the NVA. He's a little freaked out about it, and so am I. They recruited him out of college. He thought it would bring in enough money for us to get set up somewhere, but now he feels responsible for killing people."

Will finished his water and started drinking the tea. He tried to steer the conversation away from politics. "I'd be worried knowing you were alone out here at night."

"It's not so bad. Everyone around is connected to the military in some way. Most of my customers come for lunch. I stay open at night on the off chance that someone like you needs to make a rest stop. So what'll you have?"

Will had barely glanced at the menu, so he made a more thorough scan. The options weren't that appetizing, but his stomach growled. "I'll have that sandwich with the red peppers."

"Coming up." Dawn left the table and Will listened to the refrigerator door open and close, wrappers and jars unsealed, a knife hit a cutting board with successive, jarring whacks. Outside, passing headlights lit up the road. The isolation Will had experienced that day overwhelmed him as Dawn's story sunk in. He wanted to keep talking, but when she placed the sandwich in front of him, his hunger took precedence. She asked him questions instead. "What brings you out here?"

"Came to Vegas for the weekend with some friends," Will replied as he chewed.

"Vegas? You don't seem like the gambling type."

"I'm not. Guess that's why I'm out here. I mainly just wanted to get out of L.A. for a while."

"Ah, L.A. That makes more sense."

"You ever lived there?"

"Nah, I'm not a big city girl. You're not really a big city boy either, are you?"

Will raised an eyebrow and chased down a large bite of the sandwich with tea. "No, I am in fact from Ohio."

"I knew it. I'm originally from Pennsylvania. I've got family in Akron, though."

"Ever visit them?"

"Once or twice when I was a kid. Can't say I remember much about it, apart from the factories."

"Ever heard of a place called Nazareth?"

Dawn gave a confused look. "You mean where Jesus was from? You're not a religious freak are you?"

Will laughed, sensing her sudden apprehension. "No. It's a town in Pennsylvania where my guitar was made. I was just wondering if it really existed."

She gave it some serious thought. "No, never heard of it. More tea?"

"How about some coffee?"

"Sure, I'll be back in a minute." Dawn rushed to the kitchen, the bottoms of her sandals slapping against the tiled floor.

An uncomfortable silence descended. "Hey, how come you don't have any music on," Will called out to her.

"There aren't any radio stations out here. We can pick some stuff up once in a while but there's always so much static."

Dawn returned with two mugs, prompting Will to say, "I can't imagine not listening to the radio."

"I don't really mind. I used to be into music, but I can't be bothered anymore. I guess you're a musician, right? You said you have a guitar."

"Yeah, I guess I am a musician," he said, laughing under his breath.

"What? Why'd you laugh?"

"Oh, nothing. I just haven't been making much progress with it lately. I hate giving the wrong impression."

"What's the difference? If you play music, you're a musician, right?"

He smiled and nodded, self-conscious with this stranger. But she wasn't about to let him off the hook, now that she had exposed her own life. "Do you write your own songs?"

"Yeah. I've been trying to get some new ones together. Thought the park would inspire me."

"Did it?"

"Yeah, a little."

"Why don't you play me something?" Her honesty set him aglow. It wasn't sexual, just a simple recognition that he had something she needed at that moment.

"I'll get my guitar."

Will retrieved the Martin from the trunk. He removed the instrument from its case and checked the tuning before strumming a few chords. Dawn sat back in anticipation, both hands around the coffee mug. "Well, I guess I'll do one I wrote today. It's called 'Drivin' Wheel.'"

Alex couldn't get over how sexy Jessy looked, and everyone around the craps table knew it. He stared at her slender fingers cradling the dice, thinking that he was in the palm of her hand as well. His heart jumped when she threw an eleven on her first toss. She gave him a subtle wink as he placed a new bet. With each roll, his future with Jessy became defined in his mind, starting with getting a place of their own. Will would be alright if Angela were willing to take care of him, and after all, Alex thought, wasn't I the one who got off my ass and made something happen? Will was the one who supposedly had talent, and it was high time he started acting like it. Whatever happened, at least he wasn't a loser that night as he stood next to Jessy, her graceful right arm determining the fates of the dozen people around the table.

"Seven! Lucky seven!"

Will was deceived into thinking he was close to the city when he saw the lights start to burn the fringe of the horizon. But it took another hour before the desert gave way to the city limits, the small towns barely remembered snapshots, like the string of Pueblo-style beads that Dawn had offered as a keepsake, and now dangled from the Delta 88's rear view mirror. He stuck to the route he knew that took him to Fremont Street, with its permanent daylight rolling in illuminated waves through the car's interior. Past the Flamingo, it was a couple blocks to the motel, beyond the grasp of the neon tentacles. Will pulled the car into the spot in front of their room and searched for signs of life within as he cut the lights and the engine. He pictured Angela on the bed, waiting for him, and felt paralyzed. But there was nowhere left to go.

His key met no resistance in the lock. She was on the bed, staring in silence as he stood with a half-hearted smile, hoping it would convey that his defenses were down. After several painful seconds, she got up and threw her arms around him, and he drank in the florid smell of her loose curls.

He collapsed on the bed, his boots shedding some red Joshua Tree dust on the blankets. She sat across the room, eventually summoning the nerve to ask, "Are you going to tell me what happened today?"

He continued to face the ceiling, rubbing his eyes in an effort to fight off the growing desire for sleep. "Oh, I just went for a drive. It was something that I wanted to do."

"Why didn't you ask me to come?"

It was the question he had been anticipating from the moment he had walked in, knowing that no answer would suffice. "It was something personal. I needed to be alone today." He began backtracking before she could respond.

"Look, I know I should have told you guys where I was going, and I'm sorry for that. Just forget about it. I'm back now, and everything's fine."

"You got laid, didn't you? You went to one of those ranches."

The accusation forced him to sit up and laugh. "Is that what you were thinking all day? Come on, gimme a little credit." His head hit the mattress, his laughter continuing unabated.

"Fine, then tell me what you did."

"I was writing, okay? I had to get out of the city, and away from Alex for a while. Just to clear my head."

"Well, you could have taken me," she mumbled. He asked her to repeat what she had said, his growing frustration seeping through in his tone.

"Didn't you think I might want to get away from Alex and that slut too? They didn't care one bit that you were gone. They don't understand."

"Understand what?"

"What you've been dealing with."

Will exhaled and rubbed his eyes again before turning to face Angela. He could have appeared menacing if not for his fatigue. "I thought that was between us."

"It is. I didn't say anything."

The stress of the day was evident as her tiny, trembling hands reached for a cigarette. Seeing her in such a state prompted Will to take one final stab at defusing the situation. "Look, I had a good day. We're going home tomorrow morning, right? Let's get a good night's sleep and forget about it. I'll take the blame for your day, and I'll make it up to you."

Angela didn't react, smoking her cigarette in silence. The smoke drifted over Will's face, heightening his claustrophobia and making him fearful that he wouldn't be able to sleep. With much effort, Will rose and looked at Angela without expression. She gazed back, as the smoke hovered around her head like a veil.

"I don't need this much help from you," he said, as she remained stoic. "Yes, I've had a few bad moments, but I can feel that I'm pulling myself out of it."

"Where does that leave me?"

"What do you mean?"

"I mean, I've seen you lose control enough times to know what you're capable of doing. If you think you can take care of yourself, fine. But if something happens—and I'm sure it will—who's going to help you? Alex? I don't think so."

"I don't know what you're talking about."

"Precisely." She put out the cigarette and Will made a great effort to hear what was motivating her at that moment. "I can't stand the thought of what you might do when you're alone."

His frustration boiled over. "Do you want to know what I've been doing when I'm alone?" He got to his feet and bounded to the door. She heard the trunk slam, and he returned in short order, sitting on the bed with his guitar. "Here's what I've been doing." He proceeded to play the songs he had been working on, uninterrupted, none of which she had heard before. She was transfixed; he was no longer the man she had been agonizing over all day, but the embodiment of everything she wanted. The words flowed from his lips like nothing she could imagine he would speak, and they entwined with melodies that were by turns haunting and heartbreaking.

After the fifth song, he paused to ask her for a glass of water. She brought it without questioning and sat beside him on the bed before handing it to him. He drank deeply, and as he lowered the glass, she whispered, "Those songs are beautiful." He smiled in return, wanting with all of his heart to believe her. Handing back the empty glass, he noticed her glancing at the open guitar case, and the handful of yellowed pieces of paper scattered within bearing text that appeared to have been set down by an archaic typewriter. She reached down to examine one of the pages. "What are these?"

"They were in the case when my granddad gave it to me. I think they're his songs."

She snatched up more and read them quickly. "These were the songs you were just playing, weren't they?"

Will turned toward her and smiled again. "Don't tell anybody."

She gazed back in amazement before her resistance evaporated and she pressed her mouth against his. The only thing that separated them was the guitar.

"Drivin' Wheel"

Pick up your fallen faces
and try to fill the empty spaces when the day is done
If you wait I'll be there soon
And we'll spend another blue afternoon in the cold cold sun
You might pretend you've got no friends
in this cruel childish game
But turn around and hear the sound of me
calling out your name

Light me up another smoke
The time's come to make a deal
I feel like a broken spoke
In this old drivin' wheel

I keep searchin' for the words
but I got mixed up by stories I heard when I was a child
Stuck in a nowhere town, where
forgotten friends just hang around with minds gone wild
If I had another lifetime
I would let go of my lifeline
And do all the things I meant to do
Before I made you go

Light me up another smoke
The time's come to make a deal
I feel like a broken spoke
In this old drivin' wheel

We can tell our lies
to each other's eyes 'till there's nothing left to say
But later on
A brand new dawn will become a brand new day

Light me up another smoke
The time's come to make a deal
I feel like a broken spoke
In this old drivin' wheel

Chapter 5

Los Angeles / August 1970 – September 1971

From the moment she dropped the tab, Angela Carney kept close watch on everyone to see if they were noticing a change within her. She became conscious of her own actions—hand gestures, speech inflections, and word choices. After a few minutes, the passage of time had slowed down to a snail's pace. She caught herself staring at the tiki lamps marking the edge of the swimming pool and had to remind herself where she was: the latest spontaneous gathering of kids from Angela's Reseda neighborhood who didn't, and wouldn't, get jobs that summer.

Late mornings led to afternoons watching soap operas or, if enough motivation and spare change could be gathered, bus trips downtown to observe tourists before catching a matinee. As the first traces of evening fell, it was back to the familiar sidewalks separating the manicured lawns, and a brief change of scenery to someone else's version of a dollhouse-inspired room, where talk turned to boys and the fine art of smoking a cigarette. When whispers told that someone's parents were vacating their bungalow for a weekend, the myth of California summer was reborn in those who had received their new driver's licenses.

They arrived prepared at that day's designated spot, some of the girls in bikinis. Angela—not much of a swimmer—stuck with her favorite candy-striped mini-dress. With her bobbed hair, she felt like Marianne Faithfull, and tried to maintain an air of cool detachment as her friends swam. No one seemed to appreciate her efforts more than Noel. He still wore a mod suit, even though the style had long been displaced by tie-dye.

Angela's heart raced when he placed himself in the empty deck chair next to her and lit a joint. Angela allowed the thin wisps of smoke to tease her before turning to watch Noel exhale a large cloud. After another drag, he handed it to her. She took a moment to find the grip she had practiced before reclining in her chair with her thin, exposed legs crossed at the ankles. It was a moment she wished everyone there could have witnessed, but she settled for Noel's gaze from behind his wraparound sunglasses. She plucked the joint from her lips with two fingers, like a regular cigarette, and exhaled straight up.

"It's from Mexico," Noel said.

"It's good."

"You know, I've got some acid I was going to drop later on if you're into it."

She pondered for the duration of her second toke, and, handing back the joint, answered, "Sounds groovy."

Noel waited until dark to pass her the tab. Her trip came on at first like sleep, until she felt beyond control of her actions. The darkness made it difficult to react, shadow and light creating ghostly shapes out of what she knew were human beings. At times Noel had to restrain her from falling into the pool. Her only grounding was the music, the tinny wail of an endless string of 45s on a portable record player. She tried dancing with Noel, but neither could find a rhythm, and they eventually stumbled to the lawn and collapsed on their backs. Time stopped for Angela as she became transfixed on the stars. She felt Noel's fingers move through her hair, and the sensation mingled with the feel of each blade of grass on her bare legs. Occasionally, someone would walk over to check on them, to which Angela would respond with laughter as she remained supine. Noel got his feet first, and pulled her up by her arms. After making sure she could walk on her own, Noel whispered, "Maybe we should get out of here." The words seemed to come from a faraway place, but when Angela opened her eyes, Noel's smiling face hovered in front of her.

Speaking to him proved futile. Angela regrouped by reaching for something tactile—her hair—and she gradually began to feel whole again. "Yes, let's go," she muttered, placing a hand on Noel's thigh to remain steady. He guided her to the street, where his Bonneville convertible waited at the curb. He opened the passenger door and placed Angela upright on the bench seat like a rag doll.

The cool night wind restored some of Angela's bearings as Noel weaved through the empty, tree-lined streets. There didn't seem any pressing need to determine a destination. She had found serenity by allowing her head to loll, and with eyes closed, submit to the car's vibrations, even as Noel took some of the curves at dangerous speed. Still, nothing seemed real to Angela as approaching headlights flashed and vanished before her eyes. The road began stretching upward into Laurel Canyon, and Angela felt the engine race on the incline. Her body then violently shifted as they took a downslope without slowing down. The pavement broke sharply to the left, setting the car into the path of an oncoming Harley-Davidson Sportster. The impact sent the rider catapulting over the convertible, and Angela's head struck the dashboard.

A morbid silence descended, with the rider a splayed mass of denim and leather behind the car, and his bike a tangled mess of metal within the grill. Angela next felt her body being yanked to the driver's side before sensing Noel rifling through the glove box. She began weakly moaning, hearing his rapid footfalls on the asphalt as he fled the scene.

The whole mess heaped upon her under the fluorescent lights of L.A. General. When Angela regained full consciousness, she was charged with vehicular manslaughter, and many other offences beyond her grasp. What made her cry, though, was the fact that she could not remember anything.

"That's not your car."

"I don't have a car."

"You don't have a license either. Why were you driving?"

"I wasn't driving, I don't—"

"What were you on?"

"What?"

"What drugs had you taken?"

"I don't take drugs."

She withstood the questioning through the tears, feeling her clarity return as a B-1 shot kicked in.

"Where's your boyfriend?"

"I don't have a—"

"Why were you driving his car?"

She emitted a piercing wail, burying her face in her hands. The cop taking notes turned to his partner. "Better call her parents now, and get someone to bring in the boyfriend."

It later emerged that the police found Noel passed out in a bus shelter, whereupon he was similarly charged. A judge would have to sort it all out, Angela was told, causing it to firmly sink in that she had little defense beyond her own recollections, of which there were few. In court, her lawyer instructed her to accentuate her golden hair and porcelain features, to help him paint a picture of a perfect flower led astray by a cowardly drug fiend attempting to save his own neck.

"Your honor, why must we compound such a tragedy by having this unfortunate young woman suffer the injustice of taking the blame for the unthinkable actions perpetrated by the co-defendant?" The closing argument had the room enraptured. The collective conscience of all who heard it seemed to be willing the judge to render his decision.

When he returned after a long deliberation, he stared at Angela as she stood before the bench. The thought had crossed her mind more than once that perhaps she was guilty.

There was no question she had been involved in the death of another human being, however indirectly, through her careless behavior. Angela broke down as the judge began admonishing her bad decisions, prompting him to pause to allow her to compose herself.

"Although the evidence shows that one of the individuals in the car is responsible for the tragic death of a motorcyclist, there is not enough to prove that it was the defendant, Ms. Carney. Therefore, I find this defendant not guilty on all counts."

There were gasps of relief, and Angela was embraced by the horde of family members there to support her. In spite of it all, she knew she was not innocent.

The weeks and months that followed passed in a blur. There were no more invitations to parties, or even phone calls to meet for pizza. Angela's life dissolved before her eyes, but she resisted the temptation of using drugs as a crutch. Her family was ill prepared to deal with her misery, and her teachers offered no support as she was branded a pariah. Angela merely floated, refusing to eat for a time. Her once healthy figure flattened and narrowed, and she felt herself disappearing. Nothing could shield her from the ever-present assumptions and accusations.

She eventually found the most anonymous job available, answering phones for the classified section at the L.A. Times. Inquiries came in constantly, but Angela gave herself over to the work, transforming her into the machine that a part of her longed to be. Cars, boats, apartments, pianos; every day brought new voices, but always the same conversations. She reveled in the repetition, and it spilled over into her private life. Her parents seemed to marvel at how methodically she structured her day: up at seven a.m., catching the bus a half-hour later, and back home on the stroke of six, as immaculate in her pressed office attire and heels as when she'd left in the morning, betraying no sign of what might have transpired during the intervening hours. That's because nothing ever did. Her parents may have convinced themselves that her rigid contentment was happiness, but nothing about the new Angela fit the definition of the word. If they could have grasped this change as some sort of self-imposed punishment, they still believed in the divine intervention that had spared their child from a life behind bars.

The days dragged on in this manner, until one Sunday dinner Angela announced her intention to move out. This was startling to her family, but what proved more surprising was the elaboration that she would have a roommate, a girl from work, the boss's daughter, after which, Angela offered no further details.

Julie and Angela were close in age, Angela slightly older, but based on looks and personality, the age gap appeared wider. Although Angela was wary of socializing, she saw in Julie many of the carefree qualities she felt she no longer possessed. Their lunches conjured pleasant flashbacks for Angela, becoming the only times when she allowed glimpses of her past to poke through her new exterior. Julie seemed happy to have an ally at a job she had been forced to take, and did not ask questions about Angela's life beyond why she was single.

Their regular spot was an outdoor cafe on Flower Street, away from the tourist traps, but in prime position to observe other L.A. denizens. "Check out buddy in the Mercedes," was one of Julie's common remarks. At this, Angela would turn nonchalantly and spy a pair of Ray-Bans shielding a shaggy head behind the wheel of a convertible. Any eye contact would lead to a harmless shared grin before the light changed, whereupon the driver blasted the short distance to the next intersection.

"He saw us looking at him," Angela would say. "You realize I'm going to have to kill myself now."

Another day, when Julie offered, "What about that guy?" Angela discovered a young blow-dried, insurance salesman-type standing on the corner. "I know I've probably said it before," Julie added, "but this is the kind of guy I think you should be with."

Angela scowled, interpreting the remark as an insult. "And explain to me why again?"

"Because you'd have all the power," Julie replied, giggling. "A guy like that doesn't need love from you. He loves money. As long as he's got money, he's happy, right? You'd be able to make him do anything you want, as long as it didn't interfere with his money. You get what I'm saying?"

Angela reached for her glass of sangria. "Yeah, I think so, but what about me? Do you think I'd be happy manipulating someone like that?"

"It's better than having someone manipulate you."

"Why don't you go for a guy like that?"

Julie tossed her black tresses, cascading them down her back. "Come on, I'd scare him away. You on the other hand, I bet he'd pay good money for just one night with you."

Angela leaned in, feeling less inhibited by the conversation. "Why would he want me after he's paid for me?"

"That's where the manipulation comes in," Julie said, adding an obscene gesture with her fist. "After a while when he gets bored with you and starts paying someone else, you've still got him because he needs a woman to show off to his friends. He'll give you anything then, if you threaten to leave him. That's how the smart ones do it."

Angela didn't let on, but at that moment, she decided that Julie was as good a friend as she could hope for. "Do you think I'm a slut?" Angela asked, holding a toothy smile for maximum effect.

"No, of course not. I'm just saying, if you ever felt like you wanted to be one, you'd be good at it."

"Wouldn't you lose your respect for me?"

"Probably, but then again so many women who get into those kinds of relationships don't get anything out of it. I'm counting on borrowing money from you someday."

Angela shook her head and laughed. "You've been reading too many Jacqueline Susann novels."

It was a typical Tuesday afternoon when the phone rang and Angela heard an older man with a heavy eastern European accent on the line. "Hello? Yes, my dog had puppies and I'd like to put in an ad to sell them."

"Certainly, go ahead."

"Okay, they're part Rottweiler, and part something else, I'm not sure. My dog kind of got in a bit of trouble, you know?" The man chuckled at his own attempt at a joke, but Angela had learned early to not respond.

"So would you like the ad to read 'Rottweiler mixed breed puppies for sale?'"

"Okay, that sounds fine. You know, at first I thought about putting them all in a garbage bag and dropping them in the river, but then someone told me that was illegal."

When the man laughed again, Angela had to restrain herself from hanging up. She managed to get the rest of the information for the ad before setting down the receiver, her entire body gripped by tension, consumed by the constrictive isolation of her cubicle. The phone fell silent for several minutes. She remained poised to pounce the instant a call came in, a migraine gathering force in the back of her skull. Julie's voice in the adjoining cubicle provided a welcome distraction, although Angela's mind kept flashing images of those puppies being stuffed one by one into a garbage bag, the muffled yelping and fruitless scratching of tiny paws that hadn't grown claws yet.

Julie finished her call and wheeled her chair around the divider. "Did you hear that?" she shrieked. "This guy wanted to sell two tickets to the Led Zeppelin concert on Saturday. I almost told him flat out that I'd take them. Fuck this job sometimes. Wouldn't that be great to go though? Maybe I should call him back and snag them. What do you think? Wouldn't that be a blast?"

Angela stared back at Julie blankly, not fully comprehending her words.

"Well, do you wanna go?"

"Um, no. You could have fun with someone else."

Julie looked confused. Angela's phone rang but she didn't move to answer it. "You'd better get that," Julie finally said after two more rings.

Angela waited for Julie to return to her own cubicle before putting the cold receiver to her ear. The voice was barely audible. "Yes, uh, hello. I'd, uh, like to place a personal ad."

"Go ahead sir."

"Yes, well, I'd like it to say something like 'older man'—uh, better make that 'mature man seeks woman, twenty-one to thirty, for casual relationship.' Does that sound right?"

"It sounds fine sir. Please continue."

Angela called the man the first day the ad appeared in the paper. She had little trouble maintaining her composure, as he aimed to find out everything about her at that moment. She held back, suggesting they meet that night at a restaurant close to the apartment she and Julie shared off La Cienega. Angela wore work clothes to appear reserved. He was waiting at the bar, not as old as she was expecting, but, as she judged by his nervousness, conscious of his age. His crisp tan suit and sprouting hair gave Angela the impression of someone who could have worked in the movie business. But seated at a table, he told her he taught high school, then added, "I also do a little writing. I've got a screenplay I'm working on, but doesn't everybody around here?"

Angela smiled dispassionately. When he asked what she did, Angela offered her rehearsed response, vaguely referencing an unspecified clerical job at city hall. She allowed him to own the spotlight, sitting through the appetizers and entree listening to tales of his upbringing and education. When he became curious, she downplayed the existence of any excitement in her life. By the time the martinis arrived, he was ready to ask the burning question. "So what made you want to call me? The ad just came out today."

Caught off-guard, Angela bought some time by running her index finger around the lip of her glass, hoping her glowing ruby fingernail would draw his attention. "Well, like I said, I don't really meet a lot of people at my job, and you sounded interesting." He hid his beaming smile with his napkin.

They left things on an innocent note, Angela balking at his offer of a ride home, but leaving an open invitation for another date. She didn't tell Julie about the encounter, but said something after meeting him two nights later.

"I thought I'd take your advice," Angela admitted to Julie during their next lunch.

"You mean he's loaded?"

"Not exactly, but he's picking up the tab for everything so far. It's just like you said."

"How far have you gone?"

"I'm not gonna sleep with him. That's not part of my image."

"What kind of loser is this guy? You're gonna have to put out sooner or later."

"I don't know. It seems like he's having a good time. It's almost as if he's taking pity on me."

Julie laughed, attracting a few looks from the adjacent tables. "So you haven't told him anything about yourself?"

"I told him I work in an office. If he wasn't interested, he would have walked away by now."

"What do you want from him then?"

Angela looked toward the street, faced again with the harsh reality of the path that her life with men had taken; her independence drew them like a magnet, and her keen awareness of their intentions became a defense that no one could hope to penetrate. Julie's questions hung in the air as Angela continued gazing toward the Hollywood Hills, knowing that this man's dream of seeing something he'd written make it to the silver screen would never come true, just as her dreams had been destroyed by foolish choices. Whether out of revenge or a twisted sense of humanity, what Angela wanted most was to destroy him.

"I'm playing it by ear," she said to Julie. "He's not a bad guy. Maybe something will happen."

Julie raised her gin and tonic in mock cheers. "I hope it does. I can't wait to meet him." Angela accepted the encouragement, as the shadow of what she planned to do descended upon her.

She met him that night at the Aquarius Theater for a production of *Death of a Salesman*. He was excited, gushing about how much he enjoyed teaching the play, and how Arthur Miller inspired his own writing. She listened without giving any indication of how tedious she anticipated the experience was going to be. Afterward, he strained to draw her into a post-mortem of the performance as they walked down Sunset toward his car. She offered vague remarks, having hardly understood—much less paid attention to—the action. None of it fazed him as he continued to posit theories about the director's decisions. It was becoming too much for her to handle when he asked, "Could I invite you back to my place?"

She produced a smile to mask the rage she wanted to unleash upon him. "Sure, but I can't stay very late."

"Of course. Work, right?"

"Yeah, it never ends."

He lived in a Spanish-style triplex off the 101. It made her uncomfortable the moment she saw it. He was on the third floor, up a set of iron stairs that rang loudly under her heels. Inside was as expected: piles of books and records; a cluttered desk with a typewriter, and a tiny black and white television. Not a trace of femininity.

"Sorry, I should have cleaned up today," he said. "But you know what they say, a messy space is a sign of productivity." She ignored his now-familiar feeble attempts at humor. "Well, uh, have a seat. I think all I have is some beer. Is that okay?"

Angela murmured an affirmative as she lowered herself onto the tattered sofa. There were scurrying sounds from the kitchen, cans were popped and poured. He reappeared with a foamy glass in each hand, seeming unsure whether to sit next to her, or in the armchair. She accepted her glass, and he sat in the chair. "Would you like to hear some music? I've got most of Dylan's albums." He paused, looking forlorn. "I'm just trying to think of how to break the ice."

"I like the ice," Angela replied.

He drank from his glass and made his pitch. "Look, it's great to finally have you over here. I've been wondering if you'd be interested in reading some of my screenplay."

"You mean, right now?"

"Well, of course not right now. Unless you want to. I'm curious to hear what you think."

He had already told her the basic plot some nights beforehand, and she hadn't been impressed. The story sounded like his diary; a young schoolteacher fighting the system while trying to relate to his drug-addled students' needs. The last thing Angela needed was to be reminded of high school. "I can read it when I've got some more time," she answered.

He trained his eyes on her briefly before his frustration seemed to get the better of him. "I don't understand. We've seen each other a few times now, but you haven't shown the slightest interest in what I'm about. Am I boring?"

"No, you're not boring. Why would I be here if I thought you were boring? I think I'm the one who's boring."

His tone changed. "Oh no, you're incredible. You're the most beautiful woman I've been with in a long time, which isn't saying much, but still—"

"Gee, thanks."

"No, don't take that the wrong way. See, this is what always happens. I can't help saying stupid things."

"Forget it. I guess I have been a little standoffish."

"No, I've been worried that you wouldn't take me seriously as an artist unless you read my stuff."

She sensed her opportunity. "Why are you worried about that? We've only seen each other a few times."

"Yeah, but you answered my ad and didn't brush me off after our first date. That led me to assume we've at least got something in common. But I figured you couldn't respect me if you don't respect my work."

"I do respect your work. You're a teacher."

"That's my job, but I don't consider it my work. I'm a writer."

"No you're not. You haven't sold anything. You're just a teacher."

He was nonplussed. "How can you say that? You haven't read my screenplay."

"Look, what do you want from me, some sort of validation? What's it going to prove if I tell you I like it?"

"Well, I was hoping for a little support."

"Support? What could I give to you? You've got a steady job, parents, you're not on the verge of losing your apartment at the end of every month. What more do you want? You want me to be your girlfriend? If I agreed to that right now, tomorrow I'd be asking you for money. What do you think about that? This is the point where most guys run from me as fast as they can."

He was stunned, and Angela could feel a dark force gathering strength within her with every second she observed his slack-jawed expression.

"I just wanted you to know who I really am," he said, his voice cracking.

For a moment she took pity on him, and questioned why she had carried on the farce for this long. All it had accomplished was to confirm how she assumed the whole thing would play out from the start. With any luck, she hoped, she had made him face his own reality. It wasn't worth pressing the issue.

"Look," she began, "I'm sorry if I gave you the wrong impression. I thought you might be an interesting person to spend time with. Obviously, you need something I can't give you."

"But I can give you whatever you want," he said timidly. She decided to leave him with a shred of dignity. "I should get out of here. Let me call a cab, I'll wait for it outside."

Angela didn't want to tell Julie anything about that night, but it was impossible for them to keep secrets from each other. "I couldn't go on lying to him. I've been so disciplined with everything in my life in the past year, but I couldn't do that."

"What happened?"

"He was just so ... pathetic. With somebody else, maybe it could have worked out. I just couldn't see myself doing it with him."

"You mean, *doing it* doing it? Why should that be an issue?"

"I'm a virgin."

Julie nearly spit out her salad. She hadn't heard anyone admit that since the last slumber party she'd been to. It made her instantly re-evaluate everything she knew about Angela, and the end result didn't reveal much. "You can't be serious."

Angela nodded, feeling better for the admission. "Yeah. I guess this whole thing gave me a new perspective on what I'm looking for."

"Which is?"

"Someone who doesn't make *that* a top priority. Someone who needs me for other reasons."

"Good luck finding those around here," Julie scoffed as she dug into her salad again.

Angela brought the straw in her Long Island iced tea to her lips. She pondered how correct Julie was about expectations remaining unfulfilled, but as Angela watched the endless stream of pedestrians and traffic, she couldn't imagine that any of those people truly had what they wanted. The difference was, Angela thought, they were all too dumb to know the difference.

"Listen," Julie said. "I've got some friends over in Topanga who are having a little get-together tonight. You should come with me to get your mind off all of this. I guarantee you'll meet some real people who won't project any of that bullshit on you."

"They call this place the High Five Ranch," Julie said, pulling the parking brake on her Beetle. It was on a steep incline, and in the darkness it was difficult to see the house through the locust trees and thick underbrush masquerading as a lawn. No sounds could be heard until they stood at the front door. Julie knocked, and a dog's bark signaled their arrival. An enthusiastic black Labrador was the first to greet them before a tall, gaunt hippie gave Julie a hug, and Angela began tuning into voices singing unintelligible songs. "Angela," Julie said, "this is Brian." He held out a skeletal hand and smiled through a mess of whiskers. His ragged tunic gave him a scarecrow-like appearance, but he was gracious in offering anything they might need.

"Go on to the back porch," he added. "All the action's out there."

By her own choice, Angela had stayed out of Julie's personal life, and the thought of presenting herself to these people set her on edge. She stuck close to Julie as her younger friend made the rounds. Angela politely refused joints offered to her, but accepted a glass of cheap red wine Brian brought to her without prompting. Its harsh sweetness sent her throat into warm convulsions, and a second taste boosted her confidence to the point where she felt more at ease attached to Julie's unseen tether.

Julie gravitated to a small group huddled in a corner, each member holding a guitar. Angela stayed on the perimeter, cradling her glass in both hands, as they called out songs—some lasting a few bars before falling apart, and some providing a vehicle for harmonies that were astounding, if only for brief moments. Angela was invited to take a seat within the circle when a space opened up.

One of the musicians asked her name, to which she responded, "I'm Angela, Julie's co-worker. You know Julie?"

"No, but that's okay. I know you now. I'm Tim, that's David, and that's Will."

Angela made a quick assessment of each as they were introduced; Tim's thick nest of Dylanish curls and David's blonde surfer page-boy both seemed typical for California, but Will appeared oddly out of place. His dark, chiseled features suggested a rugged upbringing. He was not as engaging as the others either, barely acknowledging Angela's presence while tuning his guitar. "You guys sound great," was all she could manage to contribute.

David chimed in, "We're just messing around. We actually don't really know each other." Tim and Will both chuckled at this, Angela left out of an inside joke.

"Well, don't let me stop you," she said.

"Alright, I won't," Tim replied. He began to pick out a delicate, repetitive figure. The others noted its complexity and stayed out, allowing Tim to weave it for several minutes until Angela was mesmerized. Then, Tim's otherworldly voice emerged, breathing a melody as beguiling as the guitar part. It surged and abated like a force of nature, navigating through unpredictable turns in the music until reaching a precarious climax and fading into the night like smoke.

The others praised Tim in hushed tones at the song's conclusion. "You've been holding back on us," David said. "I guess you were waiting for the girls to show up."

Angela felt her cheeks flush, and Tim took it in stride. "Hey man, I'll hand it over. Show her what you've got."

David laughed, but Will took the challenge literally, hunching over his guitar and strumming some resolute chords. Will's song was almost diametrically opposed to Tim's. It moved with a purpose and told a story. Angela had trouble grasping what that story was, but Will's conviction drew her in as much as Tim's deviation. It was a clash between old and new Angela realized, as Will's voice rambled through his tale. She had not heard music of either sort before, and in some strange way, she felt faced with a choice.

Tim and David clapped and cheered when Will finished. David, now the anxious one, said, "What can I do to top you guys?"

"Don't worry about it man," Tim said. "Maybe it's time we did something that Angela could get in on too." David willingly agreed and banged out a few simple chords. The slow, country melody was readily taken up by Tim and Will, and by the second chorus, Angela was singing, joined by some nearby guests who likewise got swept up by the song's raucous words. They carried on for several more choruses until everyone was shouting like revelers on New Year's Eve. Tim gave David a brotherly pat on the shoulder, and even Will seemed pleased. Angela longed to display such affection.

Will continued to strum chords to himself as the other two set their guitars down and left the circle to mingle. Angela stared at him, expecting Will to say something. He kept playing instead.

"Hey. That was a really nice song."

"Thanks," he muttered.

"It sounds like you guys were meant to play together."

"Well, Tim and David are friends. They've got pretty good gigs. I think Tim's making a record and David's trying out for some TV show. Brian's had me play at his coffeehouse a few times, so he told me to come over for a jam. Where's your friend?"

"Oh, she knows everybody here. They all seem nice, but she mainly got me to come just to get me out of the house."

"Yeah, I know what you mean." Will trailed off, and he stopped strumming long enough to light a cigarette.

She was taken by his sincerity. "Where do you live?"

"Got a place off Sunset with a buddy of mine. It's a dump, but about as best as two guys without day jobs could hope for. How 'bout you?"

"Julie and I live off La Cienega. We both answer phones at The Times. I dug it for a while, but now it's getting to be a drag."

"How so?"

"I needed to escape my life and a job like that seemed like the easiest way to do it. Now I'm feeling like I'm over it and I need to get back to who I am."

Will took a long drag and Angela felt his eyes taking in every inch of her. The last thing she expected to do this night was confess to a complete stranger, but her words seemed to burn away his shyness.

"Who are you?" he asked, lodging the cigarette underneath the top string at the guitar's headstock.

She laughed defensively, feeling caught in a trap. "You don't want to know."

"Maybe you're right." Will went back to strumming, beginning a song similar to the other one he'd played, only this time it seemed more personal. He sang of bad choices and missed opportunities, struggles with his family and with himself, and of having to leave behind everything without having anything to replace it.

She didn't know the song was over until he reached for another cigarette. "Is that who you are?" she asked.

"I guess you could say that. I've got a lot of shit on my shoes."

"What are you doing about it?"

"Just trying to scrape it off a little at a time. You can never get them completely clean again. Whenever you step out onto the street, there's always something that scuffs them up."

Angela's lips spread in a wide grin. "Could I get one of those from you?" He tapped the soft pack of Marlboros and she extracted one. He struck the match and cupped it below her chin as she leaned in. The inherent grace of her movements came into sharp focus.

"Do you really want to know who I am?" she asked.

"Yes, I do," he said.

Julie came over at that moment, reeling from the smoke and wine. "Still here in the corner, huh? I didn't know you had a thing for musicians." Angela felt an unfamiliar wave of shame rise within her, and stood to talk to Julie at eye level. "Look," Julie began, "I'm a little too fucked up to drive home, so I'm just letting you know I'll probably just crash here. You cool with that?"

Angela stroked her arm. "Yeah, it's alright. Just be careful." Julie gave her a peck on the cheek and slid back into the group that was dancing to music being piped outside from the stereo.

Will said, "I can take you home."

*

"Lazy Susan"

Same old storybook romantic tale
Boy meets girl and girl makes bail
I'm glad you never tried to keep it all hid
Just don't ever explain why you did what you did

Lazy Susan, what's gone wrong?
Is life such a bore?
You just sit from dusk 'till dawn
While I walk the floor
There's more than these hard times outside your door

You still think about the days when you were out having fun
Blowin' in his ear while he played with his gun
He can't stop you anymore from doing as you please
So don't pretend that he's the one who always brought you to your knees

Lazy Susan, what's gone wrong?
Is life such a bore?
You just sit from dusk 'till dawn
While I walk the floor
There's more than these hard times outside your door

Sometimes you seem as if you're caught in a trance
Each time we talk it always feels like my last chance
I wish you'd see that I'm the man who'll make you do like you should
And I know you tell me how, baby, if you only could

Lazy Susan, what's gone wrong?
Is life such a bore?
You just sit from dusk 'till dawn
While I walk the floor
There's more than these hard times outside your door

Chapter 6

Pahrump, Nevada / March 1972

"**T**his sucks."

Alex's first impression of the Wagon Wheel caused Will to burst out laughing. "No, I mean it. This is the worst place you've forced me to come to yet. You're headed in the wrong direction, pal."

Will's amusement faded as the truth behind Alex's observation sunk in. "Well, it can't be Nashville every night," he replied. The two locked eyes for a moment, each weighing the consequences of the next words they might be tempted to say.

Alex was the first to back down. "I'm gonna get a Bud. Want one?"

"Make mine a Corona. I'll be right back." Will, still stung, walked with his guitar case to the far end of the small wooden room that possessed all the charm of a ship's hold. There were empty tables on the dance floor, and an office at the side of the stage. He set the case down, took a breath, and knocked on the office door.

"Will, you're early! It's not even happy hour yet." Rex stood in the office doorway, finishing the last few bites of a sandwich, remnants of which dotted his rust-colored beard.

"Just wanted to get here on time. I really appreciate you letting me play tonight with these guys."

Rex accepted Will's graciousness without reciprocating. Rex's surly attitude was something Will had come to expect after his initial trips to play the Wagon Wheel's open stage night. Still, he could feel that Rex genuinely liked him.

"I dunno when Butch and Billy are gonna arrive," Rex barked as he sat at his desk.

"That's alright. I figured I'd hang loose until then. Can you run me a tab?"

"Sure, just tell the bartender. I gotta finish some paperwork. Shut the door, will ya?"

Will set his guitar on the stage. His boot heels fell hard on the boards as he returned to the bar where Alex now occupied a stool. Will took a seat and guzzled the Corona that was waiting for him, as Alex said to no one in particular, "I guess we're early." The bartender didn't look up from his newspaper.

Will took another long pull from the bottle before answering, "Yeah, I guess I was a bit anxious."

"What are we gonna do?"

"I don't know, but I've got a tab and I'm gonna make full use of it."

"You fucker! You've got a tab, and I'm buying you beer? You'd better let me use it too."

"No way! In case you forgot, buying me a beer doesn't put a dent in what you owe me."

"Oh, real nice! I come out to this fucking dump—"

"Hey, keep it down!"

"—to support my friend, and I'm paying for the drinks."

"Relax, it's one beer." Will chugged the rest of the Corona and set the bottle in the damp ring it had formed on the bar. Alex nursed his beer in silence, as the jukebox switched records to Merle Haggard's "Mama Tried." Will thought of all the nights he had spent with Alex in these shit kicker joints since they'd been in California. Some of them drew an interesting mix of people, but most often it turned out to be places like the Wagon Wheel, where Will often worried about Alex causing trouble with the locals. Will had almost let it slip on the drive out how much he had grown to hate these places too. Now, as they sat in the empty bar, he had to try even harder not to speak his mind.

Will ordered another Corona, feeling the tension simmer between them. "Look, I'm glad you're here tonight. I think you'll really like these guys. They're the real deal. From Texas."

Alex tilted his head toward Will as if trying to translate what being from Texas had to do with anything.

The oppressive distance between Will and Alex was bridged by the sound of footsteps scuffling through the door. Rex emerged from the office when the two new arrivals made their presence known. Will observed the trio's easy camaraderie, but resisted the urge to impose. He instead remained at the bar until several minutes after they'd gone to the dressing room. Upon finishing his fourth Corona, Will straightened his posture. "I guess I'd better tune up."

Will stumbled off the stool, drawing glances from several recently arrived denim-and-gingham-clad patrons. Regaining his balance after a few tentative steps, he proceeded to retrieve his guitar case and head to the dressing room, leaving Alex hunched over at the bar, both forearms encircling his longneck bottle.

Alex had been feeling a cold coming on all day and his initial morning cough was building to something he couldn't control. A few cowboys scowled and scattered when he let out a violent hack that sent him into convulsions. It was enough to cause the bartender to approach Alex with concern. "Yeah, I'm alright," Alex said, waving him off. "Been feeling like shit all day. Probably should have stayed home tonight, but what the fuck else is there to do? It's kinda snuck up on me. You wouldn't know if there's a drug store around here?"

The bartender obliged Alex with a shot of brandy on Will's tab, and a promise to procure some medicine from the back room. After a few minutes, he handed Alex a bottle of Romilar. "This should get you through the night."

Alex winced after ingesting it all in one attempt, but felt a strange sense of relief. He thanked the bartender, and downed the dregs of his warm Budweiser to chase the lingering bitterness from his tongue. He felt less concerned about his present circumstances as the cough syrup's narcotic took hold of his system. Alex's thoughts drifted, until he was preoccupied with the question of why Will needed him to be there at all. When the gigs started coming after they'd arrived in L.A., there was no argument about how exciting it was to see his friend take the stage, no matter if Alex was the only one listening. The glamour faded as the slow grind of Will's chosen path became evident. But it went unspoken that Alex would be present each time, the talisman giving Will the courage to carry on with what often seemed like a pointless exercise.

Alex looked up from the bar and took an inventory of the room for the first time in what felt like hours. The scene lay out before him through a smear of smoke, masking an indistinguishable array of locals prepared for a raucous night out. The growing din within the hard-drinking crowd reminded Alex of family gatherings back in Ohio, memories that repulsed him as he stared through unsteady eyes at the assortment of beehive hairdos and cowboy hats.

Buoyed by a strange, newfound sense of determination, he turned to the bartender. "I've gotta get some air," he said, and felt his shoes hit the floor like sponges. He rethought his plan, but after a deep breath of noxious air, Alex strode to the door, relishing the cool desert night as it hit his face. He stood in the dirt by the barren highway, looking both ways in an attempt to recall the direction from which they had come. The only other object in view was a lighted building about a quarter-mile in the distance.

Will entered the dressing room to find Butch semi-conscious on a folding chair that barely supported his well-proportioned physique. A shapeless Stetson rested on two stacked guitar cases beside him. Terry, much slimmer in contrast, stood behind holding a near-empty bottle of Jack Daniel's. His face wore a grin that suggested he'd just received word from on high that a better world lay ahead.

"You must be Will, the L.A. peckerwood Rex told us about. Sit yer ass down, son!" Terry reached for another chair, and awkwardly unfolded it with one hand, maintaining his hold on the whiskey with the other. The chair hit the hardwood floor with a thud loud enough to rouse Butch.

Once Will was seated, Butch leaned in. "Don't worry, he only gets like this when we play out in the sticks. Most of the time it's better to be drunker than the audience in these places."

Will smiled out of respect, but moved his chair away from Butch with as much subtlety as he could muster. The pair each took a pull off their bottle, as Will took out his Martin and tuned it.

"That's a nice guitar ya got," Butch said. He wiped some stray drops of whiskey from his grizzled chin.

Will accepted the compliment while trying to suppress thoughts of how much Butch and Terry's songs meant to him.

"Had me an old Martin once," Butch continued, "but I had to sell it to pay off the first wife when she left me. Definitely know which one I miss the most!" Terry let out a bellowing laugh that prevented Will from responding.

"What do you play now?" Will asked when the roar subsided.

"Oh, I got an old, beat-up Gibson that some poor rummy prob'ly had to sell to make his old lady happy. They were for bluesmen, y'know. Country guys wouldn't touch 'em. You must be a country picker if ya got a Martin."

Will gave his guitar a once-over. "Well, I don't know about that. I just write songs and play 'em."

This time, Butch let out a hearty laugh, his half-lidded eyes trained on Will. "That's right, son, that's right! Yep, mighty nice guitar ya got."

Will became unsure of how to handle the situation and struggled to change the subject. "Rex told me to go on around ten. Is that cool?"

It took a moment for Butch to interpret the question. "Huh? Oh yeah, whatever ol' Rex wants is how it's gotta be."

Will looked up at Terry, leaning against a wall, but seemingly passed out. "Are, uh, you guys gonna be ready? He doesn't look too good."

Butch sat up, feigning insult by the insinuation. "Who? Terry here? He's just fine. You just do your best not to get them folks ornery and everything'll be alright. What's yer name again?"

"Will. Will Mosley."

"Will? I got a cousin named Will over in Lubbock. Sold Buddy Holly his first car. That's a true story. It was a '48

Packard that he let him have for $25. Him and the Crickets drove that thing to Clovis when they made 'Peggy Sue.' Ain't that right son?"

Terry stirred, bobbing his head and slurring, "That'll be the day."

"Aw, whadda you know? Have another drink." Butch grabbed the almost drained whiskey bottle and shoved it to Terry's lips, to Will's dismay.

"Do you think he should keep drinking? How's he gonna play?"

Butch lowered the bottle and glared. "I think you should be more concerned with how you're gonna play, son."

Will sat frozen as Terry emitted unnerving gasps for air while draining the bottle's last dregs. Butch turned to Will. "Y'see, Terry's from a place where the population never changes. Know why?" Will shook his head. "'Cause whenever a baby's born, a man leaves town."

Will couldn't help chuckling, and didn't protest when Butch asked if he'd like to hear another story.

"Well, it seems there was this newspaper reporter who'd been transferred from Dallas to a little town near Texarkana. His editor tells him that to get acquainted with the area, he should find a local farmer and do a story about him. So the reporter drives around until he finds a nice, welcoming farm, and the farmer turns out to be more than obliging. On the first day, the reporter takes notes on everything that's happening on the farm, but the thing that catches his eye is a three-legged pig. At the dinner table that night, the farmer asks if he'd learned anything and the reporter says he was fascinated by this three-legged pig. 'Well,' the farmer said. 'That pig is an amazing creature. One day our youngest boy fell in the pond and that pig made such a ruckus that I had to come and see what the trouble was. I pulled that boy out just in time.' 'That's incredible,' the reporter said, 'but how did the pig lose its leg?' The farmer offered the reporter another slice of ham and said, 'Well now, you can't eat a pig that good all at once!'"

Terry burst out laughing so hard that he collapsed on the floor in convulsions. Will laughed a little harder this time, sensing Butch was trying to gauge his appreciation of the joke. "You're free to use that one on stage tonight," Butch spat out as he lit a cigarette.

Will was beginning to feel at ease, but not enough to erase his restlessness. "Yeah, that's a funny story. Look, I need another beer. Can I get you guys anything while I'm heading to the bar?"

"Just tell Rex we're ready for another round, and bring back a couple of waitresses."

Will set his guitar in its case as he got up, prompting Butch to ask, "Mind if I have a look at yer axe?"

Will hesitated, noting Terry now passed out on the floor. Logic dictated it could be a terrible mistake, but Butch's sincere interest proved convincing. "Yeah, sure, knock yourself out."

"I don't think that would be a good idea, since one of us already has."

Will lingered at the dressing room door, observing Butch lean forward and extend his arm toward the Martin's neck. It was a painful sight. Sensing Butch about to lose his balance, Will bounded toward him and sat him upright in the chair. "Whoa, sorry kid. Guess I'm not great at judging distances. Hand me that guitar when you come back and I'll show you a thing or two." Will made sure to close his case before exiting to the barroom.

The ramshackle house drew him like a beacon, yet Alex didn't feel as if he was getting any closer, no matter how many times his shoes scraped along the highway's graveled shoulder. The walk was proving excruciating, forcing Alex to tell his brain to send nerve impulses to his legs in order to maintain forward progress. He was unmoved by the radiant high-desert night sky, or the all-encompassing silence that, aside from his own movement, was only disturbed by sounds that could have been echoes of events occurring miles away. All Alex knew was that each deliberate step was getting him to the only thing that held sway over his actions. Lights flickered from several windows, the only constant an illegible blue neon sign that hovered above the front door. Alex's frustration at being unable to read the sign overshadowed his concern over how his legs were functioning. The combination of Romilar and alcohol had wreaked havoc on all of his senses, his sight suffering the most. If it were daylight, he could have blamed the haze that lay before him on a mirage, but as the minutes dragged on, the cold desert night pierced his skin.

He picked up the pace, and as his destination came more clearly into view, he noticed faint shadows behind the curtains of the lighted rooms, and a cast-iron fence around the entrance. Outlines of cars, pickup trucks, and a few semis parked behind the house started to come into focus. Alex approached the gate and noted a hand-written sign instructing him to ring a buzzer. The gate opened, and he walked the few last steps to the front door where another sign invited him to enter. Alex stood in the foyer's harsh, artificial light, overwhelmed by countless framed photos of naked women lining the walls. The heat in the house was a welcome respite from the cold that penetrated his bones.

"Oh, honey! You look like you've seen better days." A stocky, misshapen, middle-aged woman with a nest of platinum blonde hair and a flower-print kimono greeted Alex. "Take a seat," she said, and gestured to the red leather chairs that, along with muted, piped-in samba music, gave the room a clinical atmosphere. Alex accepted, absorbing a rush of exhaustion in the process. "Where are you coming from dear?" the woman asked, her brow creased with concern.

Alex took another look around the room to get his bearings. "Uh, I came from down the road. The, uh—"

"The Wagon Wheel, dear. It's still early. Why'd you leave so soon?"

Not fully comprehending the question, Alex stammered, "Oh, I just needed some fresh air. Haven't been feeling very good today."

The woman smiled down upon him. "Well, I can surely see that. So how can we help you feel better?" He remained silent, hoping she would keep talking. "We can give you whatever you need. Just give me an idea and we can go from there. Our basic service starts at thirty dollars, if that's what suits you."

Alex, still interpreting her words through a fog, reached into the front pocket of his jeans for the money that was intended for his bar tab, as well as the gas he was obligated to pay Will for the ride home. He removed several crumpled bills, two tens, a five and a few singles, although his mathematical skills eluded him as he counted. He finally gave up and handed the whole pile to the woman, asking, "Is this enough?"

She counted the greenbacks for his benefit, and her voice dripped like honey in his ears. "You just wait here and I'll take care of everything sugar." Alex shut his eyes and surrendered to his intoxication. He imagined the thick, shag carpet engulfing his feet and creeping up his legs, wrapping his torso in tingling, woolly warmth.

In short order the woman was shaking Alex's arm. His body spasmed, and she recoiled. "It's okay honey. Sorry if I took too long, but I wanted to make sure I got everyone here for your perusal."

Alex squinted into the light. A line-up of a half-dozen women, of all manner of skin tones and shapes, stood before him in lingerie. He stared in a mix of wonder and disbelief, until a grasp of the situation burned away the cloud covering his brain. "Take your time sir. They all have something unique to offer."

Alex examined each woman with the intent of choosing the one who would make him feel the least ashamed. Some of them had clearly worked a full day, while others reminded him of past rejection. The gut-wrenching process of elimination wore on until he settled on the tall, sleek woman whose air of self-confidence and professionalism.

He extended an index finger in her direction. "I'll go with her."

"Jessy?"

"Yeah, the, uh, Black girl."

Jessy stepped forward in her stilettos as the others dispersed. She leaned down to help Alex to his feet. "Enjoy your stay with us sir," the older woman called out before disappearing down a corridor.

Alex and Jessy stood facing each other alone in the foyer. "I was told you paid for a blowjob. No point in being out here anymore then is there?"

Alex gazed back, his fondness for her increasing by the second. He logged every aspect of her features, from the sharp cheekbones that accentuated the gauntness of her face, to her bottomless ebony eyes, shaded by garish false lashes. Straight hair flowed down to her breasts, partially revealed by a push-up bra. Her full lips were painted as if to match the color of the room. Alex ignored the surface artificiality. Her real allure lay in the gentle tug she gave his hand.

"Come on, let's go to my room."

He followed Jessy down a dim hallway. Voices and music behind each door created an omnipresent muffled hum. She stopped near the end, opening a door to a small, tidy bedroom, decorated with an array of African trinkets and wall hangings. A waft of incense awakened his senses, and her first action was to light a fresh stick. "Make yourself comfortable. Don't wanna rush you, but my time's up when that burns out."

Alex sat on the end of the bed and Jessy moved in front of him, taking off her bra to free her breasts with large, dark nipples. Alex was transfixed, unsure of what he was supposed to do. "You can touch 'em if you want, baby," she said, moving closer to run her hands along his thighs. He remained still as her hands went the full distance to his crotch, rubbing the denim. "Come on baby, ain't you gonna take 'em off? Or do you want me to?" She extended her satin-coated fingernails and expertly unhinged his belt. Next came the button and zipper. "Lie back, baby. Leave everything to me." Alex did as he was instructed, placing his trust in the mattress to catch him. He gave no further resistance as Jessy removed his pants and performed the service for which he'd paid. Her valiant moans of mock pleasure went unheard; to Alex it could have been a dream.

After several minutes of laboring, Jessy climbed atop the bed until she faced Alex nose to nose. "Look boy, what's wrong?" she asked, playfully tapping his cheek. "You're the first man I ever had in here that fell asleep. This ain't no hotel." Alex struggled to raise his head, then pulled himself up to a semi-sitting position where he beheld Jessy leaning on her elbows, her glorious ass protruding above her red-stockinged legs.

Alex ran his open palms over his face and hair. "I'm really sorry. I shouldn't even be here. I took some cold medicine and it blindsided me. After I realized I'd paid, I just wanted to let you do your thing and get out of here."

She'd seen her share of young white boys before, but none were as pathetic as this one. By force of habit, Jessy had taken Alex's wallet out of his jeans while he was dozing and found it empty. She noted his driver's license info anyway.

"What was this medicine you took?"

"Romilar, the guy said."

"What guy?"

"I was down the road at the Wagon Wheel with my friend who's playing there tonight. I couldn't stand how I was feeling, so I had to take something. Then it made me wanna get away. This was the only place I could see for miles."

"You sure you ain't no junkie?"

"No, I just drank the whole goddamn bottle. I thought it would be like codeine." He laughed. "I'd heard stories about what that shit does to you, but didn't believe them until now."

Jessy had to stifle her own laughter. "Damn white boys, ya'll think you're ten feet tall when you're out here."

"I'm no fucking cracker."

"Oh, okay. Calm down. I'll tell ya what I'll do, since you've been honest with me. I'll give you a little something that'll get you back down the road. But only on one condition. You're going back to L.A. tonight, right?"

"How did you know?"

"I'll be straight up, I saw your driver's license." Alex shot her a stunned look, but her admission suggested they'd established a bond. Jessy didn't give him time to react, continuing, "I need to deliver something to my cousin tomorrow. But first things first." She got up from the bed and opened the top drawer of the bureau to extract a bag of cocaine. "This should even you out."

She did the first line off one of her hand mirrors, then chopped two for Alex. His clarity was restored instantly. "Feeling better?" Jessy asked. Alex grinned, drinking in her dark, shimmering radiance. "Good. Here's what I'd like you to do." She turned again to the bureau, this time removing a bulging brown, heavily taped envelope. "You just gotta drop this off to my cousin over in Watts. If you're cool with that, I'll call him in the morning to say expect a white boy. He'll give you something for your trouble."

"What is this, and why me?"

"Let's just say I've been having problems with my usual couriers."

Alex weighed the package in his hands, betraying no indication that he knew exactly what Jessy was talking about. All he wondered was if he would see her again. "You ever come to L.A.?"

"Yeah, when I ain't here." He moved to pick up his pants, but she stopped him before he could put them on. "Look," she said, pushing aside the envelope and grasping his wrist. "I didn't finish giving you what you paid for."

Will took the stage without an introduction. The jukebox kept blaring Webb Pierce's "There Stands The Glass,"and few in the audience took notice of him. Will checked the microphone and strummed a few chords. "Could, uh, somebody cut the music? I'm ready to start now." Scattered laughter ceased with a jolt when the bartender pulled the plug on the jukebox. Will steeled himself for the task at hand. "Hi, my name's Will Mosley, and, uh, I'm gonna play a few of my songs for you before, uh, Butch and Terry come out, so, uh, thanks in advance for listening."

A few perfunctory cheers went up as Will launched into his normal set opener, "Pretty Messed Up." The simple sentiments and rising choruses went over well enough that he kept driving along with "Coal Porter Blues," one of his granddad's numbers. He needed another beer after that, and as he put in the request over the PA, he was surprised to see Rex dart from his office to the bar, and hustle two Coronas to the stage. It gave Will some added ambition; after downing a good portion of one bottle, he announced he was going to try something new. This was met by someone from the back of the room yelling, "Play one you know," eliciting more laughter.

"Good to hear I've got one fan out there," came Will's weak retort. "Bartender, if that was my buddy Alex, you'd better cut him off. He'll probably have to drive me home tonight. Butch and Terry have been giving some drinking lessons backstage."

The first unified roar erupted from the crowd. Will soaked up this small victory and carried on with increased confidence. "This one's called 'More Than a Memory.'"

He began by strumming the chords slowly, knowing that such a wordy piece would be a test. He tried to avoid spitting out each line, instead, keeping his mind open to points in the song that demanded emphasis, while thinking ahead to the next phrase. He was not fond of songs that were structured in such a fashion, but there was something about this one that had spilled itself onto the page. By the halfway point, he could tell he was losing some of the crowd. He heard the chattering flare up, and bottles clinking more intensely. In response, Will shut his eyes and calculated how far he had left to go in the song. Each chorus became a rest stop, until he gathered all he had left for the final verse. He wasn't committed to it as the song's climax, but that didn't prevent him from ignoring his concern for dynamics and pouring out whatever it was he was trying to say. He couldn't bring himself to drag out a coda after that. The song stopped abruptly, leaving those who had bothered to follow its faint, twisting path unfulfilled.

Amid the few half-hearted approvals, a voice yelled, "You know what I liked best about that song? When it ended!"

Will tried to take the jab in stride, pausing to finish a beer before replying, "I know that's the kind of song that ain't everybody's cup of tea. But sometimes you gotta say what's on your mind, like that fella there just did. I can respect that."

"Play some George Jones!"

"Now wait, I like country music as much as all of you out there, but that's not what I do—"

"What are ya, a fuckin' L.A. hippie?"

"Nope. Well yeah, I live there, but I'm no hippie. That doesn't matter anyway. I'm just trying to play you my songs."

Will could see Rex standing at the side of the stage, arms crossed and a scowl penetrating through his beard. The fact that he didn't pull Will off at that moment gave Will an inkling he was allowed one more song.

"Alright. You want a country song? Here's a country song." Will mentally scanned his repertoire for another of his granddad's numbers he'd been toying with. All he had of it was some scribbled lines on a yellowed piece of paper. There was a definite rhythmic pattern to the verses, but Will's problem was producing a melody. He knew he was making a huge mistake, despite the opening chords settling the room down. The words rang out with an ancient tone, foreign to his own ears, images of a young boy growing up beside idyllic streams and valleys set the stage for his leaving to fight a war in Europe he didn't understand. Will had instantly connected to the words the first time he'd read them, but the song was not yet his, something he realized as the audience's hostility grew palpable. Nonetheless, he pressed on with the story until it possessed him. *"Dear father, dear father, for me do not weep / For a lonesome high mountain, I mean for to sleep / And the danger of war I intend for to share / And for sickness and death I intend to prepare."* Eventually his hands caught the melody line, but by the last verse, his voice was trembling. *"Dear mother,*

dear mother, I cannot tend your woe / Your tears and your sorrow
they trouble me so / I must be a-going for here I cannot stand / I'm
going in defense of our own native land."

Will finished the song without flourish, gave a mumbled
goodnight and staggered off-stage, brushing past Rex. Will
burst into the dressing room, his entire body shaking. It made
the job of setting the guitar in its case appear as delicate as
laying a baby in its cradle, and Terry, now fully cognizant
sipping a Budweiser, took notice. "What the fuck happened to
you out there, kid?"

Will threw himself into a chair and stared at the ceiling,
wondering what possible excuse he could give. Butch was idly
tuning his Gibson while exhibiting signs of catching a second
wind, much like his partner. "What did I tell you about getting
them folks ornery? Terry, what did I tell the kid?"

"You told him not to get them folks ornery."

"That's right. Now you and I have to go out there and put
on a goddamn show. Do you think we can manage that?"

"I dunno Hoss. How does 'You Are My Sunshine' go
again?"

Butch let out his bellowing laugh before addressing Will.
"Look kid. You had a rough night. It happens to all of us. I
heard a bit of what you were doing, and it sounded alright. But
sometimes you gotta give the people what they want until they
get to know ya a little bit. Especially out in these parts. They
don't wanna hear no folkie shit, no matter how good you are.
They just wanna be entertained. Once you get 'em feelin' that
way, then you can hit 'em where it hurts."

Will listened to the lecture with great patience, but it wasn't doing much to alter his mood. The shaking didn't abate, and his head throbbed as Butch rambled on. During a pause in the monologue, Will jumped in, if only to prove to himself that he could still speak.

"Listen to me for a second. You've been telling me stories all night. You wanna hear one of mine?" Butch's eyes narrowed in response to Will's breathless assertiveness. Terry leaned in as well. "You guys know about the white buffalo?" Both of them shook their heads in unison. "Well, there's a tribe of Indians up in the Dakotas who believe that the Great Spirit will return in the form of a white buffalo, and it will be a sign for all the tribes to unite and reclaim their lands. When I was making my way out to California for the first time, I was passing through Chicago when I heard some people talking about this, a white buffalo born on a farm in Wisconsin. I asked a guy where it was, and he told me it was near a little town called Janesville. He pointed the way and I went, for no other reason than it wasn't too far off my route. It didn't take much to locate the farm, 'cause there were a bunch of big spray-painted signs that said 'Miracle,' where the side road crossed the main highway. I could see a line of cars stretched about a half-mile from the farmhouse and I could hear drums and chanting. I figured I must have picked a good day to visit, so I left my car and started walking up the dirt road. I started to see people milling around the gates and some teepees and campfires. I was feeling a little nervous, but no one paid any attention to me. I walked over to an empty corral beside a red barn and asked a man if that's where the buffalo was, and he said yes but it was only let out at designated worship times. I asked when the next one was and he said at dusk. I was about to leave when I noticed an Indian girl, a little younger than me, sitting by herself under an oak in a filthy, torn overcoat, and playing the most beat-up guitar I'd ever seen. But somehow she was getting a sound out of it that mixed perfectly with whatever it was she was singing in her native tongue. I didn't want to disturb her, but after listening for a few minutes, I had to say something. I started tossing out compliments, and she just smiled. I asked her about the song she was singing, and she said it came to her the moment she saw the buffalo and it was the only song she had played in the week she had been there. Then she said it would probably be the only song she plays for the rest of her life. She had seen the Great Spirit made whole and this was the song He had told her to play for humanity. You can imagine how stunned I was. I thanked her and found a spot along the corral's fence. As the sun began to set, the drumming and chanting intensified until a white man, the farm's owner I presumed, walked from the house toward the barn. He opened the big swinging doors and the herd emerged. They scattered to reveal the white one, small but sturdy, hobbling along with the others in anticipation of its evening meal. The chanters were yelling at the top of their lungs, and I swear the white buffalo acknowledged them. It broke away and walked along the length of the fence where we all stood. It looked straight at me with its sad eyes as it passed."

Will paused. He had been caught up in his storytelling, unconcerned whether Butch and Terry were listening. They were, in fact, hanging on his every word.

"Gentlemen," Will said, "I have seen the face of God. And it is for that reason that I will not heed the words of mortal men."

Will picked up his guitar case and walked out of the dressing room, as Terry turned to Butch and asked, "Do you believe that shit?"

Butch opened the new bottle of Jack Daniel's Rex had sent in. "I believe it as much as all the shit I've ever told you." After taking a drink and passing the bottle to his partner, he added, "Hell, if it's true, the kid's got a lot more going for him than we'll ever have."

Will was intent on finding Alex, but Rex pulled him aside, shoving fifty dollars into Will's palm. "That was some display of showmanship you put on. Don't come back until you've learned some songs people want to hear." Will's face was rigid, but he kept his anger in check, turning away and pocketing the cash.

Alex was back at the bar, wide-eyed, and ordered a Corona for Will as he saw him approach. "Here, have one on me." After downing the bottle, and with the frustration beginning to seep out of him, he looked at Alex with a hint of desperation. "You okay to drive?"

Alex nodded.

"Good. Let's get the fuck out of here." Will remained composed, and hoped things would stay that way during the two-hour ride back to L.A.

"More Than A Memory"

There were stars in the sky, and I was feelin' kinda high
Knowin' it was all comin' true
You pledged your love to me, through all eternity
Give or take a year or two

Everybody knew the story, but it wasn't cause to worry
It could never hold a candle to you
It just got more frustratin', knowin' no one would be waitin'
When my long working day was through

I was all but forgotten, by the time you started moppin'
Up the floor of the Dairy Queen
They'd all sit there starin', at whatever you were wearin'
Or whatever was seldom seen

CHORUS: I can't recall -- ever havin' you close to me
But I can't forget -- you're more than a memory

You made up your own rules, and played them all for fools
It was close to a work of art
So when he got you with his lies, I surely was surprised
You must have wanted that from the start

It seemed a sure thing, that he'd offer you his ring
And take you somewhere far away
But how it played out, didn't leave much doubt
You weren't wanted 'round here anyway

They said that you were lovers, but I knew it was a cover
You didn't want the truth to be told
That by the time you had grown, you couldn't find a home
For a heart already bought and sold

CHORUS: I can't recall -- ever havin' you close to me
But I can't forget -- you're more than a memory

Then one night you were gone, and it didn't take long
For him to finally make up his mind
That he couldn't let you go, and had to tell you so
Before someone else treated you kind

You headed down to Dallas to move into a palace
At least that's what he said it was
But it only took a week before you left him in his sleep
Your only reason was just because

Your face began to twitch as the car went in the ditch
You were lucky to get out alive
And all that you could save, was the cross that Uncle Dave
Gave you back in '65

CHORUS: I can't recall -- ever havin' you close to me
But I can't forget -- you're more than a memory

It could have been remorse that set you off course
But I'd like to think it's something more
Like the thought of leavin' me, slaving in the factory
Every day from seven to four

I wasn't feeling very well when you called from that motel
Sayin' that you'd had enough
I thought the leavin' part was hard, but comin' home scarred
Was gonna be twice as rough

I rolled my window low, and played the radio
All the way, tryin' not to think
Now we're bleary-eyed strangers, wary of the danger
Of bein' the first to blink

CHORUS: I can't recall -- ever havin' you close to me
But I can't forget -- you're more than a memory

Chapter 7

Watts / November 1969 – March 1972

"**M**ost human behavior is learned behavior. Humans do not act from instinct as lower animals do. Those things learned indirectly many times stimulate very effective responses to what might be later a direct response. At this time the Black masses are handling the resistance incorrectly. The brothers in East Oakland learned from Watts a means of resistance fighting by amassing the people in the streets, throwing bricks and Molotov cocktails to destroy property and create disruption. The brothers and sisters in the streets were herded into a small area by the Gestapo police and immediately contained by the brutal violence of the oppressor's storm troops. This manner of resistance is sporadic, short-lived, and costly in violence against the people. This method has been transmitted to all the ghettos of the Black nation across the country. The first man who threw a Molotov cocktail is not personally known by the masses, but yet the action was respected and followed by the people. When the people learn that it is no longer advantageous for them to resist by going into the streets in large numbers, and when they see the advantage in the activities of the guerrilla warfare method, they will quickly follow this example. But first, they must respect the party which is transmitting this message."

Jessy Robinson's life changed the moment she heard Huey Newton speak, conjuring faded memories of Sunday services when she sat on hard pews, week after week in the dress her mother had sewn for her, being taught to fear God. She learned there were more tangible things to fear when her mother could no longer provide her with anything. When that reality set in, Jessy didn't need to put much thought into turning herself out; her first trick made the decision for her. She'd noticed him looking her over, and the next step was asking if he wanted it. It seemed natural; she was in complete control the entire time.

But in late 1969, she did not feel in control as she sat in the cramped living room listening to Huey. He spoke with a confidence she had not encountered since the sermons of her youth, maintaining eye contact with each participant in the same manner, while gesturing dramatically for emphasis. Jessy had come to hear Huey at the invitation of her cousin Fred, a recent Panther recruit, who organized the evening meeting at his house to discuss rebuilding Watts in the wake of the riots. No substantial dialogue occurred though, everyone just wanted to hear Huey speak about the Revolution, and give reports from the front lines in Oakland and Chicago. Jessy hung on every word, and when he concluded with a raised fist salute, her arm shot up in the air.

The room converged upon Huey, leaving Jessy unable to see him amid the crush of bodies. Fred appeared from the kitchen with a glass of water for her.

"What'd you think? Pretty incredible cat, huh?"

Jessy remained entranced and didn't respond until her cousin wrapped her fingers around the glass. "Oh yeah, that was ... a trip." The water cooled her entire body as it went down her parched throat.

The chatter around Huey grew louder as he fielded dozens of questions at once. Others repeated snatches of party propaganda, and when that went unacknowledged, they asserted themselves more loudly. Fred seemed to be talking to himself more than Jessy. "Look at what's going on. We're making shit happen, right here in my house. Would you have ever believed that was possible?"

Jessy cocked her head toward her cousin's beaming exterior. She had heard all of the words Huey had spoken, but was still too naive to fully understand them. She also knew Fred; he was the only person in her life, since her mother passed, who cared about her being on the street without passing judgment. She had vague notions about his illegal activities, and chose to keep her nose out of his business as well, but in the six months after Fred had become a Panther, she had noticed a change, although his motivation remained unclear.

"No, I would not have believed it was possible," she whispered to him.

"So, you want in?"

The address for the delivery required Alex to take multiple buses. Each time he transferred he could feel distinct physical changes in the city. The modest dwellings in West Hollywood gave way to block upon block of low rent lodgings; most appeared abandoned, although as the bus ambled along, a steady flow of kids, workers, and elderly shoppers got on board. He had not been in Watts before, having been warned to stay away. But on this bright Sunday morning, despite the cocaine and cough syrup hangover, he summoned the courage to keep his word to Jessy and trace the route to Fred's Body Shop on Wilmington.

Alex kept the package tucked in the back waistband of his jeans. It started irritating him as the ride turned into a longer endeavor than he'd anticipated. He fidgeted in the bus's small metal seat, but could not fix the situation amid the stream of passengers, a cross-section of human evolution that became less attractive with each stop. He tried to find a distraction by eavesdropping on two young drifters sitting across from him, one haranguing the other with seemingly little concern over who was listening.

"I got an aunt who lives around here," the man said, glancing out the window as the bus limped down 103rd Street. "She let me stay for a couple months. Man, it was wicked. That place was fucking huge." Alex detected sincerity in the kid's tone, and felt a deeper meaning to the statement after determining from the pair's shabby appearance that they had both been spending a lot of time outdoors.

The silent kid didn't appear to care, much less register where they were. The speaker carried on regardless. "Living outside the city, that was cool for a while, but I don't want to go back. All you can really do out there is be a fruit picker, and that's a total drag. You bake in the sun and pull every muscle. And you're surrounded by Mexicans all day." Alex glanced around to see if anyone reacted to the slur, but most of the other riders were out of earshot. "But I gotta tell ya, they do have the best weed. Acapulco fuckin' Gold, dude. If I could be guaranteed some of that every night in the bunkhouse, I'd go back to work there right now. Fuck everything else!"

Alex kept his eyes trained on the pair. Sensing this, the speaker sat smiling, revealing a few missing teeth. He continued his speech, aware that Alex was listening. "Yeah, it sure will be nice to get a place again." The quiet one still hadn't moved, instead staring at something only he could see. Alex sensed a strange bond forming and felt an urge to ask if the pair had any Acapulco Gold for sale. But the stoic air he maintained eventually got under the speaker's skin.

"What's up with you buddy? You seem interested in what I'm sayin'."

"Nah. Just couldn't help overhearing. Where do you get your shit now?"

"What are ya, a fuckin' narc?"

Alex let out a short burst of laughter. "If you don't want people asking for it, you shouldn't advertise."

The kid smiled again, knowing he'd been caught out. "I got a friend from TJ that I do a little work for now and then."

Alex decided to push his luck, in part for his own amusement. "What's his name? I'm kinda looking for work too." The kid scoffed, but Alex kept pressing. "I'm serious. What's his name?"

"His name? Look man, I dunno who the fuck you are, but you should start minding your own fucking business."

Alex held up his hands in surrender, before reaching around his back to feel the package still securely wedged under his shirt. The kid clammed up after that, and cast his eyes out the window before pulling the cord for a stop. As the bus slowed, he shook his friend awake, and the pair staggered toward the back door. The silent one stumbled out onto the sidewalk. Before he exited, the loud one took a last look at Alex, who couldn't resist waggling his fingers in return.

As the bus rolled on, Alex couldn't ignore the package digging into his lower back. A sudden twinge of panic struck, and he reached into his pocket for Jessy's crude map. He strained to locate street signs out the window, his anxiety rising with each passing intersection.

"You held a gun before, baby? Nice, ain't it? Yeah, feel that weight. It's heavier than it looks, huh?" The meeting had yet to end inside the house, but Fred stood with Jessy under the 40-watt light bulb in his garage, unable to contain his joy at the possibility of her joining the cause. He wanted to show her the benefits.

"I've seen my share of these," she said, studying the .45 automatic.

"Yeah, but it's a whole other thing to hold it. You're a different person. Don't you feel it?" Jessy didn't know how to feel. She kept shifting the pistol in her hands, caressing every part of its cold, black exterior. "Everyone's gotta have one," Fred continued. "You know what it's like on your own, but when you become a Panther, you gotta be prepared to defend yourself at all times. First thing you gotta learn is how to use that motherfucker."

Fred couldn't stand watching her fumble with it. He motioned for Jessy to hand it back to him and proceeded to go through the routine of cocking and dry firing. He repeated the motions before urging her to try. She was slow and clumsy, but managed to execute the moves and bring it up to a firing position. "Squeeze it baby. Don't pull it, squeeze it." She aimed at an auto parts poster against the far wall, alternating the target between the model's head and her tits busting out of her bikini. Jessy squeezed and the click reverberated through her body. She lowered the gun. The girl in the bikini still leaned against the car with her frozen smile. "You're gonna be a soldier, baby. A motherfucking life-taker."

Voices were getting louder inside the house, and another shudder ran up Jessy's spine.

Alex was late, and the noon-hour sun marred his vision as he stood on the corner looking for the shop's sign. The faded paint above the raised door caught his eye like an apparition. There was one car inside, but no others to suggest that this was a thriving business. Alex jogged across the street against the light, honing in on the windowless, reinforced side door that bore a simple sign: "Open—Enter." No one was there to meet Alex in the office, other than a jumble of parts, manuals, and assorted paperwork. He could hear activity in the adjacent garage—some banging, a muffled radio—and debated seeing who might be there. A hand-written sign on the desk directed him to "ring the bell for service," and a Black man in dirty coveralls appeared. He waited for Alex to speak, wiping his hands with a greasy rag.

"Uh, hi," Alex mumbled. "I'm looking for Fred." The other man didn't react, as if his mere presence was the answer. The silence prompted Alex to continue. "I've, uh, got the package from Jessy." Fred set the rag on the desk and motioned for Alex to reveal what he was carrying. With much satisfaction, he extracted the wrapped bundle and dropped it into Fred's massive palms.

"How was she?" Fred's first words blindsided Alex, stoking an intolerable mood in the small room.

"What do you mean?"

Fred sat in a wooden swivel chair, and the package disappeared underneath the desk. "I'm just sorta curious about why you're here today. I mean, she tells me to expect a white boy I've never met before, so you can understand why I might have cause to wonder who you are."

Alex shuffled his feet, pondering the correct response. "Honestly, I don't know what happened. I was in bad shape and she was nice to me. Then she found out I lived here and asked me to deliver a package. I didn't want to say no."

"You weren't curious about what was in the package?"

"No, but I used my imagination." Alex smiled hoping to ease the tension. "When someone asks me to do something for them, I try to help as best I can."

Fred, fingers enjoined behind his head, nodded. "Where are you coming from?"

"West Hollywood."

"You got your own action up there?"

Alex teetered on the verge of pleading ignorance. "Well, I'm trying to do a little acting, if that's what you mean."

"Yeah, that figures. I mean, how do you really make a living? A guy like you's gotta have some connections."

Alex started to warm up to Fred's patronizing tone, but remained unsure. He flashed back to grilling the kid on the bus and decided to stand up for himself. "There's a guy I met when I did some extra work on a zombie movie last year. He gets shit sent up the coast by boat. Lotta people in the biz buy from him."

"So you've done this kinda thing before?"

"Yeah, it's no big deal. Haven't been down here before though."

"The American Dream, ain't it? Had this shop for ten years and damned if I'll let my own people burn it down. Gotta make ends meet though, so I appreciate your assistance."

Fred ducked out of Alex's view, opening a bottom drawer in the desk, then rose again holding a wad of cash. "Hope this makes the trip worthwhile," he said, handing Alex $250 in tens and twenties. Alex accepted with a grateful nod and pocketed the cash without counting it. He turned to leave, but Fred addressed him before he reached the door. "Tell me more about this dude. He hooked up with some heavy players or what?"

Alex felt an urge to sit, but wasn't about to without being offered one of the filthy leather chairs. "I guess he knows a few, but it's none of my business. I just drop off the shit where he tells me to go."

"But you really wanna be an actor?"

Alex smiled. "Yeah man, doesn't everybody?"

Fred returned the smile. "How did you meet Jessy? Our routine usually involves truckers."

"My friend's a singer and he was playing some shitkicker bar down the road from her place. I couldn't handle that scene so I ended up with her."

"She's a special girl, huh?"

"Yeah, is she your—"

"She's my cousin. Practically raised her myself. It's nice that she's in a safe place and not on the street anymore."

Fred appeared to drift and Alex took it as a cue to leave. "Well, I guess I'd better—"

"Tell your friend I've got some business for him if he wants it. Might save me some trouble." Fred opened another desk drawer, this time at the top, and passed over a business card bearing his name and phone number alongside the shop's logo.

Alex gave it courteous once-over and put it in the back pocket of his jeans. "I'll give this to him."

"I'm interested in the movies myself. But like you said, aren't we all?" Fred let out a low, rumbling laugh that seemed to force itself out of his throat. "Hope I'll be seeing you again soon man."

"Yeah."

Alex debated shaking Fred's hand, but the dirt and grime impeded his desire to touch anything in the shop. He exited through the heavy door and the overpowering heat struck him like an oven. It took a second to get his bearings. He finally located the northbound bus stop halfway up the block. With the package gone, the money became his pressing concern. He felt the cash emitting a signal from his front pocket, calling to anyone looking for a quick score, although fortunately the streets remained quiet at midday. He steeled himself for a long wait at the bus stop with the new information he'd learned about Jessy burning in his head. Details of the previous night were taking on pastel hues. He wanted to see her, if only to let her know everything went all right, and that he was someone she could depend on. He thought about borrowing Will's car and going back. Would she be happy to see him? A glint from the bus windshield appeared from up the block and Alex dug change from his pocket. He'd better go see Carlos first. There would be plenty of time to decide on the long ride home.

She remembered what she'd been told about waiting until the wind was right. It whistled past her ears and kicked up dust in front of the target. The longer she held her aim, the more she could feel her eyes threatening to tear up. Fred told her that she needed discipline to react to the moment. And it will be a reaction, he further stressed; from now on she represents a threat to people who have more guns than the Panthers can dream of owning. The message was repeated to her over and over by Fred and other Panthers: match the enemy strength for strength. This page, straight out of *The Art Of War*, they had urged her to study. She had abandoned reading the same day she walked out of school to earn the money her mother no longer could, but she had heard enough rhetoric since Fred put the gun in her hand. Now, her instincts were talking.

Jessy pulled the trigger the moment the wind dissipated. The pistol exploded in her hands. Her entire body absorbed the blowback, muscles unwilling to relinquish her fixed position. She could not see where the bullet hit; the dust clouded her view, and Jessy lowered her arms.

"How was that one?" she asked.

Fred stood behind her, his tone anxious. "Hard to tell. Fire the rest, and try not to let your hands come up."

Jessy raised her arms, assumed the position with more confidence, and sighted the target with greater ease. She squeezed the trigger, and after absorbing the expected kick, emptied the chambers without further hesitation. Each successive pop built upon the last, creating an ominous echo. She turned to Fred as the sound faded. He beamed, and stretched out a hand to relieve her of the .45. "Let's see how you made out."

They walked the fifty yards in silence. Jessy replaced her sunglasses to repel the relentless sun. Fred's only concern was the target, and he broke into a trot as the black holes came into view. She had penetrated the center circle, and a few holes dotted the outer edges. Jessy approached at a casual pace, too slow for Fred, who called out, "You're gonna love this. One hit dead on." She shifted her sunglasses to the top of her head to examine her work. She wanted to share Fred's excitement, but the sight left her inexplicably cold. She straightened up and lowered her shades as their footprints were erased by the wind. Fred reloaded the revolver.

"Try some more."

Jessy sighed. "I don't think I want to. I know I can do it now."

Fred's expression soured. "Are you shittin' me? You think you're Annie-fuckin'-Oakley all of a sudden? I gotta tell Huey straight up that you can be counted on in case shit goes down, and I ain't gonna lie to the man. Now let's fire off a few more."

They proceeded to where Fred's Cutlass Supreme sat radiating in the late autumn heat. "You gotta get good in a hurry. We're gonna need you." It wasn't like Fred to ask her for favors.

"Need me for what?"

"Things are getting too high profile for the pigs," he said. "Politicians want 'em to send a message that they still got the upper hand. Word is they're gonna come at the headquarters with everything they've got. They might just be saying that to rattle us, but since Huey got paroled, it's no secret that those fuckers wanna send him right back in. We need as many people around the place as we can to defend it from now on. And you can't be afraid to take out a pig if you have to."

Jessy knew that it was too late to back out. "If I'm going to be a part of this, I want to meet Huey."

Fred's smile returned. "You'll meet him when you demonstrate your commitment to the Revolution." He handed her the reloaded pistol, and this time her grip felt familiar.

She cocked and aimed in one smooth motion, releasing the bullet into the dust. "Don't get your hopes up though," Fred added as Jessy prepared for the next shot. "You're at the back of the line."

She pulled the trigger before he finished his thought. She fired the rest of the clip in a consistent rhythm, the echoes reverberating off the canyon walls.

Carlos caught the bullet and collapsed against the side of the police cruiser, but failed to burst the blood pack taped inside his shirt. The director cut the scene and the prop master besieged Carlos, explaining in simple terms how to use the device.

"Look," said Carlos, "I've done this before. I just missed it, okay? Better I miss it than needing a new shirt, right?" It was Carlos's only scene, and the last shot of the day, and he was eager to get it done and get paid. He returned to his mark, this time cheating a bit with his hand poised to puncture the plastic bag. The director yelled "Action!" and with an off-camera crack, Carlos dropped his own fake service revolver and doubled over, making sure to lose his hat in the process. As he slumped against the car, he could see his blue shirt turning red.

"Cut! I guess that'll have to do, so print it. That's a wrap for today everybody. Back at five tomorrow!" The prop master, a young hippie whose only qualifications appeared to be a fascination with explosives, approached Carlos and carefully examined the stain pattern before helping him to his feet.

"That one felt pretty good to me," Carlos said. "How'd it look?"

"It doesn't matter. The kids are gonna get off either way seeing a cop get taken down by some freaks. Take off your shirt, I wanna compare this to the other ones. I think you hit the sweet spot."

The prop master helped Carlos remove the shirt and tear off the empty pouch. "Be easy with that. Fuck! They gotta think of a better way to do this. I've lost half the hair on my chest because of these little bastards."

"Hey, at least you're working."

"Yeah right. I can see those leading man parts starting to roll in any day now. Who the fuck decided to make me a cop anyway? I guess it makes sense that I wouldn't have a partner though."

With his tools in hand, the prop master scurried off leaving Carlos alone, shirtless, and dying for a cigarette as the crew cleaned up the set. Amidst the commotion he spotted Alex waiting near the trailers. Carlos walked over without betraying a whiff of how happy he was to see him.

Alex called out as Carlos approached, "Wow, that was so fucking cool how you did that!"

"Thanks. I gotta put my clothes back on. You got a smoke?" Alex produced his Camels, and Carlos navigated the two of them through the maze of trailers until they reached one designated for the stunt crew. Carlos didn't ask the reason for the meeting until he had changed into his street clothes and bummed another cigarette.

"Is there a problem with something?"

"No, just the opposite," Alex replied. "I think I've got a new market for you."

Carlos took a long, satisfying drag. "Yeah?"

"I just did a deal with a guy in Watts, owns a body shop—"

"What the fuck were you doing down there? And what are you doing making outside deals?"

Alex explained his encounter with Jessy, and Fred's offer. Carlos wasn't impressed. "I don't deal with outsiders. Haven't I told you that? It's nothing but trouble. You need muscle if you're gonna mess around with those people, and I don't have time for that. I've got my customers and everyone's happy."

"But there's a lot of cash. I could feel it when I was talking to this guy. They got a whole operation happening that's gotta be bigger than yours."

"So what the fuck do they need me for?"

"Well, for starters, I told him how good your shit is. Then I mentioned something about acting and that seemed to grab his attention."

"What about acting? You're not an actor, you're a fucking extra."

"So what? I just thought it might be a chance to expand the operation on both ends."

"Lemme guess, the guy's got a script?"

"I don't know. We didn't get into details. Honestly, I wanted to get the fuck out of there as fast as I could, but I told him I'd at least bring it up with you."

Carlos squinted through the blinds that shielded the trailer's front window. He pulled them tight and turned to Alex. "What's in it for you? There must be something. I know you're not working for me for the thrills. I'll bet it's pussy."

Alex's aloof reaction told Carlos he was right. "What do you want me to say? I haven't had much action since I've been out here. Maybe it's affecting my judgment."

Alex's desperate tone caused Carlos to gaze at him with disdain. "Hey, if you wanna get laid, just tell me. But that ain't the business I'm in. Speaking of that, you have your buddy's car?"

"Yeah."

Carlos reached for his sport jacket lying in a heap near the mirror. He extracted a bag containing an ounce of grass from the inside pocket and tossed it toward Alex. "Take this to Dennis's place on your way home."

"Where am I supposed to put this?"

Carlos exhaled a plume of smoke in mild frustration as he assessed the problem. "Here, take the fuckin' jacket," he spat. Alex made an awkward, one-handed grab. He replaced the grass in the pocket and put on the jacket—at least two sizes too big for his slim build—over his faded t-shirt and jeans. The ensemble made him appear like a guy begging to get fingered in a police line-up. "What can I tell this guy in Watts?"

Carlos had to suppress laughter as he took in Alex's disheveled appearance. "Tell him to stick to his own kind."

Jessy didn't like the routine, but there was little she could do about it. It went unspoken that she and the other women were there to serve the men and keep the house in order and run errands. The .45 was in her purse whenever she left the house. It kept her aware of projecting a strong image, which in turn helped maintain a level of mutual respect in the house. It wasn't necessary; everyone was motivated to defend the headquarters, especially at night when they would get stoned and crazy. Jessy refused to partake, having observed how people became vulnerable in that state, hatching unrealistic plans and competing in a mix of political grandstanding and illicit activities. Jessy made every effort to become invisible, taking up a post on the front porch, or in the backyard, and allowing the other night noises to provide distractions. The omnipresent echo of distant sirens kept her awake.

She was drowsing on the front porch in the pre-dawn half-light of a December morning when sirens erupted on the street. The cops had already taken up positions, and a voice from a bullhorn announced that they had a search warrant. Jessy hit the floorboards, grasping the .45 next to her cheek. The bullhorn continued to bark instructions about allowing officers to peacefully enter. Jessy couldn't hear anything from inside, but assumed that guns were aimed from all corners. She focused on the chatter emanating from the street. With her body largely hidden from view by the porch railing, she settled in, waiting for whatever was approaching. There were several more bullhorn warnings before the command came to enter the house. Boots marched in terrifying unison. Jessy fired from her prone position as the first pair came into view at the top of the steps. The lead cop fell, struck in his ankle. He blocked the path of the others, allowing Jessy to get a better view of her handiwork. The fallen cop cried out in agony amid the pool of blood spreading from his shorn foot. The shock of Jessy's attack had sent the cop's assault rifle windmilling to the far side of the porch, where it impotently rested out of reach. As Jessy braced to fire off another round, guns from the second and third floors roared to life forcing the cops to take cover. She didn't panic. The fallen cop glared at her and hurled epithets—"Fuckin' nigger bitch! We're gonna get every last motherfucking one of you!" Jessy kept her barrel trained on his face.

Her concentration was shattered by the sound of banging on the inside of the window beside her head. It was Geronimo imploring her to get to safety behind the house. She could see him screaming through the glass, but could not hear a word. The message became clear though. Ignoring the on-going gunfire, she leapt over the side railing, her tennis shoes absorbed by the tall grass. Within seconds she was on the back porch where a strategy huddle was in session. The big guns had been hauled out of the basement, including several M16s, which two of the young recruits were hastily loading. Jessy showed no signs of being rattled, and gave a strong affirmative when asked if she was all right. Leadership offered no indication that escape was an option. "We gotta hold our positions. Wait 'till we get the word that they're moving in, then take a spot inside with any kind of sightline. Get those M16s up to the attic!"

Shots blasted from both sides with regularity, until Geronimo came out the back door with a status report. "They're playing it cool now. I think we took out two or three. Jessy got one for sure." The assembled party turned as one toward her with smiles and a few pats on her shoulders. "They know we're not fuckin' around. They're gonna wanna negotiate eventually. I know it."

The standoff turned into a siege in short order. The cops had made phone calls to the house seeking surrender, but Geronimo refused to take the bait, maintaining the firm stance that they would have to level the building. Another hour went by without any gunfire. Jessy had taken over a position in her own second floor bedroom, where she had clear shots at several officers in full riot gear. A cry came from the next room as she watched others regrouping behind the front line. "Tear gas! They're gonna fire tear gas!" Everyone in the house mobilized; some ran to the bathrooms to grab wet towels, others hid out in the basement. Jessy was reluctant to leave her post, but felt abandoned. The deep, resonant blasts from the tear gas guns rang out and the canisters broke through the windows on the ground floor. Confusion reigned. A canister hit the room beside her, the smoke and fumes choking the hallway.

Jessy crammed her pistol in her waistband and tied a pillowcase around her mouth and nose. She hit the floor, crawling toward the only escape route she knew. The central stairway was engulfed by smoke, and she heard the sounds of the cops asserting control. The gas was overwhelming and Jessy knew she couldn't afford to sit still. She pulled out her pistol and tossed it into the haze of the hallway, before retreating to her room and inhaling the last vestiges of outside air that came through her window. Heavy footfalls came rushing up the stairs seconds later. Barely conscious from the fumes, Jessy faced the cops with her hands raised. One grabbed her arm and jerked her toward the staircase. He wrestled her all the way down, where she was thrown in a paddy wagon stuffed with her handcuffed comrades. No one had the strength to speak; all of their chests were heaving in an attempt to restore normal breathing. Sounds of struggle outside the van caused those inside to wail in rage. Jessy shut her eyes as more bodies were tossed in until the van reached its capacity and lunged to County lockup. She didn't see the sun again for three days.

⟋

"I didn't think you'd be back," Fred said through a conspiratorial smile.

"Well, I am."

"I suppose that means your friend wanted to give me a message."

"He wanted to know how much shit you were interested in." It was a lie Alex had full confidence in conveying.

"Hold up. Before we get into that, you've come a long way. Why don't we go smoke a joint? I've got other questions for you."

Fred, wearing the same oil-stained coveralls he'd had on the day before when Alex first visited, exited the office into the main work area where a young employee was pounding out a dent on the fender of a '67 Camaro. The ringing made an unholy racket. Alex tried in vain to ignore it, following close behind Fred as he weaved through the mess of tools and parts that littered the floor. Behind the shop was a bigger mess— piles of old tires, empty oil drums, a few stripped-down engines. Fred reached inside his coveralls to his shirt pocket, pulling out a joint from a pack of Lucky Strikes and lighting it as casually as a cigarette. He took three quick tokes before passing it to Alex.

"It's nice to be your own boss so you can do stuff like this," he said as Alex smoked. "That kid in there, he's a hard worker too, so I don't have to worry. I can concentrate on other business."

As he inhaled the smoke, Alex could tell that it was as good as the weed he got from Carlos. "Is that kid part of your outside thing too?"

"Nah. He needed a job so I showed him the ropes. Little bastard's a better body man than I am now. Might as well sell him the shop."

"Why don't you?"

"Hey, I thought I was gonna ask the questions."

Alex gave a smug grin and took another toke. "What do you need to know?"

"I gotta be honest. I'm not really interested in your friend's shit. I'm doing alright in that department. I want to talk movies."

Alex forced himself to play coy, realizing Carlos had the situation pegged. "What about the movies?"

"You said you're in the business, right?"

"Yeah."

"And so is your partner?"

Whatever command of the situation Alex felt he had disappeared. He was being cross-examined. "Yeah, he is."

"Good. You're the first guys I've met in the business and I need some help with a friend's idea. You've heard of Huey Newton, haven't you?"

"Sure, who hasn't?"

"Yeah, well let me clue you in. I'm in the Panthers."

Alex raised an eyebrow, but didn't act surprised. As far as he knew, everyone in Watts was connected to the party in some way.

"You've heard about the shit we've been involved in then too, right?"

"Yeah man, it's heavy." Alex added, "I'm on your side."

"Most people aren't right now. Huey wants to change that by making a movie."

"A movie about the Panthers?"

"Right. Something that'll give people the whole story of the Revolution so they can understand that we're trying to bring about some positive change. They made movies about those fuckin' Hell's Angels, and what did they ever do? Killed one of our brothers at that concert for starters."

Alex's buzz was amping up, making it difficult to wrap his head around the idea. "Where do I fit into this?"

"We can't do it ourselves."

Alex looked off into the wasteland of garbage that stretched to the back of the property and thought hard about how this conversation could end. Instead, Fred laid out the plan. "Look, I want to talk to your friend. What's his name?"

"Carlos," Alex responded, a haze beginning to cover him like a veil.

"All he has to do is sell my shit to his Hollywood buddies. He can keep the profits, as long as he gets the word out that Huey's looking to make something happen."

"What if no one's interested?"

"It'll be your job to make sure they are."

Alex felt trapped in the ruins around him, with Fred blocking the door.

"Is Jessy in on this?"

"Why does that matter?"

"I'd like to see her again."

Alex's bold admission made Fred glare hard at the skinny white punk showing off grim determination. "You can do another pick-up at the end of the week. I'll tell her to expect you."

The Panther Defense Fund helped Jessy and many of the others snatched up in the raid to get out on bail. The national press had a field day with the LAPD, calling the operation a botched attempt at vigilante justice. The headquarters was now off-limits, so Jessy stayed with Fred. Although she was free for the time being, she feared being in public based on real concerns of some cop taking matters into his own hands. While Fred was at the body shop, she was alone watching game shows and soap operas on his deluxe color set, a perk of his sideline business. The daily ritual was the continuing coverage of the raid on the lunch-hour news that made it clear one of the cops had been killed. The day after she was paroled, she saw her mugshot on television. The image haunted her—glassy eyes, bird's nest hair, defiant lips. She had been treated fairly at County, and followed her lawyer's instructions to claim every action as self-defense. She was surprised at how easy it was, which reinforced her belief that she'd be attacked the minute she was back on the street. But Fred didn't let her down. He'd heard what she had done, and like everyone else, told her it made him proud. He gave her space around the house and did the cooking, unless she made a point of doing it herself. He didn't bring up his concerns until they both settled into a quiet routine.

"You don't have to worry about anything, you know," he told her one night at the dinner table.

"I know."

"Everyone's on our side," he said. "The cops went too far." Jessy murmured in non-committal agreement as she ate. "It won't be easy, but no one's gonna do any hard time." He paused to chew the first morsel of his pork chop and spoke after swallowing. "There's one problem though. They're gonna try to finger you as a cop killer." Fred's tone suggested it was a fait accompli, but Jessy wasn't about to accept it, even though her dreams were haunted by images of a man writhing in his death throes.

"I didn't kill anybody," she exclaimed.

"Nobody's sure who killed who. But enough people know you fired the first shot."

Jessy cried out as the reality of her guilt broke her. Fred wrapped his arm around her shoulders. "It's alright, it's alright. You're part of the Revolution now. You'll be protected." She let out a few more tears before rallying her courage. Fred held her right hand between his palms, and she turned toward his benevolent face with misty eyes. "We've got a plan. You'll be safe. But to make sure, you're going to have to go away for a while."

"Where do I have to go?"

"That's the delicate part. We've already got you set up at this place over the border in Nevada. It's the drop-off for our shipments from Juarez. You're gonna be the new go-between until the heat dies down."

Jessy was shocked out of her sorrow, but could tell Fred was holding something back. "What is this place?"

"I hate to say it. It's a bordello."

Jessy pulled her hand from his, angry rather than scared. "Is that how it is, huh? I almost get killed and charged with murdering a cop, and you repay me by packing me off to a fuckin' whorehouse where I could get charged with trafficking? Jesus, that's some reward."

Fred couldn't defend his position. "It should only be for a few months. It won't be like when you were on the street. You'll be safe. It's a good system."

"Yeah, as long as your contacts get some pussy thrown in to sweeten the deal."

"Come on baby, it's the only option. The Man might not care about the other shit, but he sure as fuck wants to nail someone for taking out a pig. Chances are they'll find a way to pin it on you unless you get the fuck out of here right now."

Jessy stared hard at Fred while considering his plan. It meant throwing away all the training that had given her a new life. It meant returning to a life she detested, one that held no meaning. As she studied Fred's shameful expression, it sunk in that this was the best shot at getting herself off the hook. If someone had to go down for this—she could almost hear him say—there's no doubt it would be her. For Jessy, the Revolution was over.

Chapter 8

Los Angeles / March 1972

Will and Angela's encounters had been limited to his gigs in the months after they'd found each other at the Topanga party. She became a fixture wherever he was playing, either sitting nervously with Alex or, on nights he wasn't there, eagerly giving Will her full attention from a table near the stage. Will always ensured her drinks were put on his tab. Afterward, they would sometimes drift to a late-night party, but most often he would take her back to her apartment and end the night with a dispassionate kiss. It became a routine that neither appeared willing to disrupt. Then, with her apartment free for a night, and a bottle of Jose Cuervo on hand, Angela persuaded Will to come over—without the guitar—in hopes of discovering what they meant to each other. He had no trouble engaging in conversation, and by their third round of shots he'd unraveled the entire tale of the trip to California. As he picked over the details, the distant look in his eyes reminded her of women she'd met in Chino after the accident, women who had not seen their children in years, and likely never would again.

When Angela asked him about his music and what he planned to do with it, Will's mood turned darker, his frustration evident in a sudden sharp change in tone. He rejected whatever talent she insisted he possessed, instead praising names she didn't know. In desperation, she asked about his family, and his gut reaction was to say that he had none. "I don't believe you," she responded. He rubbed his eyes with both hands, as if he were trying to rouse himself from a bad dream. Angela's old, fat tabby lounged on the windowsill, paying no heed.

After enduring that painful silence, Angela relented.

"I don't need to know about your family," she said. "I'm sorry."

He shook his head, disgusted by his weakness, before looking Angela in the face. "There are things inside me I can't control," Will said softly. "Most often, they control me."

"You're saying you hear voices?"

"A voice," Will whispered. "It's always just one voice."

Angela paused, gauging the truth in his words, but Will's fearful expression said it all. "Okay, a voice. When did you start hearing it?"

"It's been with me since I've been out here. One way or another. Sometimes it's like we're in the same room having a conversation."

"You mean like this?"

"Yeah. But right now I only hear you."

She placed a hand on his forearm. He heaved a sigh before continuing in a measured tone. "I thought leaving home was the answer, but things have become worse. You're the first person I've told."

Angela moved closer, bringing her other hand to his cheek. He didn't resist. "Look at me," she said, turning him towards her. "I want to help." She moved her hand to the nape of his neck and pulled him in for a kiss, but it felt wrong to her the instant their lips touched.

He felt it too and was on the verge of tears. "I'm sorry," he said. "I know I shouldn't be acting this way. No one cared about me like this."

Angela tensed up, feeling like she'd cornered a small, wild animal. "That can't be true," she forced herself to say. He turned, realizing that such exaggeration wasn't necessary. "You mean your family doesn't care?"

She sensed the games were over as he faced her. "Well, to tell you the truth, my family is wonderful. They're too good for me."

Angela remained careful. "Do they know about your ... problem?"

"No, I couldn't find a way to explain it. They wouldn't believe me anyway. I think they know something is wrong, but they choose to ignore it."

"That must make things hard."

"I just try to avoid them. I don't think I've called home in months. Smoking dope helped for a while, but now it gives me headaches."

Angela reached for his hands. This time they folded into each other, assuming a tight grip. "How did your parents react when you left?"

"I told them that I'd made it in one piece, and that seemed enough. I'd already convinced myself they were happy to see me go."

"Well, I'm glad you made it." She shifted her body and attempted another kiss. This time he submitted. She proceeded to devour him, and he gave in. Her hands moved in a flurry around his head and shoulders. Craving more flesh, she unbuttoned his shirt. "Let's go to my room," she said.

He stood and followed her bouncing figure down the hall. He lingered in the doorway as she lit a few candles. Satisfied with the ambience, she dragged him to the bed. He fell on his back, and she resumed undressing him. With his jeans off, she pulled her flower dress over her head, revealing her skeletal frame that didn't require a bra. He was reluctant to touch her, but she paid no mind, falling on top of him and spreading kisses from his neck to his stomach.

In spite of this, Will could not get aroused. He let her carry on for a few more minutes, until she removed her underwear and made a grab for his, at which point he resisted.

"What's wrong baby," she asked after catching her breath.

"Nothing. I just... This is all a bit... unexpected. I haven't done this kind of thing in a long time."

"Neither have I. So why don't we figure it out together?"

She moved her hand between his legs and he reacted by rolling onto his side and pulling his knees up.

"I'm sorry, I can't do this," he said, and sat on the edge of the bed. Angela, now ashamed of her nudity, gathered the sheet over her. She was too stunned to speak. "I'm kinda tired," Will mumbled. "I think I'd better go home."

Angela sat paralyzed, staring at his back. "Please don't," she whispered. His head sank below his shoulders. "Don't listen to what the voice is telling you."

He collected his scattered clothing and didn't look at her until he was dressed. "Don't be angry. This doesn't have anything to do with you." He strode out of the room without looking back.

As he disappeared from view, Angela dropped the sheet and chased after him, catching his waist with both arms before he could reach the front door. "Remember," she pleaded, "I want to help."

He unlocked her hands and turned. "I know. You're probably the only one who does."

The heat inside the Delta 88 was oppressive, even with every window rolled down. Alex pushed the car down the familiar stretch of desert blacktop, seeing Jessy foremost in his mind. It was all that he had thought about since his last meeting with Fred. He'd taken some smack in order to sleep, which left an aching pain in the pit of his stomach. When Will expressed concern, Alex convinced him it was just a virus. When Carlos was able to ask why he'd been out of touch, Alex fed him a line of bullshit about acting classes.

Alex knew traffic would be light heading out Ventura Parkway to Highway 15. Within a couple hours, he could make out the sign for the Wagon Wheel in the distance, hanging in the growing dusk, and his pensiveness was replaced by a sense of relief. The lights of the bordello weren't on, but the building's iron fence was unmistakable. Alex pulled in beside two semis and walked to the front gate, where he received quick entry. This time, the old woman in the kimono approached him with a measured greeting.

"Don't you remember me?" he asked with a touch of haughtiness. She squinted, the smoke from her cigarette wafting into his face. "I was here last week. I'm back to see Jessy."

The old woman smiled, betraying her dishonesty. "Yeah, I remember you. But I'm sorry to say that Jessy's busy at the moment, sugar. You're going to have to wait. Please have a seat." She waved her free hand toward the red leather chairs against the wall of the foyer. Alex did as she requested, but couldn't conceal his frustration. "I'll let you know when she's free," and disappeared through a door with the flourish of an actress exiting off-stage.

Alex's insides went into convulsions and his mind raced with terrible thoughts of how Jessy might react to seeing him. It was supposed to be strictly business between them, and with time to contemplate the situation, he doubted she would treat him any differently than a faceless trucker. The minutes dragged on and nothing stirred aside from the occasional faint sounds of pleasure. Alex shifted in the chair, aware of the leather's vulgar squeaking. He was sweating when a door burst open and a fat, middle-aged Okie strode out, giving Alex a gentlemanly nod and tip of his baseball cap as he passed.

Alex watched him all the way out the entrance, appalled by his filthy exterior.

A few minutes later, the old hostess materialized behind the counter. "Jessy will see you now. Room seven." He rose, exhaled, and walked toward the door the Okie had come through. Once out of the old woman's sight, he took a moment to gather himself and proceeded down the claustrophobic hallway. He knocked twice, and was answered by a muted, "Come in honey." As he opened the door, Jessy tore herself from her mirror. He shouldn't have been surprised to see her in a red negligee and heels, but her image stopped him in his tracks. She got up and hugged him, flooding his nostrils with a strange mix of cheap perfume and stale sex.

"Look at you," she said. "You came back. I knew you were the right guy for the job."

He smiled and took in the entire picture, recalling unsettling memories of his first visit. "Yeah, it was a cinch," he stammered.

"Well, good. Come over and sit down." She was on the hastily made bed, legs crossed, lighting a cigarette. He took one she offered and settled in next to her, feeling more relaxed after the first drag. "Fred seems to like you," she said, turning back to the mirror.

"Yeah, I guess."

"He said you're an actor."

"Aren't we all?"

She blew two streams of smoke from her nostrils. "I bet you say that to everyone." He laughed with her, as thoughts of the number of other men that had been in her room that day evaporated. "It's nice to have someone come in who wants to talk."

"What do you mean? I've paid."

Her laughter increased. "Sorry. Miss Kitty should have told you it's my coffee break." Jessy reached to open her bureau and lifted out her works and prepared a shot. It took Alex a moment to take in what he was seeing, and the silence prompted her to ask, "Care to join me?" He nodded an affirmative and she tied him off, after which he collapsed on the bed the instant the needle went in. She attended to herself, and they each faded into their own worlds for several minutes. Snapping back to consciousness, she pulled him to a sitting position, slapping his cheeks.

"Alright, listen. We gotta get something straight. Fred explained to me that you think you can get your man to sell our shit it to his movie pals. Right?"

Alex had to peel his attention away from the body he'd been dying to hold all week. "Huh? Yeah, right."

"And you'll get the money to Fred."

"Of course."

"But the important thing is that these movie folks know the shit is coming from the Panthers."

"Yeah, totally. No problem."

He noticed Jessy momentarily eying him with slight suspicion. "You know, for a white boy, you've got a lot of balls." Her affectionate change in her tone made him take a deep breath in anticipation of what he expected would come next, although she kept him at bay. "You're really in the movies?"

"Yeah, but nothing you would have heard of," he answered. "I've only been an extra."

"Fred seems to think you're well connected."

"There's nothing I can do about what he thinks. I tried to tell him it's my friend who's the actor, not me."

"Yeah, Fred sometimes gets ideas in his head and doesn't think them through. Like putting me out here."

Alex felt the heat between them cooling. "You mean, this isn't your dream job?"

"Very funny. I got into trouble a while ago, and Fred decided that this was the best option to keep me safe. Easy for him to say."

"How do you put up with it?"

"Oh, you know, it's best not to think too much. The truckers are all the same. They want blowjobs or the exotic Black pussy routine. It's the Vegas crowd I hate. They come in wanting all kinds of weird shit. A bunch of girls together, or getting everybody tied up. I had you pegged as one of those when you showed up." Alex grinned, although he couldn't imagine what had given her that impression. "It didn't take long to see that you weren't. You were just fucked up."

"Still am." They both laughed in unison and gazed into each other's eyes. "I couldn't stop thinking about you all week," he said.

"Come on. You should know better than to say that to a hooker."

"You're not a hooker. We're business partners."

She smiled and reached for a cigarette. "You know, I hate to admit it, but you crossed my mind once or twice too," she said before lighting up.

"Come back to L.A. with me. Right now."

"I can't. I have to wait for Fred to tell me it's all clear."

"Don't you want to get the fuck out of here?"

"Sure."

"You can stay with me. Nobody would know. Tell Fred that it's part of the deal."

"He won't be happy. Once he starts making plans, it's hard to change them."

"I'll keep making the pick-ups—wherever he wants. I need to be closer to you."

Jessy took some deep drags before answering. "Get a room at the first motel you find. I'll be ready to go in the morning."

Will barely moved a muscle all night. He stared at the ceiling as Angela slept beside him, unaware of how many hours had passed since her begging had persuaded him to stay. His only desire from the moment he undressed and laid down was to disappear. The battle raged within him until the room brightened with first light and Angela's clock radio burst out with a harsh squawk that sent a shudder through his rattled nervous system. When she didn't stir, he reached over and struck the radio with an open palm. The silence calmed him, until several minutes passed and she hadn't shown any signs of awakening. He propped himself up and whispered in her ear, "Hey, don't you have to go to work?" She pulled the sheet over her head and emitted a low moan. He thought about leaving her to fend for herself, but thought better of it.

He dressed himself as she was in the bathroom, then searched her closet for a fresh outfit. He set out a plain black miniskirt and pale blue blouse. They were on the bed when Angela lurched into the room, eyes barely open. "Put these on."

She doubled over in laughter at his attempt to take control. "Yes sir, right away!" Will paced the room as Angela dressed, consumed with getting her out of the apartment as quickly as possible. She tried to calm him while buttoning the blouse. "Just hold tight, I haven't put on make-up yet."

Will stood behind her at the bathroom mirror as she applied eyeliner and lipstick. "That's enough, we need to go. I got your purse."

Angela ignored his outburst as she slipped into her thick-heeled office shoes. Will hustled her onto the street. When he opened the passenger door for her, she flopped on the bench seat, seemingly unmoved by his growing agitation. "Hey, you gotta tell me where to go," he said, shaking her.

"Alright, take it easy. Turn left at the end of this street and then right at the lights. For God's sake, don't speed. Damn. Why did I drink tequila? I'm sorry to make you do this."

Will glanced over and smiled for the first time that morning. "It's okay. I just don't want you to get in trouble."

She let out a pointed laugh. "I think everyone will know what happened when they get a look at me."

Will laughed with her, as downtown traffic began congesting. He got as close to the newspaper office's entrance as he could and double-parked. She hesitated, unsure of how to make a proper exit.

"You look great," he finally said.

"Thanks," she replied, before pressing her lips to his. She got out of the car without another word and galloped up the concrete steps, the click-clack of her shoes audible over the street noise.

Will pulled away from the curb, suddenly at a loss as to how to spend the rest of the day. The feeling lingered as he drove to his apartment. He parked and stretched, his body absorbing the rising morning heat. He thought of lying on the brown, patchy lawn, but summoned the energy to plod up the three dark flights of wooden stairs. He was careful to keep quiet, assuming that Alex was in his room, and stared out the kitchen window as his coffee brewed. The neighborhood almost seemed livable at this time of day, he mused, as he observed kids running along the sidewalks, ignorant of the drama that frequently occurred over the course of the night. He lost himself in the simplicity of the sun reflecting off the windows of other buildings, their tenants emerging in plain uniforms carrying lunch boxes, and walking the short distance to the corner bus stop.

The percolating coffee pot brought him back to reality and he sat at the kitchen table with his cup. No longer interested in the outside world, he dwelled on how he was now too awake to sleep. The kitchen was a disaster area as usual. With nothing to occupy his time, Will started cleaning. He heard Alex stir and make a clumsy journey to the bathroom as he washed the dishes. Alex was in the kitchen after a few minutes, looking distressed in his soiled robe.

"What are you doing up this early?" Alex asked.

"I just got home. Thought I'd make myself useful."

"Thanks for waking me. You have a gig last night?"

"Nah. I was over at Angela's."

Alex dropped himself at the table as Will continued to wash and dry. "Really? How'd it go?" Will thought he heard a note of jealousy in Alex's question.

"It was fine. She got loaded on tequila so it ended up a little strange. I couldn't leave her in the state she was in."

"You're such a gentleman."

"What was I supposed to do? She's a nice girl and she has a thing for me."

"You must like her too. Why else would you have stayed?"

"Maybe I do like her, but that's not what I'm looking for."

Alex yawned. "Well, I tell ya what, I'd take it if I were you. Feels like we've been missing out on everything lately."

"What did you expect, a beach party every night?"

"No, but look at you. You've got a chick that obviously digs you, and you get freaked out when she gets you over to her pad and wants to jump you? Jesus, you're living the dream."

Will turned his back to Alex and kept drying the glasses. "It's not that simple."

"Well, whatever. I'm sure you'll figure it out. The coffee still on?"

"Help yourself."

Alex grabbed one of the mugs that Will had just replaced in the cupboard. He filled it and sat at the table. "Look, it's good that I caught you. I gotta borrow the car."

"When?"

"Sunday."

"What for?"

"Carlos got me another job as an extra. Some kinda cowboy flick. I've gotta be at Pioneertown bright and early."

Will turned. "Look at you, a fuckin' cowboy. Nobody back home would ever believe it."

"I know, I know. Make fun of me all you want, but I'm paying my share of the rent this month."

Will set down the dishrag and crossed his arms. "Okay, but remember that if anything happens to the car, you're paying for that too."

Alex gave a cursory nod of acceptance and got up again. "Thanks. Maybe I will go back to bed after all."

Each time he surfaced, his hair in his eyes, Alex strained to see whether the shore was coming closer. Eventually, the current captured him and he eased off, his body propelled over the waves like a piece of driftwood. During a lull, he treaded water, squinting in the face of the punishing sun. Objects on the beach appeared black and formless, mere dots that danced teasingly out of reach. Alex caught a glimpse of Jessy in between blinks, as if he were operating an old wind-up movie-ola machine. She stood tall and proud in a bikini, her thick black hair blowing in the sea breeze. She must see me, he thought. She's waiting. He started moving again, building momentum until the next wave. It took longer to recover each time he repeated the process. The shore was a blur hovering above the surf, and he felt his strength dissipating. He couldn't distinguish Jessy from the other figures on the beach. With much effort, he called out.

"Jessy!"

A faint reply came in return. "Swim!"

Alex's arms were lead pipes. She called out every few seconds, but it took all his energy to raise his head. All that remained was the hollow echo of her voice.

Alex was awakened by the roar of a Harley-Davidson kicked to life outside his motel room. He lay on his back in the sweat-soaked bed, gathering his senses until the rider peeled out of the parking lot and the engine's low rumble faded. Alex didn't have to meet Jessy for another hour, and there was nothing to do except stew over the new course his life was about to take. The emptiness within him was crushing, a smack hangover that had covered his brain with a thick fuzz. He tried not to think, but as the minutes dragged on, he careened between the best and worst case scenarios that could come from his new arrangement. Before thoughts of prison or a worse fate consumed him, he decided to escape his present confining existence.

"Have a nice day now," the old man in the motel office said when Alex checked out and handed over the room key. Will's car started with a nasty growl. Alex forgave himself for being early as he made the short ride down the highway to the gated house. Upon arrival, he chose to stick to the plan anyway, parking as close as he could get to Jessy's window and announcing himself with two sharp blasts of the horn. She pulled back the curtain to give him a wave, and a few minutes later, came around the front of the building, dressed in jeans and a sweatshirt. She greeted Alex with a wet kiss on the lips that erased his anxiety, and he pulled onto the highway in a cloud of dust.

"Man, you're a little excited for so early in the day," she said over the wind rushing into the Oldsmobile's open windows. "How did you sleep?"

"Didn't really. The motel gave me the creeps. Did you talk to Fred?"

She hunched her body to get her first cigarette of the day lit. "Yeah, I did."

"Was he mad?"

"Well, he wasn't happy. I told him it was all your idea." Alex was unable to conceal his horror, but she ran her palm up and down his rigid right arm to let him know she was in control. "Come on baby, gimme a little credit," Jessy cooed. "This is my decision. He knew he wouldn't be able to keep me out here much longer. I told him I'd take my chances."

"What about me?"

"What about you? You're not the one taking a big risk. All you have to do is hold up your end of the deal and not mention to anyone where I am."

"But Fred knows about us."

"Fred knows what about us?"

Alex couldn't answer, as stress dug its claws into him again. "I know that you and Fred are Panthers."

Jessy swiveled to look Alex in the face. "Is that going to be a problem?"

"No, I guess not."

"Good, 'cause that's my business."

"I want it to be my business too. If I'm going to be involved with you guys, I have a right to know."

"What do you want to know?"

"Why are you out here and not in L.A.?"

She waited until his eyes refocused on the road before speaking. "They think I killed a cop." From the second he heard these words, he understood that all of the other questions that had been strangling his thought process were meaningless. The car's interior closed in around him. "I didn't want to tell you about any of it, but you're right, you do deserve to know."

She finished the cigarette and flicked it into the breeze, then leaned out the window to let it blow through her uncombed hair. They drove a mile in silence before he said, "I'm glad you told me."

"Are you afraid of me now?" she responded.

"Actually, I think I love you."

Jessy stared at him hard for a long time. "Did you ever think that might be a big mistake?"

Alex sighed. "No. My life seems to be about making other people's crazy dreams happen. You're the first person I've met out here who's given me a purpose." She fell silent, and he started regretting what he'd said. "Don't be so quiet. You're making me feel like a total idiot."

"It won't be easy, being with me," she forced herself to say. "But if we stick together, we can both have our freedom." She raised her left hand up to his shaggy blonde mane, stroking him with motherly care. "Baby, don't worry. You and I are gonna shock the world."

Will spread out the yellowed sheets of paper on the long, low table as he had many times before. There was a process to it now; pages that weren't typed stood out because of the effortless regal penmanship that arranged the verses in rectangular sections, with the occasional key signature added. Will had tried to ignore these notations, instead reading the words each time and allowing their cadence to seep into his brain. He had composed music for some, but needed to view each page to induce the full effect. He could pick up the guitar once he was within the safety of this world. He no longer felt any expectations, or any pressure to follow others' examples. The chords cascaded from his fingers at these times, and on this Sunday afternoon with no distractions, Will found a melody straight away.

He played it repeatedly as his eyes darted from one page to the next in search of a combination of words that fit. Time stood still as the work progressed. The sun dipped and cast a golden hue through the living room's unshaded windows. Will pressed on, having settled on a set of lyrics, and proceeded to get inside the phrases to a point where he could convince himself that he had written them. By the time the encroaching darkness forced him to turn on a light, he had the new song committed to memory. Will treated himself to the next to last Miller High Life in the refrigerator. He drank it near the window, observing the changes the dimming light brought to the street as the song replayed itself in his head.

He was unaware of the trance-like state he was in until the telephone snapped him to attention. It was Angela. They hadn't spoken since their night together at her apartment. "Hi, how've you been?" he said, trying to not sound caught off-guard.

"Oh, I've been alright. Just thought I'd see how you were doing."

"I'm fine. Did some work today on a new song and I think I got it together."

"That's great! What are you doing now?"

"Um, just having a beer."

"Do you feel like going out?"

"Alex has my car."

"Well, I could come over to your place."

Will paused, summoning a cheery response. "Yeah, sure, why not?"

Angela arrived a half-hour later, glowing from a brisk walk and carrying a bottle of wine. "I figured you wouldn't have much to drink."

"You didn't have to do that."

"Don't worry. I just wish you would call me."

Will felt the tinge of an argument stirring, but let it drop as they took up positions on the couch, drinking from tall juice glasses. "I'm sorry, you're right. I've been busy trying to work on a new set."

The topic of his music brightened her attitude. "Does that mean you've got some shows lined up?"

"Yeah, the Ash Grove and the Palomino this month. Doug says he'll try to get me an opening slot for James Taylor in a few weeks."

Angela set down her glass and threw her arms around Will's neck. "That's wonderful! This is exactly what you need."

Will, content with her reaction, sipped from his glass. "Are you thinking about getting a little tipsy tonight?"

She smiled to hide some slight embarrassment. "No, of course not. You sound like you think I'm a raging alcoholic."

"Well, it takes one to know one."

She leaned back in thought, as the silver blouse she wore radiated in the dim light. "What do you mean by that?"

He felt caught in a lie. "Nothing. It's just one of those lines that always seems to fit when you can't think of anything else to say."

"I'd say you don't know much about me at all," she said.

"Is that bothering you?"

"A little. You haven't seemed too interested."

"I've told you I'm not looking to get burned again," he said.

"And you think I am? I've made it clear that I want to take care of you."

"You only say that when you're drunk."

"That doesn't make it any less true."

He could see that his coldness was riling up her emotions. "I can't give you anything in return."

"I'm not asking you to. I've made some big mistakes in my life and I'm still paying for them in my own way."

Will moved closer, holding her as the first tears formed in her eyes. "Don't tell me what you've done," he whispered. "It doesn't make a difference. I want to know you as you are right now."

Their lips came together, and Will felt something meaningful this time. After several minutes of holding each other in silence, he asked if she needed another drink.

"I'll have a beer if you've got any."

"There's only one Miller left. I guess we'll have to split it."

"Thanks. Don't get up, I'll get it."

Angela padded to the kitchen on her bare feet, and Will listened to her retrieve the bottle and open it with a familiar burst. He heard more footsteps.

"Where are you?" When she didn't reply, Will rose and moved to the hallway that led to the bedrooms. Angela was waiting for him, dangling the bottle in her hands.

"What are you laughing at?" she asked.

"You look like a little girl with that bottle."

"And I bet that's what you'd like," she replied while approaching him. "You'd like a little girl, wouldn't you? A drunk little girl that you can have your way with."

"You shouldn't say things like that."

"Why not? That's what every man wants. Is that too painful to admit?"

"It's not true."

"Then why did you say it?" She stood against him, holding the bottle between her breasts, and looking up into his face in adoration. He reached in to take the bottle and set it on a shelf. She didn't move. "So, am I your little girl?"

Will brushed the curls from her forehead. "Yeah, you're my little girl."

They embraced again and kissed deeply. Will didn't hold back, and neither did Angela, tearing at his shirt and coaxing him into the bedroom. As he was about to surrender, Will heard footfalls on the stairs. Next came the key scraping open the lock. Alex was home, and had someone with him. Will pushed Angela away as gently as he could and mouthed an apology. He was not prepared for the woman that came through the door. "Will, this is Jessy."

She greeted Will with warmth and complimented the apartment. Angela peeked around the corner, prompting another introduction when Alex caught a glimpse of her. The four remained rooted where they stood until Alex saw the open bottle of wine.

"Hey, mind if we have some of that? It's been a long day."

Will stared hard at his friend before answering. "Yeah, we'd all better have a drink."

✓

"Angel Of Avalon"

He was called to arms in the spring of '17
The snow was almost melted and the trees were almost green
I watched him march down main street looking strong and fine
He was only one of many who were dear friends of mine

I saw her in the crowd as he passed slowly by
Much to my amazement, she didn't bat an eye
I knew he was forsaking her in her time of need
'Cause in his pocket was a letter she never got to read

They called her the Angel of Avalon
Her singing filled the valley like the whistle of a train
I can't believe I'm such a long time gone
And I won't be coming home until I hear her voice again

I was too young to follow them into the bloody fray
So I did the best I could to help her live from day to day
It wasn't very long before she drew me to her side
And I was there when she got the news that the man she loved had died

We struggled through the autumn 'till the winter storms returned
I couldn't bear to leave but in my mind the bridge was burned
That night I booked my passage on the freighter Rosa Lee
And by the time the sun had risen, that ship was out to sea

They called her the Angel of Avalon
Her singing filled the valley like the whistle of a train
I can't believe I'm such a long time gone
And I won't be coming home until I hear her voice again

Now I'm twenty years a sailor and I've been most everywhere
The hardships have been many, but nothing can compare
To the day I got the message, thought I prayed it was a dream
That they found her in the barn, swinging from a beam

They called her the Angel Of Avalon
Her singing filled the valley like the whistle of a train
I can't believe I'm such a long time gone
And I won't be coming home until I hear her voice again

Chapter 9

Kern County / May 1972

"**A**lright, everybody get ready! You're about to be dusted!" Alex stood in line with his fellow actors, all three wearing prison uniform costumes with their hands cuffed in front. They raised them in unison when the grip switched on the big fan, summoning a thick cloud of dust and dirt. The move prompted the assistant director to yell, "Keep your hands down! You're supposed to look like you haven't bathed in a month. I know that's nothing new for some of you, but we gotta do it anyway!"

Alex did his best to follow the order, feeling a sensation of being buried alive overtaking the exhaustion he had yet to shake. A full night out with Jessy was necessary to celebrate his first day of shooting, damn the consequences. They each had a fix a couple of hours before Alex had to drive Carlos' Honda to the 6 a.m. wardrobe call. He was last to receive his ill-fitting overalls and work boots, but arrived embodying the defeated and wary state of mind of a young prisoner, along with sporting the proper look of three-day stubble and a bad haircut courtesy of Jessy.

After the dust cloud settled, he felt a personal bond beginning to form out of the literal bond with his fellow actors, George and Brandon. The director, Bill Naud, had granted his old friend Carlos' favor by giving the part to Alex, who was doing everything possible to demonstrate he'd earned the right to be there. During their brief introduction, George had told Alex he had studied in New York and had a few minor credits in serious films, but inevitably fell into the Blaxploitation world when it became clear he wasn't going to be the next Sidney Poitier. Brandon revealed he had been a child star during the late Fifties and couldn't get anyone to take him seriously as an adult. Yet, his fine facial features and deep blue eyes bore a resemblance to a young Robert Redford, and everyone involved in the making of *The Sky Is Falling* was comfortable casting him as the lead, when expensive options weren't attainable. Brandon projected an air of humility that Alex picked up on from their first exchange. When Alex told him it was his first speaking role, Brandon dismissed his concerns with a laugh. "Just do what you're told and you'll get all the work you can handle." George was standoffish at first, unwilling to believe these two pretty white boys could portray criminals, but was soon put at ease by how serious Alex was taking a role most actors could do sleepwalking.

The opening scene involved the three of them being transferred in a windowless Dodge van. Larry Turkel, a veteran of westerns dating to the Thirties, played the lone prison guard. He had most of the lines, a rambling soliloquy explaining why kids today wouldn't have survived the Second World War, and that taking away Americans' God-given right to bear arms was leading the country toward disaster. When he said, "Hell, that's against the First Amendment," Alex had to pipe up and say, "Second." The rest of the day's shoot consisted of Turkel's character stopping the van in order to relieve himself, a move that allowed the three prisoners to incapacitate him and escape on foot to nearby Edwards Air Force Base, where they would creep onto a B-52 and free themselves of their shackles with a hatchet.

Most of the afternoon was taken up by shooting the three of them running through the desert scrub. Alex's muscles were aching by the time the crew shifted to setting up shots in and around the decommissioned B-52. Alex was lying on the tarmac, wishing he had sunglasses to fend off the late afternoon sun, when the click of the assistant director's megaphone signaled a break while the crew set up the first shot inside the bomber. A wave of relief washed over Alex, interrupted by someone kicking the sole of his boot. He propped himself up on his elbows and squinted at Brandon's crown of auburn waves glowing in the heat haze. "C'mon get up, it's Miller time."

Alex grabbed Brandon's extended hand and brushed some of the dust from his prison outfit. "I heard a few people say they couldn't tell us apart," Brandon said, leading the way toward the cast's trailer.

Alex laughed, feeling genuine warmth behind the comment. "I'm sure it's just the costumes. Or maybe they want me to be your stunt double."

This time Brandon laughed. "Nah, I think we finished the physical stuff for today. The rest is gonna be shot inside that fucking plane." He cocked his head to glance at the massive aircraft. "I wonder how many Vietcong that thing wiped out?"

Alex let the question hang in the air, reluctant to contemplate the horror. Brandon indicated their arrival at the trailer with a short, specific knock, but opened the door without waiting for a response. George was wedged behind the table inhaling a joint. Alex and Brandon joined him on the cushioned seats as he blew smoke over his shoulder out the window.

"Got a workout today, didn't we boys?" George handed the joint to Brandon, so Alex answered.

"That's for sure. I had no idea our escape was that big a part of the script."

"It's not," Brandon replied, trying to hold the smoke in through clenched teeth. "They just need enough footage for cutaways." He handed the joint to Alex. "It's actually a miracle they got it all done in one day. I did this spaghetti western in Spain last year—three weeks in the desert on horseback, everybody speaking different languages. What a nightmare that was. This movie's gonna be a piece of shit, but at least it won't take long."

George appeared to concur, leaving Alex confused over what was motivating the two of them besides a pay cheque. Then he remembered the other reason why he was there. "This is good dope. Where'd it come from?" Alex directed the question to George as the joint completed its circle, and was surprised when Brandon answered.

"It's Acapulco Gold. I know some musicians who get it from bikers."

Alex paused, recognizing this was the opportunity he'd been waiting for all day. "That's cool. My best friend is a singer."

"Oh really," Brandon responded with genuine interest. "What's his name?"

"Will Mosley."

Brandon's brow furrowed as he ran through his mental Rolodex. "Where does he play?"

"Oh, the Troubadour, the Palomino, the Ash Grove, wherever he can get on stage."

"Huh. I've probably seen him, but can't recall if I have at the moment."

"That's alright. He doesn't have a record out yet or anything."

"Well, find out when he's doing his next show and let's go check it out."

"For sure." The conversation seemed to reach a natural conclusion with an awkward silence hanging over the table. It was broken by George flicking his Bic to relight the roach just as Alex worked up the courage to say, "Look, I got another friend in another line of business. How are you guys fixed for, uh, anything besides weed?"

George, caught off-guard as he inhaled, coughed out a small cloud. "You serious?"

"Well, yeah. I got a great connection, and thought you guys might be short."

Brandon chimed in. "What d'ya got?"

"Anything you want." Sensing his opening, Alex leaned in and lowered his voice. "In fact, I can get you coke from the Panthers."

George couldn't stifle a laugh. "What the fuck are you doing mixed up with the Panthers?"

Alex kept his composure. "It's a special deal for privileged clients."

The trailer door was barraged at that moment and a loud voice outside yelled, "Guys, we'll be ready for you in five."

George took one last hit off the joint and said to Alex, "Look, let's get through these scenes and we can talk about that stuff after. I'm sure we'll be out of here quickly if you don't screw this up, okay?"

Alex nodded, and the trio exited the trailer into the controlled chaos of the set where Bill Naud was finalizing the lighting set up. The tall, slim director gave the actors an encouraging greeting when he finally noticed them. "Good work today boys. We're going to get you sneaking onto the plane, then we'll call it a day, okay?" He turned his attention to the camera set-up without any further acknowledgment of the actors, and a production assistant showed them their marks and reattached their handcuffs.

A few yards away, another group of actors dressed in air force uniforms found their places. The scene was arranged to depict the flight crew receiving their orders from their commanding officer on the tarmac, their backs to the three prisoners climbing the bomber's steps in the gathering darkness. After a few excruciating minutes, the AD's megaphone clicked again. "Quiet on the set please!"

The only voice after that was Naud's. "OK, so everyone knows what to do? No need to rehearse. Let's try to nail this one quickly."

Alex took a deep breath and tried to ignore the weight of his manacles. He had been placed in between George and Brandon in order for them to set the pace. Naud gave the command to roll sound and camera, and as he yelled "Action!" The actor playing the Air Force colonel recited his lines in a powerful roar. Alex froze, but Brandon gave him a subtle push as George began to lead them toward the bomber. Alex lost his footing halfway up the steps, creating a large metal-on-metal clang as he tried to maintain his balance.

"Cut! What happened up there?"

Alex was too embarrassed to answer, forcing Brandon to yell back, "Just had a slip on the step Bill. No big deal."

Several painful seconds passed before Naud called out, "Okay, let's do it again, and please be more careful!"

Alex whispered a thank you to Brandon as they returned to their places. This time the shot went off without a hitch and Naud called a wrap on the day with a notable sense of accomplishment in his voice.

There was palpable relief among the three actors as well, although no words were exchanged until they were in the trailer and in their regular clothes. Brandon pulled out three cans of Budweiser from the small refrigerator and they returned to their spots around the table. George had been pondering Alex's proposition. "Can you bring me a half-key of coke tomorrow?" he asked.

Alex gave a terse nod. "Cool," George responded. "I'll have five grand for you." With that, he drained his beer and exited the trailer, leaving Alex and Brandon staring at each other in mock disbelief.

"Didn't think it would be that easy, did you?" Brandon said, lighting a cigarette.

Alex chuckled, although his thoughts honed in on connecting with either Jessy or Carlos as soon as possible. He took a long sip from his can. "How about you? Can I get you anything?"

"I wouldn't say no to some China White if you could get your hands on it."

Fred knew he shouldn't watch Jessy dance, but she was a natural, able to tap into some primitive urge within him. He could see that she was aware of every movement she made, down to the subtlest glance. It was all calculated, perfectly timed to the music. Fred maintained a position near the club's door, in fear of being spotted. She aimed her attention at the handful of heads scattered around the front of the stage, men who gazed at her like hungry dogs as she fondled her breasts and, in crucial moments, lifted each of them to her own tongue.

Fred resisted being aroused by recalling the times he had picked her up on corners and in alleys, beaten or strung out. She always bounced back, always tried to become a better person. Now she was a legend within the Panthers' inner circle; the mere mention of her name evoked the grim day of the shootout. No one but Fred knew that this same Jessy was now dancing for small bills.

Jessy's demeanor altered the moment the song ended. She picked up her scattered pieces of clothing and rushed off the stage in her sequined platform heels. Fred hurried to meet her before she vanished into the dressing room. He tapped her shoulder without warning, prompting her to spin around with a shocked look. "Fuck! You should know better than to do that," she said with clear restraint.

"I do know better. And I also know that you can smell a pig," he replied, trying to laugh off his mistake.

She responded with a cold stare. "Come on, we can talk in here."

Jessy put her crocheted dress back on and began retouching her make-up. Fred stood inside the door waiting for the report he'd been promised. "Don't keep me in suspense. What's the little white boy been up to?"

She stared at the mirror, applying more lipstick. "Well, for starters, he's been moving the stuff."

"To the movie types?"

Jessy smiled at her cousin's crudeness, and made an extra effort to enunciate her words. "Yes, to the movie types. They're all apparently enjoying it immensely."

"That's good."

She turned from the mirror, sensing Fred's hesitation. "What did you really come here to talk about?"

Fred took a quick glance behind him before leaning in. "There's an idea floating around."

Jessy returned to her own reflection. "Oh yeah, what's that?"

"Some of us feel like we're losing the public relations war. We need to remind folks that the cause is still righteous. The people in charge want to make a movie."

Jessy laughed out loud. "Well, if that don't beat all. You can't be serious."

"If those fuckin' Hell's Angels can do it, why can't we?"

"Okay, but how are you planning on getting this movie made?"

"For starters, through your boy's connections."

Jessy shot Fred another cold glare. She couldn't dismiss the idea outright, but her mind raced with the likely complications that would come with getting Alex heavily involved. Fred wouldn't look away, as if coaxing an answer from her.

Jessy's façade eventually cracked. "What exactly do you want me to do?"

"Tell Alex what I told you, and say we need his help to make it happen. We'll give him whatever he needs."

She turned to the mirror, sighing. "I don't want him to feel like he's being used. He's been good to me." Her tone left little doubt that she was accusing Fred of doing precisely that to her.

"For fuck's sake, it's a simple request," Fred responded, trying to keep his frustration in check.

Jessy took a few seconds to collect herself, her aloofness returning in the process. "Fine, I'll ask him after I'm done with my shift. You should go."

"I don't like you bossing me around."

"Well then, you'd better start treating me with a little more r-e-s-p-e-c-t."

"That boy's changing you. Don't forget where you come from."

Jessy's eyes narrowed before she barged past Fred. "And don't you forget that I put my life on the line for you and everyone else."

⌐

Angela arrived on time. The apartment's deadbolt snapped open, but she had to let herself in as Will had already returned to re-stringing his guitar and studying the array of lyric sheets spread out on the glass-topped table in front of the sofa. Angela approached with trepidation.

"Almost ready?"

"Gimme a minute." He tuned the last string and the guitar shimmered when he strummed some random chords. Satisfied, he eyed the papers.

"What's the matter?" she asked, breaking the silence.

"Trying to figure out what to play tonight."

"Well, can't you do that when we get there? We should leave now." Will straightened his posture as he set his guitar down, his face showing real concern. "Don't worry," she said. "Just do your best stuff like you always do. The new songs can wait. Why are you so nervous? It's only the Troubadour."

"Remember that guy from Elektra who gave me his card at the James Taylor show a couple weeks ago?" Angela didn't, but she nodded. "I called him today and he said he'd be there tonight with some other people from the label."

"That's wonderful!" She bounded to the sofa and kissed his cheek. "They're paying attention. That's what you've been wanting, right?"

Will faced her with a reluctant grin. "Yeah, I guess it is."

"Well then, we'd better not keep them waiting." Brimming with optimism, she kissed his lips and helped him pack. "Should we take a cab?"

"Sure, I don't care."

"Okay, I'll grab one. See you downstairs."

It was a short ride, but as they arrived at the club, she was overtaken by a new sense of purpose in their relationship. She opened the doors for him and stayed close as he approached the stage. It was another prime opening slot, this time for Ry Cooder, and Will didn't forget to thank those responsible after he did a quick sound check. There was nothing left to do after that but kill time in the empty dressing room.

"I guess they must be out having dinner," Will muttered. The usual tub of beer was full and loaded with fresh ice. He grabbed two Coronas and busted off the caps on a tabletop.

Angela touched her bottle's long, clear neck against his. "Here's to a great show, whether they like it or not."

They sat side by side on molded plastic chairs and finished the first bottles in short order. "How do you feel now?" she asked, unafraid now to nestle her body against his.

"I'm alright. I'm just gonna do what I always do."

"That's right. Don't forget it."

Will got up and brought back two more beers. He took long pulls, lost in thought, while Angela nursed hers, observing him at the same time. These silences terrified her. She imagined the voice speaking to him. He didn't appear tormented though, and after several minutes she envied his serenity.

"You know," he said, "I'd thought that being able to do this for a living would make me happy. Everyone in my family has had to work hard all their lives, and it never got us anywhere."

"That's nothing to be ashamed of."

"But it was having to work for someone else that always got to me. I don't think my dad ever came to grips with that. It made him an angry person. I knew since I was a little kid that I didn't want a life like that. But I couldn't explain that to him. I just left."

"He let you go. You don't owe him anything."

"I owe him an explanation."

"Fine, but you can't be concerned with that. After tonight, you'll be able to tell him that everything is working out. You're doing what you want to do. He should respect that."

"That's the thing. I'm not sure what he respects anymore."

Will seemed to drift again as a few members of Cooder's band came in, making a beeline for the beer. Will didn't offer any small talk, and Angela, feeling out of place, introduced herself with a smile and nod. The room filled up over the next several minutes, and the growing haze of nicotine and marijuana smoke was beginning to affect Angela when the stage manager appeared through the crowd to tell Will he had ten minutes to get ready. He rose, and Angela felt a familiar sense of anticipation, as he took her hand. The contact rejuvenated some of her self-assurance. Her excitement intensified as they stood at the side of the stage with a view of the packed room.

"Is it okay if I watch you from here?" she said, clinging to his arm.

"Sure," he replied, distracted. The stage manager re-materialized, signaling Will with a pat on the shoulder to follow him up the steps. The lights stayed off until Will strapped on the Martin and gave a nod to the wings that he was ready.

"Ladies and gentlemen, first up tonight is a very talented young man who's become a favorite here at the Troubadour. We think you'll enjoy him too. Please welcome, Will Mosley."

Angela got a lump in her throat hearing the applause. What these people were seeing wasn't the Will she had just been with, she thought, but someone who had the power to move them in whatever way he chose. He began, and she tried to listen as if she hadn't heard the songs before.

Alex and Carlos sat in a cafe on La Cienega drinking coffee. Darkness had descended and the place was empty, save for a few nighthawks perched at the counter, lost in personal turmoil. Alex still felt a rush from his productive day, and drank from his mug more out of courtesy than need. "So, you've had your shot at the big time," Carlos said. "That's more than most of us get."

"I wasn't ready for it."

"Nobody is."

"It was nothing like I thought it would be. It didn't feel like I gave them anything."

"It's quite possible they thought so too. You'll find out when you see yourself. If you see yourself."

"I ruined a long take."

"Look, it's done. No need to dwell on it. Trust me, Bill's forgotten about it. You just have to try your best again tomorrow."

"Is that what you've always told yourself?"

"Nah, I gave up trying a long time ago. I just need to work every once in a while to stay in the union's good books and make some new connections whenever necessary. If I worried about shit like getting parts in any movies other than Bill's, I would lose my mind."

"What do you think I should do?"

"Well, I'm not going to tell you to give it up now that you've had a taste. I'll just say, look at the other options you have." Carlos lit a Marlboro. Alex took the hint and changed the subject.

"George wants a half-key of coke, and Brandon wants some China White. If I can't get it from you, I'll get it from my guy in Watts."

Carlos exhaled through his nose and gazed at the ceiling. He spread his arms across the span of the booth's vinyl seat. "You're putting the screws to me now, huh? You and your friend are gonna put me out of business?"

Alex fumbled with his Zippo. "There's more to it than that." He lit his own cigarette and took a deep drag. "He's a Black Panther, and he wants your help. If you agree it could mean you won't have to do any of this shit anymore." Carlos furrowed his brow, but made no further moves to prevent Alex from talking. "Remember when you asked if he was being nice to me because he had a script? Well, you were almost right. The Panthers want to make a movie, and they need to talk to the right people."

Carlos glared back, dumbfounded. "You want me to make a Black Panthers movie?"

"No, no, no! We just need to get them meetings. They say they can take it from there."

"Even you should know it's not that simple. But if I do agree to help, what do I get out of it?"

"Whatever it takes to make you happy."

Carlos placed his elbows on the table, as if recognizing the sudden power shift. Alex could sense his unwillingness to do someone else's bidding. "I can get to Roger Corman through Bill Naud, but what am I asking for?"

"All you need to say is that Huey Newton wants this to happen."

"That's all, huh?"

Alex nodded in silent consent, and the pair returned to sipping their coffee.

Carlos eventually got up the nerve to speak. "You know what advice I would give if you want to seriously start working? Get off that fuckin' junk. You can get away with a lot of shit in this town, but not that." Alex hunched over and rubbed his forearms as if he'd been blasted by a cold wind.

Carlos's sympathy seemed to catch Alex by surprise. "I don't have to get it from you, if that would make you feel better."

"I don't want you to get it from anywhere, period," Carlos said. "And now you spring this Panther thing on me. You're forcing me to put my complete trust in you." He paused, measuring his next words. "I think they've got you brainwashed."

Alex restrained himself from lunging across the table. "Don't ever say that again."

"Okay, take it easy. I'll see if I can talk to Roger next week."

The two endured several more tense minutes, as neither was in any hurry to do what needed to be done next. Carlos muttered, "If this goes bad, I swear …" before taking a deep breath and reverting to his usual tone. "Did Bill ask for any more weed?"

"Nope."

Carlos reached into the inside pocket of his suede jacket and passed two Kodak film canisters to Alex under the table. "I'm gonna call him and tell him you're coming over now with these. They're on the house. Hopefully it'll help with this Panthers thing. Pay the check."

As Carlos made his way to the café's pay phone, Alex sneered, "You're a fucking prick."

Well, here you are again, taking your turn at playing the star. You may have fooled that poor naive girl, though. What did you do to her? No time to worry about that now. This is all about those assholes in front of you. Keep selling that ignorant farm boy shtick. If they want to pay you for providing that illusion, I guess you'd better give it to them. That girl is so goddamn empty that you've become some kind of savior to her. She sees you as her purpose in

life. Is that what you came out here for? To become someone else's project? No man, it was all about the freedom to be an artist, or whatever it is you think you are. Start considering doing something else, because it's not gonna get any better than it is at this moment.

Will bid the audience goodnight and the applause was noticeably louder than when he was introduced. Some even stood in appreciation or banged their beer bottles on the tables. It all washed over him as he stumbled down the short flight of stairs next to the stage where Angela stood with open arms. He was drenched in sweat and their embrace dampened her face and hair. Will took her hand and led her to the dressing room, as *Music From Big Pink* blasted from the PA and roadies prepared the stage for Ry Cooder's set.

"Everyone loved it," Angela said once they were alone in the hallway and could speak in normal tones. "I'm so proud of you."

He squeezed her hand tighter in recognition, and held the grip all the way to the door, whereupon he faced her. "I should have told you this a while ago, but thanks for everything you've done." Her glistening face took on a holy glow in the fluorescent light. They embraced again, and he kissed the curls on top of her head. For a moment he thought he wouldn't let go.

In the dressing room, the cloud of smoke had thickened on the ceiling and many loud conversations were in progress. No one noticed Will until the stage manager burst in, handing him his guitar case and a clean towel. "Amazing set Will, really," he said in his urgent, clipped tone. "There's some guys from Elektra that want to see you."

"Tell them to come back here." Will raised his eyebrows at Angela, handing her a Corona. "I guess this is it." She nodded, as some of the other musicians approached with congratulations.

Lucas led the group, clearing a path for two older men dressed casually for the occasion. Lucas had his hand extended well before Will could shake it. "That was fantastic," he said, pumping Will's arm. "I want you to meet my bosses, Jack and Paul."

Will felt an electric charge as he greeted the older men. "Lucas told us about your last show here, and we've been waiting for the chance to see you," Jack said, traces of a New York accent still evident. "That was a nice bunch of songs you did."

"Thank you very much," Will replied.

Paul jumped in. "I've been told you haven't recorded before."

"No, just been doing gigs by myself."

"You don't have a band?"

"No."

"Well, that's not really a problem," Paul said, to Jack more than anyone else. "Who's managing you?"

"No one. Never thought I needed one."

The two men laughed at the same time, and Lucas joined in. "Look at this kid," Jack said. "Out here on his own. Where are you from again?"

"Ashtabula, Ohio."

"Beautiful! I love it! You've reached the final frontier, my boy, but you don't sing like you have. Everyone who comes here always gets wrapped up in the vibes right away, the mythology. A lot of them have done well with that, but it's getting a little repetitive. You sound like you never left the hills. Are there hills there?"

"Not really."

"Doesn't matter. You made me care about what you were singing."

Paul glanced at Will in silent agreement, and Lucas grinned, seemingly sure of the kickback that was to come his way.

"How many songs would you say you have?" Paul asked in a serious tone.

Will tabulated the handful he had written, plus his granddad's. "I dunno, maybe twenty-five or thirty."

"That's great. Enough for a couple of albums right off the bat."

Will's concentration wavered as Jack and Paul speculated. He wanted to believe everything they were saying, but he began feeling invisible as the conversation intensified. He glanced at Angela who stood apart from their small circle, and refocused as he sensed her drinking in the moment.

"How about we go to the studio and record some demos, Will," Paul said. "Just do exactly what you did tonight, and we'll see where things go from there."

Will studied the beaming faces surrounding him, stopping at Angela's. Her eyes were wide and shining, urging him to speak. "Okay, let's do it. Gimme the time and place and I'll be there."

The group celebrated with a round of beers before heading to the main room for Cooder's set. Will and Angela joined the rest of the Elektra contingent at a large reserved table near the stage. He was self-conscious sitting that close to the stage, unable to comprehend that he had been up there only minutes before. The feeling subsided when Angela clutched his hand and whispered, "See, I knew tonight would be the night." Will stared straight ahead, trying to lose himself in the sound of Cooder's slide guitar, as it tore through the room like an emergency telegram coming over the wire. They've already forgotten me, Will thought.

The booze kicked in when the lights came up. Jack and Paul hadn't stopped paying for rounds, and Will came close to nodding off a few times. Partially revived by the light and commotion of the exiting audience, he turned to his new benefactors.

"Look, I really appreciate that you like my stuff, but I can't promise I'll be the next Jim Morrison."

All three laughed, while Jack piped up. "Hey, you keep on drinking like this and you've got a fair shot at it."

Paul added, "We don't want you to be anything other than who you are. We're the ones that have to live up to our promises. We'll be in touch about the studio time. Likely next week, okay?"

Will saluted them with his whiskey and fell sideways into Angela's lap.

Alex cut the Honda's lights as he turned off Lookout Mountain Road and saw that Bill's gates were open, indicating the director was expecting him. Alex could see activity inside the house and walked purposely up the stone path to the front door. A barefoot hippie girl in a tank top and cut-off jeans received him, then showed him to the main room where Bill sat at his editing table, running through the day's rushes. "He never stops working," the girl whispered to Alex. "It's a good thing you showed up. He really needs to take a break."

The faint sound of her voice snapped Bill out of a trance. He spun in his chair, and Alex instinctively took a step back. "Oh, Alex. Good to see you," he said, getting up to shake hands. "I really appreciate you making the trip."

"No problem," Alex said, handing over the film canisters. Bill ran a hand through the silver hair dangling to his shoulders and broke into a wide grin.

"I suppose Carlos informed you that this is ..."

"Yeah, it's all cool. Look, I wanted to thank you again for the opportunity to be in this movie."

"Don't mention it. You did fine today." After a brief lull, the director said, "Hey, why don't you have a look at yourself while I roll one. Come over here and sit down." Alex deposited himself in the leather swivel chair, while Bill leaned over to cue up the scene. "Just push that button when you're ready," he said, as he turned his attention to the joint in progress.

Alex took a breath and started the machine. There he was on the small screen, appearing nervous, before Bill's off-camera voice called out "Action!" He watched the take in disbelief. It was nothing like he had imagined it when surrounded by the crew. Even his wooden cadence couldn't diminish the overall effect. By the next scene, he was completely taken in by how the light accentuated his features, noting details like a budding double chin, and the protruding ears that he managed to keep covered with hair. After seeing a clip of the three prisoners entering the bomber, he stopped the machine and turned toward Bill, who was putting the finishing touches on his own bomber.

"I guess you'll be using these," Alex said with mock confidence, hoping to get confirmation that he wouldn't be left on the cutting room floor.

"Not necessarily," the director replied, his face shrouded by smoke. "We'll have to see how things go tomorrow. I guess no one's told you yet that we've decided to kill you."

"What?" Alex's shock at hearing this was intensified seeing Bill trying to stifle a laugh.

"Don't worry about it. This script isn't coherent. I'm going to have to make sense of it when we're editing. It really has nothing to do with you."

Bill held out the joint as a peace offering as Alex became resigned to his fate. "Yeah, I suppose not," Alex said, taking the joint. "I guess that's why you're the director." Bill stayed silent on the couch while Alex smoked, seemingly unmoved by his dejection. After passing the joint back, Alex struggled to get the conversation back on track. "I really hit it off with George and Brandon today. Learned a lot from them in a short amount of time. They said I should meet Roger." Alex paused to see if Bill could sense this was a lie. When no indication was forthcoming, he played his highest card. "Do you think you could give him a message?"

"What's that?"

"Carlos wants him to know that if he needs anything, we're happy to help him out."

"What, stuff like this?" Bill said, his voice betraying a note of concern.

"No, uh, coke actually. We've got a new connection in South America. It's coming in through the Black Panthers."

Bill snorted, shooting out two thick streams of smoke from his nostrils. "Jesus, what's Carlos getting mixed up with them for?"

"Oh, it's all legit. It all kinda happened because of me, in fact."

Bill continued to eye Alex with suspicion. "Okay, so why is a nice boy like you getting involved with them?"

"It's a long story, but everything's cool." To elaborate, Alex could only spout off the rhetoric Jessy had been feeding him. "The Panthers are trying to do good work. But when you're fighting the system, the only way to make things happen is to get money from outside. That's where I've come in. Just trying to spread the word."

"You're telling me you believe in what they're doing," Bill asked.

"Yeah, of course. The Revolution is alive."

Bill smiled, baring his gleaming teeth as he passed the joint. "You don't sound totally convinced. There must be something more to it."

Alex was pinned down. "Well, truthfully, it's got to do with a movie idea."

"Ah, here we go."

"I'm sorry, I should have come right out and said it. You must have people bothering you with shit like this all the time."

"I do, but here we are. Might as well tell me the idea."

Alex took one last drag and composed himself. "Okay, first of all, this is from the highest authority in the Panthers." Bill nodded while relighting the roach. "As you know, they've been having some problems lately, public relations-wise. The Feds and the pigs have been doing everything they can to fuck things up. What they need is to get the people back on their side. They need to be seen as heroes. They need to make a movie."

Bill took it all in before raising his eyebrows in mock astonishment. "That certainly is some idea. What do you want me to do about it?"

"Whatever you can," Alex replied, a little too eagerly.

Bill coughed as he laughed. "I gotta tell you, I honestly can't see anybody wanting to touch a film about the Panthers. It would be career suicide."

"What about those movies about the Hell's Angels that Roger made?"

"That was a different time. Back then they represented an appealing ideal."

"And the Panthers don't?"

"They want to kill white people! I can't think of anything less appealing."

"No! See that's where things have gotten fucked up. All this violence, with Manson and everything, it's been a distraction from the big picture. Sure, there's been some incidents with the Panthers, but they were all in self-defense."

"And dope had nothing to do with it?"

Bill's question stopped Alex in his tracks, but he felt too close to making his point to give up. "Dope is not what they deal in. But for the purpose of getting this movie made, they figured it would be the best way to get a foot in the door."

"I'm not the guy to do it," Bill finally asserted.

Alex, satisfied with the argument he'd presented, answered, "I wasn't expecting you to be. Like I said, I'm just getting the word out, and maybe you could too." Alex reached into his jean jacket and pulled out the small baggie of cocaine he brought for this precise moment. He dangled it in front of Bill. "Here's a present from Huey. If you want more, let me know."

Bill examined the baggie, before setting it on a neutral spot on the table. "I still can't see anyone having big enough balls to make a Panther movie," he said before falling silent. Alex didn't move, confident that he'd sparked Bill's imagination. His hunch proved correct when Bill continued, "Maybe it wouldn't have to be about them specifically. Maybe it could be about an organization remarkably similar to them." After observing Bill wrestling with the new idea for a few minutes, it seemed to Alex that the director was about to spew forth a detailed synopsis. Instead, Bill shifted his focus to the bag of coke. "Alex, I think I know some other people you might want to talk to about this. Let me get back to you in a week or so. But I'll see you in the morning on set."

Alex got up from the leather swivel chair and shook hands with Bill before going. As he started the Honda, he came to the firm conclusion that all of this was too important to leave in Carlos's hands.

Angela savored her utter contentment as the cab pulled up to Will's building. He had passed out, forcing her to shake him when they came to a full stop. "Baby, I need some money to pay the man," she cooed. Will groaned, plunged a hand into his front pocket, and fished out some crumpled bills. He handed the pile to Angela and she smoothed out four singles for the driver.

Will needed prodding to get out. "Okay, we're home now," she snapped, retrieving the guitar from the trunk before yanking Will's arm until he spilled onto the sidewalk. The driver pulled away as soon as he heard the back door slam, leaving Will sprawled on the pavement.

She nudged him with her tiny sandal. "I can't carry you up there. If you can't make it, you're gonna have to sleep out here tonight." Will rolled over onto his stomach and she sighed. "Oh, that's lovely. Come on, get up before someone calls the cops." Will placed his hands in a push-up position and got to his knees. From there, she was able to help him to his feet, although he still required her for balance.

They stood motionless, Angela supporting his full weight. The block was calm enough to hear the distant rumble of jets breaking through the smog out at LAX. Streetlights cast shadows upon the jagged cobblestone walk that led to the front entrance, their dark shapes merging into a new entity that crept to the steps until blackness consumed the door.

After a few minutes, Will was coherent enough to find his keys and make the laborious trek up to the apartment. There was no sign of Alex. Will collapsed on the sofa, and Angela joined him, nuzzling her head under his chin. "Everything feels good now, doesn't it baby?" she said. "This is how it's supposed to be." Will's breathing was deep and measured. She checked to see if he was asleep, but found him staring through half-lidded eyes. "What's the matter baby? Aren't you happy?" When she realized he was unable to formulate an answer, Angela helped Will to his feet again and led him down the hall to his room. He fell onto the mattress and she took off his boots, leaving him to sleep in his clothes while she curled up beside him.

See, what did I tell ya? She thinks she's got it all figured out. This is how she wants it to be. You had your moment and now she's having hers. Kinda makes you wonder who's getting the better end of the deal doesn't it? Yeah, you fooled them all tonight, and look what's

it got you. You're not getting out of this anytime soon. So, what are
you gonna tell her? She's waiting, asshole. Are you happy or what?

"It's Time"

It's time --
Time to get that feelin'
That you've always been concealin'
Though every day it's harder to reveal

It's time --
Time to move that mountain
As the hourglass keeps countin'
Down a life you never really felt was real

Shadows fall across the path of victory
Flowers in the dust are all that I can see
They told me if I bet, there'd come a time I'd win
Now I answer every question, where do I begin?

It's mine --
But you can have it if you want it
I'm sure you're gonna flaunt it
I didn't need it that bad anyway

It's fine --
Fine for what you're knowin'
But your cards are plainly showin'
The Queen of Hearts has given you away

Shadows fall across the path of victory
Flowers in the dust are all that I can see
They told me if I bet, there'd come a time I'd win
Now I answer every question, where do I begin?

It's time --
Time to start believin'
In the word I've been receivin'
Tellin' me to get on outta here

It's time --
That we saw things as they are
Before they went too far
I want it whispered softly in my ear

Shadows fall across the path of victory
Flowers in the dust are all that I can see
They told me if I bet, there'd come a time I'd win
Now I answer every question, where do I begin?

Chapter 10

Hollywood / May 1972

Bob Richardson arrived for the meeting and was reaching for the sugar bowl of coke when Bert Levine stopped him. "Wait a sec. You gotta try this." Bert pulled out a quarter-gram bag from his desk and Bob took two whiffs with the aid of the small gold spoon attached to a chain around his neck. It knocked him back into the thick leather chair, his eyes widening to the size of dinner plates. "As good as dentist shit," Bert said. Bob nodded in uncontrolled ecstasy. "Roger turned me on to it. You won't believe where it came from."

"Where?"

"The fucking Black Panthers."

Bob was shocked to hear Corman's name mentioned as the source of this discovery, and could only respond to his partner's enthusiasm with a cursory, "Wow, that's crazy." After the initial coke rush faded, Bob let the matter drop, chalking it up to another of the strange twists the pair encountered on a daily basis. He wanted to get on with the meeting, but Bert remained fascinated by what had fallen into his lap.

"I mean, Roger comes by yesterday, straight off the set—"

"How's he coming along with that, by the way?"

"Oh, he said it's going great. Right on schedule, as usual. Which was why I was surprised to see him. I figured he'd be working. You know how he is."

"Yeah, sure."

"So he shows up and gives this to me, saying it's the best shit he's ever had. Coming from him, I had to believe it. I ask him where he got it, and he says it's from Bill Naud. You remember him? He's shooting something for American International right now at Edwards Air Force Base."

"Bill Naud? That guy was working the second unit before we were born. What the fuck is he doing mixed up with the Panthers?"

"It's not him, it's this kid in his cast. He's got a pipeline."

"You're saying that Bill's cast a Panther? That doesn't seem possible."

"No, no, it's a white boy, if you can believe it. But here's the best part. He said the Panthers want to make a movie. And they want us to meet with Huey Newton!"

Bob let out a burst of nervous laughter. "The Panthers want Bill to direct it?"

"Who the fuck knows what they want to do. But if we get enough of this coke, the thing will pay for itself."

"You're serious?"

Bert poured a small amount from the baggie and chopped out two lines with a business card bearing a name he no longer recognized. He inhaled the first line before saying, "No, of course not. But I've been thinking about it. Maybe we should start attracting Black audiences."

"You mean do more of that *Superfly* and *Shaft* shtick?" Bob replied in between snorts.

"See, there you go with the negative stereotypes."

"It sounds to me like you're talking about exploitation. I shouldn't have to remind you that we create art."

"But that's the point. We could do something artistic, the same way we did it with Peter and Dennis. We've talked about this before; it's not just about creating art. The art comes from capturing the spirit of the times. The Panthers are part of the zeitgeist, and we can't ignore it. It's a complicated story that demands to be told."

"It's not where we come from, Bert. If you want to do something complicated, we might as well make a film about Manson. If we do a Panthers movie, people are gonna think we're just as crazy as they are."

Bert snorted his second line, and tilted his head back to savor the residue dripping down his throat. His body sated for the moment, he said, "Bill's connection can put me in touch with Huey Newton. I'd like to have a meeting with him."

"Jesus Christ, first the coke, now this? What happened to running a legitimate business? We'll have the cops all over us. Huey's probably under surveillance twenty-four hours a day."

"Yeah, but he's a free man. This is America. He can associate with whoever he wants. Either way, we'll keep it quiet. I'd like to bounce around a few ideas and then maybe take him to the screening room."

"Oh yeah? What are we gonna watch?"

"Find a print of *The Battle of Algiers*. I have a feeling it'll be right up his alley."

1

"Hello?"

"This is a collect call from—"

"Will."

"—do you accept the charges?"

"Yes."

"Hi Mom, it's me."

"Oh, good lord Will, is it really you?"

"I'm sorry I haven't called."

"Are you okay?"

"Yeah, I'm fine."

"Where are you?"

"I'm still in L.A."

"You're not in trouble?"

"No, I already told you everything's good."

"Why haven't you called?"

"Mom, don't get upset."

"But we've been worried sick. It's been months."

"I know, I know, I said I'm sorry. You shouldn't worry. Mom, look, I haven't called because I haven't had anything to say."

"What does that mean? What's wrong with just calling to say hello?"

"Is Dad still mad at me?"

"No. He's been just as worried as I am."

"Really?"

"Yes. He wants to talk to you."

"No, don't! Not yet. I just wanted to tell you that I've been busy. I've been working."

"You've got a job? Oh, thank goodness."

"No, I'm playing music. That's my job."

"Oh lord. When will you realize that that's no way to live? Why won't you let me send you some money?"

"Because I don't need it. I'm playing a lot, and I've got some good news. It looks like I'm gonna make a record."

"A record? How can you afford that?"

"Mom, listen, I'm not paying for it. A record company wants to record me. They're going to pay for it. Mom? Do you understand? You'll be able to listen to me on your record player."

"When are you coming home?"

"Mom. Didn't you hear me? I'm going to be making a record. I'll send it to you when it's finished."

"Why can't you come home? It's because of that Alex isn't it? I always knew he'd get you into trouble."

"Mom, calm down. Alex is doing fine too. I hardly see him. He's doing his own thing."

"Who's taking care of you? Are you out there by yourself?"

"I don't need anyone to take care of me."

"Do you have a girlfriend?"

"No, but that's got nothing to do with anything."

"I've heard about what goes on there. You should come home. There are lots of nice girls here that you could settle down with. You shouldn't have broken up with that Janet. We really liked her."

"That was a long time ago, Mom. You gotta forget about those things. I'm a different person now."

"How can I believe that if I can't see for myself?"

"I'll be home soon, I promise."

"Here, your father wants to talk to you."

"No! I gotta go. I'll call again next week. Tell him we'll talk then. Goodbye Mom."

Alex sat in the apartment on Kirkwood that Fred had rented for Jessy, anticipating her return from the club. She'd given Alex the spare key and he'd made himself at home, despite Jessy's place being a small, dark and dirty step down from his own apartment. They were shooting heroin on a daily basis, and every other chore revolved around those precious few minutes. They tried to fix together, in a twisted notion of a family dinner, and used her works, which, at that moment, teased him from the coffee table. He alternated between running his hands through his hair, and rubbing his eyes and ears relentlessly.

The dull thud of the front door opening and shutting roused him like a cat hearing a bird rustle in the bushes. The steady thwack of heels on linoleum confirmed his joy, and Alex stood to greet her. Jessy could only reciprocate with a weak smile, as she tossed her purse, kicked off her shoes and headed to the bathroom. Alex returned to the sofa, his anxiety unabated. "Baby, you want me to cook up for you?" he called out as the water started running. Sweat bubbled on his forehead when she didn't answer. He couldn't wait.

Alex produced the stash and had a spoonful ready to cook when the water shut off. In seconds, Jessy was next to him on the sofa, stone-faced. "Could you hold off on that shit for a few minutes?"

Alex's hands, one holding the spoon, the other a lighter, trembled. "Um, actually I can't baby."

"What did you do today?"

"Aw, c'mon. Do we have to get into that? Let me take care of this first."

"Fuck. Here, let me do you." Waves of energy coursed through his nervous system as her bare knee collided with his denim-covered thigh. She leaned across his torso to cook the shot. The strip club's aromas in her hair mixed with butane fumes. Everything his senses took in brought him close to salivating.

"Well? Where am I supposed to stick this?" she said, holding the syringe at the ready. Alex snapped to attention, whipped off his belt and coaxed out a vein on his left forearm. His teeth dug into leather as the cold metal slipped under the skin with impossible smoothness. She injected the load, and the belt dropped from his mouth as his head listed like a leaking balloon. Within five minutes, his eyes refocused. He smiled while reaching out to caress her cheek. His touch was cold upon her warm flesh, causing her to recoil.

"You feel better?" she asked.

"Oh yeah, baby. Now how about we do you?"

"I'm gonna wait a while. I need to ask you if you've been getting anywhere with the movie." She spoke like a nurse to a car accident victim.

"The movie? Oh yeah, that was the news I had."

"Why couldn't you tell me before?"

His eyes rolled demonically. "I dunno. Priorities, baby."

"Get it through your junkie-ass head, this movie is your only fucking priority."

Her simmering rage couldn't be dismissed, and Alex saw her capacity for violence for the first time. "Okay baby, take it easy. You have a bad night or something?"

"Sort of. Just tell me what you've been doing."

"Alright. Bill talked to Roger Corman and he talked to Bert Levine over at Columbia and—you're not gonna believe this—he wants to meet with Huey. What do you think of that?"

"Is this guy a big fucking deal or what?"

"Baby, this is the best thing we could hope for! This guy obviously gets it—"

"'Cause I ain't gonna have Fred give Huey no jive-ass story that some clown wants to meet him. He's got enough—"

"Baby, listen. If this meeting goes well, then we've done our job. We're in the fuckin' clear."

"What makes you so sure? What if nothing comes of it?"

"Hey, we're not producers, are we? You get word to Huey about the meeting, and let the rest of them figure out what to do next." Alex reached out, and this time she closed her eyes and allowed his clammy fingertips to brush a strand of her ironed hair from her face.

"Are you sure that this guy wants to have a meeting?"

"Positive, baby. Why would I make something like that up?"

"Okay. I gotta call Fred. Leave the gear out." Alex stretched his legs out on the couch, thinking of the sex they would have if he could make it to the bedroom.

Huey could not have conceived a film like this, one that understood that there were two stories behind every revolution. As he sat watching *The Battle of Algiers* in Bert's screening room, he realized he had been playing the game the media wanted him to play, forcing people to take sides by deeming him either an enemy of the people or a freedom fighter. Lately, even he was having trouble making that distinction. To alleviate such concern, he would remind himself that rarely did these descriptions prove accurate, since revolutions succeeded through concentrated acts of violence that exposed the inherent hypocrisy of the Establishment. As that violence played out on the screen, his mind raced with memories of the early days in Oakland, and how he and the party's founders faced the same moral dilemma as Ali. Could they commit themselves to the platform, and more importantly, could they convince others to commit to it? Huey was captivated by the story's passion and conviction from the outset after noting the director's Italian name, and his analysis became clouded as he envisioned this man being shaped under Mussolini's fascist rule. As the tight scenes of street clashes built, one on top of another, Huey felt the walls of the small screening room closing in. The Casbah turned into downtown Oakland on those nights when he ventured out with his loaded .45 tucked in his jacket, knowing he'd encounter several opportunities to use it. He saw himself in Ali—the individual struggling to overturn a system unconcerned with the individual. The only thing that set them apart, Huey surmised, was that the man on the screen was up against a foreign nation imposing its will, while outside Bert's office, America was attempting to rid itself of a similar shame, instituted by the founding fathers. The film also caused Huey to question whether any of the pigs and politicians secretly respected him. If these weird Hollywood guys did, then anything was possible. After all, revolutionaries founded America. That stance remained the core of Huey's public image. But only revolutions in line with America's interests seemed to earn any credence. Goddamn, he hated to see his brothers getting wasted by the fucking Vietcong. There was no point in them being there. That hurt most, knowing the brothers were on the wrong side. As the film reached its climax, with the guerrillas facing imminent death, Huey saw the agony in Ali's face and for a moment forgot this was an actor struggling with the obvious question the character needed to answer—"Was it all worth it?" Huey had yet to ask himself that question, but he knew he would, perhaps sooner rather than later.

The screening room plunged into darkness as the projector clicked off, before someone turned on the lights. Huey, sitting in the middle of an empty row in front of the others, rubbed his eyes as they adjusted to the brightness. Bert called out from the back of the room, "What did you think?"

Huey stood and walked up the aisle to where the pair stood by the door. "That was a good fuckin' movie, man. Powerful."

"I thought you'd like it," Bert gushed. "In fact, I'm really glad you did. I wouldn't want to waste your time."

"Nah man, if I didn't like it I would tell you. I don't get to see many movies anymore anyway. Must be nice having this place where you don't have to put up with people talking through the whole picture."

Bert nodded and waited for Huey to offer any further insights. When none were forthcoming, he looked toward Bob. "Well, I suppose we should head to the refreshment stand."

The fact that Huey sat through the entire film seemed enough to calm the nerves Bert and Bob each displayed when Huey arrived, and Huey himself had to mask how star-struck he was walking the building's carpeted hallways, the walls lined with framed posters of films he hadn't seen. He chose not to come with bodyguards, since he assumed no one would expect him in Hollywood. He also didn't want to intimidate Bert and Bob any more than they already were. Theirs was a different kind of power, and Huey wanted to learn how they used it.

They entered an office—a big one—and Bert sat behind the immaculate oak desk. Bob gave Huey the choice of which plush leather chair he preferred, and Bert produced a sugar bowl, now filled with the Panther coke.

"I gotta say thank you for being generous with this," Bert said, chopping out several lines on a small mirror. "It's the best shit we've had."

Bob agreed with a serious nod.

"Glad to hear it," Huey said, before sucking up a line through the rolled-up twenty-dollar bill Bob had handed him. The other two men followed suit. In the aftermath Huey could feel an unspoken bond had been forged, as if they were all thirteen years old, sharing their first cigarette.

Huey began feeling conscious that the coke was making him appear cagey, but Bert didn't seem to notice. "I gotta say again that Bob and I are honored to meet you today. What you've managed to accomplish through all of your struggles is nothing short of remarkable."

"Well, thank you again."

"I know we come from two different worlds, but I think deep down we have similar intentions to do good things." Huey pondered the possible hidden meaning behind Bert's words. "I'm assuming you don't know anything about the movie business, so I'm not going to bore you with what Bob and I do on a day-to-day basis. What it all comes down to is this: If we believe in something, we'll find a way of making it happen. I think that's where we have some common ground."

Bob jumped in, as if needing to clarify his partner's point. "We wanted you to see this film today because we think we could turn your story into something similar."

The coke took hold of Huey's jaw, impeding his speech. "Yeah, I was getting that impression."

Bert reasserted control of conversation. "Good. I figured we wouldn't have to spell things out for you. The movies we make aren't black and white—pardon the expression— they're about real life, which is more complicated. The days of John Wayne killing Japs and Indians are over, thank God. You should know that better than anyone." Huey detected Bert's patronizing tone, but let it slide. "But enough about our ideas. We should be asking how you envision this thing."

Huey hesitated. He took another inventory of the office, noting the Oscar on a shelf behind Bert. "Well, I'm sure you know that we've had our backs up against the wall lately. We were making some real progress for a while, and I think that's when the pigs started getting scared. It didn't help that these other motherfuckers came along with their own agendas and started causing shit. It made us look bad, ya dig? We gotta get back to something real. Show where it all began. That's what I'd like to see."

Bert and Bob both listened intently, although Huey wasn't sure if he was getting the message across. Bert ended the suspense. "That was one of the best pitches we've heard in a long time."

Huey smiled, but remained unwilling to offer his complete trust. "Where do we go from here?"

"We start putting it together," Bob said. "It's going to take some investment to get the right people involved. If you're prepared to pay for it, we'll do what we can to provide you with whatever you need."

Huey bristled at the mention of money. "If I'm gonna pay for it, I'm gonna have to move a lot of that shit," he said, glancing at the sugar bowl.

"We don't have a problem with that, do we Bob?"

"None at all."

"How about one for the road?"

Huey sank into the chair, feeling as deflated as the leather. "No, I'm good."

"Okay, Will, that's enough for today. Nice work." Slipping off his headphones, Will felt like Neil Armstrong removing his helmet and catching that long-awaited first breath of pure oxygen. At the same time, he felt comfortable within the dimly lit isolation of Sunset Sound's studio B. The song he'd played was now on tape forever, he thought, nostalgic for the world of six hours ago, before Paul hit the record button.

Will's contemplation was disrupted by Paul's voice crackling over the intercom. "Do you want to come in and hear this, or what?" Will set down the Martin and entered the control room through the huge padded door. The tape was rewinding in a blinding whirr, as the engineer navigated a path through the maze of knobs preparing a rough mix. Paul, his job as producer over for the time being, greeted Will with a satisfied expression. "I think we got something pretty cool here kid," he said, motioning Will to the leather sofa, the only hominess in the room's clinical atmosphere.

The tape skidded to a halt, and a jarring clunk sent Will's first shimmering chords through the speakers. The sound pinned him against the sofa. The engineer's simple adjustments gave the performance an ethereal quality. It didn't sound like a record. It was bigger, deeper, more detailed. He could pick out every nuance, every hesitant strum, and each time he had to make a split-second decision whether or not to reach for the higher register in order to resolve the melody.

As the songs rolled on, each bookended by Will's nervous false starts and count-ins, the second-guessing became excruciating. By the fifth track, he knew he wanted to do it all over again and anticipated a similar judgment from Paul. But the older man continued to listen in silence, occasionally swiveling his captain's chair in Will's direction to indicate with an eye or hand gesture a moment he particularly enjoyed. Will reacted with a courteous smile, but Paul's enthusiasm didn't do much to ease Will's disappointment. At the conclusion of the eighth track, the tape stopped with the familiar thud.

Paul was on the verge of gushing. "You done good, kid. What else can I say? There were moments where I was... transported."

"What happens now?"

"Well, I'm going to dub a copy and really give it a good listen to see if anything could be improved. But mostly it'll be to get some ideas for other instruments."

Will's thoughts spun with the prospect that this was going to be a real record. "What do you have in mind?"

"Oh, I'll call in my usual crew. Fonfara, Benno, Mundi. They'll be able to sweeten things." Will didn't recognize the names, but Paul kept talking. "The great thing about these songs is that they fit together as a whole." He laced his fingers to illustrate the point. "It's going to make a great *album*, but the trick is going to be finding that one song that will be an invitation to embrace the full experience." Hearing this caused Will to question Paul's motives for the first time, and the producer seemed to perceive a twinge of fear in his young protégé. "But we're not going to worry about that right now. I shouldn't have even brought it up. You're an artist, not a pop star. Once people start hearing your stuff, believe me, they'll want to record it. We'll let Linda Ronstadt have the hit, and we'll cash the checks." Paul let out a conspiratorial laugh. "Look, I know this is all happening fast, but believe me, I wouldn't be working this way if Jack and I and everybody at the label didn't believe in you. You've seen the artists we've worked with. Some of them sell a lot of records, and some of them don't. The bottom line is we put out music we think is good. Go home and relax. Have something to celebrate. I'll call you after I've spent some time with these songs. If you happen to have anything else you think might work with this vibe we've got going, we can lay it down."

Will rose and shook Paul's hand, feeling like he'd been talked into buying aluminum siding. The transition from the studio's tomblike interior to the blinding late afternoon sun sent a dull throb through his skull. Inside the scorching Delta 88, he thought of one song his granddad had left him, but hadn't figured out a way to perform, something about radios in heaven. If he could make it a hit, Will mused, maybe his granddad would get to hear it.

Alex parked Carlos's Honda behind a Quonset hut off the road that led into San Pedro's Downtown Waterfront. The single security light above him illuminated the cabin cruiser docked a hundred yards in front of him. He sat in the car for several minutes, expecting to detect some movement, but nothing stirred. Alex began walking toward the boat, feeling the cool, salty night breeze on his face. Several glowing orange cigarette tips appeared as he adjusted his stride, hoping to conduct the transaction as quickly as possible. He stopped at the end of the landing to await instructions from three stocky Mexicans, all bearing the wear and tear of several days at sea. Alex had made pickups at the docks before, but these were three new faces. "Is that Carlos' boy?" one asked.

Alex shuddered as the words shot out over the water, prompting him to keep his voice down. "Yeah. Should I, uh, come aboard?"

"As long as you have the money."

Alex tapped a breast pocket on his jean jacket. "Right here."

A flashlight's narrow beam hit him. "Pull it out."

Alex reached across his chest with his right hand, keeping his left raised as a natural precaution. He produced the wad of cash held together by two elastic bands. The beam lowered and disappeared, and the man ordered him to come on board.

Another Mexican flicked his cigarette butt into the dark abyss surrounding the boat, saying, "This trip is getting harder each time."

Alex attempted to sympathize. "I'll let Carlos know."

"You don't have to. We've let Carlos know. See, the problem is not bringing things here." The speaker paused. "The problem is returning without what we were promised. Give me the money."

Alex obeyed. He could hear the bills being shuffled but could not see the action. A heavy sigh indicated the counting was over. "Carlos has come up short. It could not be you who miscounted, could it?"

Alex began to tremble. "He didn't tell me how much it was supposed to be. There's never been a problem before."

The speaker took a few steps out of the shadows, revealing his ruddy complexion. A stench attached to his army surplus outfit wafted into Alex's nostrils. Standing in front of Alex, the Mexican's head only reached Alex's chin. "Look, we don't blame you," the Mexican said with mock sincerity. "But you must understand that this is very frustrating for us. Carlos has been sloppy lately, things that I'm sure he hasn't told you. But we have a message we would like you to tell him."

Alex stuttered, "I-I-I'll tell him wh-wh-whatever you w-w-want."

"It's not that simple jefe. Carlos is family, and we have done business together for a long time, but even family has its limits. To make matters worse, he no longer shows us the courtesy of meeting in person. He sends you, his poor naive young gringo errand boy, knowing full well how we will react."

The blood drained from Alex's head, as the man continued. "You know there are sharks in these waters, yes? We see them all the time, even close to the harbor. Very majestic they can be. I wonder if Carlos knows this? Maybe you can give him that information too."

The Mexican grabbed Alex in a bear hug and called out to the others, "Tie him up!" One lassoed his wrists and the other his ankles. They carried him to the stern and tossed him like a rolled-up carpet. Alex's scream was deadened by black salt water filling his mouth. His nightmares came true.

The Mexicans had left some slack in their ropes, and Alex kicked his legs loose first, allowing some upward propulsion until he could slide his hands out. He lunged for the surface, and the men on the boat cheered as his head broke above the water. They continued to taunt him until he climbed atop the pier, one yelling out a parting shot as Alex staggered toward the Honda.

"Don't forget to tell Carlos about the sharks!"

Chapter 11

West Hollywood / May 1972

Will had started taking refuge in the Troubadour's front bar on days when he couldn't get any work done. He'd noticed many others using it as a similar method of escape, but Will had no interest in commiserating, despite feeling accepted into the L.A. music scene's exclusive club of miscreants and misanthropes since word of his record deal had circulated. That hit home when the bartenders started treating him with more respect, but nothing prepared him for the tall, wild-eyed stranger who took a seat next to him, and initiated some small talk after ordering each of them bottles of Budweiser. Will looked up to say thanks, but couldn't get the words out once he registered who it was. "My god, you're Gene Clark."

"What gave it away?" Gene's demeanor put Will at ease and they both shared a laugh. "You're Will Mosley, right? I saw you open for Ry. I dig your stuff, man."

"Wow, thank you. I can't believe it's actually you."

"Don't mention it, the scene is smaller than you think. I heard through the grapevine that you're recording for Elektra. Congrats, they're good people. I'm not supposed to tell anyone, but we've been talking to them about doing a new Byrds album. It's possible we could be label mates."

Will had to pause in order to process this news, but began opening up when Gene asked how the recording sessions were going. This led to Will revealing some things about his background, which Gene took as a cue to reflect on his own mid-western roots. They drank all afternoon, but Will lagged behind. Still, each round seemed to bring them closer, until Will's vision of them talking as equals was altered to one of a beaten-down veteran dispensing his war stories. As Gene's speech began slurring, Will hung on every detail of missed opportunities, bad deals, and friendships torn by greed, jealousy, and excessive behavior. "That's something you've got to look forward to," Gene said with a decrepit laugh. Will couldn't admit that it was already happening; his relationship with Alex was, for all intents, becoming non-existent. He was navigating this new world of recording studios and contract negotiations on his own.

The truth was, he spent afternoons at the Troubadour not to get out of his stifling apartment, but so Angela couldn't find him. She was at her office, taking directions from voices on the telephone. He knew at what time she would be home, and when she would call him to check in. Sometimes she would insist on coming over, other times he could dodge her by feigning a creative spark that needed to be stoked.

As Will continued to soak in Gene's stories, the underlying lesson appeared to be that it was the present moment that mattered. Each of Gene's hard-luck tales symbolized another chance he had used up, another bridge he had burned. It struck Will that by the time Gene's former band had recorded "So You Want To Be a Rock 'N Roll Star," Gene was out of the game. "There are a lot of people out here with good intentions," he told Will at one point. "But they don't know the rest of the country like you and I do."

Several more denim-clad longhairs milled around the bar, including a few who recognized Gene and gave him an appreciative greeting. "See what I mean?" he said after the two of them had their solitude restored. "You always get the pat on the back before the kick in the teeth."

"But what about all the people like me who will always love your music?"

Gene finished another beer before answering. "You can always make records, even if no one buys them—if that's all you want to do. You can keep changing the chords, but you can't change the world."

Their conversation sputtered after that and they both sulked over the bar for several minutes until Will said he had to leave. He laid down a twenty-dollar bill and slid off the stool to his feet as the thought struck him that Gene expected him to pick up his tab. "It was great to meet you," Will said.

Gene looked up through drowsy eyes. "Yeah, I'll keep an ear out for that record of yours. I hope it all goes well for you. I really do." His sincerity was touching, although Will walked away with a sense of foreboding. That sense continued to grow as Will resumed stewing over Paul's thoughts on the tracks, while walking back to his apartment. His conscious decision to withhold any news from Angela only made him feel worse.

The phone rang minutes after Will walked through the door. Something told him it was Angela calling, although it wasn't yet five o'clock.

"Where have you been? I've called a few times."

"Aren't you at work?"

"It's been slow. I thought I'd see how you're doing."

"I'm doing fine. I went out for a while, and now I'm back."

"Did you hear from that producer guy?"

"No. But I wasn't here anyway, so it doesn't matter."

"Jesus! Why aren't you staying by the phone? You know he's supposed to be calling."

"I'm not gonna sit here all day waiting for the goddamn phone to ring. I've got a life."

"What was so important?"

"Why do you have to know everything? Paul and I will talk in good time. It's not like he's gonna forget about me. I think you should go back to work."

She changed the subject without hesitation. "What are you doing tonight?"

"I dunno. I don't feel like going out."

"Can I come over?"

"I don't think so. I might try to come up with some new stuff."

"Fine. I'll call you tomorrow."

"Sure."

Will hung up, rubbing his temples. Angela seemed more invested in his life than he was. He wanted to hear other music, anything to divert him from the dark night he knew loomed ahead. He idly flipped through his records, and pulled out The Byrds' *Mr. Tambourine Man*. He took a second to admire the cover, examining the noble figure of Gene Clark staring back at him, all pageboy hair and Greenwich Village swagger, the perfect combination of Lennon and Dylan. The vinyl spun and the title track began with its crackling jangle. Will recalled hearing it on the radio when it first broke across the country, that long lost summer of his sixteenth year.

But when Gene's low register launched into "I'll Feel A Whole Lot Better," Will felt something stir inside him. No wonder Gene never topped it. Yes, Will thought, I'll probably feel a whole lot better when you're gone.

Alex arrived at Carlos's apartment as the haze over L.A. regrouped for the start of another day. He pounded on the front door.

"For fuck sakes, keep it down," Carlos snarled in his robe while pulling Alex inside.

Alex unleashed his rage. "So, you're shorting your supplier now and leaving me to take the heat? Real fucking nice."

"I guess I miscounted," Carlos said.

"I don't think so. They said you've been getting sloppy, but they let you off the hook because you're family. Not me though, they tied me up and threw me in the fucking bay! Just admit it, you were setting me up."

The truth in Alex's words stung. Carlos hated being manipulated by anyone, much less Alex. His gut told him that dealing with Panthers along with his Mexican connections was a recipe for disaster. Eliminating the middleman was the convenient excuse for a way out, although he was relieved that they didn't do anything more drastic to Alex. The kid had been put in his place, and that was the important thing.

Carlos stayed calm. "How could you think I was setting you up? I made a bad mistake and I apologize. I guess they kept the shit?"

"Of course they did! But it doesn't matter, and you wanna know why? Word's getting around, man, that the Panthers are gonna corner the market with their coke. So what the fuck are you gonna do?"

"I'll straighten things out."

Carlos noticed the telltale signs that Alex needed a fix—sweating, pacing and uncontrollable hand gestures. He waited until Alex asked for it. "It's the least you can fucking do."

Carlos reached deep inside himself to find his most compassionate expression, the one he used for the bit part as a priest in *Hollywood Zombies*, and resisted the urge to call Alex "my son."

"Of course," Carlos said. "Don't worry, everything will be all right." He produced his works, and the mere sight seemed to erase the recent trauma from Alex's mind. Carlos made Alex inject himself, which he accomplished with some trepidation, still unsure of his technique. The rush triggered the sleep that Alex had been keeping at bay for several hours, and Carlos took the Honda to San Pedro to get his package back.

'Well, here we are again wondering how do we begin.' How's that for an opening line? At least it rhymes. You're not thinking about writing an actual radio hit, are you? Do you even listen to the radio anymore? I don't know what that record company weasel was doing putting that thought in your head. For once I have to side with you. Do what you wanna do, and let them take it or leave it.

I can't. I have to at least make an effort.

What? Didn't you hear? I'm agreeing with you about all your 'stand by my principles' shit. It's not like the world needs another moronic pop song. You'll be a one-hit wonder. All this hard work, down the tubes in six months.

I just gotta come up with something to show him I've got the ability.

Why don't you ask your new drinking buddy to help you out? I bet he's itching for another shot at the big time. Maybe you should steal one of his ideas just like you stole all the others.

That's not fair. Those songs are my birthright, and it's my duty to perform them.

You don't know the meaning of the word. What about your duty to stand by your family, or your friend? Do you even know what kind of shit he's gotten himself into?

He knows he can come to me if he's in trouble.

Oh, does he? And what about this girl? I guess having someone completely devoted to you isn't enough.

It's all **too** much. She doesn't understand the position I'm in. Neither can Alex.

Okay, back to this again. You want another good line? How about this: 'The battle lines are drawn but there's nothing going on?' There you go, you've got half a verse. It's even got a nice, lilting flow to it. Put three chords over it and you're done.

Stop. I've got to concentrate.

Look, you said it yourself that it's impossible. You haven't got it in you to be a hack. It's all about integrity, right? Well, let me clue you into something; as long as you're playing your grandfather's songs, you're living a lie.

It's not true.

It is, and you know it every time you're on stage. You can hear it in the applause. Everyone likes those songs better than your own. Do you think you'd be making a record if not for those songs? Do I even have to ask?

He'd want it this way. He'd be proud of me.

What's going to happen the next time you meet one of your has-been idols and he tells you what a great songwriter you are? Or more realistically, when your mother starts bawling with joy over the fact that your name is on a record? Are you gonna tell the truth?

Shut up.

You're surrounded by liars. And it's turning you into a bigger one than you already are. So, most of your shtick is based on your grandfather's music. Fine. Just don't hide it.

Angela knows.

I know she does, and I bet that really gnaws at you, doesn't it? That's why you've got to be careful with her. Just put up with it a little while longer.

Nothing good can come of it.

You need her.

Please, stop.

The phone rang at about ten the next morning, its announcement shattering Will's short-lived peace. He was still in his clothes, lying on the sofa. The coffee table was littered with paper chronicling a series of false starts that had degenerated in accordance with the depletion of a fifth of Wild Turkey. The bottle stood amongst the scraps like a cathedral within the ruins of a bombed city. Will answered before the phone could sound another alarm in his head.

"Will? It's Lucas. Sounds like I woke you. Sorry about that. Did you have a gig last night?"

"No, I was just ... trying to ... write some new stuff."

"How'd that go?"

"Oh, fine. There's a few ... promising ideas."

"Great, can't wait to hear them. Hey, I wanted to get in touch on behalf of Paul. He's been working with the tracks, and he's really excited about the whole vibe. We want you to come in today and let us know what you think."

"Have you heard them?"

"No. It's gonna be my first time. Hopefully we'll all be able to get a sense of direction for you after this. How's two o'clock for you?"

"Shouldn't be a problem."

"Great, see you at the office, and feel free to play us the new stuff too. Ciao."

Will surveyed his surroundings with the self-disgust that came with the absence of a normal sleep cycle. He could no longer differentiate a new day from the last. The Martin occupied the stuffed chair, observing him from its upright position. Will gathered up the paper, knowing that, in spite of the effort, he'd produced nothing meaningful. Taking to his bed for a few hours seemed the only option, but footsteps in the stairwell delayed his progress. It was Alex. They both took hard looks at each other.

"Get into one last night?" Alex asked, looking at the empty bottle.

"Yeah, it appears so."

"Angela come over?"

"Nah, I was trying to write."

"How'd that go?"

"Not too good."

Alex sniffed. "Christ, why don't you open a few windows," he said.

Will remained passive. "You don't look so hot yourself."

Alex yanked up the front window and muttered, "I almost got killed last night."

"Fuck, what happened?"

"I went to do a pick-up for Carlos, and these guys tried to drown me. Carlos set me up."

"Holy shit. Well, thank God you're alright." Alex ignored Will's attempt at empathy, and after a few tense seconds, Will continued. "Maybe it's the sign that you should get out of that fucking business. Take an acting class like you used to talk about." Those words also went unheeded and Will could sense the wheels turning in Alex's brain. "Look, I've got a meeting with the label this afternoon, so I gotta catch a few more hours of shut-eye." He turned to Alex before exiting the room. "I'm glad you're alive."

The lights of Bert's house shone a beacon from atop the cliff that bordered Stone Canyon. Fred swung the Lincoln Town Car onto the dark, winding road that led up the mountainside. Huey sat in back, his trusted bodyguard, Sonny, taking up the passenger seat with his massive frame. Huey had a sense that greater numbers on his side would make him more comfortable during the meeting.

Fred found the laneway that brought them to the house. A colorful assortment of sports cars amassed in the sprawling courtyard. Music and raucous laughter seeped through the curtained windows. When Fred rang the doorbell, a striking young mulatto girl with blue eyes, dressed like a servant, let them in without question. She pointed to the source of the uproar, and heads turned when the trio materialized in the large den, a more extravagant version of Bert's office.

Bert bounded from his chair to shake Huey's hand. "Glad you could make it. Everyone's been dying to meet you." He proceeded to introduce the rest of the party, among them Bob Richardson and a host of actors and writers that none of the new arrivals recognized. They acknowledged the others with courtly manners, all except Sonny, who took up a sentry position, statuesque, to the side. His shoulder-holstered .44 went unnoticed underneath his heavy black sweatshirt. A few people got up without being asked, allowing Huey and Fred to sit on the large, sectional sofa. Bert changed the record to Sly and the Family Stone's *Stand*. The coke was being partitioned when he returned to the circle, as if all had been waiting for Huey's arrival to break it out. Everyone did a bump, then Bert broke the wall of silence.

"We've got some ideas," he announced. Huey nodded as a sign to proceed. Bert passed a signal on to one of the writers, who launched into a rambling description of Oakland in the early Sixties, unconcerned with Huey's potential criticism of its accuracy. The character of Huey himself, along with his cohorts Bobby and Eldridge, was described as humble, yet determined to play the bad hand he'd been dealt.

Bob took over at that point, speaking with directorial authority. "We want to do it documentary-style, just like the Algiers movie you saw. I think it can work that way. We'll cast the lead roles, but you can use your own people for everything else. I'd like to shoot in Oakland, but if it's too tough, we can do it all here. I figure recreating the riots is going to be the hardest part."

After a few others had chipped in further ideas, Huey felt a genuine disconnection to everything that was happening. It wasn't until the budget question came up that they sought his opinion. "So, what you're saying is you can get started on this as soon as I start giving you some money?"

"Yeah, basically," Bert said. "The studios wouldn't want to touch anything like this."

"Have you asked them?"

Bert had his answer prepared. "I don't have to. The people who run these companies only know about you guys from the news." He paused before adding, "That's going to be the whole point of this movie, to open up peoples' eyes and minds to your struggle. This is gonna be a work of art that makes a lasting statement, like *Guernica*, or, uh, what was that other Spanish painting of the guy getting executed?"

"Goya," someone yelled.

"Yeah, I know he did it, but what was it called? Forget it. Doesn't matter. What I'm saying is, I've convinced everyone here that this is a project that needs to be done, and we're gonna do it."

"But how is anyone gonna see it if the studios won't put it out?"

"Huey, trust me, there's other avenues we can explore. If we play in the big cities where you're respected, word will spread. This thing's got cult hit written all over it. Then we take it to Cannes—"

Fred couldn't seem to keep himself from interjecting. "James Caan? Dude from *The Godfather*?" The room erupted in laughter.

"James Caan," Bert responded. "Yeah, that's funny. No, Cannes in France. It's a big showcase for the European market. They'll eat this thing up. Anything made in America that's subversive, they go nuts for over there. You'll be a big fucking star, and probably be able to make your money back within a year if we can do it for under a million. That's just for starters. This thing could make money for you for years to come if it turns out anything like I'm hoping it will." Bert looked around the room for support and received unanimous nods.

Huey paid close attention to Bert's self-confidence, maintaining regular eye contact—a good sign—while the concept of how to raise a million dollars rattled in Huey's head. It was easy to say, but hard to picture. Huey did a quick mental inventory of Panther assets: the drug operation, guns, clubhouses, vehicles, donations; it all had to add up to something close to a million. Maybe, if he excluded the organization's ever-present legal expenses. The only answer was to keep the coke coming. Supplying all of these Hollywood chumps was important, but to make real dough, the shit would have to spread further. He made a mental note to talk to Fred about that cousin of his. She'd gone way beyond the call of duty already, so she'd automatically draw the heat. As his scenarios started to spin out of control, Huey sensed the gathering waiting for him to say something. "If I say let's do it, what comes next?"

Bert sat back, relieved. "These guys will put a script together, and we can start doing some casting. Got any thoughts on who you'd want to play you?"

The question had not crossed Huey's mind, and his contemplation drew some nervous giggles, as if everyone else in the room had known for years who would star in their own life stories. "Honestly, I can't think of anyone."

"Don't worry about it. Just thought I'd throw it out there. It's probably better if we find some unknowns anyway. It'll give it a more realistic feel."

A few separate conversations flared up at that point, and names were thrown around. Bert remained fixed on Huey, and stood when Huey asked to be excused, gesturing to Fred and Sonny to come with him. Fred was visibly agitated as the young mulatto girl led the trio to the dining room.

"I don't know about this," Huey said. "I'm feeling out of my league with these guys."

Fred replied, "Man, they're giving you whatever you want as long as you pick up the tab. This is what you've been dreaming about."

"Keep your voice down motherfucker. Yeah, that's exactly what doesn't feel right about this. It's too easy. No one's ever gone to this much trouble to do anything for me." Huey lost himself in thought, then stared at Fred. "How have the shipments been?"

"Smooth as can be. Jessy's been takin' care of business."

"Why didn't you tell me she was back in town?" The perfectly timed bombshell finally shook Fred's composure.

"She, uh, she—"

"Come on man, I've got it on good authority that she's dancing in some dive on the Strip. Why isn't she in fuckin' Nevada?"

Fred took a breath, as he deliberated which version of the truth he should tell, his or Jessy's. "She couldn't hack it no more out there. She begged me to come back. What was I supposed to say? I feel like we owe her that much."

"Have you forgotten that she's public enemy number one? She gets a cop killer rap laid on her and we're all fucked."

"I know, believe me I know, brother, but she's got it under control. I trust her."

Huey scowled his disdain, before laying a comforting hand on Fred's shoulder. "Look man, you've done a good job so far. But you're gonna have to be completely fucking straight with me if we're gonna raise a million dollars. Ya dig? High gear. I'm probably gonna have to get personally involved. Get rid of the shit you're sittin' on. The next shipment is gonna be big. These ofays gotta see that I can walk the walk."

Fred nodded, and Huey strode back to the den. The chatter ceased. "I'll raise the money," Huey said, and a joyful exhalation altered the overall mood of the room. Bert rose to shake hands with his slender, manicured fingers. They could relax for the rest of the night, perhaps even get wrecked. Still, Huey knew his first thought the next morning would be that number rattling in his head. One million—easy to say, hard to earn.

Alex offered Will a half-hearted good luck as he left for the meeting. The desire for sleep overwhelmed him the instant he was alone. Before he took to his bed, Alex noted how Will had been rearranging the living room during his prolonged absences. Alex was conscious of disturbing its contents, but his room was still his room, and he toppled like a bowling pin onto the untouched bed. He awoke as the last rays of sunlight cast long shadows, and got up, groggy and hungry.

Alex walked the many blocks to Jessy's club, trying to focus his thoughts on her and not Carlos. But with each step, the picture of her in his mind was burned away by the compulsion to retaliate. He was not a violent person, despite what the drugs had often led him to believe. He'd come to the conclusion some time ago that he was a coward and a masochist, while convincing himself the drugs kept those failings hidden.

Still, Carlos must have taken him for an easy mark from the moment they met, Alex reflected as he walked. Alex's instincts were as sharp as they had ever been during the initial days after he and Will had arrived in L.A., and he shed his sheltered mid-western attitude in a hurry. The dream was laid out before him, tangible, and he made progress each day, pursuing every passing mention of an audition. He'd read the lines he'd be handed, and quickly became accustomed to rejection, but at each casting call he'd meet guys who taught him not to take things too seriously. Work was just a distraction from more important things like getting laid, something that seemed to come easily to every guy Alex encountered.

It didn't appear to interest Will, and Alex began associating with new companions who took him to Santa Monica and elsewhere, entire days often spent stoned on the best weed he'd ever smoked. It was real Acapulco Gold, not the impotent remnants the dealers sold back home. As Ohio kids, he and Will didn't know better. But as soon as Alex could tell the difference, he wanted all he could handle. He was told to get it from Carlos Montez, supplier to the stars, friend of the workingman. Alex called Carlos the first time from a payphone on the pier, saying he'd be willing to start dealing if it would give him a discount. It was a bold request; too bold to come from a cop. Carlos eased him in, with Alex digging into his savings to purchase his stash. It's an unforgiving business, the older man assured him. He said the same about the movies as he showed Alex his personal memorabilia, the posters bearing crude renderings of monsters, alien life forms and motorcycle gangs. Alex needed to know the secret.

"Could you tell me how to, uh, get my foot in the door?" It was a job like any other, Carlos explained, but his ambivalence couldn't sway Alex. He persisted until Carlos finally relented.

"I might need some help, if you're looking for something to occupy your time."

Within days, Carlos had Alex on a regular schedule of movie set drop-offs. At first, Alex didn't even think about what he was doing; being in the middle of the action raised his belief that eventually he'd get the break he desired. But when nothing materialized, Alex became more aggressive, seeking out actors directly, rather than the crewmembers that typically made the buys. When he expressed his frustration to Carlos, the older man consoled him by offering Quaaludes, and when those didn't work, heroin. By that point, Alex was becoming a familiar face within certain Hollywood circles, with his presence on some sets welcomed, and on others shunned.

The memories churned in Alex's mind as he got to Sunset. He tried to erase them with thoughts of what everyone back home would think of him now, going to meet his Black Panther stripper girlfriend to talk about the political bullshit that had entangled them. He recalled the old song Will often played about the blues killing a man by degrees.

Alex arrived at the club and settled into its aura of abject failure. Jessy was waiting tables, and Alex observed her from an inconspicuous corner. She took his order, returning promptly with a Jack Daniel's and soda. "What happened?" she asked, staying in waitress character. "I thought you'd be there when I got home last night."

"Things got ugly with Carlos." Just saying the asshole's name caused bile to rise in Alex's throat. "I can't talk about it here."

"Are you okay?"

"Yeah, I got some sleep, so that helped."

"I was worried. Something was telling me you were in trouble." Her tenderness caught him off-guard and erased some of the lingering bitterness. It also reconfirmed that she was the only thing he could depend on.

"Sorry, I should have called, but I was too out of it."

"Well, thank God you're okay. You gonna hang around?"

"Yeah, I need a few drinks."

"Alright, I should be able to get off early." He couldn't resist a glance at her ass bobbing in time to her stiletto-heeled steps as she departed. For the first time all day, he felt safe as he watched the dancer on stage, a petite brunette with ironed hair that reached her nipples. She could be from anywhere. He wanted to hear her story, to compare notes. Was she as confused and frustrated as he was?

A figure passed through his field of vision. It was Fred on his way to the bar. He stopped, waiting for Jessy to notice him. Alex observed them talking for several minutes until Jessy pointed him out and Fred approached.

"It's good that you're here," Fred began, after taking the other chair at the small table. "The movie's a go."

"That's great," Alex replied, unsure of how he should take the news.

"Yeah, we got these heavy dudes on board and they're gonna tell the story right." Alex was unnerved that he wasn't being thanked for his role in the deal, but realized the reason why as Fred continued. "We're still gonna need your help, though. Huey's making a huge score to pay for everything, and it's gonna be too much for me to handle by myself. I gotta ask you and your man to carry some of the load."

Alex hid his disbelief at the impossible timing of this request. "How much?"

"A few keys at least."

"Jesus. What's in it for us?"

"Ten per-cent," Fred said without missing a beat. Alex mulled the offer over, not knowing what the exact figure could be. All he knew was that it meant at least one more meeting with Carlos. The thought reignited his rage, but there was nothing Fred needed to know about that, not yet anyway.

"I'll see what I can do."

Fred leaned across the table. "Now listen here, you get things squared away by tomorrow and tell Jessy." Fred rose and whispered a final word in his cousin's ear before leaving the club. Alex hadn't moved, and Jessy brought him another drink, on the house.

"What was that about?" she asked.

"Looks like I've got more work to do."

"Pretty Messed Up"

You came here tonight and you don't know why
She ain't your type and you ain't her kind of guy
You shoulda turned and ran
Just in time to be too late
You're at the end of the line and you're gonna have to wait
To grab what you can

The train has left the station and the ship has set sail
It's a desperate situation, every plan has failed

You're thinkin' about all the excuses you gave
Now you're runnin' on empty with one foot in the grave
You ain't gettin' away

You come for the party but you don't wanna drink
You open your mouth but there ain't no time to think
You might as well stay

'Cause somewhere in this place, there's a girl that you been missin'
With lipstick on her face just like the last time you were kissin'
She was so pretty, pretty messed up

You're gonna follow the wind to where the weather's warm
You say it's all that you've wanted ever since you were born
You'll make it somehow
There's plenty of ways to catch an easy ride
But there's only one girl who will stay by your side
It can't be over now

'Cause somewhere in this place, there's a girl that you been missin'
With tears rolling down her face just like the last time you were
kissin'
She was so pretty, pretty messed up

Chapter 12

Hollywood Hills / May 1972

The music was foreign, its rhythms striking him as the same blue-eyed soul that everyone had been copying since Otis played Monterey. The bass player was too jazzy, taking unnecessary flights and walking all over the melodies. The guitarist showed off like he was John McLaughlin at a Miles Davis session. Will's own voice seemed to struggle for space against these outside forces trying to bury it.

He sat at the conference room table wedged between Jack and Lucas. Paul operated the reel-to-reel. "Remember Will, these are just rough mixes," he had said at the outset. "I wanted the guys to lay down something that we can work with. Try to listen with an open mind." Will did, for about the first minute, until all of his expectations slipped away. His hopes of capturing his ideal performance appeared unattainable, now that Paul was hell-bent on taking things in an unfathomable new direction.

Will couldn't bear to hear any more by the third song, but continued nodding whenever he felt someone's eyes upon him. In his periphery he could see Lucas tapping his fingers in time, and Jack listening stoically. Will's eyes held steady on Paul, who seemed lost in the details of the sound. Will wasn't prepared to give an honest answer when Paul stopped the machine and asked, "What do you think?"

Will's heart sank, but he forced himself to answer. "It's good. A lot of it, anyway." The others' silence urged him to elaborate. "I mean, some of those parts added a lot, but some things sounded a little strange. I guess I wasn't expecting you to do that much. Were those strings that I heard at one point? Man, I thought, okay, he'll put on bass and drums, maybe another guitar, and that'll be cool, but that was something else man. Yeah, that was something else."

Will trailed off, and Jack jumped in, exerting his naturally soothing influence. "We had to make a decision whether you're better suited to be an AM or FM artist. We love these songs, but the way you do them—" He paused in search of the proper description. "It's as if you're from another time and place. We felt like we had to modernize you a little bit, you know? Give the kids something they can relate to. Believe me, it's for the best."

The pronouncement wasn't a complete blow to Will's confidence, but he was unable to respond with any authority. "I understand this probably wasn't what you were expecting to hear," Paul interjected. "Like I explained, we're far from being finished, but these are the raw materials and I want you to be happy with it. Are you?"

Will shifted in his seat. "Yeah, sure," he shrugged.

"I'm not convinced."

The mounting pressure forced Will's frustration out. "I said it's fine. Look, you guys know more about this stuff than I do, so whatever you think is best makes sense to me."

Jack put a fatherly hand on Will's shoulder as he stood up from the table. "Remember, we want what's best for you. I've got to make some phone calls, so I'll let you guys finish up. It's gonna be a great record, Will."

Jack's departure took some of the tension out of the room. Paul filled the seat his partner had abdicated. "He's right. I know you're used to doing things in a simple way, and you can keep doing that when you play live. Actually, I think that'll give people two different perspectives on your music, which will probably excite the critics. This record is all about putting you in the same league with Dylan and the rest. You deserve to be there."

The bullshit was piling up, and Will was happy to let the matter drop. He had a few new songs ready to try out on them, but the mood of the room suggested it would have been a waste of breath. His real objection stemmed from the thought of how his granddad would have reacted to hearing what these stoned freaks had done to his songs. Could he have even comprehended it? Will kept returning to what Gene Clark had told him about Californians being unable to understand what the rest of America was about. Paul had produced a lot of hit records, Will mused, but did he truly get the stories I'm telling? Maybe I don't know either, and I'm too chickenshit to admit it.

Paul could see Will disintegrating in the leather office chair. "Hey, don't worry about this. Jack's right, people are gonna flip when they hear this record. Besides, you've got plenty of good songs. Trust us with this one, and you can do whatever you want on the next one. That's a promise." There was indeed something trustworthy about Paul, despite his unhealthy pallor, a result of too many days in recording studios and too many nights in clubs, although his work ethic was at odds with the general attitude Will had encountered within the scene. He saw compassion in Paul's eyes, but also something that suggested more to this arrangement than he had dared to imagine. The message seemed to be that the songs weren't relevant to the big picture. "This is how the business works, Will. You'll get used to it soon enough. Now, why don't you go out with Lucas for a drink, and he can tell you about other stuff that's going to happen."

Lucas touched Will's shoulder right on cue. Will turned toward the younger man, whose bright countenance reminded him of kids back home who made the rounds on Saturday mornings looking to mow lawns or wash cars for a few bucks. "Wherever you feel like going, it's on me."

"See what happens when you get an expense account?" Paul added, punctuating the comment with a playful jab to Lucas's midsection.

"I guess we'll go to the Troub," Will said. "That's where I feel most comfortable."

"Cool with me. We'll take my Mustang."

It was the car Will had long desired, and riding in one was the next best thing.

"You must feel like Steve McQueen in this," Will said to Lucas as he weaved through traffic toward Santa Monica Boulevard.

"Yeah, I was lucky to find a job that allowed me to get one of these. I'm sure you'll be able to get one too eventually. Maybe something even better."

Will spent the rest of the trip pondering that possibility, and felt at ease listening to the hum of the Mustang's engine. After arriving at the Troubadour and finding a table, Lucas excused himself to use the pay phone. "Thought I'd invite a friend to meet me after we have our little confab. Remember Cyndi? She was with me when I met you."

Will flashed back to that night a few weeks prior, and recalled the young pushy blonde who kept bumming cigarettes. "Yeah, I think I know who you're talking about," he said, unable to mask his disinterest.

Lucas changed the subject anyway. "You looked a little shell-shocked at the office."

"Yeah, that's fair to say. I didn't know this is how you made records."

"Well, I don't really know much about that either. My job is to make sure people hear them once they're done."

"When do you think that will be?"

"A couple months. But here's the big news. We've set up a tour for you to build some hype. I'm gonna blitz all the cities to get the press to come out and see you. If we get some good ink from that, the next thing you know, radio will be all over the record and you'll come back a hero."

Lucas went into detail for the next several minutes. It all made sense to Will, but he had to remind himself that he would be the one on stage each night. It was too surreal to imagine. "And here's the best part," Lucas continued. "I got Jack to agree to let you take the train. Isn't that groovy? I think that suits your whole vibe. It's gonna add so much to your image; you'll be like an outlaw blowing into town. I'll have the press there to meet you at each stop."

Will was still having trouble placing himself inside the picture Lucas was painting, but felt some relief in knowing he wouldn't have to do the cross-country drive again. "How far east will I go?"

"To Boston. All the major markets. You'll be back in three weeks."

"Is there a show in Cleveland?"

"Probably. I'll have to check. Why?"

"I'd like to see my family. They live nearby. I promised my mother."

"I'll make the arrangements." Something about Lucas's efficiency seemed condescending to Will, as if he wasn't a person but a product that Lucas was intent on selling.

That feeling began to wane as they sat drinking and making small talk for the next thirty minutes, waiting for Cyndi to arrive. When she burst into the bar, many of the regulars fought through their stupors to stare at her in her tight, striped mini-dress. She breezed by the oglers and took a chair beside Lucas, who said, "You remember Will, don't you sugar pie?"

She extended a long, slender hand, and offered a glittering smile. "Of course." Will took her hand, which appeared more delicate than he recalled. She slid it across his palm in the subtlest manner. "I hear you've come a long way since the last time we saw each other."

Something about her made it appear to Will that she had aged several years. "Yeah, I guess I have. What have you been doing?"

"Oh, making the scene, as usual." She nudged Lucas for emphasis, and he looked away in embarrassment. "Anyway, I can't wait to hear your album. Lucas tells me it's really great."

"Isn't it his job to say that?" Will's attempt at a humorous dig landed flat, prompting him to backpedal. "Yeah, I think it's turning out all right." He drank from his bottle of Bud. "What do you two have planned for tonight?"

Cyndi fluttered her big blue eyes at Lucas. "Well, I thought we might hit the Rainbow and then see what happens after that," he said.

Cyndi put both her hands on the table, as if she'd completely ignored Lucas's suggestion. "Let's go dancing at Rodney's! Will, come with us, it'll be a blast."

He gauged Lucas's reaction, but the younger man appeared non-committal. Will was in the mood for more drinks, as long as he didn't have to pay for them. "Feel like dipping into that expense account Lucas?"

"Sure, why not? That's what it's for."

Jessy heard a tinge of fear in Alex's voice for the first time. "Maybe we should lay off this shit for a while," he said.

"You serious?"

"Yeah. I've been thinking all day that it's starting to fuck me up."

"I'm surprised to hear that. You seem to enjoy it."

"Is that supposed to be funny? I mean it, I feel like I need to make some changes in my life, or—Jesus, I don't even want to imagine what might happen."

Jessy tried to rein him in. "This is about Carlos, isn't it?"

"Well, fuck, the guy tried to have me killed. What am I supposed to do, let it go?"

"You don't know for sure that was his intention."

"It doesn't matter. He doesn't want to take responsibility for anything anymore. I don't ever want to be in that position again. Step one is to clean up, and second is to free myself from that asshole."

"Step one is easier said than done."

"What do you mean? You seem like you can take it or leave it."

"I've been around it my whole life," she said. "At a certain point you figure out how to manage it, as long as you've got a good supply. See, you let Carlos pay you off with his shit, and that was a mistake. I wasn't about to say anything, though."

"Why not? I thought we were in this together baby? Why aren't you looking out for me?"

"Hey, I am, but don't forget I've got my own problems. Whatever arrangement you and Carlos have is none of my business. You know I can get you shit whenever you want it."

"You're right, I'm sorry. There's too much going on. I'm having trouble handling it."

"It's okay," she said. "We'll get through this. Listen to me, I'm gonna get clean with you. We'll do it together. Then everything will be alright and we can get on to doing the other stuff that needs to be done."

"You mean it?"

"Of course. Look, Carlos's cut of this big score will be ten per cent, right? Sounds to me like that would be enough for us to be able to get away from all this. You hear what I'm sayin'?"

"What about Fred? What about Huey?"

"They'll get their money. That's all they care about. They want me out of the picture as much as Carlos wants you gone. If I go to the slammer, their house of cards could collapse."

"What about the movie? I think it's a good idea. I was hoping to be a part of it."

"Jesus, you actually believe that they're gonna make that happen? All I know is when you see a chance to pull yourself out of a hopeless situation, you'd better fucking take it."

"Is that what you saw when you met me?" Alex was on the verge of tears.

"Come on baby, don't think that way. Maybe I did, but that hardly matters, does it? Look at what we've become."

"I don't know, what have we become?"

"Stop it. You said you want to change your life, right? Right?"

"Yeah."

"You want me to look out for you? This is me looking out for you."

"What about Carlos?"

"You gotta play it cool for a little while, just until everything is set up and we got that money in our pockets. This is a deal he can't refuse, and you gotta sell it to him that way. You understand?"

"I can't do it. I'll be too tempted to hurt him. It's gotta be somebody else. Fred, maybe."

"Okay. If that's how it's got to be, I'll set it up. Now come here baby. The next few days aren't gonna be easy, but I'll be right here. Whatever you need, I'll get it for you. We're gonna be fine."

Alex whispered, "Do you love me?"

"Sure I love you baby. Start thinking about where you want to go once all of this is over. I could see us in Florida. Or maybe Hawaii. That would be beautiful, wouldn't it baby?"

"Yeah, it sure would."

Will had heard about Rodney's English Disco, but everything about the place defied all of his expectations. He followed Lucas and Cyndi as the doorman waved them in. Seconds later, they were on the dance floor, being assaulted by Day-Glo spotlights and a raw pounding beat.

When he was able to catch Lucas's ear at the bar, he yelled, "Do you know this song?"

"It's T. Rex. They're the hottest thing in the U.K. right now. We tried to get them, but they signed with Reprise."

"Sounds really cool."

"Yeah, I know. It's part of a new trend over there. It's called glam rock—guys wearing make-up and dressing like chicks. You heard of David Bowie? He's gonna be massive over here soon too. I've tried to turn Jack and Paul on to all that stuff, but I guess they're still folkies at heart—no offence. I think they still feel burned for signing the MC5 and The Stooges. But it's obvious that this is the way things are going in music. Times are changing. Just look around this place."

"Maybe I should start wearing make-up."

Will directed his comment at Cyndi instead of Lucas, and she shouted back, "I'd be happy to show you how," before sipping her pink martini.

Lucas handed Will a gin and tonic as he watched Cyndi swaying to the sound, heedless of everything else around her. She belonged in this place, and soon approached Lucas with a silent command to get out on the floor. He turned to Will. "Come on, grab a chick and shake it up a bit."

"Nah. I've never been much for dancing. I'll be fine."

Lucas didn't put up any resistance when Cyndi pulled him into the crush of gyrating bodies. Will propped himself up on the bar and dug the spectacle when the DJ next spun The Who's "Substitute" at top volume. He caught glimpses of Cyndi amid the other mini-dresses. She moved effortlessly, becoming his high school fantasy made real. Will couldn't take his eyes off her, and his heart swelled whenever she glanced back at him. All that soon mattered were those split seconds when their eyes would lock, and if they held it too long, one or the other would smile coyly for transgressing the evident rules of the game.

It could have gone on all night for Will, but after another song, Cyndi and Lucas returned to the bar, breathless, ready for another round. "Looks like a lot of fun," Will said.

"Ooh, check out Mr. Musician over here," Cyndi chided. "Too cool to dance."

He fell for her in that instant, hard. He no longer cared what she meant to Lucas; there was something undeniable going on that was sweeping him away. "Maybe after another drink."

"Yeah, right. I know your type. Always want to be in control. I think it's time you let go a little bit. I'm going to the bathroom to smoke a joint, and I suggest you come with me."

Will looked at Lucas, but the music had muffled his exchange with Cyndi. "All right, let's go."

Cyndi grasped Will's hand and with her other hand she gave Lucas a be-right-back pat on the shoulder. She cut through the crowd and Will had to find his own path when she released her grip. She was leaning next to the bathroom doors when he caught up. "What's it gonna be, your place or mine?"

"I've never been in a ladies' room."

"No one's ever called me a lady. Quick, while there's no one around."

He hardly had a chance to admire the foreign pink decor before she pushed him into a stall and barred the lock. Cyndi giggled at the naughtiness of it all, nose to nose with Will. She produced a toothpick-like joint from an unseen pocket in her dress and asked Will for a light.

"Did you roll that?" he asked.

"Um, no. Why? Is it done wrong?"

"I can't imagine we'll get much from it."

"What if I told you Lucas rolled it?"

"Well, either he's a cheap bastard with his grass, or he's not as cool as he thinks he is."

"That's for sure."

"Which part?"

"Both."

Will lit the joint and sucked hard to draw something from it. He'd smoked nearly a third before handing it over. Cyndi tried her best as well. Smoke escaped her lips as she giggled and offered the joint back to Will. "No, keep it. You barely had any."

She took two more drags before leaning into his ear. "Are you gonna dance with me now?"

Will smoked what was left to the roach and tossed it in the toilet. "Sure, why the hell not?"

Cyndi purred "groovy," as she reached behind his back to unbar the door. He fell out of the stall, landing on his ass in full view of two girls checking themselves in the mirror. They resumed their work upon seeing Cyndi stumble out after him. Back on the dance floor, everyone was bouncing to the Raspberries' "Go All the Way." Cyndi maneuvered Will into a comfortable spot and placed her hands on his hips. She brought her mouth close to his ear. "I want you to come home with me."

He gently replied, "Pardon me?"

"I want you to come home with me. Tonight."

"You can't be serious." She grinned and nodded. "What about Lucas? He's driving. I thought the two of you were, you know—"

"I am whatever I want to be." She moved her hands up to Will's shoulders and sealed her proposition with an open-mouth kiss. He withdrew, convinced that Lucas was watching. He couldn't walk away from his good fortune, though. They kept dancing, in spite of Will's nagging fear that Lucas was about to blindside him.

He made a break for the bar as the next song began. "I need a drink."

She tailed him. "Me too!" He was relieved to find Lucas engrossed in a conversation with a fellow hipster.

Will ordered another gin and tonic for himself and a pink martini for Cyndi, who groped him without restraint. "Jesus, he's standing right there," Will hissed.

"Don't worry about it. Everything's cool."

Will drank, trying to appear nonchalant while losing himself in the music. The weed was impotent, just as he had suspected. Still, it had unleashed something within Cyndi. She was on the dance floor by herself, engaging with guys and girls alike. There was no way around it, Will thought, he had to play this situation out to the bitter end.

Lucas kept talking, as other regulars congregated at the bar. Will felt a jolt of resentment for being excluded, but assured himself that he didn't want to know who those people were.

Cyndi jogged back, coming to rest at Will's side and reaching across his body for her martini. She downed it in one gulp, saying, "We going or what?"

"I think you should ask the driver."

Cyndi threw herself against Lucas' back, cooing into his ear, "Can you take us home now?"

"Hey, I'm talking to some people here."

"This is a drag. Let's just go."

He looked to Will, who gave an apathetic shrug. "Alright, come on."

Cyndi sat between them in the Mustang. Lucas broke a tense silence by asking for directions to Will's apartment.

"Just go to my place," Cyndi jumped in.

"But I gotta drop Will off first."

"No you don't."

Will recoiled in his seat as a wave of guilt washed over him. All he could do to detach himself was stare out his window. To Will's relief, Lucas seemed to accept it as if it was a common occurrence, and silence reigned again as they drove to Cyndi's building near Griffith Park. She gave Lucas a peck on the cheek when they arrived. Will set aside his lust momentarily, replacing it with empathy toward Lucas over the damage Cyndi was wreaking on him. But as the Mustang pulled away, all of Will's anxiety went with it. Alone on the stoop, he wanted whatever was going to happen between the two of them to begin, but she said, "Let's take a walk over to the park."

Within ten minutes they reached a bluff overlooking a large portion of the famous L.A. landscape that Will had only seen in movies until that moment. He took it in as he sat next to her on a sheltered grassy patch. "I haven't forgotten how you treated me the last time we saw each other," she said, her tone now sober, but more reflective than accusatory.

He became defensive. "What do you mean?"

"When I saw you play at the Troubadour. At the end of the night. You were a total asshole to me, then you stormed out."

"I did?" He paused to consider his words, and opted for the easy way out. "Honestly, I don't remember. I must have been pretty hammered."

"Yeah, right."

"So why are you friendly all of a sudden?"

"I guess I wanted another chance to see if you really are an asshole. Haven't seen any signs yet."

"I'm sure Lucas thinks I am."

"Shit, forget about him. You don't want to know that story."

Will's curiosity got the better of him. "So there was something between you two?"

"I don't belong to anybody. I don't ever want to belong to anybody." Her declaration was a standard warning he'd heard before. "I don't want to have kids either. All these goddamn rules you're supposed to follow, it's just meant to keep people tied down."

An image of Janet flashed in Will's mind. "Well, it's good that you believe in something."

"Yeah, I guess. That and music. I could never be a musician, but I understand what you're all about."

"You know, I read something once that said music is the obvious proof that God exists."

Cyndi laughed. "Wow, that's one of the dumbest things I've ever heard."

"You don't believe in God?"

"No way. My parents were Jesus freaks. They tried to force me to swallow all that shit. Don't tell me you're one of them too."

"I suppose 'yes' is the wrong answer?"

"Funny, you don't look like one."

"That's because I'm not. I'm just wondering why it's such a big deal if I am."

Cyndi stretched out her bare legs, crossing them at the ankles, as she gazed at the sparkling city below. "It's because I get fed up hearing people talk as if they know everything. It's incredible how they can think that the universe was created by an old dude up in the sky."

"It wasn't."

"How are you so sure?"

"Would you believe me if I said I've seen His face?"

"No." Will was jarred by her outright rejection of what he'd said, but remained calm. She seemed to sense his simmering unease, and casually changed the subject. "It's so beautiful here, don't you think? This is my favorite spot in the entire city."

Cyndi moved on him then, their mouths inseparable except for brief gasps of oxygen. Her hands moved from his hair to his chest, trying to find an opening that would reveal flesh. He gripped her hips to keep her steady, his heart racing out of pure joy.

Her hands found the straining top of his jeans. She unfastened his belt and buttons, then dove inside, squeezing tightly. He fought to suppress his moans, but it was impossible once she had completely revealed him. She descended between his legs, working her tongue slowly. Her teasing sent tremors through his limbs, but he settled down as her mouth established a steady rhythm. He found himself unable to hold back, and at that moment she relented, sitting up and pulling off her dress in a single motion, before sliding herself down his shaft and emitting a sigh that stopped time.

It took only seconds for Will to explode inside her. They lay on their backs in the aftermath, staring up at the few stars that could be seen through the smog.

"Thank you." He knew before the words were out that they sounded self-serving.

"You're welcome," she replied. "Come on, it's starting to get chilly."

He observed everything with clarity not present when they first arrived. It didn't take long for her to compose herself. She appeared ready to go back downtown before last call, a prospect that terrified him. However, she didn't say anything on the walk back to her apartment, leaving Will wondering what she thought of him now.

It wasn't until they were in sight of her building that he considered what needed to happen next. "I guess I have to figure out how to get home."

"Oh yeah. I'd ask you to stay over, but my roommate's got friends here, and well, you know." He waved off her excuse, since spending the night wasn't an option. Still, he couldn't comprehend her sudden aloofness, and was struck by the notion that she had the entire encounter planned in order to get back at him for his initial crassness. "There's an all-night grocery store two blocks that way," she said. "You can call a cab from there."

All the joy Will had felt was completely drained as they stood facing each other. He studied her face in the shadow of the streetlight until she took a step forward and craned her neck to bring her mouth to his ear.

"I try to get them just before they become famous," she said, before turning and walking briskly to the front door.

Carlos was wary of showing his face on the street since suspecting Alex was spreading the word that he was peddling inferior shit. The batch of coke that Carlos managed to recover off the boat seemed fine to his taste, though. The Mexicans had remained in the harbor, as if what they'd done to Alex was merely bait. Carlos had left his .45 in the car, one of the hardest decisions he had ever made. He flashed a bankroll instead as he approached the boat, and no further words needed to be exchanged, apart from Carlos receiving a terse warning that his cousins back home expected him to do better.

That would only become harder with the Panthers cutting into his business. As he drove to Fred's Body Shop for their scheduled meeting, Carlos was consumed by thoughts that he'd be squeezed out somehow, most likely by Alex. The kid seemed desperate enough to risk his own neck in order to take control of the operation. This scenario churned in Carlos's brain as he waited in the Honda across from Fred's. A bus arrived in short order and Alex got off, moving with a keen sense of purpose. Carlos leaped out of the car to catch him before he reached the shop's door.

"Hey!"

Alex wheeled around and seemed stunned. "Jesus! Where did you come from?"

"Just got here. We should go in together."

"Yeah, good idea," Alex said coolly.

Their simultaneous arrival didn't seem to matter to Fred. Alex made the introduction and Fred shook Carlos's hand. "So this is the famous actor I've heard so much about."

Carlos deflected Fred's weak attempt at charm with a confident smile. "Yes, I am."

"Well, have a seat. I know you came to talk business and I appreciate that." Fred locked the front door, then the inner office door, although the ever-present sound of bodywork still bled through. "Okay, here's the deal," Fred said to Carlos. "We've got an agreement to make our movie, as long as we fund it ourselves."

"And by 'ourselves,' you mean the Black Panthers."

"You got it."

"Who are your partners?"

"Well, I'd rather not say. They prefer to remain anonymous with this project. I'm sure you'd know who they are though."

Carlos shot a glance at Alex, as his bullshit detector flew off the scales. Fred seemed to sense the rising tension between them. "I should have thanked you first for helping us get this far. You've been the reason that this is happening, and I'm glad to finally tell you that in person, on behalf of everyone."

"Get to the point."

Fred's face darkened. "All right, here's the fucking point. We gotta get this operation moving, so we're gonna have to bring up a whole lotta shit in one trip and get it on the street as fast as possible. Our young friend Alex has told me that you have the capability to do just that."

"What's my end?"

"Ten per cent, plus whatever you need for incidental costs. If all goes well, I can guarantee you at least fifty grand. On top of that, I bet you always wanted to be a movie producer. Well, here's your chance."

"What if I don't want to be a movie producer?"

Fred sat back and glanced toward Alex, as if he could explain Carlos' hostility. "Hey man, we got a good thing going. Believe me, you're already a hero within the movement. Sure, this is a major risk we're asking you to take, but you'll be rightfully compensated for it."

"Maybe I don't give a fuck about your movement," Carlos said. "You ever think that? Maybe I'd like to see all you niggers hang."

Fred stood up. Alex couldn't decide whether to restrain him, or protect Carlos. "So that's what this is about," Fred growled. "Name your price you spic motherfucker."

"I want a hundred grand, plus expenses. Alex and I can pick up the shit."

"We've already got that arranged and I'll be coming too. Not that we don't trust our good pal Alex."

"Fine. We got a deal?"

Carlos felt a rush from observing Fred visibly squirm while contemplating the offer. Carlos remained stoic until Fred blurted, "Alright, you'll get your hundred grand. And not a fucking penny more."

That was something, wasn't it? Was it everything you hoped it would be? I'm getting the feeling it wasn't. Caught you by surprise, huh? She had her way with you, didn't she? Man, it was a thing of beauty how she had you right from the start. I mean, when she fed you that bullshit about not wanting to belong to anybody— you should have seen your face! You should have known right then that this was a big mistake. Granted, you would have been an even bigger jackass to walk away. But it's like I've always told you, you're not man enough to do it without any strings attached. Now look at yourself, you're actually regretting it. It's better having things turn out this way than ending up like that Lucas chump, being there for someone like a fucking prop they use only when they have to—like an umbrella, or a walking stick? Oh, wait. Isn't that what Angela is to you?

Shut up.

Yeah, right. No point in bringing her up now when she could actually do you some good.

It isn't about her.

Then let me guess, it's that chick's thing about religion, right? How can a person be so spiritually empty? What made you so high and mighty all of a sudden?

I know God is real.

Just because you saw that white buffalo?

I didn't ask for any guidance, especially from you.

There's nothing you can do to shut me up. Right now you should talk to Angela. Don't forget you've got that tour they want you to do.

I don't think I'll be able to get through it.

I'll tell you this much, I'm sure she'd at least appreciate an invitation.

Yeah, you're right.

You know I am.

⟋

"Golden"

You said it's too soon to say goodbye
You said you're too afraid to fly
From where I stood, there wasn't a cloud in the sky
And when I think of you it's golden

Although you're gone I don't seem to care
'Cause what I wanted was never there
But still I dream of running my fingers through your hair
And when I think of you it's golden

I never thought I could be untrue
With all the things we used to do
Like sitting under trees with the light shining through
And when I think of you it's golden

Chapter 13

Ashtabula / June 1972

Will couldn't restrain himself from calling Angela first thing in the morning. He was certain she would call him anyway. Familiar lyrics became jumbled in his head—*By the time I dial the six, she'll be rising / She'll let it ring, and wonder if it's me*—as he reminded himself that this was about taking the initiative.

She answered on the eighth ring. "Hello?"

"Hi, it's me."

"God, it's nice to hear from you. I tried calling last night but you weren't home."

"Yeah, that meeting with the label ended up going long."

"Everything's alright, I hope."

"About as good as can be expected."

"That doesn't sound very encouraging."

"They've been doing some stuff to the songs. It's fine, but it's gonna take me a while to get used to it."

"Were you arguing about it? Is that why you were out late?"

"No, no, there wasn't any argument. Lucas wanted to take me out for a few drinks and talk about what he wants to do when the album comes out."

"That sounds more like it. What's going to happen?"

"I can't remember the details, but I've got to ask you something."

"Anything."

"Think you can get a few weeks off work?"

"Yeah, I've got some vacation time I haven't used. Why?"

"They want me to go on tour. By myself. Take the train to Boston and back. I need somebody to go with me. Or else I don't think I'll be able to handle it."

Angela's tone turned dreamy. "Of course, baby. I'm so happy you asked me. When are we leaving?"

"Next weekend. The first gig's in San Francisco."

"Oh, wow! I've always wanted to go. This is gonna be amazing."

She was talking like a schoolgirl, and Will hadn't expected her enthusiasm to get out of hand. "Look, I'm still trying to let it all sink in," he said. "We'll talk about it when I get the full schedule. Just let me know if you have any trouble getting the time off, okay?"

The spark in her voice was extinguished. "Okay. I'll quit if I have to. Maybe even kill my boss."

"Jesus, don't go that far," he said, trying hard to appreciate the joke.

"I was just kidding."

In a way, he knew she wasn't.

The ensuing days dragged on with bleak regularity. Will got into the unusual habit of answering the phone, knowing that it would be Lucas with information on the itinerary. After their first chat, during which Will was relieved the subject of Cyndi didn't come up, they managed to remain focused on the task at hand. Will told him he'd invited Angela to accompany him, and Lucas didn't question it. He seemed relieved to hear Will wouldn't require the added expense of a road manager.

Will had no desire to engage in any other social interaction aside from these calls. There would be plenty of that to come on tour. All he could do to prepare was play the songs—all of them—each day, over and over, until a logical running order emerged, like one long song that was impossible to forget. He often lost track of time as he rehearsed; when the living room took on an orange glow, it was a sign that he would soon have to turn on a lamp to see his lyric sheets. He was reminded of that day's date only when he read newspapers during daily outings for chop suey or a burrito. He convinced himself that this mundane repetition would come in handy on the road. It had to.

Then Alex turned up. Will barely heard him enter the apartment; his friend was a wraith, pale and gaunt, his jeans and t-shirt hanging on his limbs.

"You look terrible," Will muttered.

"So do you. I feel fine, though. How about you?"

Will had to think about it. "I'm alright, I guess. I'm going away for a while. On tour. Been getting ready for it."

Alex's response was muted. "Oh, that sounds cool. How long?"

"Three weeks."

"Funny, I'm going away myself for a while. Taking a little trip to Mexico." Will showed little interest, and Alex didn't say anything more about it. Will's next comment caught Alex's full attention.

"I'm gonna stop in back home. Have to tell the folks that I'm a big star now. Do you want me to tell anybody how you're doing?"

Alex paused and Will detected his friend fighting back tears. "If you see my family, you can tell them I say hello. And that I'm clean." Will hoped the admission was accurate, but Alex fled to his room before Will could probe any deeper. He thought of calling out to Alex, but couldn't detach from the mounting pressure of the tour.

Will returned to the sanctuary of his songs, and Alex trudged back to the living room within a few minutes holding a duffel bag packed to capacity. "I don't know if you heard me before when I said that I'm clean."

"I heard you," Will answered while playing some random riffs on the Martin.

"You know, Jessy has really helped me. I'm sure it's been bothering you that I've been spending more time with her than around here, but we're doing things that are going to turn both of our lives around."

Will kept strumming. "I'm really glad to hear that. I am."

Alex stood listening for several minutes before picking up his bag. "Take care of yourself out there," he said, reaching for the door.

"Yeah, you too. See you when I get back."

↙

San Francisco Chronicle – June 3, 1972
Latest L.A. Songster Aims For Simplicity
by Jim Clements

Last night saw the Bay Area debut of the latest participant in the current L.A. singer/songwriter sweepstakes, Will Mosley. The hugely hyped 24-year-old's first album for Elektra Records isn't due until the fall, and that showed in the sparse attendance for both of his hour-long sets at The Boarding House.

For those who had caught the word-of-mouth, they were treated to some fine, original tunes that evoked some of the down-home storytelling of Robbie Robertson. Of these, the best were "Angel Of Avalon," and "The Dying Soldier," which, like Robertson's "The Night They Drove Old Dixie Down," turned back the clock without veering off into a dull history lesson.

However, at other times Mosley sang with the confessional tones of his L.A. brethren, which overall provided a nice balance to his material. Talking to him between sets, Mosley admitted to still being a little shy on stage, but happy to be out on his first nationwide tour.

"It's all a big learning experience for me right now," he said. "I've been playing music for a few years, but this is really the first time that anyone's paid attention to me."

Mosley's self-effacing honesty in conversation seemed a logical extension of his musical approach. "I'm really not trying to be anything other than who I am," he says. "I'm actually from Ohio, and it's been odd to discover how many other guys in L.A. are from the Midwest. Maybe there's something about that that I miss and want to put into my songs."

No matter what the magic formula is, those who missed out on hearing Mosley this time should be ready to snap up his new album. It's too soon to tell, but judging by last night's performance, it may prove to be one of this year's best collections.

After a day on the train Will began to enjoy the scenery, at ease with Angela at his side. She had also settled down after the excitement of the first show wore off. The orchards along the tracks receded into the scrub of Nevada and Utah, places so barren that no songwriter had ever found any romance in them. They were both sleep-deprived—the club's hospitality had extended late into the night—but he was comforted that she hadn't felt the need to protect him. As Will fought his hangover, he felt envious observing Angela at rest, sedated by the hum of the train wheels. So far, she was displaying the wits and stamina to make sure they stuck to the itinerary. Yes, Will thought, it was the right decision to invite her.

He closed his eyes and leaned his head against the window, the sunlight warming his face. Even blind men know when the sun is shining, he mused, before slipping into a painless slumber. He awoke to discover the foothills of the Rockies looming on the horizon. His stiff neck was compounded by Angela's full weight pressed against him. He nudged her then navigated past to the bathroom. She was awake when he returned, deciphering their route on her map.

"Know where we are?" he asked.

"No, but it's getting late. We must be close."

The train pulled into Denver a half-hour later. A wild-looking hippie kid, the kind that seemed a vanishing breed in California, met them on the platform.

"Hey, I'm really looking forward to the show tonight," he said to Will, who sat in the passenger seat of the kid's cavernous Ford Fairlane station wagon. "We've been hearing a lot of great things about you."

"Thanks. That stuff's really out of my control. I'm just hoping that people dig what I do."

"Right, right. Listen, if you've got a minute when we get there, I was hoping you could talk a bit for a story I want to do for the campus paper. I'm taking anthropology, but I'm kinda the music critic around here too."

"Cool. Yeah, sure, whatever you want to do."

"Right on. I really appreciate it." The kid went on at length describing the town for the rest of the ride. Will tried to appear interested, but became fixated on what he might reveal in the interview. He eventually had to interrupt the kid's monologue.

"Hey, I just realized that you haven't heard my songs yet. You still want to do an interview?"

"Yeah, it's fine. I figured I'd just ask some general questions, then I'll tie it all together after I see the show." The wagon turned onto the fortress-like grounds of the campus a few minutes later.

Arts Section, University of Colorado (Boulder) Campus Press, June 5, 1972
Will Mosley Comes to Play, Not Protest
by Craig Hoyle, music reporter

The few who attended Will Mosley's gig at Macky Hall on Saturday night know who he is now, but I still have to assume that most of you don't. That's likely to change in a few months once his debut album hits the streets and launches the L.A. native into the growing ranks of "the new Dylans."

Whether that's something that appeals to you or not should be irrelevant, as most of Mosley's songs—as evidenced by how he held the small crowd in the palm of his hands for over an hour—possess their own unique, magical qualities. Safe to say, it was a thoroughly enjoyable show, but I was more interested in getting to know Will Mosley, the man, for the benefit of all of you who will undoubtedly be digging his music shortly on your turntables.

CH: Judging by what your label is saying, you're the next big thing. How does it feel?

WP: Well, I don't necessarily agree with that. I'm just hoping that people enjoy what I do.

CH: So you're saying that it's all hype?

WP: I don't know. I guess I'm just learning what hype is. I'd never heard of it until I moved to L.A.

CH: Do you feel that your music is filling the void left by Dylan?

WP: I've never thought about it that way. I mean, I like Dylan a lot, but I've never believed I have anything in common with him.

CH: So you wouldn't call yourself a protest singer?

WP: No, not at all. I guess, if anything, I've only tried to be as good a storyteller as Dylan is.

CH: What's your view on the war in Cambodia?

WP: (Long pause) I'm not sure what to say to that. I obviously think it's time we got all our guys out of Vietnam, if that's what you mean. I don't know what's going on in Cambodia.

CH: Were you eligible for the draft?

WP: Actually, no. I went to Kent State for a while.

CH: Really? Were you there when the massacre happened?

WP: No. That was just after I left. I was in California by then.

CH: What did you think when you heard about it?

WP: Well, I was sad, of course.

CH: Did it inspire you at all?

WP: Not really. I think Neil Young summed it up better than I ever could.

CH: What does inspire you?

WP: Well, like I said, I just try to write simple stories about ordinary people. Sometimes they're about me, but mostly I think that the concerns we all have today are the same as they were fifty or a hundred years ago. As you can tell, I'm not really up on current events anyway.

CH: What's your position on legalizing drugs?

WP: I can't really say I have one. I think people should be allowed to take whatever they want as long as it doesn't make them hurt someone else. I mean, certain drugs definitely cause bad changes in people, so maybe they should be illegal. I haven't tried everything, so I can't say for sure.

CH: Is there any message that you're trying to get out to people?

WP: Not that I know of. This tour I'm on is really the first time I've played for people outside of L.A., so I'm just hoping to get through it in one piece. If it helps to get people excited about my record, all the better, because I'm really proud of it. I'm happy to leave messages to other people.

CH: Thanks Will, and good luck.

WP: Much obliged.

There you go, not the most exciting guy in the world, but don't worry, I'll save you a seat the next time he's in town.

Chicago was overwhelming. Will got off the train at Union Station looking like a refugee after some improper sleep. Angela was frayed as well, but riding a rush of accomplishment in getting him through the first days of the tour without incident, but navigating a major metropolis sent her maternal tendencies into overdrive. She inventoried their belongings as they waited for a ride to the gig. After ten minutes, none was forthcoming, and she anxiously scanned the itinerary for a clue. All it showed was the club's name and address.

"I guess we'll have to take a taxi," she sighed. "Oh God, you look so tired." He was propped up on his guitar case, with his head resting on his folded arms. He could only respond by raising his eyebrows and giving a weak nod. "You didn't sleep at all, did you?" His head moved side to side. She got behind him, threading her arms between his torso and the guitar case. She held him as everything around them remained in constant motion.

✔

Chicago Sun-Times, June 7, 1972
Young Singer Is a Fresh Voice In Folk
by Peter Walker

The Earl of Old Town has hosted its share of famous artists over the years, not to mention launching Messrs. John Prine and Steve Goodman in more recent times. It wasn't surprising then that, based on such a track record, the regulars were enticed last night to check out the unknown Will Mosley, said to be the next great west coast troubadour. Although his first album on Elektra Records is not due to arrive until the end of summer, he is already on the road giving audiences a preview, or at least attempting to prove that he can live up to the praise that some have already heaped upon him.

However, Mosley appeared like an ordinary denim-clad kid when he ambled on stage with just his acoustic guitar. The respectably sized crowd seemed to surprise him. Before he played a note, he remarked, "Wow, you can't all be here to see me," which elicited some supportive cheers in return. That set a positive tone for the rest of the evening, as Mosley ran through songs, presumably from the album, for the next hour, most of which echoed classic folk music themes of heartbreak and loss.

At times he clearly drifted, yet Mosley remained engaged overall and the audience responded in kind. Even the aforementioned Goodman was spotted giving his enthusiastic approval. Mosley's naivety surfaced again when he was called back for an encore and blatantly claimed that he didn't know any more songs. At someone's loud suggestion of doing something by Hank Williams, Mosley tentatively attempted "I'm So Lonesome I Could Cry." Unsatisfied by ending the night with that, he announced, "Here's one for a friend back in L.A.," and performed an unusually moving version of The Byrds' "I'll Feel a Whole Lot Better," to rapturous applause.

While still rough around the edges, Will Mosley showed that he has boundless potential and may shortly become an important new voice in folk music.

He grew depressed about the little things. Chiefly, the fact that she was dressing in the same manner as he was every day. Jeans, t-shirts, and sneakers had replaced the mini-skirts, half-buttoned blouses and high heels that he was used to seeing, the stuff that never failed to arouse him, no matter how much she ordered him around. They shared a different kind of closeness now, a product of her new role. He caught himself deferring to her in almost every situation, and it was easy. By Detroit, he needed a shield. Sleep remained hard to come by, causing the radio and press interviews to be terse, unflattering affairs. He didn't need to be told that he had to rally his spirits for New

York, but she told him anyway as the train made more frequent stops in the industrial heartland.

"Remember when you asked me that one time if this was the real America," he said hazily somewhere in Pennsylvania, while transfixed by the rotting structures and endless acres of haphazardly stored waste that crept up to the tracks. "There it is, if you want to see it."

"What do you think about it?" she asked, looking at him instead of out the window.

"I really don't know anymore."

She made him sleep after the Philadelphia gig, declining an invitation from their host to see the Liberty Bell the next day. Instead, she called Lucas and got the label to pay for a hotel room.

"I thought you guys would have begged for this sooner. I'm impressed," Lucas said, his voice clipped over the long-distance line.

"I figured you'd want Will at his best for New York."

"You're a smart girl, and you're doing an excellent job. Try to call me more often."

They slept in separate beds. In the morning, Will was serene, but felt a distance creeping over him. They each had the hotel's continental breakfast, and the artificial environment led to their first casual conversation in days. "I used to fantasize about living in a hotel when I was a kid," she said, scooping wedges from her grapefruit. "I don't know where it came from. Maybe some book my parents read to me. I imagined it would be like a big playground. You could do anything and there would be someone there to clean up after you. And then all the guests arriving all the time, dressed so elegantly. I wanted that—this—to be my world." He picked up what he thought was a subtle suggestion. He himself was getting sick of spending nights on the floors and sofas of strangers. Angela finally asked bluntly, "Do you want to stay in a hotel in New York? Lucas said it would be okay."

Will didn't want to feel entitled to any of it, because he knew he wasn't. "Well, if it's fine with him."

He sipped his coffee, observing the lunch crowd steadily filling up the lounge. He felt like an intruder, snapping out of it when he saw her looking as if she had transformed into her ten-year-old self. "You know, it's alright to act like a star a little," she purred. "When are we going to get a chance to live like this again?"

The idea repulsed him. Was this the best he could hope for? An anonymous room, and bland, overpriced food? He lit a cigarette and rolled his eyes. "I'm not a star. Never will be."

Her smile didn't waver. She clearly had a different opinion.

The Village Voice -- *June 15, 1972*
Will Mosley, The Bottom Line, June 12
by Richard Finkle

While we may be fortunate to still call ourselves the home to many of the country's best singer-songwriters, the recent upsurge in talent coming from L.A. has threatened to put us all under its laid-back spell. Will Mosley is the latest gentrified rustic to break away from the denim hordes, but (thankfully) he's not just another Jackson Browne.

That was the general expectation Monday night at The Bottom Line for his New York debut, a rather over-inflated event, considering his record label, Elektra, isn't putting out Mosley's first album for another few months. Why? Who knows, but if it's anything like Mosley's hour-long set, it couldn't have been hard to produce.

The reticent young artist took the stage without any fanfare, and responded to the smattering of applause with only a meek hello. But by his third number, an impossibly ancient-sounding original ballad entitled "The Ohio Valley," all preconceived notions could be tossed aside. I hesitate to use the word "authentic" to describe Mosley, because in today's commercialized post-Woodstock music world, everyone understands that they have to play the game to some degree.

Yet, despite the talk that has slowly been building up around him, Mosley truly appeared unaffected by it all. A few times, he even looked distracted between songs, as if momentarily losing the thread of some overarching story he was trying to tell. It was at those times that a palpable feeling spread throughout the audience to help him recover, just to maintain this unanticipated experience they had all more or less stumbled into.

Contrary to this description, Mosley didn't need much help to right himself, and certainly didn't ask for it. By the end of his set, it was like we were watching a kinescope of some previously unheard folk singer who would vanish back into the mists of time the second he left the stage. Mosley's eventual exit wasn't quite as dramatic, as he was brought back for two encores, the last being his only recognition of any contemporary influence, a version of Tim Hardin's "Black Sheep Boy," dedicated to "an old friend back home."

It's hard to believe that Mosley has packed so much living into so few years, and hopefully his album has managed to capture at least a fraction of it. If every show he plays is as moving as his Bottom Line appearance, he may soon seek out a less demanding line of work.

Attn: Lucas Finch / Elektra Records PR, Los Angeles CA
From: Linda McLean / Elektra Records NYC
Re: transcript of Will Mosley interview on WBCN Boston, 6/13/72

[Announcer]: OK, we're back, and as promised we've got a special treat here in the studio. A young man from L.A. on his first cross-country tour, Will Mosley.

[WM]: Hi, great to be here.

[Announcer]: Well, we're glad you could drop in. You're performing at Oliver's tonight, right?

[WM]: Yeah, that's right.

[Announcer]: And this is your first time in Boston?

[WM]: Yeah, I've been on the road for, I guess, a couple weeks now, and it's been amazing to see all these places I've never been before.

[Announcer]: Now, I should say that most people out there are probably wondering who you are. I understand that you've just made your first record, but it won't be out for a while.

[WM]: Yeah, I'm doing this tour to sort of introduce myself to people and hopefully get them familiar with some of the songs.

[Announcer]: How's that been going so far?

[WM]: It's been great. I mean, I didn't expect a lot of people to come out, but every audience has been really nice.

[Announcer]: So how would you describe your music for anyone who might want to see the show tonight?

[WM]: Well, I suppose I'm not doing anything out of the ordinary. I just try to write songs that tell interesting stories.

[Announcer]: Who are some of your influences?

[WM]: I actually like a lot of old, obscure country and folk singers. I don't really listen to much current stuff.

[Announcer]: So you wouldn't say that you're part of the current scene in L.A.?

[WM]: I guess not. I mean, I'm friends with some of those guys, but I've never felt like I fit in anywhere I've been. Maybe that'll change when the record comes out, but mostly I just stick to doing my own thing.

[Announcer]: Alright, well why don't you give everyone a sample of what that is right now? This is Will Mosley live on WBCN.

[WM performs "Angel of Avalon"]

[Announcer]: That was beautiful. Is that going to be on the album?

[WM]: Yeah, that one's called "Angel of Avalon."

[Announcer]: And what's it about?

[WM]: Well, pretty much just what it says. It was a story my granddad told me one time that stuck in my head.

[Announcer]: Fantastic. Well, unfortunately we're running out of time, but thanks so much for coming in Will. Once again, it's Will Mosley at Oliver's tonight starting at 10 p.m. Normally we'd play one of your records, but since you don't have any yet, is there anything you'd like to hear?

[WM]: Um, yeah, maybe some Van Morrison would be nice.

[Announcer]: No problem, we've always got Van handy. Here's "Into The Mystic," and stay tuned for news at the top of the hour.

⟍⟋

Whenever he drove home from Cleveland, either with his family or by himself, there was a sign on the highway that told him he was close to Ashtabula. The huge, billboard-like monstrosity on top of a bluff beside the Interstate advertised Mosley's Meat Products. All of Will's friends assumed that was his family's business, although it wasn't true. He may have been distantly related to the company's founders, but there was no point in speculating; his friends would believe what they wanted to believe. What affected him most about the sign, though, was the woman's face, which provided a human touch. She was the company's trademark, likely conceived in the thirties or forties, judging by her features. There she was, forever providing a beacon with her enigmatic smile, Mona Lisa-like in its own wholesome, midwestern way. As he grew to recognize the important role she played in his life, Will began wishing that they did share some relation. She was too precise to be a mere artist's rendering. It was a family company, so perhaps she was the owner's daughter or niece, singled out for her obvious beauty, and eager to put her face in front of millions of eyes out of sheer loyalty.

But Will wasn't going to see her as the train crept toward Ashtabula. The tracks were laid on the north side of town, closer to the factories along the shore of Lake Erie, and far away from the Interstate where his distant relative kept her watch from the billboard. She was not going to witness his homecoming, and the more he thought about it, the more it saddened him. It could have also been the rain. A steady late-spring downpour had blown in over the lake, streaking the train's windows and marring the view of other landmarks he was curious to observe and point out to Angela. She seemed pensive about their imminent arrival, still flipping through a fashion magazine that she'd finished reading the day after buying it in New York. She had asked Will if his parents would be in Cleveland to see him play the last show of the tour, but he'd merely shrugged, and the night unfolded like all the rest. Although anticlimactic following the previous gigs, Will was on familiar turf and didn't need to rely on her encouragement. The small crowd loved him, and that appeared likely enough to get them back to L.A. unscathed.

Still, Will was unsure if it was enough to get them through the meeting that was about to take place. When he saw his parents sheltering beneath an awning on the platform, they appeared noticeably older. Will fumbled with his guitar case and bags, and neither of his parents moved to help him, nor did they react to seeing Angela. They stood side-by-side, immobile, waiting for their son to approach. Angela kept close, seeming terrified at what might transpire after they set down their baggage.

Will's mother spoke first, a choked welcome, and extended her arms for an embrace that Will weakly reciprocated. "And who's this?" she asked after letting go, her face vibrating in an effort to hold back tears.

"This is Angela. Angela, this is my mom and dad."

Will's father kept shifting from one foot to the other. "Why don't we get the hell out of this rain?" No one dared to challenge him. They followed his lead through the empty station to the parking lot where a light blue Crown Victoria sat on its own.

"New car?" Will was proud that his parents' lives had carried on in his absence.

"Yeah. Traded in the Buick," his father replied. "The Olds still running?"

Will felt some common ground being restored. "Actually, yeah. I've tried to take care of it like you said."

"Good. She always was a reliable set of wheels."

Will and Angela settled into the plush back seat. He wanted more than anything to start telling her about the old neighborhoods, but couldn't think of how to include his parents in the conversation. Instead, silence permeated, until the car slid into the driveway.

Inside the house, Will's mother stated, "We didn't know you were bringing someone. I wish I could have been better prepared. Angela, I hope the guest bedroom will suit you. Will, your room is just how you left it." Angela flinched at the thought of them making any sort of fuss over her, and followed Mrs. Mosley up the stairs with her bags. Will and his father stood in the kitchen, together for the first time in two years.

"So, big shot, she's your L.A. girlfriend?"

"No. She's just helping me out on this trip. I didn't want to travel alone."

"I bet you didn't."

"Jesus, Dad. Do you have to?"

"Well, what do you expect me to think? You take off, and we barely hear a word. You won't even talk to me. What the hell did I do that was so bad?"

Will took a deep breath, his absent years dissolving at the sight of the same kitchen utensils hanging on the wall, and the same spice containers sitting on the counter. "I know, I'm sorry. It's my fault. I figured you were disappointed in me."

Mr. Mosley stared hard at his son, and Will sensed the old man had thought for a long time about what this moment would be like. Will steeled himself for a blow to the head, but his father stood before him, humbled in a manner that would have been unimaginable before Will had left. He wrapped his arms around his son, saying quietly, "Don't feel that way, Will. It's good to see you."

They let go of each other at the sound of Angela coming down the stairs. Noting her presence, Mr. Mosley said, "Mrs. Mosley should probably start getting dinner ready. We can get to know each other better then." At that, Mr. Mosley ducked out of the room.

"I think we're going to take a walk around the neighborhood, Dad," Will yelled after him. "We'll be back in a bit." Will didn't wait for a response. The rain had receded into a fine mist, giving the houses on the street an identical ambience. He led Angela in the direction of the high school, as if it were still the center of his universe. He wanted her to see everything through his eyes, and somehow convey what the rundown corner stores and empty playgrounds meant to him.

"You're sorry you came back," she said.

"I would have had to sooner or later."

Will suddenly saw that there was nothing unique here to any kid's upbringing. He anticipated seeing friends every time he turned a corner; they might have still been in town, but he didn't really care to know. Alex's absence was most palpable, causing Will to feel even more like a stranger with Angela in tow. She barged into his thoughts, asking, "Where are we going?"

They were close to Replay Records, as good a destination as any. Jimmy, the owner, was stunned to see them. "Holy shit, I don't believe it! He walks in here out of thin air. I must be seeing things."

The reception instantly lightened Will's mood. "Had to make sure you're still teaching the kids about the devil's music, Jimmy."

"I've been hearing about this kid who just signed with Elektra. Wait, don't tell me you're playing around here?"

"Yeah, we were in Cleveland last night. It's been crazy. I don't feel like I'm ready to be doing this stuff yet."

Will finally caught a glimpse of Angela standing off to the side. "Oh, Jimmy, this is Angela. She's been helping me with the trip."

"Nice to meet you. So when's this record coming out? I wanna put it all over the store." Jimmy turned to Angela. "I can't believe he used to come in here all the time just to listen to stuff and read magazines all day. Now I'll be playing his record for everyone else and making him rich. Just doesn't seem fair." They all laughed, until the pull of Will's new life dragged them back into the present. "How long are you here for?" Jimmy asked.

"Just came in to see my folks, then we're heading back west tomorrow."

"Jesus. Well, I'm glad to get a few minutes with you anyway. For fuck sakes, why don't you call me and tell me what's happening? You know it means a lot."

"Yeah, I know Jimmy. I'll keep in touch better from now on."

Several customers came and went, but Jimmy paid no heed. He continued to pepper Will with questions about L.A. and musicians he had met, as Angela stood by and admired the scene.

"God, I'm sorry Jimmy, but my Mom's making dinner and we'd better get back."

"Sure. I'll send you my review of the album."

"I really hope you do. Look, do me a favor."

"Anything."

"When the records come in, drop a copy off at my folks' place." Will scribbled down the address.

"No problem Will. You take care of yourself."

"You bet. Maybe you could come out to see me sometime."

"Yeah, maybe."

They shook hands vigorously and Will ushered Angela outside where twilight was descending. "They'll probably think I took you somewhere to make out," he said to her as they walked.

"What's wrong with that?"

He gave her a quick peck on the cheek. "I guess seeing Jimmy made it all worthwhile," he said, as if finally providing a sufficient answer to her question of how he felt about being home. "There's only a few things left here that mean anything, and that store is definitely one."

"What about your folks?"

He didn't respond until he saw the porch light that somehow shone brighter than the others on the street. "I'm not coming back after today."

Coal Porter Blues

Shovel in another load of coal
I heard the engineer say
If we don't get there by morning
They're gonna lock us both away
Don't let me catch you drinkin'
Or trying to get some sleep
And tomorrow night I'll guarantee
You'll get a midnight creep

I leaned into my shovel
And I dug into the coal
My back hurt like the devil
And a shadow crossed my soul

No one could hear me holler
No one could hear me moan
As I thought about the girl I left
Waiting all alone

The train it kept a-rollin'
And my tears began to flow
As I leaned against the window
And watched the morning glow
As we hit the city limits
The whistle blew its sound
And if I had my way right then
I'd-a turned that train around

Chapter 14

San Miguel / June 1972

*A*lex and Carlos arrived at the pier ahead of the agreed upon meeting time, an hour before dawn. They left the Honda in the empty parking lot and walked toward the launches. Identical boats were moored at each, and swaying masts provided the only noticeable movement in the darkness. The pair was drawn toward sounds of preparation on a 40-foot cabin cruiser, and the noise ceased as they got halfway up the wharf, prompting Carlos to shoot a look of concern toward his partner. Alex called out, "Ahoy," and a flashlight lit up, followed by a voice that beckoned them aboard. The light shifted to illuminate the small gangway.

The captain emerged, a bearded fireplug of a man, who could have been mistaken for someone stepping off a ship at Ellis Island a hundred years earlier "You must be my crew. I'm Murray. Get yourselves squared away down below. I'm almost ready."

"Nice boat," Alex said.

"Yeah, she's a beaut, ain't she," Murray replied from the cabin. "I sold it to our film producer buddies last year, but they decided to keep me as captain whenever they want to take her somewhere. It's a nice arrangement. I still enjoy being out on the water."

Carlos entered the cabin and asked, "Have you been to this place before?"

Murray was checking the instruments, seemingly oblivious to Carlos's presence behind him. "Yeah, we've been to San Miguel a few times. It's a nice trip."

"I just want to make sure you understand why we're going," Carlos said. "This isn't a fucking pleasure cruise."

"Look, Bert explained it all to me," Murray said, remaining focused on the task in front of him. "Everything's taken care of."

"I wish someone would have explained that to me," Carlos replied, visibly irritated. "You'd just better get us back with the fucking cargo, 'cause if any shit goes down, I won't be responsible."

Murray took Carlos's outburst in stride and offered him coffee from a large Thermos. Within a few minutes, Carlos heard footsteps on the dock. Cup in hand, he leaned out of the cabin and saw Alex giving Fred a hand to come on board. If Murray looked out of place on the boat, he was an old salt compared to Fred, who, clad in his Panther garb, took great care with each shaky step.

"Some fucking crew," Carlos spat out as the four stood on deck.

"You ought to watch that talk, or this is gonna be one unpleasant little adventure," Fred responded, placing a hand under his left arm, where he kept his .38 Special.

Murray appeared unfazed by the simmering tension and took command. "Well, we're all here," he said. "Let's shove off."

Fred went below and Carlos took up a position alone at the stern, leaving Alex standing next to Murray. "I guess you're my first mate," the captain said. "Help me untie the moorings."

The vessel glided out of the inner harbor as the dawn's first rays sliced along the shoreline, draping the Hollywood Hills in amber.

The sun was scorching by noon, tempered by the sea breeze, the passengers lulled into a tranquil state none were used to on land. With Murray at the helm, the trio lounged shirtless in the cockpit. All sets of eyes were hidden by aviator shades, and empty cans of Miller High Life were tossed into the ocean with regularity. Mid-afternoon, Fred lit a joint that Carlos accepted with some disdain. Fred responded, "Relax man, this'll be a milk run." Carlos nodded, unsmiling, taking a deep toke before holding the joint out to Alex.

Alex paused to observe the thin line of smoke trailing up from Carlos's fingertips. Something inside him reacted violently to the notion of getting high, and he surprised himself by brushing away the joint with a weak flick of his wrist. Carlos passed it back to Fred without shifting his gaze from Alex. "What the fuck's wrong with you?" Fred asked, and expelled a cloud of smoke through his nostrils. "You afraid we're gonna get busted out here?"

"I'm trying to stay clean," Alex stated. He paused before reassuring himself, "I am clean."

"Well, isn't that something," Carlos said. "You're finally taking my advice. No wonder you look like a piece of leftover fish. What brought this on all of a sudden?"

Alex looked at Fred, aware he was about to speak of the man's cousin. "It was Jessy who convinced me." Fred looked up, passing the joint to Carlos.

"She got you clean, huh?" Fred seemed unconvinced. "What about her? She ain't said nuthin' to me about getting clean."

"I asked her to help me. What she does is her own business."

"Things better stay that way too."

Alex felt defensive. He hadn't wanted to bring up Jessy's name during the entire trip, and now that he had, he knew it was a mistake. But thinking of her reminded him that he had to keep Carlos and Fred from killing each other, and if that meant letting them gang up on him, then he would have to deal with it.

Alex watched the two of them finish off the joint, and attempted to read their motives throughout the exchange. Both wanted the money for different reasons, but as soon as Carlos got his, Alex knew he'd likely do something dangerous to cut ties between them for good. Fred wanted the Panther movie made, and as far as Alex could tell, couldn't care less what Jessy did after that. She and Alex knew their ultimate goal, and he knew not to let that out of his sight. "I'm going down for another beer," he said. "You guys need one?"

"Of course, my little cabin boy," Carlos replied, his bloated body at ease. Alex thought of staying below after pulling three cans from the cooler. The space had a secure, homey feeling that beckoned him to sleep. They each had individual bunks, but Murray assured them that they would arrive at their destination before the following dawn. Alex tramped up the stairs into the late afternoon light to find both Carlos and Fred drowsing. He set the beers beside them, unopened, and went to see the captain.

Murray wasn't doing much beyond keeping the boat moving at a steady clip in the calm waters. He cast a noble figure, even with his slight frame. Alex stared out at the ocean before them, and for several minutes tried to see what Murray might be seeing.

"Never thought I'd do something like this," Alex said.

"Pretty gorgeous, isn't it?" Murray spoke as if his thoughts didn't dwell on anything beyond his charted course. That illusion was erased in short order. "Look, I'm doing this as a favor to Bert, and I don't wanna stick my nose in where it don't belong, but—" Murray was momentarily distracted by something miles ahead that could have been nothing. "You guys don't seem like you have any reason to be together other than, I don't know, business."

Alex sensed worry in the small man's voice, and spoke with an acknowledgement of the trust that had been established during the brief time they'd known each other. "That's fair to say," Alex replied, without adding anything further.

"Bert told me what this is about, so I know what I have to do to come through on my end of the deal. I don't mind telling you that Bert and I have set up stuff like this before, and part of the bargain is that I do the heavy lifting." He fell silent, checking the gauges and making mental calculations. "I'm prepared for a lot of eventualities. I guess what I'm wondering is, should I expect something … unexpected?"

Alex kept his eyes trained on the vast stretch of ocean as he listened. His growing fatigue made Murray's words sound like they were coming from a far off place. It took Alex a long time to respond, as he once again questioned his purpose for being on the boat. But Murray's candidness had won him over. "I don't think you need to worry about anything. If there's trouble between those two, I'll handle it." Alex's words drifted into the wind and he fell into a trance brought on by the endless blue and green vista. "I think I'll take a nap," he said after a few minutes. Murray remained impassive, showing no signs of fatigue as his hands gripped the wheel.

Carlos scrounged in the cooler for a sandwich, rousing Alex out of what had been a satisfying sleep. He raised himself to a sitting position on the cot, catching a glimpse of Carlos's doubled over hairy torso. Carlos produced a wedge of salami and cheese, sniffing it like an animal before stuffing it all in his mouth. Seeing Alex awake, he spoke as he chewed. "Man, you should see that sunset out there. It's un-fucking-believable."

Alex yawned and ran his hand through his hair. "Yeah, I'll be right up."

The light had dimmed to a neon orange and Alex drank it in. "It's worth it just to see this," Fred mumbled.

"Yeah," said Carlos, "it's like staring into the eye of God." Alex agreed, the weight of the mission put aside for the next several minutes. But soon the natural light disappeared, replaced by the artificial beams that Murray switched on without warning. The shock snapped them to reality and their shared restlessness became palpable. "Where the fuck are we?" Fred asked nobody in particular. Receiving no answer, he yelled to Murray, "Hey Captain! We in Mexico yet?"

It was the first time in hours that any of them had raised their voice. Murray yelled back, "We slipped over while you guys were asleep. We're halfway there."

Fred looked out at the dark water in disbelief. "Sheeit, I ain't never been out of the country before."

"Don't look much different, does it?" Carlos replied, his voice betraying signs of intoxication.

"Guess you would know, huh? When did you sneak in?"

Alex froze at Fred's remark, anticipating how Carlos might respond. But to Alex's surprise, Carlos took it as an opportunity to reveal himself. "My father came after the war to work in the orchards," he began. "There was good money to be made then. After a few years when he'd saved enough to get a small house, he bribed a truck driver to come and get us. Me, my mother, and my sister. We were stuffed in that trailer like cargo for what felt like days. I can't stand being in enclosed spaces ever since." He took a breath and sipped his beer. "But we made it, and we were all together again."

"And they lived happily ever after," Fred interjected.

"Hardly. It wasn't long after that the agents swept through the farm my father was on, and rounded up everyone who didn't have papers. They were all deported right away. My mother, God bless her, had already started the immigration process for us, but they wouldn't do anything for my father. They wanted his job. The small plane they put him on was overloaded and it crashed in a canyon. We didn't even get to bury him."

Alex was stunned, while Fred blurted out, "Jesus Christ." No one said anything more, allowing Carlos to gather his thoughts.

"From that point on, I've said fuck this government. A man should be free to work to support his family. I did what I had to do to provide until my mother passed and my sister moved out. I'm a citizen of this fucking country now, but I don't agree with how it treats its people."

"Maybe we got more in common than you think, man." Fred brought a cigarette to his lips, the ember illuminating his face as he sucked the filter. "Things need to change for everybody. The powers that be don't want any of us here. That's why we've got to fight them."

"Well, you keep fighting them your way, and I'll fight them mine."

The glimmer of empathy faded and the two men retreated into their silent mutual distrust. Alex needed to detach himself, and went to see Murray. The wheelhouse door was open. Murray stood at attention, his face radiant in the light of the radar screen.

"Don't you ever sleep?" Alex asked.

"I took some stuff that'll keep me going until we get there. It won't be much longer. Hand me my Thermos, will you?"

Alex obliged, his admiration of the little captain changing to a feeling of inadequacy being in the man's presence. He was about to depart when Murray said, "I could hear your friend telling his story. Seems like everyone who gets wrapped up in this kind of shit has some reason like that for doing what they do. That's why I try not to judge people when I meet them. Even the most fucked-up ones have some kind of humanity deep down. Although most of the time it's best not to look too hard, if you know what I mean."

Alex smiled. He was already trying to forget Carlos's humanity. "Those guys, they're the type that are easy to pin down," Murray continued between sips of coffee. "You, on the other hand, I'm not so sure about."

"I haven't been too sure of it myself lately," Alex responded. "I've tried starting a new life a bunch of times, but no matter what I do, it keeps getting harder. And the shit I have to do to survive keeps getting stranger. It almost feels like I'm cursed. The more I want to make myself a better person, the worse things get." Alex couldn't hold back. "I've got this friend who's a singer, and he just signed a big record deal. He's out playing gigs across the country right now, and the stupid thing is, he doesn't even want to do it. Look at where I am, and you tell me that life's fair."

"Sounds like you might have found a way out."

Alex paused. "I have. But it's not gonna go down here."

"Are you sure? I might be able to help if I knew what you had in mind."

Alex's thoughts clouded over. He couldn't believe how Murray had read him. The notion struck him that he shouldn't say another word. He had to say something though. "Look, forget all that shit. I'm not planning anything apart from trying to get some sleep."

He heard most of Murray's reply as he exited the cabin. "Whatever you say. I'll wake you when we arrive."

On deck, Fred was trying to get Carlos to talk about the movie business, and Alex's sudden reappearance provided Carlos with a suitable distraction. "What's our Cap-ee-tain saying?" Carlos inquired. "You like his company better than ours?"

"I've never been on a boat before. I like to learn how things work."

Carlos let out his first laugh of the day, setting Fred on edge. "Is that what you're gonna do with your money? Buy a boat and become a sailor? You should join the Navy. Ah, but they're all fags. Nothing to do on the high seas but fuck each other up the ass."

"Hey cocksucker, my uncle was in the Navy! Say that again, I fuckin' dare ya." Fred was standing over Carlos but Alex couldn't see if he had pulled his gun. What he could see was Carlos grinning without a trace of fear. Alex silently urged Fred to do what he hadn't been able to do himself.

Aloud, he said, "Jesus guys, Murray says we're almost there. I'm sure Carlos was kidding." No one made a move.

"Yeah, right, just kidding," Carlos hissed through clenched teeth. Fred sat back down in his deck chair, and looked up into the starry night.

Alex took a deep breath. "I'm going to bed," he said, before any more words could be exchanged. He threw himself on his bunk and embraced the soothing ocean swells. His thoughts turned again to Jessy, and he wondered if at that moment she was thinking of him. She had to be, he concluded, after those endless days of nursing, encouraging and mothering she put in to get him clean. He was helpless throughout it all, and ashamed because of it. Still, he fought hard, for the sole purpose of making it onto the boat with all of his faculties intact. It was the only way he could save her life the way she had saved his. The pangs came from time to time, signified by the sweat, but all it took to eradicate them was the thought of her stroking his brow with the same gentleness she used to display while shooting him up. He imagined her on the boat, lying topless on the deck, the beads of ocean spray clinging to her dark flesh, shining like polished mahogany. There would come a time when that picture would be real, in some place where no one would have the courage to search for them, like Cuba. All it had to be was hot, so he could see her body shining in the sun. He rolled over, burying his head in the pillow. He gave his senses over to the darkness, and let the consistent rocking of the hull usher him off into a foggy, dreamless sleep.

The rocking had ceased by the time Alex awoke. Light from above filled the quarters, and a moment later, heavy footsteps descended the stairs. A drawn and weary Murray stood before him. "Welcome to Mexico. I gotta rest now." He collapsed on the opposite bunk, fully clothed, leaving Alex to ponder what awaited him. The boat was tied to a crudely constructed pier that stretched to an untouched beach. Beyond was thick grass and underbrush. There were no other immediate signs of civilization in either direction along the shore.

Carlos and Fred stood on the unstable wooden structure, and marveled at the immeasurable space. Fred asked, "How the fuck was he able to find this place?" Carlos didn't answer as he approached Alex to help him over the side. Fred's bewilderment continued. "Do you think they know we're here? I can't see the house."

Carlos replied, "Who else can they be expecting?" He looked haggard to Alex, more the worse for wear than Fred after the exposure to the elements. The trio trudged up the beach, with Alex unable to detect any lingering signs of animosity. The vegetation grew taller and the path became less defined as it led upward, before ending at a wide glade. At its center was a sprawling Spanish-style villa. Huey's bodyguard Sonny stood on the porch, his massive hands making his binoculars seem tiny. Fred broke away to greet him, and they exchanged a personalized handshake. Alex couldn't hear the words passed between them, and he and Carlos continued to approach with caution. As the house came into full view, Alex could see the shadow of a Lincoln Town Car parked at the side, and a variety of cases strewn around the grounds. It looked like an abandoned film set. He had no idea what time it was, but he assumed it was too early for the occupants of the house to be up.

Fred introduced the others to Sonny, who motioned them inside. Additional camera and lighting equipment was piled in each corner of the ground floor. The remnants of dinner, including many empty bottles, littered the main seating area. Alex was afraid to disturb anything. He and Carlos both observed as Fred stormed around, the sound of his boots on the hardwood floor loud enough to wake the entire house. "Jesus," Fred complained. "You'd think there'd be some kinda welcome."

A door opened on the second floor, and Bob Richardson, in nothing but boxer shorts, materialized at the railing. After acknowledging the new arrivals with a wave, he returned to his room and a few minutes later stumbled down the stairs fully clothed. Formal introductions were made as Bob heated up the coffee pot and Fred cleared the large table of sauce-stained plates, overflowing ashtrays and other debris.

"Glad to see you made it all right," Bob said, tipping back his cup. "But we all know that Murray's quite a sailor."

"When did you guys get here?" Fred asked.

"A couple days ago," Bob replied. "Huey got the deal out of the way straight off. We've just been waiting for you guys to show up."

"So the shit's here?"

"Yeah, it's in the trunk of the Town Car."

Fred exhaled before continuing. "You tried it I presume?"

Bob answered with a broad smile. "Don't worry, it's fucking good."

They proceeded to make small talk, with Carlos showing some curiosity about the film gear. "This stuff's been lying around for about a year," Bob responded. "Peckinpah shot something a few towns over, and this was his home base. Typical Sam; things got crazy and the crew ended up leaving behind all this shit. Good thing we didn't have to pay for it. Anyway, I thought that while it's here, I'd get a head start on the project by getting some footage of Huey telling stories. It'll help out with the script, or at least be some kind of historical record." As he spoke, Bob repeatedly eyed Carlos. "Man, you look familiar. You do any acting?"

Carlos answered, "Yeah, I've done a bunch of things here and there. Whenever there's a role for an ugly Hispanic, I usually get a call."

"I knew it! But I'm trying to remember specifically what I've seen you in."

"Probably in some of Corman's things. Russ Meyer too."

"Yeah, that's it! I got my start with Roger. I made it up to being his AD on the last thing I did with him. Jesus, you can't swing a dead cat in Hollywood without hitting someone who's worked for him." Bob refilled his cup and lapsed into fond memories until Fred changed the subject.

"So, uh, what's Huey been telling you?"

"Basically his life story. I just turn the camera on and let him rap about whatever he feels like."

Alex saw a look of concern sweep across Fred's face. "Nothing, uh, incriminating I hope?"

A voice shouted from the second floor, "Freddy, my man! You and your boys made it." Huey was dressed in his Panther casuals—black t-shirt and cut-off jeans—as if he were on vacation. "Fuck, I hope there's some of that smokin' java left. Mornin' Bobby." Seeing everyone there together clearly had him in a bright mood. "And these must be the fine folks who have made it all possible," he added, extending his hand to Carlos and Alex. "You have no idea how much your help is appreciated."

Although Alex had been on edge in anticipation of meeting Huey in person, Huey paid way more attention to Carlos. Alex's image of Huey suddenly changed from the godlike figure Fred had described, to just another hustler who talked a better game than the rest. Alex could tell the false praise was making Carlos ill at ease, but he managed to maintain a pleasant exterior in order to ask the burning question, "So, Mister Newton, when do we do our business?"

"Are you serious man? You've just had a long trip, you're in a tropical paradise, and that's all you're thinking about? We got all the time in the world, brother. Let's at least enjoy one day without having to worry about that shit. It ain't goin' anywhere. Now, why don't we whip up some breakfast?"

Alex tensed up, aware that Carlos didn't want to waste time, but everyone now seemed caught up in the general cordial atmosphere.

"Allow me," Carlos said, rising from his chair. "Huevos rancheros is my specialty." Alex let the tension ease by reassuring himself that all of them would get what was coming to them.

↗

B. Richardson / Panther Film Log 06/06/72

I filmed Huey telling stories about the nights in '65/'66 when the shit first started going down in Oakland. I've come to see how much he loves being the center of attention, and all day he wanted us to get high with him. We broke out the peyote after dinner, and I got Huey to sit down for the camera immediately after. He started off slowly and casually, and as the drug took hold, he became visibly sensitive, like a massive open wound. But he didn't break, instead bent on entertaining the rest of us. I kept leaning in, trying to coax out the truth rather than a performance. When the peyote took full effect, he started rambling on about Dylan—"I used to listen to that dude a lot back when things started getting heavy, especially that Mr. Jones song." Note: see if we can get that for the soundtrack.

He went off about Eldridge being the one who was "really down with it." My interpretation: you start shit with cops and you'd better not be a pussy about it. Huey asserted that everything Dr. King and Malcolm preached didn't mean shit when you're hustling. Key line: "Every Saturday night could be your last, you know? Is that what being a free man's all about? It sure ain't what they teach you in church, or what all those motherfuckers yell about when they go out to march."

Huey stated unequivocally that he's always been the brains, using as an example something Eldridge told him that until he became a Panther, he never gave a shit whether or not he went to prison. I'm hearing all of this as an opening voiceover: Huey sitting inside a big house, seeming out of the reach of the forces trying to stop him. The camera pans away to a gun barrel pointing directly at him. It fires a bullet, but misses. He starts to run, and more bullets whistle past. He stops and turns to face the gunman. He has to stand and fight.

I stopped filming Huey after about twenty minutes. Everyone was transfixed by his words, but of course we were all high by then. Nothing notable happened until we came down a couple hours later. Huey seemed shattered by the experience. He kept repeating, "No matter what I do, I'll still be a fucking hustler." Fred consoled him, and I saw for the first time the kind of loyalty Huey inspires in others. Like Ho Chi Minh. That's got to be at the heart of the film. Fuck it if it means I never work again.

When Alex awoke, for one fleeting second he imagined himself on the same golden shore Will used to sing about. Then he realized he was on the beach, fully clothed and aching, surrounded by wails and chirps that emanated from the nearby brush. The sun beat down with an almighty force that surely inspired primitive man to worship. Alex bowed to stretch his back, arising with arms extended and chest swelling, ready to face whatever lay ahead. He gazed toward the boat, wondering if Murray had slept through the previous day. Alex thought of going on board to check on him, but the need for water was more pressing.

He could hear voices inside, beyond where Sonny stood guard. Alex entered to find them all, including Murray, attacking another meal that could have been either breakfast or lunch.

"I've been getting some great stuff," Bob said. "I mean, last night was just what I was hoping for, if only for narration, you know? All we'll have to do is flesh out the stories visually. It'll be fucking groundbreaking."

"Excuse me," Fred objected. "All this is being done under the influence, man. There's gonna be shit in there that the pigs are gonna think they can use. I mean, I already gotta keep my cousin under wraps for what she's done. Some of this shit gets out, she ain't got no hope of a fair trial if they catch her."

"It's my story, man," Huey grunted. "I got a right to tell it."

Alex's arrival put an end to the debate. "Jesus, we thought we'd lost you," Carlos said.

"I woke up on the beach. I can't remember going out there."

"I made sure you were alright," Murray said.

Alex couldn't decide if thanks were in order, but he offered them anyway before asking the entire table, "What happened to me?"

Carlos chuckled in spite of himself. "That's a good question. I was wondering that about myself too."

The others laughed knowingly.

"Peyote," Bob said. "It's something you gotta do when you're down here. Helps you get in tune with the environment.

Otherwise, the paranoia will make you wanna blow your brains out. People here have known that for centuries." Bob handed Alex a glass of water, and gestured him toward a platter of bean burritos.

Murray checked his watch. "If we load up now, we'll be back by tomorrow night. I think that'll work best."

No one objected, but Carlos couldn't seem to let it be. "Before we do that, can I assume that Mr. Newton's supplier is satisfied?"

Huey gave him a quizzical look. "Yeah, of course. Everything's on the up and up with these cats."

"Okay. Because I want to assure Mr. Newton that I will live up to my end of the bargain, and I will not appreciate any accusations to the contrary. In return, I will expect Mr. Newton to honor his end of the bargain."

Alex stopped chewing his food, as Fred's frustration with Carlos appeared to reach its limit. "Fuck, man," he shouted, "how can you talk shit like that now?"

"Cool it, Fred," Huey jumped in. "The man's concerns are justified. But what he may not yet understand is that we ain't in the business of ripping people off, and likewise do not tolerate anybody who does. If you don't believe me, I can always get Sonny to explain it in plainer terms." Huey exposed his white, movie star teeth. "Perhaps you boys should do as Murray says and get on with your work."

Alex admired another sunset from the deck as they sailed home. Fred and Carlos no longer spoke to each other. Fred stayed down below close to the heavy trunks containing the cargo. Carlos was in the same cockpit chair he'd occupied on the way down, apparently content staring out at the watery expanse. Alex lingered a few feet behind.

"I know you think I set you up," Carlos said without taking his eyes off the ocean. "But I never wanted to be in this business. I wanted to be an actor, just like you. On the other hand, I have relatives down here in Mexico who depend on me. They could have made other connections in America, but I'm someone they trust unconditionally. Our arrangement has worked out well so far, and you've been a big help with that. The truth is, I've wanted to see you succeed, but I don't think you understand that the more you've tried to go out on your own, the more risk it's placed on me. Now you've got me mixed up in this Panther business, and I don't know how I can resume my own operation when it's over. The only way I see this ending is with the two of us parting ways. Once you get your share of this deal, I never want to see you again."

Alex stared at the back of Carlos's head, thinking of what he and Jessy had planned. He didn't doubt Carlos' sincerity and placed a hand on his shoulder. "Thanks. You've done more for me than most people have." Alex knew he was speaking the truth, but still feared his words rang hollow, as he flashed back to the terror of nearly losing his life underwater.

Alex made a beeline to his only refuge, the cabin where Murray stood at the wheel.

"Steady as she goes, huh kid?"

Alex was trying to compose himself. "What? Oh yeah, that's some kinda sailing term, right?"

"It can mean a lot of things," Murray replied. "It can mean sticking with your plan. Or it can mean, do what people say you should do to get your life right."

"Why do you care about what happens to me?"

"Look, I told you before I don't want to stick my nose in, but I gotta tell you that after spending time with these guys, I think you're in over your head."

"Oh, you do, huh?"

"I just picture this ending bad for you, that's all."

"What, you some kinda fortune teller or what?"

"No, but I know that when a pack of wild animals gets attacked, it's the youngest that gets eaten."

"Thanks for the tip. Thought I could find some peace and quiet in here."

"Okay, I get it. You're gonna do what you have to do. Just remember that you don't have to do it right away. That's all I'm gonna say."

Alex remained in the cabin as the boat skimmed through the darkness. He pondered whether he had it in him to follow through with the plan. But he knew for certain that there was no way he could hold back Jessy.

"First Time on the Highway"

First time on the highway I was 19 years old
I tell ya boys, I was sure was scared and cold
First time on the highway I was lonesome as I could be
Next time on the highway gonna be the death of me

First time on the highway I had a freight train as my friend
I thought I'd never see my dear old mama again
First time on the highway I went from sea to shining sea
Next time on the highway gonna be the death of me

First time on the highway I made a pretty good run
Didn't need no razor and I didn't need no gun
First time on the highway I got lost in Tennessee
Next time on the highway gonna be the death of me

First time on the highway I didn't have a dime
But down in New Orleans I still had a pretty good time
First time on the highway boys I sure felt free
Next time on the highway gonna be the death of me

First time on the highway I caught a ride in Ohio
Eighteen wheels were smokin' all the way to Buffalo
First time on the highway I saw my hangin' tree
Next time on the highway gonna be the death of me

Chapter 15

Los Angeles / June 1972

"**D**id you see what they wrote about you? This is exactly what we were all hoping for. You did great out there." As Lucas rambled, Will could hardly bear to keep the receiver pressed against his ear. He offered some glimmers of enthusiasm, but these only encouraged Lucas to divulge more of what he wanted to do when the album was released. Will finally insisted they meet at another time to talk about it, and Lucas hung up after reminding him, "Believe me, you're gonna be huge."

Will contemplated that possibility as he breathed the stale air within the apartment. The only evidence that Alex had been there was a scrawled note saying he'd returned from Mexico and everything was fine. Will had been looking forward to at least a few days away from Angela when the train arrived back in L.A., but tried not to show any signs until the moment they separated outside his building and the cab took her home. She gave him a quick kiss, accompanied by a promise that she'd call after catching up on her sleep.

Will had dropped his things inside the door and flopped on the sofa, succumbing to the illusion that he hadn't left at all. Will wasn't sure how he was supposed to feel. His ambivalence kept his guitar in its case. He saw no point in rehearsing, or forcing himself to write anything new.

Angela called late Monday afternoon, sounding well rested. "Hey, whatcha doing?"

He let out a deep breath before replying. "Absolutely nothing. Just sitting here bored out of my skull. You home from work?"

"I'm home, but I didn't go in today. I think I slept for about fourteen hours. How 'bout you?"

"I slept alright, but I feel about the same."

"What's the matter?"

"I don't know. I'm not sure what to do with myself."

"Well, that's understandable. We just spent three weeks on a tight schedule. I'll come over, then we can go out somewhere."

He set the phone down with a surprising sense of relief. She came through the door an hour later looking as refreshed as she'd sounded on the phone, and back to her California uniform of sundress and sandals. He resisted making a bad joke out of it by rubbing his eyes in disbelief, but she threw her arms around him before he got the chance. She stayed close on the sofa, her legs tucked beneath like a child.

"What should we do?" she asked, reaching to stroke the nape of his neck.

"If I knew, I don't think we'd still be sitting here."

"You know what I was thinking on the way over? You showed me the places where you grew up. I should show you some places where I grew up."

"How far do we have to go?"

"Everything's close by. I should have just said let's go for a walk."

The cool early evening air and soft light made him forget his self-imposed incarceration. They strolled toward Hollywood Boulevard, Angela leading the way. As they passed over stars on the Walk of Fame, Will admitted it was a part of the city he hadn't bothered to notice since he'd been there.

"It's funny how you don't do the touristy things in the places you live," he said. "Alex and I never once talked about seeing the sights for fun. I just started stumbling upon things. They didn't look like what I imagined them to be, so I didn't pay any attention after that."

Angela seemed encouraged by his openness. "What did you imagine them to be?"

"I don't know. Less man-made or something. It's like when you go to Mount Rushmore and you're expecting to see these giant heads floating in space. But they're so... small. It makes you realize that it was just a bunch of human beings who made it." Will paused to take in their surroundings. "I mean, look at all of this. Does it inspire you? I want to know the things that weren't made by human hands."

They walked a block in silence until they passed Grauman's Chinese Theatre and Angela found a reason to change the subject. "I loved doing the touristy stuff when I was a kid," she said. "I think here it's like an initiation, because everyone knows someone who's in the business, and that's all that everyone talks about."

"Who did you know?"

"My mother had an uncle who did some kind of technical work at MGM. Nothing spectacular. But there were a couple of times when I was really small that we got to see him on the lot. I can't remember what the picture was, but all the activity was something I couldn't begin to comprehend. It was like magic. Maybe that's why I'm still drawn to things that seem like magic to me. Like the first time I heard you play." She laced her fingers with his without breaking stride. He didn't resist, but didn't feel comfortable either. She kept talking. "I think there are plenty of things that have always existed just to inspire us. What about your granddad's songs? You never heard him actually sing them, so you really have no proof that they're his. Who knows where he got them? But look at what they've done for you. Because of them, you're probably going to make more money than he ever dreamed of."

Will clenched his fist as soon as she mentioned the songs, squeezing her hand hard. He had managed to repress the secret throughout the entire tour, in every interview and every casual conversation, only to have her now throw it back in his face. His palm began to sweat.

"Ow," she said, and tried to pull away, but Will didn't let go.

"Those songs are mine now. I don't want to ever hear you say anything about them being my granddad's again."

"Okay, you got it," she said, sounding confused by Will's sudden hostility. He relaxed his grip, and she leaned her head against his shoulder as they walked into the fading light. Angela resumed pointing out all of her old hangouts until they approached the Troubadour, and the immediate pleasures of a cold beer took precedence over a trip down memory lane.

They had entered the Long Beach Inner Harbor shrouded in pre-dawn mist. The homecoming brought Alex no joy. He was already thinking of the work he had to do over the next several days, as Carlos and Fred unloaded the cargo once Murray had docked. The two even shook hands, a gesture that Alex presumed was intended to remind each of them of the trust still required to fully complete the operation.

Fueled by a last rush of adrenaline, Carlos and Alex packed several suitcases of cocaine into the Honda, which started with a cough. Alex asked to be taken to Jessy's apartment.

"You're gonna have to be available at all times as I get the packages prepared," Carlos said.

Alex turned toward the passenger side window rather than look Carlos in the face. "I know. Jesus, can't I go see my woman and let her know I'm alive first?"

Carlos displayed no apparent concern. "I'm making calls as soon as I get home. I don't want to have this shit in my house any longer than I need to." Carlos spoke as if convincing himself, but Alex didn't need any reassurance. He counted the blocks passing by until they were in Jessy's neighborhood, with its rows of identical triplexes. "Just be ready," Carlos said as Alex stepped out onto the sidewalk. The Honda pulled away, and Alex heard Carlos shift gears violently at quick intervals up the street.

Alex found his key and entered quietly, knowing that Jessy would be asleep. After his initial noises failed to announce his presence, he moved to the bedroom where she lay, covered up to her neck. He pulled the sheets back one by one, until she was exposed in only her white cotton panties and tank top. She rolled toward him with both arms extended, eyes closed, and pulled him down by his collar for a deep kiss. She began removing his clothes and within a few agonizing seconds he was inside her. It felt new and pure. There was no hesitation in his movements, despite his exhaustion. Everything about him seemed strong and confident, and for the first time in their relationship, she came to climax before him. After she subsided, she worked to get him off, and they both lay on their backs, spent.

"So I take it everything went well," she said, staring at the ceiling.

"Yeah. I guess phase one is finished."

"How was Huey?"

"Nice guy. Really smart. I can see why you think highly of him."

"No troubles at all?"

"Not really. I was worried about Fred and Carlos a few times, but it sorted itself out. The captain was a really good guy. Barely saw another boat the whole trip."

"Good. So Carlos is still—"

"Expecting me to be his errand boy until the shit's gone. Yeah, there's no fucking doubt about that. He said to be ready."

The words weighed heavy on him. Jessy brushed the hair from his brow. "Don't worry baby. You've come so far. You can do this one last little task. After that, you can leave it all to me."

They stayed in bed for the next twenty-four hours, happy to explore each other's bodies again, until the phone rang like an alarm.

"Take a cab over, I'll pay for it," Carlos murmured down the line, the effects of some long hours evident in his voice. Alex arrived to find several dozen baggies of white powder neatly arranged on the kitchen table. "This is just the start," Carlos said, pausing to admire his work. "I gotta say, now that the hard part is over, this whole thing couldn't have worked out any better." He let out a laugh that mutated into spastic coughing, forcing him to put a hand on the countertop to support his girth. Carlos shook his shaggy head, as if revived by smelling salts. "Dios mio. The doctors say this shit'll kill you, but they don't say when, eh?"

Alex expressed little sympathy. "You kept some for yourself, I take it?"

"Of course. The spoils of war, my friend. Get used to it."

"How much?"

"Enough to keep me happy so I won't have to go back to fucking Mexico again anytime soon, that's for sure."

"You're charging more than usual for this shit then?"

"Don't worry, everyone knows this is a special offer. It's not that much more, and besides, all these cats can afford it."

Alex paced the kitchen, sensing his plans starting to unravel. "You cut it with something. I know you did." He stopped and looked into Carlos's dark, unflinching eyes. "Tell me what the fuck you cut it with! I need to know. Keeping secrets is what almost got me fucking killed before!"

Carlos sidestepped Alex and poured a cup of coffee without offering any to his guest. After a sip, he summoned an authoritarian voice. "What do you care? You just have to get the money. You're planning to tell the Panthers I cut it anyway, just so they'll retaliate."

Time sped up and Alex became rooted where he stood. He didn't know how to answer Carlos's accusation. "If I was a rat, I would have done it a long time ago." This partial admission put a smile on Carlos's face, until Alex added, "But that's not the point. I know that once I hand over the money, you're gone, right?"

Nervous tics bubbled under Carlos's cheeks. He offered an unexpected ultimatum. "If that's the way you see it, then I don't need you. I can do it all by myself. Go on, get out right now!"

Alex froze. "I have to do this. I need the money."

Carlos fixed Alex with a cold stare. "I know you do." He allowed the words to resonate within Alex before adding, "Now start getting this shit out there so we can get on with our fucking lives."

Alex started filling a duffle bag. Carlos handed him the car keys, along with a scribbled list of names, locations and quantities.

This scene repeated over the coming week. Alex made constant trips to Laurel Canyon, Topanga, the San Fernando Valley, and elsewhere. He crashed sets in search of PAs. He dropped in at late night parties where actors and musicians awaited him. He was welcomed into recording studios and editing suites. The guards at Paramount let him through, no questions asked. Everyone seemed happy, especially Carlos when Alex returned with bulging rolls of bills. The next round of baggies was always ready on the table. He saw Jessy whenever he could spare a few minutes and her soothing touch became necessary to revitalize him. After the first few days, he caved in and told her about Carlos's tactic to maximize his take, and she became furious. "You can't tell Fred," he pleaded. "That'll blow the whole thing. He'll kill Carlos." She didn't question his reasoning. "We won't have much time to act after my last run. Carlos is ready to disappear."

"How much longer, baby?"

"I don't know. I guess it'll be over when I walk in and see nothing on the table."

Pick up that fucking guitar. This is the life you chose. You're no good for anything else.

That's not true.

You haven't done anything to make me believe otherwise. Why do you have to throw everything away?

You must know. Why don't you just tell me? It'll save me a lot of trouble.

You've got something seriously wrong with you.

Gee, that's a big surprise. How could it have taken this long for you to say that?

You're all alone now, you know that, right? No more family, no more Alex. There's only that girl, the one who for some reason still builds her world around you. That doesn't mean anything to you yet?

It's starting to. I know I've been a fool. I'm trying to change. I think I do love her.

No, you don't.

Fuck you! You're the one who's been telling me all along that she's the only thing that can save me. I realize that now. I want her to help me! You were right, okay? Is that what you want to hear?

She could have helped you if you had listened to me the first time. Now it's too late. She doesn't love you. She only loves the music.

No! I don't believe you!

She's in charge. She's planning your future as we speak.

What's wrong with that? I wouldn't have made it through that tour without her.

If you can't do it without her, how will you be able to do any of the other things you'll have to do by yourself? You can't even pick up your fucking guitar now. Go ahead, call her! Maybe she can come over and put it in your cowardly hands.

Shut up! I love her.

Face it, you're not cut out for this life, and you're gonna have to break it to her. And how do you suppose she's gonna take it? Adios amigo.

No, you're a liar! I don't care if she only loves the music. That's enough for now. I have to make it work. It's all I've got.

If that's all you ever believed in, you would have written another album by now.

I can do it. I will do it.

No you won't. You want to know why? Because I wrote those fucking songs for you.

Granddad?

⟋

If he hadn't been tailing the yellow Honda, Murray still would have had no trouble spotting Alex. He only had to stand on the corner of 32nd and Figueroa for an afternoon to see Alex pass by a half-dozen times. That would have been easier than trying to keep up with Alex's surprising adeptness behind the wheel, skills that managed to keep the traffic cops off his back. The Honda might as well have had "cocaine delivery" painted on its doors.

He ran addresses of Alex's drops to pass time and wasn't surprised to hear the names of movie stars and other high-placed people come back to him over his radio. These facts weren't essential anymore. His surveillance of Carlos had made the case as close to airtight as the DA could hope for. Murray was going to miss being around the show business people; it was a shame how they were so easily swayed by dope. All Murray had to do to penetrate Bert and Bob's circle was lean on one of their coke connections to provide a phony backstory about Murray being his supplier. When they met, Murray laid it out that he'd be happy to cut out the middle man and become their sole supplier, something that would have tipped off anyone who didn't possess the egos of Hollywood executives. Murray took full advantage, knowing that if he played things right, he'd take down half of Hollywood. The coup de grace was selling them the boat, a move Murray convinced them would be advantageous if they ever needed to make a quick escape. They left the paperwork in Murray's hands, signing for whatever was necessary, although nobody bothered to notice that the boat was registered to the F.B.I.

Things were different with Alex. Murray felt a strange desire to protect him from the moment they'd met. It was the kid's involvement with the Panthers that had the potential to break the case open wider than Murray could have imagined. Murray was certain to be a national hero if he nailed Huey. He just had to figure out a way to get Alex to give it all up before doing something stupid. Murray formulated his plan throughout the days he tailed Alex, waiting for the right moment to reveal himself. Alex was in constant motion, pausing only to get gas or a cheeseburger. All the while, what he'd said at sea about his own plan to extricate himself from the situation echoed in Murray's mind. The frantic activity was building up to Alex's final solution, and Murray held his breath whenever Alex made it back to Carlos's place. Each time, he expected to hear shots, but each time, Alex hustled back to the Honda and headed out to make his next round of drops. Murray just wanted to know when it was all going to end.

He resorted to calling Bert to ask about the status of the Panther film. This led to a one-sided conversation about how amazing it was going to be. Murray talked to other bureau agents who were monitoring the Panthers, but none knew anything about a film. Murray had enough evidence on Carlos to bring him in anytime he wanted, but there was more to this than eliminating a single trafficking operation. Alex was the only one with all the answers.

Lucas picked a rare gray Tuesday morning for the album cover shoot. Will arrived late at Zuma Beach after Angela insisted on tagging along. The photographer, an old pony-tailed hippie named Harvey, was setting up, and greeted them with a wide grin, creasing his face into a detailed map of wrinkles.

"Sorry we're late," Will said. "We're not used to being up this early."

Harvey replied, "Don't worry, I know about rock and roll time. I've been waiting for the sun to poke through anyway, but it doesn't look like we're gonna get any. It might work out for the best. Jack played me a couple of your tunes and they sounded kinda moody to me. In a good way, of course."

Will smiled. "Thanks. I wasn't sure what you had in mind, but I'm open to whatever you want to do." He caught Harvey glancing at Angela, and introduced her.

Harvey turned his attention to their location, his eyes scanning the scattered bits of debris along the beach, rather than Will's appearance. Will was dressed for the cool weather in a denim shirt and tattered corduroy blazer. His dark hair was limp and greasy, and a week's worth of stubble covered his face.

Harvey led them toward a large driftwood log wedged into the beach many yards away. "You two look good together," he offered as they trudged through the wet sand. "I'm tempted to have you both in the shots. It could be like a California version of *The Freewheelin' Bob Dylan* cover. You know what I'm talking about?"

Will explained the reference to Angela, and she rolled her eyes in response. "Yeah, I know. I used to have that record." Harvey circled the log, then told Will to place himself however he felt comfortable. Will sat and awaited further instruction, but Harvey commenced snapping.

"Are you sure this is okay?" Will asked after a minute.

"Yeah, it's great. You look just like you sound. Turn your head to the ocean if you want." Will did so, conscious of every flinch he made whenever the shutter clicked. He hoped to evoke the grim determination he admired in pictures of his heroes, which helped make the experience more bearable.

"Why don't you try smiling?" Angela blurted out after Harvey had gone through his first roll.

"What?" Will answered as if she was speaking in another language.

"Just take a few smiling. You've got a really nice smile. It's a better reflection of your personality anyway." Will didn't believe it, but he adjusted his position on the log and looked straight into the lens with a forced grin. "No, no! That looks stupid. Here, look at me." Angela crossed her eyes and stuck out her tongue. Will nearly fell off the log in laughter, and Harvey snapped away.

"There, that's your album cover," Angela proclaimed.

The shoot continued at an unhurried pace. Harvey contorted himself into every conceivable position, and Will became curious to know what he was seeing through the lens. During a break to change rolls, he asked, "You've been doing this for a long time, huh?"

Harvey clapped the back of the camera shut. "Yeah, I started out shooting in the jazz clubs in Frisco back in the Fifties. That's the music I really love. When everything changed to rock and roll, all the work ended up down here. I've made a lot of good friends though, and they all seem to enjoy getting their picture taken."

"Do you think I could become one of those guys?"

Harvey lowered his camera. "Well, from what little I know about you, I'd say you're one of the more serious young men I've met in a while. I can tell you're more like those jazz cats I used to know. And because of that, I'd say to be careful. If you don't dig the sun, you'll end up on a dark path, you know what I mean?" Both Will and Angela listened intently. "You ever hear of a cat named Chet Baker?" Will shook his head and lit a cigarette. "He was the king shit with all the jazz heads. He had it all man, looked like James Dean, blew like Miles, and got more pussy than Sinatra. Pardon my French." Angela let out an embarrassed giggle. "But he was looking for something else, something that doesn't exist out here. Something to remind him of who he was deep down in his soul. The only place he could find it was in junk, ya dig? And once he found it, he couldn't pretend to be anything else anymore."

"What happened to him?" Angela asked.

"He split for Europe, someplace where you can live with a habit and people won't judge you."

"Just so you know, I've never done that shit," Will said.

"Never suggested you did. All's I'm saying is that certain people were meant to live here and certain people weren't. I don't know you well enough to say, so my advice is that you should make up your mind about it by the time people start shoving more contracts in your face. It can be a nasty fucking business." Will flicked his cigarette butt toward the water, lost for words, while Angela shifted her feet in the sand. "Well," Harvey continued, "didn't mean to be a bringdown. I should try to get a few more shots and that should be enough."

Will stood up unprompted and walked toward the shoreline. Harvey continued snapping Will's isolated figure against the bruised panorama. Angela watched in silence. When the first wave lapped against the toes of Will's boots, he stopped at the water's edge, feeling himself sink in the mud.

Harvey yelled, "Turn around! Stay right there, but just turn around!" A part of Will didn't want to obey the command, but he turned, replanting his feet in dry sand. The evidence of where he had previously stood was swept away by the next wave. He saw the glint of Harvey's lens, now fifty yards away, and waited to be told that it was over.

"I don't know what they're gonna want to use," Harvey said, "but there should be plenty to choose from." He looked into Will's eyes. "Don't take what I said before too seriously. Just stick with this little girl here and you'll be fine." He stepped back and raised his camera one last time. "Here, let me take a couple of you two together, just for posterity. You can keep them for yourselves." Will and Angela glanced at each other and moved closer. Angela put on a broad smile. Will remained a study in blankness. Harvey gave no further direction, focusing and clicking the shutter twice in rapid succession. "There, that makes me happy." He pulled them both into an embrace before throwing his bags across his back and lighting out to the parking lot.

Will felt the void of his absence right away.

"I think that went alright, don't you?" Angela offered.

All Will could manage to say was, "I'm hearing the voice again."

Alex was still operating at a relentless pace after the first week. Jessy worked endless shifts at the club to keep herself occupied. At the conclusion of the latest long day, Alex dragged himself into her apartment, and was greeted by the smell of marijuana and the sound of Bobby Blue Bland's *California Album*. Jessy sprawled on the sofa, joint in hand, her bare legs stretched over the coffee table. Only a single button was done up on her blouse, and he had to step around her stacked-heel shoes lying haphazardly on the floor. "Hi baby," she said after exhaling a plume of smoke. She kissed his cheek and offered him the joint. He thought fleetingly of his pledge to stay clean, but within a few minutes they were both sedated. Conversation wasn't necessary. They reclined shoulder to shoulder, their heads cushioned by each other's hair. Alex tried to look outside himself and observe the tableau. It was a perfect moment; he could feel her love for him in all of its purity.

The sound of the stereo kept Alex grounded until they finished the joint, whereupon the familiar fantasy of he and Jessy lying on a tropical beach embedded itself within his mind. It was as vivid as it had ever been; Alex's inner world was flooded with light, as if the ceiling had fallen away. His euphoria was fleeting, however, replaced by an image of Carlos flanked by a host of faceless figures bearing down upon him.

Alex's screams roused Jessy and she cradled his head until he caught his breath.

"It's okay baby, I'm here."

Alex opened his eyes and took in his surroundings, resting his gaze on Jessy's beatific smile. He forced himself to speak. "You won't let anything happen to me, will you?"

"Of course not sugar. We've made it this far. Just a little further to go."

You know who I am.

No. It's not possible.

I want you to be the person I didn't get a chance to be.

I don't know what that is.

Don't bullshit me. It's all in the songs, even the ones you wrote yourself. That's when I knew you could do it.

I would if it got you out of my head.

I'm all you've got left.

No, it's not true.

We've been through this before.

I want my life back.

It was never yours to begin with.

Stop!

I'm here to help. We'll get through it together.

Why can't I see you?

You have seen me, many times, you just didn't realize.

Were you the white buffalo?

We'll be face to face again, trust me.

You're a liar! Nothing you've ever said is true. You think I'm some pawn in this twisted game you're playing. I won't do what you tell me anymore. I want my life back.

A life with that little controlling bitch?

I refuse to listen anymore.

I've got nothing more to say. But don't ever forget.

⏤

"Waitin' For the Future"

There's a crack in the window and a stain on the floor
The virus keeps spreadin' from door to door
It can't be heard and is seldom seen
A souvenir from a place you've never been

The kids are all grown and the money's all gone
And he's been waitin' for the future for far too long

With your face to the wall and your back to the whip
You got no choice but make the trip
From Wichita Falls to the Mexican Gulf
No one's satisfied 'till they get enough

The kids are all grown and the money's all gone
And he's been waitin' for the future for far too long

Don't use my hair to build your nest
Don't break my heart if you know what's best
There ain't no room for your picture on my shelf
And that window just might have to fix itself

The kids are all grown and the money's all gone
And I been waitin' for the future for far too long

Chapter 16

Joshua Tree / June 1972

Only a half-dozen baggies remained. The number made Alex's pulse accelerate. The next stage of the plan was imminent. He maintained his composure, asking Carlos for a coffee while rubbing his face to stave off the sleep he craved.

"Why so few today?" Alex asked.

"This is it, man. It's all gone." Carlos offered a toast with his mug, and they both drank while staring at the last vestiges of their partnership.

"This shouldn't take me too long."

"No, it shouldn't. What, you want to go celebrate after?" Carlos's voice grated on Alex as he thought ahead of where Jessy said she would be.

"Well, if this is the last time we're gonna see each other."

"Don't start getting sentimental on me," Carlos spat out. "I'll have the money ready for you when you get back. Then you'll be free. Free to help your friends make their fucking movie."

Alex's temper rose. "Just make sure it's here," he growled, before swallowing the rest of the coffee and packing up the coke.

"Don't you want to know where you're going?"

Alex realized he needed to stay calm, rather than entertain thoughts of dumping the shit on the first corner he found. Carlos handed over the day's itinerary, scrawled out in his usual crude handwriting. "I expect to see you in four hours at the most."

"You'll see me when you see me. Have a nice fucking day."

Alex stormed out, hearing Carlos call after him, "Ah, spoken like a true leading man! You could be the next Clint Eastwood if you want to!"

Alex slammed the door of the Honda, cranking the key hard and revving the engine until all four cylinders screamed in unison like a Cessna. He laid a trail of rubber on the street as he set out for the first film set drop-off.

Alex's peel-out shook off Murray's drowsiness as he sat in his car across from Carlos's building. He didn't get much of a chance to catch up. Alex tore through every intersection on his path to the freeway, forcing Murray to run several yellow lights. A conscientious driver would have noticed this sure sign of a tail, but Murray suspected Alex was lost in his mission.

The set in Irvine was a large house with spacious grounds. Murray hung back while keeping the Honda in view. Within twenty minutes, Alex was heading for the Paramount lot. Murray lingered as Alex exchanged friendly words with the front gate security guard. The wooden barrier lifted and the Honda entered after expelling a small cloud of exhaust.

A half-hour later, the yellow car reappeared, dashing toward the Strip. Murray stuck to Alex the whole time, as he had been trained. His experience told him that something unscripted was occurring when Alex pulled into a Texaco station to use the pay phone. Whoever he was calling didn't answer. When Alex got back on the road, he slowed to a leisurely pace. Murray followed him to Sunset, where Alex entered a strip club without his duffel bag. Murray's mind raced with possible explanations. For the first time in his surveillance, his curiosity got the better of him. He followed Alex on foot.

⟨ornament⟩

"Ladies and gentlemen, next up I'd like you all to welcome someone who got his start on this stage not so long ago. His first album will be coming out soon on Elektra Records, so enjoy this opportunity to see him for free while you can. Let's hear it for Will Mosley!"

The stage was familiar, but the applause was not. It rang more hollow than the other places he'd recently been. The Wednesday night hootenanny mainly attracted other musicians, coming to drink without guilt on a night off while scoping out the competition. Will hesitated as he stood before the microphone. He checked the tuning on the Martin, an action that lowered the noise in the room down to the hum of conversations at the bar.

He needed to be on stage that night. The isolation of the apartment had been grinding him down, dulling his senses to the point where Angela looked as if she were encased in plastic. He felt no desire to touch her, and knew he wouldn't feel anything if he did. Playing for someone—anyone—was a last resort to provoke an emotional response within him. He went to the Troubadour without telling her. No one appeared more surprised than Doug at seeing Will turn up early to get himself on the performers' list. Few artists whom Doug had helped humbled themselves by waiting among those who lined up outside the club every week with their acoustic guitars, all with the faint hope of gaining what Will now possessed. Will's explanation to Doug when he got to the front of the line was honest: he just needed to get out of the house.

He had not planned what he would do, but he settled into his granddad's songs when his hands struck a ringing G chord to confirm he was in tune. In that instant, Will decided it was the last time he would play any of them. One after another the songs echoed around the room. The loose chatter had ceased as he began, with all eyes and ears aimed at the stage. The focused attention from his peers didn't affect him. Will wanted to believe that he was possessed, whether by his granddad or whoever it was who wrote those songs, but he'd assured himself that wasn't true. He was the only one on stage, singing words he no longer cared about.

By the third song the chatter sparked up, while those waiting in the wings began preparing for their sets with a heightened sense of confidence that they could show up the guy with the record deal. By his final song, even Will could feel himself struggling to get through it. At its conclusion, he quietly thanked the audience over token applause. He brushed past the singers in line, avoiding eye contact. In the dressing room, the sense of failure radiated through him in waves.

He placed the Martin in its case and took in the unknown faces around him, some older, but not lacking in youthful ambition. He heard the lies long before they were spoken.

"Hey man, I really dig your stuff."

"I heard you really kicked ass on tour."

"Wow, you're on Elektra? What the fuck are you doing here with all us nobodies?"

"Hey, do you think you could give my tape to someone there?"

Will answered with vague platitudes until those who wanted a piece of him backed off out of either fear or respect. He then picked up the guitar case and slipped out the back door, feeling at peace breathing the night air.

Jessy was bussing tables for the dinner crowd when Alex came in. She tuned into his agitated state and dropped her tray on the bar, a move that drew the ire of two patrons waiting for their beer before the next dancer came out. Jessy met Alex in a corner where they wouldn't have to strain to hear each other over the music. Another man in a Dodgers cap had entered behind Alex, but dashed in the direction of the bathrooms. She detected Alex's pulse racing as they stood face to face. She placed her hands on his shoulders to ensure he spoke directly into her eyes.

"Well?"

"I just dropped off the last package. It's all gone."

"You still got the cash on you?"

"Of course. I told you I'd get you before I went back. There was no answer at home, so I figured you were here."

Her hands jumped from his shoulders to his cheeks and she pressed her lips against his. "Good work baby. We're almost home free. Sit down and relax. I'll get you a drink. I'll need a minute to get ready."

He nodded and took a table close to the bar, sharing some of her joy. She brought him a scotch and soda, and the first sip coated his system like a balm. The music was cranked up as the dancer took the stage. She was one of the older ones Alex had seen before; one of the few, like Jessy, willing to work for the meager wages of the dayshift. With some of the load off his mind, Alex became lost in thinking she was dancing only for him.

Murray sat across the room, taking advantage of some shadows with his Dodgers cap pulled low over his forehead. Even the other waitresses didn't seem to notice him. He kept his eyes on Alex enjoying his scotch, as well as the dancer and her heaving black breasts. Murray had to be in position to ensure the kid didn't get hurt, but it was too late to let him off the hook. The kid would flip; Murray was convinced of that. He didn't want to see Alex do hard time, although that would be next to impossible for the DA to accept. He'd have to take the kid down himself if he could, and somehow show him the high road.

Jessy emerged from a back room dressed in jeans and a black sweatshirt, a large leather purse slung across her torso. *Jesus Christ*, Murray thought, *it's the fucking Pantherette, the cop killer*. The pieces were falling right into Murray's lap. His anxiety grew. Jessy sat across from Alex and they leaned their heads in close together in what appeared to be intense strategizing. At one point, Alex's index finger traced some unknown patterns on the table, and Jessy nodded. Then they both rose and strode toward the front door. Murray followed them to the street and watched the yellow Honda tear away from the curb. He hustled to his car and radioed for backup to meet him at Carlos's pad.

"You wanna tell me what happened last night?" They sat at an outdoor cafe in Echo Park where Lucas had insisted on meeting Will for coffee. Lucas had waited until they were settled before asking his burning question.

"How did you hear about that?"

"Come on Will, you know that that audience is musicians and guys like me. I got a couple phone calls this morning."

"From who?"

"You want me to snitch? What is this, high school? The point is, a lot of people thought you bombed last night, and you know how word gets around. Now, if you had an off night, that's fine. You're entitled to your share like everyone else. I'm just curious if something else is going on."

Will lit a cigarette. He struggled to formulate an answer, wondering what Lucas was expecting to hear. Finally, he spoke. "I guess it was just a bad night."

He could feel Lucas' disappointment. "Is that it? Look, I don't want to make a bigger deal out of this than it deserves to be, but we're starting to get some momentum. Everyone's heard great things about the tour and they're waiting with bated breath for the album to come out. So, what do you do? You go out and act like some fucking amateur. People don't forget these things, believe me. So, what was it? Were you stoned? Drunk?"

Will remained silent.

"It's okay if you were. I mean, you wouldn't be the first."

Will shifted in his chair, feeling a sudden urge to unburden himself. "I needed to get out and do something, alright? It was the only thing I could think of. Maybe it was a mistake, but I can't wait much longer for this record. I don't know what else to do."

"I know, I know, but if you're going to do anything like that, you should tell me first. We'd prefer it if you didn't play any more gigs in L.A. until the album's shipped. We're planning on making a big splash with ads in the trades, and if we get a little radio play, that'll get some new faces out to see you. You'll finally be doing your own night at the Troub, and it'll be spectacular. I can imagine it's tough laying low until then, but believe me, it'll pay off. You just gotta hang in there for a few more weeks. If you need money, ask us."

Will stubbed out his cigarette and lit another. "Thanks, I appreciate that, but I seriously don't know how much longer I can stand it."

"Will, it's the business. I don't make the rules. We just want things to work out as best they can for you. I don't know how many times I need to tell you that. Trust me, you'll have plenty to do when the album comes out."

"That's what I'm worried about. I can't stand the thought of going out in front of people and playing those songs. I realized that last night."

"But Will, they're great songs."

"Maybe, for someone else."

"What the fuck is that supposed to mean? They're your songs."

"Yeah, I suppose."

Lucas seemed at a loss. "Look, why don't we start putting your band together? That'll easily give you something to do for a few weeks. We can forget about doing the solo thing and come out of the gate playing some rock and roll. How does that sound?"

Will offered with a noncommittal shrug, hoping it would be enough to shut Lucas up. It did appear to satisfy him enough to jog his memory about the manila envelope in his shoulder bag. "Oh, I almost forgot. Harvey wanted me to give you these." Lucas slid the envelope across the table. Inside were two black and white prints of Will and Angela on the beach. For the first time, Will saw what they looked like together. Seeing Will engrossed in the images, Lucas said, "I've got to get back to the office. Remember, everything's gonna be fine. I'll talk to Paul about the band, and we'll get that going. We'll talk soon."

Will raised his hand in a half-hearted goodbye. For several more minutes he sat staring at the photos, the figures now strangers to him.

Alex eased the Honda into Carlos's driveway. Jessy lay in the back seat, concealed. Alex exited the car, and Carlos greeted him at the door, dressed casually in a peasant shirt and blue polyester pants. Alex felt composed as he watched Carlos flutter between rooms, double-checking that everything was in its proper place. Alex glanced through the front window and caught a glimpse of Jessy observing from inside the Honda.

Carlos grinned with self-satisfaction as he collapsed in a stuffed chair, beckoning Alex to sit on the sofa. "We have come through the fires together, eh my friend? You have been loyal and honest with me, and for that I am grateful. Now, if I can get today's total from you, we can settle up the rest." Alex reached into his bag and produced a familiar roll of bills secured by an elastic band. Carlos removed it and rifled through the take in short order. "Well done. Yes, everything is as it should be. I'll be right back."

Carlos jumped from the chair and darted to the kitchen where Alex knew he was gathering the rest of the money. Alex turned to the window and waved at Jessy. Carlos returned with a brown briefcase, opening it on the coffee table to reveal bills arranged in even stacks. Carlos extracted one and handed it to Alex. "This is yours. The rest is for the Panthers." Alex sifted through the bills slowly, listening for the first sounds of Jessy slipping through the front door. Carlos stared at Will, his legs twitching uncontrollably as Alex continued to fumble with the stack of cash. He snatched the money back out of Alex's hands. "You want me to count it? Jesus, did you go back on junk today?"

At that moment, Jessy materialized from the hallway, her outstretched hands gripping the .44 that was aimed at Carlos's head. The bills he was holding scattered around the room as he threw his arms up, his face breaking into a terror sweat.

"We want all the money," she said. "Get it now or I swear to God I'm pulling this fucking trigger." Carlos couldn't speak. He nodded but did not rise from the chair.

"What are you waitin' for, motherfucker? Baby, get him on his feet."

Alex yanked Carlos up from under his right arm, but Carlos swung his left hand, clubbing Alex in the head. The room erupted in screams as both men fell to the floor, upending the coffee table. Jessy watched helplessly as Carlos forced his way on top of Alex and pummeled him, his fists drawing streaks of blood.

"Get the fuck off him, or I'll kill you," she screamed, but Carlos didn't stop.

Jessy turned the pistol over and brought the butt squarely down on the top of Carlos's skull. He keeled over, unconscious, and Alex crawled away, staring up at Jessy who cringed at his damaged face. Alex didn't care. They need to focus. "The fucking money," Alex murmured. "Gotta pick it up."

"What do we do with him?"

Alex kept snatching up the bills on the floor. "I don't give a shit. Waste the cocksucker."

Jessy aimed the pistol again, as Carlos began to stir. He rolled up against the bookshelf, knocking some of its contents to the floor. He stared at Jessy through glassy eyes, croaking out a laugh watching Alex scrambling to gather up the money. "You had this planned all along, didn't you, you fucking scum," he slurred. "You wanna kill me, but you get your fucking bitch to do it? What kind of man are you? I tell you, you aren't a man. You never were."

Alex stopped and looked at Carlos through swelling eyes. He was too angry to speak. He wanted to stick a knife through that bloated gut, but instead began to sob at his body's unwillingness to obey his mind. Carlos now laughed without restraint.

"Shut up," Jessy said. She held the gun out to Alex, but he couldn't meet her eyes. All he could do was keep picking up the bills, one by one. Carlos worked himself into a sitting position, thin ribbons of blood trickling down his forehead.

"Okay, so you kill me now, huh?" he said, gasping for breath. "You've done this before, I bet. You and your friends are gonna change the world with violence. Look where it's got you? About to kill a defenseless man."

Jessy's hands started to twitch, but she kept the gun aimed at Carlos. Alex got to his feet and stood next to Jessy, his pockets stuffed with cash. Carlos shifted his gaze to him. "It didn't have to come to this," Carlos said.

"You only wanted to use me."

"You got your share. And I was about to set you free. But that wasn't enough. Now you have to kill me."

"We don't have to do anything. Where's the rest of the money?"

"In the freezer."

Alex stumbled as fast as he could to the kitchen and retrieved a plastic bag crammed with Carlos's share wrapped in butcher's paper. He said to Jessy, "Let's get the fuck outta here. We got what we need."

Jessy remained unmoving.

Will wasn't answering his phone. Angela had called at regular intervals and could no longer force her fingers to dial. She had lost focus at work. A constant concern over his wellbeing overrode her tasks. She took breaks by herself but was unable to eat, much less carry on a normal conversation with her co-workers. She had resisted calling him from her desk, but after one futile last attempt at the end of her shift, she gathered her belongings and dashed for the elevator.

Upon arriving by taxi outside Will's building, she threw the driver a ten-dollar bill and didn't wait for the change. She ran toward the front door in her short heels, her footsteps ringing on the familiar creaking staircase. At the apartment door, she made three quick, sharp knocks, holding her breath until she heard a low rumble on the other side. The locks were unfastened and her heart swelled before she took in the full picture of the living room. Torn and crumpled pieces of Will's song lyrics littered the floor, but he had gone to the kitchen to make tea, leaving Angela to take a seat on the sofa with much hesitation.

"You didn't pick up the phone," she called out after a few tense moments. "Did you know it was me?"

"I've had some things to do," he responded. "But I knew you'd come over."

"You shouldn't take me for granted."

"Who said I was?"

The kettle whistled, and in short order he placed a serving tray on the table and filled two cups. He was eerily content, ignoring the torn lyric sheets, and she didn't press the issue.

"I'm sorry for being worried," Angela finally offered. "Is it the voice?"

He took a sip and winced as the hot water scalded the roof of his mouth. "No, I don't hear it anymore."

"How can you be so sure?"

"I told it to go away."

Angela covered her face with her hands in disbelief, then leaned forward and gripped Will's knees. "Listen to me, we have to stop all this for good. You need help, more help than I can give you. And you have to get it before the album comes out, because by then it might be too late."

He stared at her, his face blank. "I don't need help," he said in a measured tone. "I've made my life right." She didn't pretend to comprehend what he meant. "I'm getting out of here," he continued.

"You found a new apartment?"

"No. I'm getting out of L.A., getting out of music, getting out of all the things that have been making me crazy for the past two years."

Angela's tears flowed as she grasped the enormity of Will's statement. "You can't be serious. It's all just beginning. What about the album?"

"It's a complete fraud. You know it as well as I do."

"What about all those people who—"

"Who what? Love me? Don't even think that. It's the music that's doing it to them. It's the music that I loved at first too. But I can't go on believing that's who I am, because it isn't. Those songs don't belong to me anymore. Someday, they'll find their way to somebody else."

"What about me? You can't leave me. I love you."

Will didn't respond, and the drawn out silence gave Angela hope that he was struggling to find the right words. Yet, her silent urging was in vain.

He took a deep breath before saying, "I have to leave, and that's all there is to it. I'll never forget everything you did for me."

She wanted to run from this nightmare, but understood that, if she did, she wouldn't see him again. Angela wiped away her tears and steadied herself.

"You need to live your own life too," he said. "Now's your chance."

She thought of everything she'd endured up until meeting Will, and how becoming a part of his world had helped her overcome it all. But it was still a world that often terrified her. She couldn't trust Will to do what was best for him, but looking at him now, she could see a more complete human being beginning to emerge from ruins.

She felt tears welling up again as she placed her hands on his. "I promise to keep your secret if you'll come back to me."

"Thank you. But we don't need to keep secrets anymore." Will assisted Angela to her feet and led her to the door. A cool, late afternoon breeze greeted them outside the building.

"I always wanted to tell you that I loved you too," he said, brushing the curls from her forehead as he liked to do.

"Why didn't you?"

"I guess I didn't want to admit it until now."

"We can be happy together if we try."

"I have to try something else first."

"What? Where are you gonna go?"

"I don't know, but I'll always know where you are."

They embraced until Will released her. He took a few steps back, then turned and went back inside and the door shut and locked.

Murray heard a shot. He was in his car, parked in his usual hidden spot at the curb. The LAPD backup he'd requested still hadn't arrived. He unholstered his service revolver and took cover behind the Honda. The front door swung open and Alex ran out, his face awash with horror. Murray stood up and aimed his weapon. "Freeze Alex! F.B.I., you're under arrest!" Alex dropped to the ground.

"Who fired the shot," Murray yelled.

Alex was on the verge of hyperventilating. "It wasn't me. Oh God, please don't kill her!"

"Just stay down Alex. Don't move and everything will be alright." Murray cursed the lack of support with each protracted second that passed. He finally heard a wail of sirens coming from several blocks away.

Jessy was unable to move, even as she heard the sirens approach. Time had stopped after she'd pulled the trigger, and she no longer knew what to do. Her instincts told her to flee out the back door while there was time. There had to be a way for Fred to get her to a Panther safe house. All she had to say was she shot Carlos in self-defense—he was going to kill Alex and take all the money. It wouldn't matter what Alex told the pigs. But she couldn't afford to lose any more time. She would have to punish herself later for abandoning Alex.

Jessy slid the gun into her jeans, slammed the briefcase shut and bolted out the back door with it. She scaled several fences before spotting a line of trees concealing a dry storm drain—her only escape route.

Murray couldn't risk entering the house until the uniforms were in position. By now, the street was aglow with squad cars.

He got Alex to his feet, asking loudly and clearly, "She still in there?"

Alex gaped in amazement, muttering, "It's not you. It can't be."

"I told you to get out while you had a chance." Murray cuffed Alex and led him back to his car. He made a final plea to Alex before tossing him in the back seat. "I know you were doing what was best for the two of you. That was gonna be to your benefit. But she's just fucked that up for good."

Alex jerked his head up at the sound of shotguns being cocked by the cops preparing to storm the house. One of them yelled into a megaphone for Jessy to come out. Murray stayed by Alex, studying his reactions. "She still in there Alex?" he asked again.

"She wouldn't leave me."

"Yeah, you're probably right."

Murray ran to one of the cruisers and ordered an all points bulletin. He couldn't let her get away now.

The morning after Will said goodbye to Angela wasn't as difficult as he thought it would be. He had taken a Seconal from the bottle Alex had stashed in the medicine cabinet and awoke clear-headed as if she were already a distant memory. His mind seemed eager to ponder new things, like getting rid of his useless possessions and ditching the apartment. He needed to locate Alex before he could do any of that. Will found Jessy's phone number on a piece of paper amid the pile of unpaid bills on the kitchen counter, and tried calling. The endless rings felt like a betrayal.

For the next several hours, Will obsessed over where Alex could be. The phone rang, and for once he didn't hesitate to pick up. He couldn't make out the voice on the other end initially, something about L.A. County Jail. Then he heard Alex state his own name.

"Jesus Christ, you're in jail?"

"Fuck man, you gotta help me. This is fuckin' serious."

"What happened?"

"I can't say. You're the only one I could call. They got me a lawyer, but you gotta come see me. Please."

"Yeah, sure, don't sweat it. I'll be right there."

Will felt detached from himself as he waited in the sterile lobby. When they finally called him in, Alex looked more shattered than Will had anticipated. They spoke through telephone receivers, separated by glass.

"God, it's good to see you," Alex said.

Will nodded. "So you've talked to a lawyer?"

"Yeah. I'm in deep shit anyway you look at it. The Feds were tailing me from the moment I came back from Mexico."

"Jesus. What about Jessy?"

"Some shit went down and she's gone. They're looking for her. Carlos, he's gone too." A pause hung in the air. "You're all I've got left, man. Can you get me outta here?"

Will looked deeply into his friend's bruised and battered face, the face that always beckoned him to sneak away on Friday nights to drink beer under the bleachers and play pool the next afternoon, the face that got him through the cross-country drive and convinced him that they could survive in L.A. Will looked into that face and said with assurance, "I'll get you out."

Jack couldn't hold back his concern when Will requested the balance of his advance. "You'd better not be using this to buy drugs, Will. I've been down this road with many other artists. You've got a long career ahead of you, don't start mortgaging it now."

Will stood puzzled before the older man's desk. He was hoping to avoid an explanation, but still played coy. "No, I seriously need it. It's a personal matter."

Jack didn't let him off the hook. "What then? Medical bills? You wanna buy a new car? It's no problem, I just want to know in case I can help some other way."

Jack's sincerity finally made Will relent. He produced the piece of paper on which he'd written the names and numbers of Alex's lawyer and bail bondsman. He looked it over once more before handing it to Jack. "I want you to take all the money and give it to these guys, so my friend can get out of jail. I've arranged it already."

Jack glanced at the paper then stared at Will open-mouthed. "You're serious?" Will nodded. "You never cease to amaze me Will. I hope the next record we make won't be this dramatic." Will laughed under his breath and turned to leave the office. Jack called out after him, "I've got a band for you.

All top-notch guys. You'll love 'em. We start rehearsals next week. I'll call you."

Will shot back a nod, but kept walking past the other offices and the receptionist. He felt safe again once behind the wheel of the Delta 88. The back seat was jammed with clothes, and everything else he deemed essential, only a handful of albums, as well as some books, a small box of letters, and enough non-perishable food to last a week at most. He already knew he'd be on the road longer than that, but his immediate destination was east through the desert toward Joshua Tree.

Will drove without turning on the radio. Outside the city, the ever-present hum of the engine and rush of air coming through the windows soothed him into accepting that this was the right decision, the only decision that could provide the freedom that every song he admired—hell, every work of art—always promised. Whether he could use that freedom for something meaningful wasn't important. Everything he did from that moment on would be a work of art.

It was nearing dusk when Will stopped at the front gate of the park, and chatted with the ranger on duty. "Just wanna see the sunset," Will said.

"Yeah, should be a beauty. Always convinces me that there's a higher power."

These words echoed in Will's head as he took the winding road at a slow pace, almost ashamed at disturbing the coyotes who stared back at him like old friends. He pulled into the dirt beside Cap Rock, popped the trunk and pulled out his guitar case and a can of gasoline. The Martin rested inside, just a piece of wood with six metal strings. Taking a deep breath, he poured out the gasoline, took a few steps back, and threw a match. The heat hit him hard in the face, but after a few seconds of holding his ground, Will took in the full sight and smell. As the initial plume of black smoke dissipated, he heard the harsh cracking of the Martin's death throes. The flames kept him warm as darkness descended.

Attn: Lucas Finch / Elektra Records (Publicity)
Re: Will Mosley review, Creem (Oct./72)

Will Mosley
Angel of Avalon (Elektra)

This is one of them cosmic cowboy records. On the back of the album cover, right up there in the upper left corner, is a liner note from someone in the biz who obviously knows more than I do. I can't read who it is, cuz Elektra has embossed upon it in gold, "DEMONSTRATION: Not For Sale." But what he says about this kid is something about wind and flesh and blood. Well, hell, who cares? Ernest Tubb never had to meditate.

Got the words to the songs printed on the record sleeve, so us literary types don't even have to listen to the sucker. First cut looks like a goodun': "You're thinkin' about all the excuses you gave / Now you're runnin' on empty with one foot in the grave." Makes you feel good all over, doesn't it? Yeah, sort of, well, glad to be alive. I know a creep down the street who once

made me eat a sesame-seed cookie. I am gonna give him this
album to pay him back.

    Nick Tosches

"The Ohio Valley"

In the Ohio Valley
There lives my blue-eyed Sally
She keeps the cabin warm
'Cause the baby will soon be born
You know I love her madly

By the Ohio River
I pledged all the love I could give her
She said it's all too fast
We were never meant to last
I did my best to forgive her

I found a Delta Rocket
The driver forgot to lock it
I set out to take a ride
Just to show I could provide
The gun was heavy in my pocket

In the town of Cincinnati
There lived a man named Matty

I killed him for his pay
And tried to run away
But the sheriff soon had caught me

In the Cleveland Penitentiary
Doing one less a century
I write her every day
Just to say that I'm okay
And to hope she's just as lonely

In the Ohio Valley
There lives my blue-eyed Sally
She keeps the cabin warm
'Cause the baby will soon be born
You know I love her madly

Author Bio

Jason Schneider is the author of six books, including That Gun In Your Hand: the Strange Saga of 'Hey Joe' and Popular Music's History of Violence, and 3,000 Miles (A Novel). He has been writing about music since 1994, with his work appearing in Exclaim!, Paste, Shindig, The Globe & Mail, the Toronto Star, and many other outlets. He currently resides in his hometown, Kitchener, Ontario.